Dark

Waters

An Abraham Hart investigation

By

Max
Elwood

To Ellie, for believing.

Copyright © 2025 Max Elwood
All rights reserved.
ISBN: 9798301607103

One

The phone in his pocket was buzzing again, but Abraham ignored the pulsing handset to focus on the back of Hristo Nikolova's head.

He could picture Nikolova's face without seeing it; he would be smiling, but subtly, almost imperceptibly, because Nikolova knew a jury would not look favourably on a defendant revelling in a floundering prosecution.

The Right Honourable Mr Justice Belton stared expectantly at the prosecutor from the Bench, his chin on clasped hands, eyebrows raised. 'Well, Mr Cranbourne?' came the baritone voice.

Abraham closed his eyes and attempted to control his breathing, tried to clear his mind of the building anxiety. But the pressure remained, and the only distraction came from the phone that was still vibrating against his leg, a vibration that put him in mind of an electric current.

An image sprang into his head, one of Nikolova strapped to a wooden chair. He pictured wires, a metal skull cap and an old-fashioned lever with a red handle. He imagined the lever being pulled by a sombre prison official, releasing a current that grew in intensity.

He thought of burning skin, gritted teeth and liquifying organs. Abraham wished for Nikolova a slow, painful death.

When the phone stopped pulsing, Abraham opened his eyes. His gaze was still aimed at the back of the defendant's head, but everyone else in court was focussed on the panicked expression of Peter Cranbourne, whose mouth was moving but from which no sound emerged.

Abraham felt his heart beating faster, sensed his stomach, along with a chance at closure, dropping away.

Cranbourne turned his head to confer with the dark suited woman next to him. Indistinct whispers could be heard, whispers that grew steadily more tense.

'Mr Cranbourne,' the irritated judge bellowed, 'you have called a witness to the witness box. Protocol dictates they now appear to answer questions.'

'Of course, Your Honour,' replied Cranbourne, a single bead of sweat escaping from under his horsehair wig. 'Only, I'm afraid we seem to have misplaced her.'

Sat in the public gallery, surrounded by a handful of absorbed law students, a selection of note-taking reporters and some half-interested members of the public, Abraham Hart continued in his attempt to stare a hole into the back of Nikolova's head.

When the defendant turned Abraham wondered if Nikolova had somehow felt his murderous stare. But, sat towards the front of the gallery, he saw a woman with long hair the colour of caramel. She flicked a Burberry scarf over her shoulder, smoothed the creases from her tailored cream jacket then, raising a well-manicured hand, gave a curt nod towards the defendant.

A girlfriend, maybe? Certainly not his wife.

Out of the corner of his eye Abraham noticed a colleague glance in his direction. Kelvin Strathmore held eye contact, contorting his face into a question; *What are you doing here?*

Abraham ignored him. He wasn't working this trial. Kelvin had been assigned the court case and would file the story once proceedings had concluded. In fact, Abraham wasn't working any trials. He was meant to have attended a mayoral function at City Hall that morning, something about air quality. Or maybe knife crime. He couldn't remember. Then he had a meeting with the editor at noon, one which had been oft-delayed, always by him.

Abraham glanced at his watch; 12:31pm. Now he knew who'd been trying to call him for the last twenty minutes.

But, instead of meeting his boss, here he was, squashed into the cramped gallery of Southwark Crown Court. The lure of Nikolova's trial had been too strong, and the hope that the man's freedom would be withdrawn, his businesses shut down, too enticing.

After some back and forth between Cranbourne and the increasingly exasperated judge, the jury were instructed to take lunch while both the prosecution and defence counsel were summoned to speak to Belton in private.

Abraham watched the jury being escorted from the courtroom and the rotund figure of Nikolova's defence solicitor strolling towards the judge's chambers. Peter Cranbourne, head down, a look of disconsolation etched into his face, followed.

'Don't look good,' said Kelvin, who had approached Abraham, a Marlboro already between the index and middle finger of one hand, a silver Zippo clutched in the other.

Abraham nodded solemnly, shrugging on his overcoat.

'Slippery bastard, too,' added Kelvin, flicking greasy brown hair out of his eyes with a sudden snap of his neck.

'I suppose he can afford equally slippery solicitors. I mean, if Nikolova's worth as much as you think he is, the fat guy he's sitting next to down there isn't some court-appointed nobody.'

'I don't *think*,' said Abraham, emphasising the last word.

Kelvin nodded slowly and placed the unlit cigarette in a corner of his mouth. 'Maybe it's really *not* him though, you know. My source says they've had a hell of a time getting anything concrete. Shell companies, offshore accounts, burner phones, nothing linked directly, hardly any of it admissible… if it *is* him, he's a clever bastard.'

Abraham sighed, his energy and fight expelled in one breath. 'He's a clever bastard.'

'The ace in the hole's the missus. Seems convenient that she's been "misplaced".' Kelvin made air quotes with his fingers. 'Anyway, what're you doing here? Thought Rachel told you to give this a wide berth coz of, well, you know.'

Abraham did know but couldn't muster the strength to say anything. Instead, he gave Kelvin a thin smile and walked away.

Outside, in the cool October air, Abraham walked to the rear of the court and found a wooden bench overlooking the Thames, one which sat directly opposite the imposing, grey bulk of HMS Belfast. He swept away biscuit crumbs and a half-eaten sandwich and sat down to watch water the colour of builder's tea slide past.

Abraham had written hundreds, probably thousands of stories over his career. Too many had featured sadness, suffering and the pursuit of personal gain, whatever the cost. At forty-six-years-old and with twenty-five years in the job, he had more knowledge of the darker side of life than many but, whatever he was reporting on, from abuse in care homes to human trafficking or prostitution rings, he had been at a remove. While always empathetic, he was able to compartmentalise. If he hadn't, those millions of words would have buried him long before now.

He felt the buzzing of his phone again and reached into his suit. Staring at the screen he noticed four missed calls from Rachel Somerfield, his editor, and a text message from Kelvin.

THEY'RE COMING BACK IN.

Abraham tipped his head back and blew out his cheeks. Had it been an hour already? The thought of returning to the courtroom caused a tightening in his chest. His colleague had been right, it didn't look good, and he wasn't sure he could stand to watch the prosecution flounder further, trying to land a punch on Nikolova.

Slowly he stood up, navigated his way past the tourists, the joggers and the early afternoon dog-walkers, and made his way to the front of the uninspiring brown brick building.

As he approached the entrance his phone vibrated once more and, this time, didn't stop. Abraham assumed it was Rachel again, calling to find out where he was. He already knew he was too much of a coward to answer it but, fishing the device from his pocket, he saw a different name filling the screen.

He swiped to answer. 'Shiv?' said Abraham. 'Everything ok? Evie ok?'

'Yes. Though it's no thanks to you, is it?'

Abraham momentarily stared at the screen again, as if the reason for his wife's anger might be illuminated there.

'What have I done?'

'It's what you haven't done, wouldn't you say?'

Abraham sighed. 'At some point one of us is going to have to answer a question. You're obviously angry but I don't know what about. Is it the car? I think the MOT's due. Did I say I'd book it in?'

Though they were roughly forty miles apart, if he closed his eyes Abraham could see Siobhan shaking her head, her mane of perfectly braided hair swaying slightly, and her flawlessly lacquered maroon lips pursed into an angry pout, forcing out an almost inaudible sound that was a mixture of annoyance and resignation. Mostly the former.

'You were supposed to take Evie to her interview this morning. You said you'd be here first thing. That you'd taken the day off. Would spend the whole afternoon with her. Instead, I had to cancel a meeting with a client and rush her there myself.'

Abraham swore under his breath and looked at his watch, as though that might help. Like he could turn back time. 'Shit! I'm so sorry, Shiv. Christ, this trial, work, being up here, I just, you know, it slipped my mind. I'm sorry. How can I make it up to you?'

'Why are you apologising to me? It's your daughter you let down. Again. How could you forget something so important? It's her first job, Abraham. The beginning of the rest of her life.'

'I know, I know, I'm sorry. How did she get on?'

Abraham heard a sigh, followed by a pause. He hoped it was his wife calming down rather than her preparing to deliver bad news.

'She thinks it went well,' Shiv finally said. 'They asked about her qualifications, why she wants to get into teaching, her goals. She liked the school. It would only be two days a week at first, but if she does well, and likes it, who knows?'

'That's great. Can I speak to her? Is she there?'

'She's angry with you. With good reason, too. She's getting a celebratory Frappuccino from Costa.'

'Right, course. I'll call her in a bit.'

'Abraham, you need to sort yourself out, for Evie's sake as well as your own. She needs you. This isn't over.'

'Us?'

'What?'

'Do you mean "this isn't over" as in, we're not over?'

That pause again. That shake of the head.

'No, Abraham, I didn't mean that,' said Siobhan, anger rising now. 'Being Evie's father is what I meant. Just because she's technically an adult doesn't mean she no longer needs support and love. And she's still coming to terms with the separation, too. You need to be there for her.'

Abraham watched as a bird swooped down to the pavement, grabbed what looked like a remnant of croissant in its beak before returning to the smog-filled but surprisingly blue sky. 'I know. I will. I'm sorry. It's just work and, you know, our situation. And mum. And Grace and —'

'I can't deal with this, Abraham,' Siobhan interrupted. 'Grace and your mum died years ago. It was tragic, and I miss them too, but your eighteen-year-old daughter is alive. She's well and, God willing, she has a future ahead of her. If you keep living in the past, then you're going to miss it.'

Abraham was about to apologise again but realised his soon-to-be ex-wife had already hung up.

Two

*A*lissa had read that a smile was as much in the eyes as the mouth. Staring at the young woman looking back from the smeared mirror, she wondered if she seemed happy, whether her eyes would betray her.

She could hear Craig in the kitchen, searching through cupboards, the scraping jars and jostled packets, becoming more pronounced, angrier. Could a noise be angry? she wondered. Probably not, but she recognised the sounds as a precursor.

'Have we not got any bread?' came the shout. As much an accusation as a question.

The smile in the reflection disappeared behind dust and grime. She had learned in the last week that, whatever the question, no answer would suffice. That it wasn't really a question at all, but a warning shot across the bow. 'Have you put out the rubbish?' 'Did you change the alarm setting?' 'Is the washing machine broken?'

It was 7:15am. Twenty more minutes and Craig would need to leave to get the train. It was unlikely she could stay in the bedroom for that long. The thought crossed her mind, though another arrived almost simultaneously; if he *was* made redundant, he would be here all the time. The weight that lifted when he closed the front door behind him would be gone and the eggshells she currently walked on would crack and crumble into skin-piercing shrapnel.

The door opened suddenly and the smile that reached no further than her lips quickly reappeared. 'You hear what I said?' asked Craig, stepping into the room.

Alissa feigned surprise. 'No. Sorry. What's wrong?'

Craig was handsome in his suit, she had to admit that. He looked smart and cultured. He looked like a grown up. Silly, really. He was a grown up. At twenty-three-years-old he was five years older than she was. They were both grown ups, she supposed. Legally, at least. When she moved in nine months ago, she'd felt very mature. Her first home, barring the one she had shared with her mum.

Craig had been as excited as her. They'd spent a whole weekend cleaning the flat, rearranging furniture so that she felt comfortable, like she belonged. They'd driven to the IKEA in Lakeside to look at double beds and side-table lamps and new cutlery.

Back then Alissa supposed her eyes did look happy. OK, so it wasn't the biggest flat, or the nicest building, and the next-door neighbour was a bit of a creep, and her mum wasn't convinced this was a good idea, but nothing was ever perfect. Craig was kind and attentive, college was going well, and she'd been kept on part time at the company she'd done work experience at.

'Bread,' said Craig, staring at her. 'Have we got any?'

'If there's none in the cupboard then no, I don't think so.'

'I thought you were going to get some.'

Alissa wasn't sure why he thought this. She hadn't said anything of the sort. He hadn't asked her either. She didn't know how to answer, but then it hadn't been a question.

'It's fine,' he said, making it sound anything but. 'It's not like I've got a full day's work ahead of me. S'pose you're just preparing for when we're on the poverty line.'

Craig stomped out of the room and back towards the kitchen leaving Alissa to brush the long brown hair of her grimy reflection. Maybe her mum had been right, maybe she was too young to play the dutiful girlfriend, the proud homeowner, the dinner party hostess. Though they weren't the roles she had signed up for. They weren't even the roles Craig had handed to her. But she had enjoyed attempting to inhabit them. Up until recently, at least.

It would change, she told herself. Once Craig found a new job or was told he was to be kept in this one, it would go back to how it was. And, until then, she just needed to work hard, play nice and be understanding.

She thought of the picture her mum had hanging in the hallway of her house, an image of a powerful wave encircling a cursive script that read 'This too shall pass'. *She whispered the four words to herself before replacing the brush on the dresser, standing up and making her way to the bedroom door.*

The bang as the front door slammed shut made her jump and she called out for Craig. No answer. Never leave home under the cloud of an argument, her mum always said. Easy to say, not so easy to achieve, not when one person is constantly on the lookout for something to argue about: bins, broken washing machines, bread.

Alissa turned on the radio, poured herself some muesli with a splash of milk and ate as Harry Styles sang about the sign of the times. She automatically scanned the room for her phone, wondering whether she should text Craig, something upbeat, tender. Then she

17

remembered she'd left her phone at work. It felt strange to be without it. Had felt strange all last night, too. What did it say about her that she was already having withdrawal symptoms after less than twelve hours?

She finished her breakfast, placed the bowl and spoon in the sink and checked her reflection in the mirror one last time. Then, as she was about to leave the flat, she walked back to the sink and washed up the bowl and spoon, placing it on the sideboard to drip dry. There was no point leaving any reason for Craig to be mad at her when he got home from work that evening.

She pulled on her cream-coloured coat, shrugged her rucksack, the one Craig had bought her for Christmas, over her shoulder and opened the front door. It was only 7.30. She'd be early for college, but she could sit in the common room to revise, or maybe Em would be early too, and they could talk about Saturday night. Craig was heading off to Newquay for a stag weekend and she and Em were planning to go out to get wasted.

As she pulled the door closed Alissa wondered whether a weekend away might cheer Craig up, bring him back to himself. She wasn't concentrating and flinched with shock when someone spoke.

'Boo!' said Matt Hallstaff into her left ear. He was close, too close, and she could feel him breathing on her neck. She remade the smile that didn't reach her eyes and turned to their neighbour thinking, this too shall pass.

Three

Abraham didn't return to the courtroom that day and, apart from leaving a grovelling voice mail for Evie, who hadn't picked up when he'd called, he had purposely avoided his phone in case he was tempted to contact Kelvin Strathmore for an update on the trial.

He spent much of the afternoon aimlessly wandering the streets of London, studiously avoiding intermittent calls from Rachel Somerfield before returning to the Premier Inn in Aldgate, which had been his home for the past three weeks, since Siobhan suggested they have some time apart. After an evening staring-at-but-not-really-watching a variety of cooking programmes while eating a pre-packed sandwich from M&S, he decided to go to bed. Evie still hadn't called him back.

Abraham slept fitfully, images of Hristo Nikolova and Evie intermingling in his dreams, one laughing from above, the other staring mournfully from below. He woke just before 6am and, unable to get back to sleep, decided that now would be the perfect time to start the running regime he'd been planning since arriving at the hotel. By the time he was back it would be late enough to call Evie

He climbed into his unused training kit, brushed his teeth and ran a comb through his short brown hair, ignoring the increasing number of strands that came away in the comb. He got as far as the door to his room, where a near-pristine pair of Nikes sat, before deciding he didn't have the energy to pound the streets of east London. It took him twenty-five minutes to remove his running gear, take a shower and slide into his suit.

Still not even 7am, and not wanting to wake Evie if she were asleep, Abraham decided to head to the office. *The Chronicle* was situated in London Bridge, a short walk from Southwark Crown Court. It was on the opposite side of the river to Fenchurch Street train station which would, ordinarily, take him directly out of London and east, to Essex, to Southend, to home.

Joshua had offered to put him up while he and Siobhan 'worked towards rebuilding the sacred union of marriage'. But Joshua was a Catholic priest, and Abraham knew all the sanctimonious preaching he would face meant he'd end up killing his brother after a few hours, let alone a few weeks. The church might frown upon divorce, but murder was a real no-no.

Not that he'd actually told Joshua about the separation, but his brother was often referred to as 'resourceful' by his friends and parishioners. Not by Abraham, though, who simply said he was a nosy bastard. Whether Siobhan had told him voluntarily or after prolonged interrogation he didn't know, but it meant that his dad must know and, likely, half the city by now.

Staying nearer home would have been more practical for both him and Shiv, and certainly for Evie, but if his wife needed space then, in a fit of pique, he'd decided to give it to her. It also drastically cut his commute for what he thought - or hoped - would be a week or two, and it also coincided with Nikolova's trial, in which he had a vested interest.

It was a Friday, so the streets were less busy than usual. The now popular 'work from home' approach to life was one of the few welcome results of the Covid pandemic. The roads were still in semi-darkness as Abraham walked south towards Tower Hill station and the imposing structure of the Tower of London. Even this early there were tourists, mainly American he noted, taking photos of each other with the huge edifice in the background, the sand-coloured bricks like a sturdy beacon among the more impermanent metal and glass structures around it.

He trudged along Lower Thames Street and at London Bridge crossed the river that ran like an impressive stain through the city. He made his way through partially dug up pavements and harassed-looking office workers who, like him, were trying to get an early chokehold on the day. As he walked, he listened to the sound of a city coaxing itself to life. At Grind, he bought a large filter coffee and an almond croissant.

At the smart, if impermanent, steel and glass edifice that housed *The Chronicle*, Abraham nodded to the security guard keeping watch over the entrance, tapped his ID card on the gate and made his way to the fourth floor where rows of messy desks featured a smattering of people either starting early or finishing very late. He nodded to a few of them, each drinking from cups of coffee even larger than his. As he crossed the grey carpet tiles to sit at his usual desk a voice he recognised shouted his name.

Abraham looked around to see the loping figure of Kelvin Strathmore striding towards him, a mug of something steaming in his hand.

'Have you actually been home since yesterday?' Abraham asked Kelvin, who looked like he'd slept in his clothes and whose hair hadn't seen the contents of a shampoo bottle for some time.

Kelvin ignored the question, instead asking one of his own, 'What happened yesterday?'

Abraham looked at him, cocking an eyebrow.

'You didn't come back in. Sent you a text.'

'Sorry. Family emergency.'

If Kelvin was interested in the reasons behind his colleague's no show, he didn't press it. 'Didn't miss much. Soon as they came back, Belton adjourned for the day. Didn't look too happy either. Not like the defendant and his brief. They looked like they'd just dropped a tenner but found a tonne.'

News of the prosecution's problems put Abraham even more on edge. As a journalist he had no direct connection to the trial itself, but he had worked tirelessly over the previous two years on the issue of county lines drug trafficking.

He had spoken to addicts and their suppliers. He had talked to families struggling with loved ones dealing with addition. He had interviewed community leaders fighting the problem, and kids - some as young as eight - recruited to ferry illegal substances from one part of the country to another. Abraham was invested in the outcome of this trial in more ways than one.

During the course of Abraham's investigations Hristo Nikolova's name had occasionally been mentioned. It was usually by former dealers now living their lives at His Majesty's pleasure, but was always off the record, and always whispered, as though he may be lurking somewhere in the shadows, listening. It was rumoured that he was the mastermind behind the majority of cocaine and heroin that found its way onto the streets of east London and the towns and cities across large parts of southeast Essex.

Outwardly, Nikolova was a 56-year-old half-British half-Albanian businessman who had shares in a diverse array of companies that included - but were not limited to - meat packaging, haulage, sanitation and construction. Abraham had attempted to unpick the financial dealings of Nikolova. He'd even convinced the *Chronicle* to hire a forensic accountant to help and, though her findings had proven to be illuminating, they were not the smoking gun Abraham or his employers had hoped for.

This, he assumed, was the same scenario in which the authorities found themselves. Small cogs in the county lines machinery were often prosecuted. On occasion, more substantial moving parts of the business also received the full glare of the law. But one of the men many believed – but no one could prove – was the engine at the heart of the issue was free to go about his seemingly legitimate business. At least until Mrs Nikolova stepped forward to speak to both the press and the authorities.

'They'll find her,' said Abraham, in an attempt to convince himself as much as Kelvin. 'They wouldn't be so stupid as to let her out of their sight for long.'

Kelvin emitted a low chuckle that stayed at the back of his throat, like it was embarrassed to show its face. 'British justice system,' he said, taking a tentative sip from the still steaming cup. 'Stupid things are done by clever people all the time. S'pect we'll find out soon though. Court's back in session at nine.' Kelvin checked his watch. 'See you in there?' he asked as he made his way back towards his own desk.

'Not sure,' Abraham replied to Kelvin's back. He didn't know if he could stand to look at Nikolova's smug face for any length of time.

At just past 8.30am Abraham decided that it was late enough to risk disturbing his daughter. He found an empty meeting room and sat on one of the uncomfortable metal chairs that surrounded a too-low wooden table. He stared at the framed front pages from decades past as he pressed the icon below the photo of Evie on his mobile, one he'd taken last summer, when he, Siobhan and Evie had gone to Mallorca for a week. The lingering aroma of stale coffee and tuna sandwiches lurked in the room and Abraham thought about opening the door to let some air in, but privacy trumped comfort and he stayed where he was.

The phone kept ringing and Abraham was about to give up when it finally connected and a groggy voice on the other end of the line mumbled a hello. Not a good start if he'd woken her up.

'Evie? It's Dad.'

'You do know how mobiles work, right Dad? Your name comes up when you call. Even your photo.'

Definitely not a good start.

Abraham closed his eyes and inhaled deeply before replying. 'Yeah, course, just, you know, old habits. Sorry, did I wake you up? Bit early, maybe?'

'No, you're alright,' replied Evie, 'couldn't really sleep so been awake for a bit.'

'Right. Sorry. Only, you sounded a bit, you know, groggy.'

When he first moved out of the family home Abraham wondered why he immediately felt so nervous when talking to his daughter. He tripped over words, peppered sentences with phrases he'd never uttered before, and seemed to apologise every few seconds. He quickly realised that he felt nervous because he was nervous.

'Just not feeling that great, to be honest. A cold or something.'

'You sure it's just a cold? Maybe we need to get it checked out, you can't be too careful about these things.'

'Oh, is that right?' Evie replied. '*We* should make sure I'm alright. *We*, as in you and me? Only, I thought that was the plan yesterday, when *we* were meant to take *me* to my interview, only *you* didn't bloody turn up.'

Abraham could hear his daughter's voice cracking, and it was only then he realised how much he'd let her down. No, he was lying to himself. He'd known months ago, probably years. He'd known when Evie was just ten years old and her aunt had died and he'd missed the best part of a year of her life as he worked and drank, and drank and worked, in a bid to forget his part in Grace's death.

He'd known when she was twelve years old and her grandmother died and he worked and drank, and drank and worked, in a bid to forget how his mother was dead, in part, from a broken heart after losing her only daughter. And he'd known all the while since then, as he let his marriage flounder and his family drift away even as they held out their arms, reaching for him, trying to get him to grab hold.

'I'm sorry,' he said.

'You're always sorry, Dad.'

If Abraham had an effective response to his daughter's justified disappointment, he didn't have time to articulate it before she ended the call, leaving him silently staring at the handset, wondering how else he could set fire to his life.

It wouldn't be long before he found out.

Four

Abraham remained in the meeting room trying to control the surge of anger he could still feel crashing around inside him. The death of his younger sister eight years previously was still an open wound that each member of his family found difficult to touch. They all dealt with it in their own way and, sometimes, when they weren't looking, distracted by some other tidbit of news, the memory of her absence went unnoticed and the hole she had left was temporarily filled. But never for long.

His mother had withered away for two painful years after Grace's overdose, shrinking into herself until only a shell of Marion Hart remained, and then not even that.

Grace's then-boyfriend, Brody Lipscombe, had also fanned the flames of discontent. Abraham couldn't bear to hear his name, let alone see his face. But Brody was apparently now a recovering drug addict under Joshua's protective wing. According to his brother, the man who had dragged their little sister down into the gutter, who turned her into someone she wasn't, who urged her to steal, to beg, and who paid for that final, irreversible hit, was now striving for forgiveness and working towards redemption. It made Abraham feel sick.

All this had been dragged back to the surface with the court case against the man who had undoubtedly supplied the dealer who, in turn, supplied Brody who had then shared his ill-gotten purchase with Grace.

A hard rap on the glass of the meeting room startled Abraham, who had lost himself in joyless thought. He looked up at the round face of Bryan Meard, the newspaper's Culture Editor, peering in at him. Meard raised his wrist, tapped his watch, mouthed two words - 'Editorial meeting' - then wandered off.

By 8.50am the heads of different departments - news, sport, business, culture, showbusiness - along with some of the more senior members of staff, were headed towards the large meeting room for the usually brief but occasionally fractious gathering about the following day's publication.

While the Saturday supplements were overseen by a separate editorial team, the main paper was still the domain of Rachel Somerfield, the *Chronicle*'s weekday editor, a fifty-nine-year-old Scott who, while small in stature, barely reaching the shoulders of Abraham's six-foot frame, was a big presence both in her own newspaper's building and beyond.

Somerfield had edited many national dailies, a smattering of Sunday editions and was the outgoing chair of the Press Association. Her reputation was for quality, incisive journalism, and she had a well-known disregard for citizen journalists, 'All those no marks with phones and a poorly maintained YouTube channel or, God forbid, a blog.'

While Abraham respected and feared Rachel in equal measure, his opinion of her deputy, Spencer Milton, was less positive. Unlike many of the *Chronicle*'s staff, Spencer had not worked his way up through local and regional reporting. He hadn't attended summer fetes, written about golden wedding anniversaries, or disclosed the effects over-subscribed local food banks had on a community. In fact, Abraham was certain he had never even heard of a food bank and had definitely never spoken to anyone who made use of them. Spencer was what Abraham called a hereditary reporter. His father, Alfred Spencer, now Sir Alfred, sat on the board of the *Chronicle* and had been its editor for many years before embarking on a career in politics, chiefly as a communications consultant for the Tories and, when Spencer decided to follow in his dad's footsteps, a door seemed to open for him on command.

Admittedly he had started as just another reporter on the showbiz desk but, able to get numerous exclusives with a coterie of minor royals and other well-heeled professional partygoers, all of whom he'd either been to private school or Cambridge with, he was soon promoted through the ranks as other less connected but more deserving members of staff looked on.

Abraham tried not to dislike him for this fact, after all, nepotism was as old as humanity. Instead, Abraham disliked Spencer because he was a sanctimonious prick with little talent and even less empathy. He was a man who, in an editorial meeting, had once challenged the relevance of the paper's 'Help for the Homeless' initiative because, 'Give them an inch, and they'll take a mile.' This was said with a thin smile and a hollow laugh. When the mask slipped, as it had done then, Spencer showed himself for the man he really was.

The oval table in the meeting room was almost full when Abraham got there. Cups of coffee sat in front of each person, notebooks were open and pens were poised as Rachel waited for the stragglers to take a seat.

'Come on, in you come,' she said, 'we've all got better places to be.'

Abraham was the last to arrive and the only seat left vacant was the one next to Spencer. He grudgingly made his way towards it, careful not to catch his colleague's eye for fear of instigating conversation.

The next fifteen minutes passed relatively uneventfully as Rachel asked the paper's various section editors for updates on stories and plans for upcoming features and interviews, as well as sharing information about the performance of stories on the paper's website.

Eventually, Rachel looked at Abraham and asked him what the special investigations team was planning. The team to which she referred consisted primarily of Abraham, alongside a predetermined budget for freelancers. Depending on the subject matter they were examining, Abraham would speak to a pool of writers he trusted, or experts in that particular field, and would commission articles accordingly.

Sometimes Abraham followed a trail that led nowhere, as had happened two years previously when he attempted to uncover information about malware ransomers. The practice of locking a company out of its own software, crippling it until a hefty ransom was paid, always via untraceable crypto currency, was becoming ever more prevalent and costly to businesses across the globe. But tracing the ransomers themselves was next to impossible and many of the businesses affected didn't want to talk to Abraham on the record in case it spooked their customers. After a month of research Rachel pulled the plug, telling Abraham to move on.

'I want to continue digging into the county lines problem,' Abraham said.

Rachel locked her eyes on him over her the rim of her thick, black designer glasses. Her lips, which were never without lipstick the colour of a good claret, were pursed. 'Been done, don't you think?'

'I don't think we've scratched the surface, to be honest,' Abraham replied, trying to keep his tone neutral. 'We've laid out the problem, spoken to a lot of former dealers, and to the Force about their plans to tackle it, but there's so much more; the former addicts, the current addicts, the families who've been devastated by this...' Out of the corner of his eye Abraham could see Spencer shaking his head slowly, the hint of a smile playing at the corner of his mouth. '...this plague that's devastating communities...'

Rachel cut him off. 'I agree it's a major problem, but there's a risk we're becoming campaigners rather than reporters.'

Spencer was nodding now.

'And what's wrong with that? It's such a big issue, one affecting so many people across the —'

'Poor people,' interrupted Spencer in his clipped, nasal whine. 'People who don't buy the newspaper or pay for the site subscription, and people to whom the advertisers aren't really speaking.'

All eyes turned towards Spencer now, as he picked up the mug in front of him and took a sip, smiling at Abraham, innocence personified. 'No offence,' he said.

Abraham realised his right foot was tapping uncontrollably on the carpet tiles beneath the desk. He looked from Spencer to Rachel, waiting for her to say something. When she didn't, he turned to Spencer. 'You think only poor people are drug addicts, you dickhead?'

'Abraham!' warned Rachel, waving an index finger in the air before using it to push her glasses back up her nose. 'I know you have skin in this game, Abe, but I think we may have gone as far as we can with this. For now, at least.'

Abraham held up his hands in lieu of an actual apology. 'Look, Rachel, if nothing else, we should be following up on the trial. Whatever happens, the effects of this situation are endemic.'

'Oh, you've not heard?' said Spencer, trying and failing to keep the pleasure from his voice. 'The case against Nikolova's been dropped. Insufficient evidence. Kelvin emailed just now.'

Spencer held up his phone and looked at Abraham with a mixture of faux pity and triumph. Abraham froze, his mouth half open, unsure whether to be more offended by what Spencer had just said, or the way in which he'd said it. When he recovered enough to react, he couldn't focus on the phone screen Spencer was waving around so turned back to Rachel, hoping that she would contradict him.

Instead, she just nodded, though at least she had the good grace to look sorry.

'Well, even more reason to double down. People are still dying, communities are crumbling. It's murder on an industrial scale.'

'More like natural selection,' Spencer mumbled, loud enough for Abraham to hear but indistinct to everyone else in the room.

Abraham wondered if those four words were said to provoke a reaction. After the millisecond it took for that thought to form, settle in his brain and undergo examination, he believed that they were because, otherwise, Spencer was a sociopath. Abraham didn't know how Spencer was expecting him to react, but he didn't think he'd expect a balled right fist to be swung in his direction.

Abraham felt like the last decade was somehow culminating in this moment. In his mind's eye he envisioned his fist connecting with skin, his knuckles feeling bone impact on bone, his ears picking up the celebratory crack of a jaw as it splintered beneath his punch. His heart was sounding a charge and his emotions, which he'd stirred into a rage, seemed to be overwhelming the internal wall that he'd successfully built after his sister's death.

Abraham had interviewed his share of people who had talked about watching themselves from above, about how they seemed separated from their body when they ran back into a burning house, jumped into a busy road to save a distracted child or plunged a knife into an abusive husband. Until this point, he'd thought it was a figure of speech but, sitting around that conference table, Abraham was looking at himself seething with anger. He saw the clenched fist, the gritted teeth, the smug, self-righteous visage of Spencer Milton.

He saw what he wanted to do, what he should do.

Instead, his ethereal self watched his real self say, 'Sorry, yes, you're probably right, Rachel.' It witnessed Spencer snort a condescending laugh and looked on as the meeting progressed to the next point of order.

'How was the City Hall event?' asked Rachel. 'I think a half page should cover it, don't you?'

The visceral fight and passion had now evaporated, and Abraham looked at his editor, giving a meek smile.

'Ok,' she said, 'I think we've covered everything. Go, make me a newspaper.'

The assembled crowd started to move, chairs dragged, phone calls were begun. 'Abraham,' Rachel added. 'Can you come to my office, please?'

Abraham remained seated, eyes aimed at the table, a docile nod of affirmation all he could manage.

As the room emptied the last one to leave, bar Abraham, was Spencer, who tucked his iPad Pro under his arm and said, 'No offence, Abe, but two-bit drug stuff, it's just not sexy anymore, you know?'

Five

'*Matt!*' *said Alissa, holding a hand to her chest. 'You scared me.'*
  '*Sorry, babe,*' *he replied, winking, 'couldn't resist. How's my favourite neighbour?'*
  Encountering Matt Hallstaff was one of the risks of living with Craig. They had been neighbours before she had moved in and, while not best friends, exactly, they were a similar age and on good terms, occasionally sharing a drink in one or other of their flats, or playing the Xbox till the early hours.
  Initially Alissa had reacted to Matt with the same open friendliness as her boyfriend did. She had, she supposed, trusted Craig's ability to judge a person's character. She soon realised that had been a mistake.
  'Looking gorgeous, as ever,' he said, looking her up and down, as if she were wearing a tight-fitting dress as opposed to her usual attire of jeans, trainers and a hoodie, which were entirely covered by her coat. 'Off anywhere special?'
  'Just college. Then work later,' she replied, raising the shoulder on which her rucksack hung to indicate a change of clothes held within. 'You?'
  Alissa cursed inwardly for asking a question that would only prolong the conversation. She knew where he was going. Dressed in his work trousers, grubby boots and an overcoat while carrying a toolbox, there was only one place he could be headed.

'Just work, you know. All ok in there,' he said, nodding towards the front door of Craig and Alissa's flat. *'Thought I heard some raised voices earlier.'*

Alissa noticed he was standing on his tiptoes, as he often did when they met. He was leaning against his front door as he did so, trying - but failing - to make it less obvious. Alissa was tall, almost 5'10', while Matt was a couple of inches shorter.

He smiled. It reminded her of a snake, ready to strike.

'All fine,' Alissa smiled back, looking at her watch. *'Just running a bit late, that's all.'*

Matt took no notice of her hint, instead leaning forward slightly, close enough that she could smell the coffee on his breath. *'You know,'* he said quietly, like they were sharing a secret, *'if you ever need a shoulder to cry on, even a place to stay if things get a bit... heated... you can always let me know. I'd happily sleep on the couch. If you wanted me to, obviously.'* That smile again.

This was not the first time Matt had suggested such an arrangement. Nor was it the first instance of him effectively trying to elbow Craig out of the picture. Over the months she had lived here he had often told her she was too attractive to be going out with Craig, that she should be a model, not a college student and that he would know far better how to keep her happy than the man she was living with. Putting aside the fact that Alissa didn't find this short, skinny man with a wiry beard attractive in the least, it also made a mockery of Matt and Craig's so-called friendship.

She should have told Craig about their neighbour's behaviour long before now but, initially, she wanted to give him the benefit of the doubt. She'd wondered if it *wasn't that he was a creep, but that she'd simply misunderstood his type of humour. That notion had passed, but so too had the time to tell Craig. She worried that if she brought it up now he would think it was some sort of ploy to make him jealous, or to undermine him. No, she would just have to grin and bear it. For now, at least. Maybe she could ask Joshua what she should do when she next saw him.*

'That's very sweet, Matt,' she said, 'but there'll be no need. Everything's fine. I'd better go, don't want to miss my bus.'

Alissa turned from Matt and made her way to the staircase. She could feel his eyes on her until she stepped out of sight.

***

Walking into the common room 40 minutes later Alissa was pleased to see Em was already there, head buried in a book about Martin Scorsese.

'You're keen,' Alissa said. 'Teacher's pet.'

Em looked up and smiled, her shock of tight black curls pulled back from her oval face with a hairband. 'That's rich coming from you,' said Em, now affecting an approximation of a posh accent, 'Miss 'I've Got a Job in a Production Company Don't You Know' Peters.'

The two girls hugged a greeting, and both sat down on the rickety old sofa. 'It's hardly a Hollywood steppingstone,' said Alissa. 'Unless Hollywood is looking for someone who can order lunch and remember what coffee everyone drinks without referring to notes.'

'Don't underestimate that skill. Like an army, the film industry marches on its stomach. How's it going there, anyway?'

'It's fine, I suppose. The guy who runs it, Lewis, is nice. Gave me some advice about our film. Well, he criticised it, but in a nice way. Said we needed more "creative flair".'

Em rolled her eyes. 'He gonna stump up the cash for that?'

Alissa smiled, the first genuine one of the day. It felt good. 'Wouldn't have thought so. But he gave me an idea I'm working on.'

'Care to share?'

'I'll show you when it's ready, don't worry.'

'What about Craig?' asked Em. 'Any improvement?'

The smile faded, replaced by a deep sigh. 'Let's not talk about it. Let's plan for Saturday instead. Meet at seven for pre-drink drinks, yeah? Then, what, into Leigh?'

'I'm on a budget, Al. I can't be splashing the cash in swanky wine bars.'

'No, it's ok. We'll head to the Broker for a couple. Maybe the Mariners. Someone'll buy us drinks, you know what it's like.'

'Buy you drinks, maybe.'

The two girls smiled mischievously, excited about their weekend plans. Plans that would never come to fruition.

Six

Hristo Nikolova had remained seated, hands clasped, elbows resting on the scratched wood of the defendant's table, when the judge dismissed the trial. He hadn't celebrated, hadn't hugged his solicitor, nor clenched a fist in quiet victory. There was nothing to celebrate. His appearance in court was an embarrassment to him. The mere threat of incarceration already a punishment.

Now it was over he could acknowledge he had not been too concerned about the outcome. The trail he had left was well concealed and, even if found, so convoluted he was confident no one would ever truly unravel it. It was his wife who had been the piece of the puzzle around which the authorities had built their picture.

It was a shame, he thought, seated in a small room somewhere deep within the court's labyrinthine interior, he and Mariana had been well-suited. Initially, at least. But greed could change people. Greed and fear. She had represented one, he the other. Together greed and fear had conspired against her.

His solicitor sat opposite him now, a sharp haircut, Savile Row suit and Rolex watch. Hristo wondered how much of who this man was came down to the exorbitant fees paid by people like him. But those fees had got Hristo nowhere. It hadn't been deft oratory or clever manipulation of a jury which had seen the case against him fall apart. Instead, it had been Erjon.

When results were needed, it was always Erjon.

It had pained him to instruct his most trusted employee to find Mariana. He had hoped it wouldn't come to that. But hope was for the foolish, the weak and the unprepared. Hope would get you caught, get you killed. So, before the printer ink on the warrant for his arrest had dried, Hristo had been prepared. Where his ex-wife was now, he didn't know, didn't want to know. The only person who did was Erjon and, no matter how hard you might try to control The Wind, it bent to no man.

'I suppose we might say it was a stroke of luck that Mrs Nikolova decided to run,' said the solicitor, with a laugh that sounded like a he might be having a mini stroke.

Hristo couldn't remember his name. He guessed at Quentin, or maybe Caspar. They should make them wear badges, he thought.

'Of course,' the solicitor continued, suddenly aware that he needed to shoot down the notion that luck played any part in the outcome, 'we'd have beaten it regardless. Just means it didn't take as long.'

Another mini stroke.

Christian? Hristo wondered.

'You're a free man, Hristo.' The solicitor seemed to be under the impression they were friends. 'They'll have you out of here shortly. Few T's to cross and I's to dot, that sort of thing, then we'll have you back where you belong.'

Hristo ran a hand over his head. Since being arrested he had been unable to shave his scalp as often as he would have liked. A sound, like the sea dragging itself across the sand, played in his ears as he felt the tiny bristles catching on his palm. He pulled the same hand down over his forehead, across his eyes, his long nose and the thick black beard on his face. 'I would like to see my associate,' he said.

It took longer that Hristo would have liked for those Ts to be crossed, but he made no complaints. There was no point in doing so. These things took as long as they took and complaining would likely only make them take longer. When papers had been signed and documents checked Hristo eventually found himself inside the comfortable cocoon of his black Mercedes-AMG, Erjon at the wheel.

Hristo had a driver, someone whose job it was to be sat where Erjon was. But while the driver didn't have the skills Erjon possessed, Erjon could drive, and there was no need for extra ears to be party to their conversation.

'You did well,' said Hristo.

'I did as asked,' Erjon replied.

Hristo nodded. 'Painless?'

'Does it matter?'

No, he supposed it didn't. He wondered if he was getting soft in his old age. He was only fifty-six, but in the world in which they lived, fifty-six was to be celebrated. 'Is anyone looking?'

'Does it matter?' Erjon repeated.

'No,' he said. Mariana would never be found.

'Will you miss her?' asked Erjon.

Hristo thought about the question. 'I'm not sure,' he eventually said.

Erjon nodded. 'You still have Diellza.'

'That's different,' Hristo countered. 'And the business?'

'Everything is fine,' said Erjon.

'What about the journalist? He was problematic.'

Erjon, his cold eyes fixed firmly on the London traffic, shrugged his lean shoulders. 'Mariana had spoken to him. She won't speak to him anymore.'

'Do we know what she said?'

'We know what he wrote. It's unlikely he didn't use what he had. There would be no sense in waiting.'

More nodding. Erjon was a man of few words. Much like Hristo. Maybe that was why they understood each other. 'Are you staying in London?'

'I can.'

A final nod before Hristo leant his head back on the soft leather headrest and closed his eyes. Having The Wind around could only be beneficial.

'Just in case,' he said. 'Just in case.'

Seven

Abraham sat alone amid a bank of four seats on the 10.41am train from Fenchurch Street. The train wasn't particularly busy but those entering his carriage had made the decision to sit elsewhere. Abraham put that down not to the one unopened can of Stella sitting in front of him on the grey plastic table, but to the three empty ones stood beside it.

He'd noticed the disapproving look he'd received from a middle-aged woman who'd got on at Upminster and, in return, had held out a can to her with a smile. She had quickly moved through to the next carriage.

He stared out of the window at the thick grey skies above the open fields whizzing by, and at the smattering of blurry cows standing idly within them, before cracking the last ring pull and taking a healthy swig. He wasn't a big drinker, but after his conversation with Rachel, and before he'd bought a train ticket back to Essex, he'd felt the only sensible thing to do was get drunk.

The *Chronicle*'s editor was not one for histrionics. She didn't shout at people, scream obscenities or threaten retribution. She didn't need to. She had the respect of her staff and the experience to deal with situations calmly and effectively. This she had done by telling Abraham she was offering him a leave of absence. When he politely refused, she told him it wasn't really an offer.

'I don't know what's happened to you, Abraham,' she had said, sitting behind the sleek glass desk in her corner office, the framed front pages of the *Chronicle*'s more recent big stories staring down at them. 'You're here, but you're not really here. And you've missed too many assignments over the last few months. I know they might not be high-end investigative pieces, but the mayor's press conference was important. We all have to pull our weight. You know what the industry's like at the moment.'

Abraham did but said nothing.

'Kelvin said you were at the trial.'

Abraham had given a thin smile.

'I know what happened to your sister. I know this whole situation with Nikolova, with county lines, it's personal, but it can't be an excuse, Abraham.'

Abraham had continued to say nothing.

'I've spoken to HR and they've recommended a leave of absence. Personal time.'

Rachel said some other stuff. Something about wanting to support him, about mental health, about being sorry and that the door was not being closed, but Abraham wasn't really listening. He was thinking that he was sorry, too; sorry that he'd ever heard the name Brody Lipscombe, sorry that Hristo Nikolova was able to get away with mass murder, and sorry that he hadn't had the guts to hit Spencer Milton when he had the chance.

As he stepped out of the editor's office to a sudden silence and a collection of badly disguised stares from the people sitting close by, he realised that he'd been the last to know about his fate.

Abraham took another swig of beer as the familiar views of this part of Essex flickered by; the fields and farms, the crumbling wreck of Hadleigh Castle.

Marion and Victor Hart had initially lived in Westcliff, the neighbourhood bordering Southend Central. Both had originally hailed from east London, moving to the Essex coast when they had Joshua, deciding that London was no place to raise a child. Abraham had arrived soon after his brother, followed by Grace much later, and entirely unplanned. By that point his parents had moved to their current, slightly bigger house on Cambridge Road, and had been there ever since.

Marion and Victor had immediately loved living outside the capital. They embraced life by the sea, the smaller but closer-knit community spirit, and especially the church, which had always been a part of their lives, but which became more central after their move. They rarely went back to London, only venturing there for occasional theatre visits or shopping trips at Christmas. It was ironic, really, because since he'd started senior school, Abraham had wanted nothing more than to leave Southend behind and move to London.

He'd achieved that dream by being accepted on a graduate scheme at the local paper, the *Southend Gazette*. Two years of training and three as a cub reporter later, Abraham bagged a job as a junior at the *Daily Mirror*.

It was at this point his career almost came off the tracks. He nearly threw everything away after getting involved with some old school friends who turned his head away from journalism and towards more nefarious avenues.

Siobhan, by then his girlfriend, steered him back. She salvaged his nascent career by convincing him not to waste the passion and the talent he had been given. He refocussed on the job he loved and moved to London with Siobhan, working his way through a series of jobs before moving to the role he had, that morning, unintentionally vacated.

In those twenty-five years he had moved to London, got married, moved back to Essex and had a child who he didn't see nearly enough of.

Abraham carefully heaved himself off the train when it finally stopped at Southend Central and made his way towards the old house, sucking in lungfuls of air in a bid to clear an increasingly foggy head.

The house was a tall, thin Edwardian construction that, like Abraham's career, had seen better days. The white render at the front was cracked and peeling, the gutter was leaking dirty rainwater down the discoloured brickwork and the small front garden, though tidy, was unloved.

But the sight of his home, despite its lacklustre kerb appeal, made Abraham feel nostalgic for his childhood. It even engendered in him a fraternal warmth towards Joshua, with whom he had a fractious relationship, especially over the previous few years after his brother's insistence on accepting Brody Lipscombe's supposed contrition at face value.

Despite living only a few miles away, in Eastwood, Abraham seldom visited his childhood home. He would usually blame work or, when Evie was small, the pressure of parenthood. Later he'd attribute it to dance class, and netball practice and school homework. Really, though, it was just work, and the fact that he couldn't bear to be in the place where he and Grace had spent so much time together.

After the death of their mother, he'd promised himself, and Joshua, that he'd make more of an effort. His dad was independent, mobile, a better cook than Abraham would ever be, and still as sharp as a tack, but he was also seventy-eight-years-old and living alone. He'd last been home at Easter, six months prior, and he could feel the pangs of guilt at his lack of physical contact with his aging father gnawing at his insides.

His front door key was somewhere in the bag slung over his shoulder, so he pressed the doorbell, heard the distant chime, and waited. A few seconds later he could hear the shuffle of feet on the other side of the door. Then it swung open and Victor Hart, dressed in a navy, cable-knit jumper, black jeans and a pair of brown moccasin slippers, stood, mouth open in surprise. 'Abraham! What a surprise,' he said, instinctively looking at his wrist. 'Shouldn't you be at work?'

Abraham wanted to say that, yes, he should be at work but as he seemed to be having some sort of existential crisis the *Chronicle* had let him go, or as good as. He could also add that, far from this being a surprise visit, he may need to move back into his old room if the *Chronicle* didn't allow him back. Or if his wife filed for divorce, which was looking increasingly likely.

'I took the day off,' he said.

The old house hadn't changed much since his last visit. Not that he had expected it to. The hallway walls were still covered in the flowery wallpaper that Abraham remembered his dad hanging around 1985, just before Grace was born. It was faded in the places that caught the sun, and there were black marks, scribblings and noticeable dents in more than a few areas, some of which were due to the various Hart offspring, others that had simply appeared over the years, like bruises that never healed.

A glass jar of potpourri sat on the telephone table halfway along the hall, next to the landline phone with the extra-large buttons. Marion had embraced the fad for containers of aromatic dead plant material in the early 90s and, so far, her husband had decided to keep up the tradition. For all Abraham knew it could be the same pot.

He dropped his bag in the hall and, as with any visitor - and Abraham felt more a visitor than a former resident - the next stop was the kitchen. Victor still referred to the off-white units and double oven as 'the new kitchen', despite it being installed in 1999. It smelled like a mixture of cooked meat, boiled vegetables and Mr Muscle, and was tidy, if worn, with nothing out of place apart from a slew of NHS-headed letters sprawled across the kitchen table, a magnifying glass lying next to them. The smell alone made Abraham feel like he was nine-years-old again.

'What's all this?' he said.

Victor attempted to tidy things away, shuffling pages into a neat pile. 'Oh, nothing. Just the usual vagaries that come with getting old. I don't recommend it, son.'

'I'll bear that in mind.'

'You been drinking?' he asked, the old man's sense of small undiminished by time. 'Anything wrong?'

'What? No. I had one on the train. Day off, you know. Different rules.'

'If you say so. How's Shiv and Evie? And are they coming too? Haven't seen either of them in a while, you know.'

'She's doing ok thanks, Dad. Still job hunting, so we're keeping our fingers crossed. She might come over later,' Abraham lied.

'That's wonderful,' replied Victor. 'I've been praying for her every day. God willing she'll be in the job of her dreams in no time.'

Abraham nodded and apologised for not coming down more, which Victor brushed off with a wave of his large but bony hand and asked if there was anything he could do to help out.

'Well,' said Victor, opening the fridge and removing a large Tupperware container, 'if you want to help, you could take this over to your brother.'

'What is it?'

'A casserole.'

'He's fifty-years-old, Dad. You shouldn't be making his dinner.'

'It's not for him, it's for Carol. You remember Carol, the housekeeper? Lovely woman, and such a tragedy about her daughter.'

'Her daughter?' said Abraham. 'I don't even know who Carol is.'

'Yes, you do,' said Victor. 'Anyway, I'm afraid it was drugs. Accidental overdose.'

'Christ!' said Abraham.

'Abraham!'

'Sorry. And this is for her?'

'It's only been a week since the funeral and she's back working already. Says she needs to keep busy. I can understand, of course I can. But she's not looking after herself. We all had each other after Gracie. Carol's on her own.'

Victor placed the Tupperware container in a cloth bag and handed it to Abraham. 'If she's not there, give it to Josh, he'll make sure she gets it. Plus, he'll be happy to see you.'

Abraham started on a sarcastic laugh that was curtailed by one of his father's stares.

'You can take my car if you want, you're still on the insurance.'

Abraham didn't want to mention the four cans of Stella, so said he fancied the walk.

Eight

*A*lissa's lectures finished at noon and after grabbing a sandwich from the cafeteria she changed in the toilet and got the bus from outside the college, back along the London Road and towards Spotlight.

She'd been lucky to get the work experience place over the summer. Mrs Johnson, her Media teacher, had recommended to all her students that, before they embarked on their final year of A Levels, they'd be well-advised to bolster their CV with some real-world experience in the industry they wanted to break into.

Great idea in theory, but southeast Essex was hardly a hotbed of film and television production, and Spotlight was the only company that had any kind of presence in the area. Few people knew what they actually did behind the slightly shoddy-looking glass-fronted office that was opaque enough to keep out prying eyes, but it was a place many of them passed every day. Alissa hadn't wasted any time, knowing that it would likely be everyone's first port of call when thinking of places to approach.

Only, no one else did think of Spotlight. Or, more to the point, no one thought of work experience at all. Most students were too busy enjoying the summer, meeting friends, boyfriends or girlfriends or going on holiday. Working for free as, essentially, a glorified waitress, wasn't at the top of most people's agenda. But Alissa wasn't most people. Even Em had shrugged at the thought of working for no pay over the holidays.

Within twelve hours of Mrs Johnson suggesting they think about a week or two's placement, Alissa had visited the offices, met with Lewis Maynard-Jones, the Managing Director of the company, shown him her CV and her (admittedly limited) film work, and had secured two weeks at the end of the summer holidays.

By the end of those two weeks, she'd made countless coffees and was on first name terms with the people who ran the sandwich shop a few doors down, but she had also picked up some invaluable knowledge about budgets, location recces and mood films. When Lewis asked her if she wanted to stay on for a couple of days each week, for a modest hourly wage, she'd been ecstatic and agreed immediately.

She had got on with everyone at the company since she'd started. Well, almost everyone. Francesca was proving a harder nut to crack, which was a shame because she was the person closest in age to Alissa. Lewis's Executive Assistant was a very pretty, chic-looking 23-year-old who had been at Spotlight for almost a year, but who often acted like she owned the place. She was the gatekeeper to Lewis, as well as to Lewis's wife's, who was a partner in the firm.

Francesca got annoyed if you didn't make an appointment to see either via her. She'd once pulled Alissa to one side after she'd popped her head around Lewis's office door to ask if he wanted a drink, saying Lewis was never to be disturbed without her explicit say-so. Francesca was efficient, no doubt, and took her job seriously, but was territorial over access to the company founders, especially Lewis.

Despite the likelihood of a less than warm welcome from Francesca, Alissa was even more keen to get to work than usual because of the project she had put in place at the end of her shift the previous day. Lewis had asked her what she was working on at college, so she had shown him clips of the film she and Em were putting together. It was a piece for Halloween, a short film about a spooky house and the barely seen inhabitants within. It was more a mood film than anything with a narrative, but Lewis had said it needed more creativity. 'Use what's around you,' he had told her. 'Think of things that can add that creepy, inhospitable element. Use different techniques, too. You don't want to throw everything at it, but people will want to see what you're capable of.'

Alissa had listened intently. She was disappointed that the response to her and Em's work hadn't been more fulsome but was determined to improve the film by taking on board what Lewis had told her in the office's boardroom, which didn't seem to have been cleaned properly in years which, after taking in Lewis's advice, had given her an idea.

'Afternoon,' Alissa said, smiling at Francesca as she walked through the entrance of Spotlight.

'Didn't know you were working today,' replied Francesca from behind her computer, the smile unreturned.

Alissa tried to laugh the comment off. 'It's Thursday. I always work Thursday.'

Francesca shrugged. 'Hadn't noticed.' Then she turned her attention back to the screen in front of her.

Alissa just nodded and made her way to her usual desk where she dumped her rucksack and hung her coat over the chair. The office was quiet. David, the company's Chief Financial Officer, was the only other person here and he was, as usual, lost in something on his computer screen, his oversized headphones covering his ears.

There were still a lot of staff members she hadn't met. Most, in fact. The company's website listed fifteen full time employees - a mixture of producers, directors, researchers, account people and admin staff - but Lewis had said that the company was so busy that they were often on shoots. Plus, many of them whose roles didn't require them to be on location worked from home. A situation that apparently existed even before the pandemic had changed working practices across a host of industries.

'Anyone in the boardroom, Francesca?' Alissa said across the room.

The Executive Assistant's mane of long, dark brown hair swished in the air as she turned to face Alissa, who was reminded of a shampoo advert. 'What do you want the boardroom for?'

Alissa bit her tongue as a reflexive swear word travelled upwards, towards her lips. 'I don't want the boardroom,' replied Alissa, putting extra emphasis on the word 'want'. 'I left something in there last night and I'm checking whether I can get it.' Alissa tilted her head to one side and delivered a smile that was soaked in contempt.

Francesca turned away, once again focussing on whatever was on her screen, and Alissa took that as unspoken permission. She knocked on the door before entering, just in case. It was the only room in the office that didn't have glass walls, and she wouldn't put it past Francesca to not tell her there was an important meeting happening to get her into trouble. When no one responded to the second, louder knock, Alissa tentatively pushed the door open and stepped into an empty room.

It was a long but thin space with a large wooden table in the centre and six black office chairs set around it. A conference call system sat in the middle of the table, wires snaking from it, and a 42-inch TV hung from the wall to the left. Shelves holding reference books, coffee table tomes and a series of DVDs were either side of the TV. Alissa recognised films by Martin Scorsese, Billy Wilder and Frank Capra, but her focus was on what lay on the very top shelf.

Before reaching up she checked the area between the top of the TV and the ceiling, nodding with satisfaction at the perfectly intact cobweb that hung there. Then she wheeled a chair over, carefully balanced herself on top of it and retrieved the item that would be the death of her.

Nine

Our Lady of Lourdes Roman Catholic church was a ten-minute stroll through the backstreets of Southend, across the main high street, then another ten minutes' walk further east. Abraham had walked these streets countless times in his youth; to friends' houses, to bars, to fast food restaurants, to girlfriends and prospective girlfriends. He'd walked them again as a cub reporter for the *Southend Gazette,* speaking to the city's inhabitants about burglaries and car thefts, sick children, elderly parents, and a hundred other things that make up the disparate contents of a local newspaper.

Hundreds of times in the past Abraham had openly criticised Southend and its surrounding areas. He'd poured scorn on those who'd never left, been cynical of those who'd arrived from other places, and told friends and colleagues in London that he was glad to have escaped. But, after leaving London and moving back, he was protective of it. He wouldn't stand for criticism of Southend from those who had never lived there. He became defensive when people cracked Essex jokes, or even parroted things Abraham himself had once said. It was, after all, his home and, for all its faults - of which he knew there were many - it had been good to him and to his family. At least, up until it took Grace.

Against all odds, the low sun had somehow forced its way through clouds the colour of a two-day-old bruise and, though not warm, the light gave the buildings around him an uplifting glow. It lit the red brick flats sitting above the shops on the high street, and the reflections on the windows sparkled like pools of clear water. The crisp air helped freshen Abraham's head from the remaining alcohol fog and, in an attempt to completely shift the nagging thud that had descended, he turned right, strolled beneath the railway bridge and made his way to a chaotically decorated coffee shop where he bought a double macchiato to take away.

Ten minutes later, after passing an array of charity shops, a newsagent and a development opposite the church that was in the middle of being build, he crossed the road and stood in front of the large, orange brick structure that was Our Lady of Lourdes.

A series of cordylines stood guard along the perimeter like spiked sentries and, next to them, a statue of the Virgin Mary, arms open in welcome. To the left of the church was a large, detached house built from the same orange brick; the rectory in which Joshua lived. Parked outside it was the blue Volvo Joshua had been driving for years.

Abraham had not been to his brother's church since Grace's funeral and, as he walked towards the main entrance, echoes of that day called out to him. They reminded him of a sky that had been cobalt blue, of a relentless sun beating down on the congregation like it wanted to sear the memory of that day from their minds. They recalled solemn faces, parched flowers and the whispered words of sympathy from people he barely remembered or had never met.

Most of all the echoes reignited the pain that had etched permanent lines across his parents' faces and which had reached inside Abraham's chest to wrap its frozen fingers around his heart. It had squeezed hardest on that day and, though its grip had slackened over the years, it still had a firm hold. Abraham was glad, because that pain-filled squeeze reminded him of his sister, and of the part he played in her death.

He entered the church, passing through the small porch that was filled by a wooden table, a variety of leaflets strewn across it, and into the nave. Rows of dark wood pews lined the large space, each with a pile of books neatly stacked at one end. There was a closed door on Abraham's left which, he knew, led to the sacristy, where the priest kept his vestments and changed for the service. A huge, stained-glass window dominated the far end of the building, an image of a crucified Jesus, both beautiful and terrifying, bearing down on the altar and everything else.

He was immediately hit by the lingering aroma of incense and burning candles, smells he associated with his childhood. And it was cold, too. Colder inside that out. Abraham wondered what it might cost to heat such a large, open space when the price of fuel was so high. Nothing, he decided, if you never turned the heating on.

'Thought that was you.'

The voice made Abraham jump, and he almost dropped the cloth bag containing the casserole. He turned and faced his brother, who was wearing black trousers, black shoes and a black clerical shirt with a white dog collar, every inch the dapper clergyman. He looked the same as he had six months previously; slim, bearded and with small dark eyes that peered out from silver-framed glasses.

'God, you scared the shit out of me,' said Abraham, placing his right hand over his chest.

Joshua gave him a stern look.

'Sorry. Just slipped out. Wasn't intentional, honest. I come in peace.'

'Well, that's good,' replied Joshua, 'because peace is one of our main tenets. What are you doing here, anyway? Not that it's not good to see you.'

'Day off,' said Abraham, staring at the floor. 'Thought I'd visit. Not been over for a while.'

The two brothers looked at each other, six feet apart but a lifetime of history between them. Neither was ever quite sure how to react upon meeting; fraternal hug? Casual nod of the head? Often a greeting was simply ignored but, on this occasion, Joshua took a step forward and offered a hand. It wasn't much, Abraham knew, and something most siblings wouldn't think twice about but, for them, it was a rare cessation of hostilities.

'So, what brings you to church? If you've come to confess, I'm afraid I have to meet a parishioner in a couple of hours.' Joshua's smile wasn't exactly warm, but Abraham recognised that his big brother's attempt at humour was an olive branch.

Abraham glanced at his watch. 'I'd love to stay, but I've got a character assassination in fifteen minutes, followed by an attack on democracy at half past so, you know... Dad asked me to bring this over,' he said, raising the bag slightly. 'For Carol.'

Joshua's face darkened, like a shadow had passed over it, and the smile which had only recently bloomed sunk away. He nodded, taking the bag. 'That's very nice of him, and I'm sure Carol will be very grateful. She's

—' Joshua paused, searching, '— not herself at the moment.'

'Can't blame her, though, can you? Not after what's happened.'

'You know about that then?'

'Dad told me. Sounds terrible. Did you know her? The daughter, I mean.'

'Not well, no. I baptised her, presided over her confirmation and I occasionally see her waiting —'. Again, Joshua paused, the shadow darkening. 'I occasionally *saw* her waiting for her mother, but she wasn't a parishioner, much to Carol's dismay. She was friends with Evie though, I think. At college together, so Carol has told me. How is Evie?'

'She's fine. Job-hunting'

'Well, anyone would be lucky to have her. I bet she was glad to see you.'

'Who?'

Joshua gave Abraham a confused stare. 'Evie. You've been to see her, haven't you?'

Abraham shuffled his feet, still staring at the floor. 'Well, no, not yet. Called in on Dad first.'

'Right, well, when you do see her,' replied Joshua, emphasising the verb, 'pass on my love. And to Siobhan too. How is Shiv?'

Abraham noticed the sly stare and over-egged smile, a trademark Joshua move that he thought might get the recipient of said stare to open up. Abraham wasn't falling for it but knew it meant Shiv had spoken to Joshua about their marital issues.

'Fine, fine,' he said, unconvincingly. 'I'll pass on your best when I see them.'

Joshua nodded, equally unconvinced. 'Listen,' he said, taking another half step closer and checking over his shoulder as he did so. 'I probably don't need to say this, but just in case.'

Abraham waited for some sort of rebuke or unwanted advice, for a pointed barb at his lack of marital commitment or fatherly concern, but the anticipated lecture didn't come.

'If Carol sees you,' Joshua continued, 'if she asks you things. Just treat her with kid gloves. Like I said, she's not herself and, really, she hasn't come to terms with what's happened. I told her she shouldn't be back at work yet, but she was insistent, and, well, just remember she's in shock, and grief hits everyone differently. Try not to engage.'

Abraham was unsure what his brother was talking about so just nodded. 'You did the funeral?'

'I did, yes. Last week. She was baptised in this church as a baby, and she had her funeral here, too. She wasn't religious but it was her mother's wish. Alissa left no indication of what should be done in the event of her death.'

Abraham let out a sarcastic laugh. 'Jesus, what eighteen-year-old does?'

Another stern look. Another apology.

'That was her name, was it? Alissa? Poor kid.'

Joshua made a noise that Abraham couldn't translate. 'Poor mother, I would say.'

Abraham wasn't sure what his brother meant by that. It sounded accusatory in some way, an unspoken reproach of young Alissa Peters. He wanted to ask but he decided that, while their often fractious relationship seemed, for now, to have found an even keel, it didn't make sense to rock the boat.

The brothers stood facing each other, each wondering what to say next, the extended pause between them as awkward as it was familiar. Abraham knew from experience that the next fail-safe area of conversation would be around their jobs, with Joshua eventually asking what story he was working on at the moment? Abraham didn't want to talk about work any more than he wanted to talk about his marriage and, in a bid to avoid having to lie about it, instead clung to a different untruth.

'I'd better go, Josh. Said I'd help dad with some stuff around the house,' he said, retreating from the church. 'I'll see you later.'

Joshua nodded, then pushed his glasses further up on his nose. 'Right-oh,' he said. 'I was planning to visit Dad tonight. Don't suppose you'll be there, will you? I suspect you'll be in Eastwood with Shiv and Evie.'

It was a leading question. A fishing expedition. Instead of rising to the bait, Abraham simply shrugged, raised a hand in goodbye, and walked back the way he'd come.

He hadn't got far from the church when Abraham heard his name being called. It took a few seconds for it to register because the person, in a quiet but insistent tone, was saying, 'Mr Hart! Mr Hart!' Only his bank manager called him that, so the words drifted through his consciousness without stopping to make themselves known. When they eventually did, Abraham turned to the source of the noise and saw a woman coming towards him, waving a thin arm.

It wasn't only her arm that was waif-like. Her entire body looked like it had been filtered down so that it had just enough space for her vital organs, but no more. She didn't look unhealthy, simply diminished, like she was in the process of fading from the world. She wore a mauve cardigan over a white t-shirt, a pair of black jogging bottoms and some slip-on training shoes. Her brown hair, greying at the roots, was tied back and it looked like she hadn't slept in days.

Abraham didn't need to ask for a name as Carol Peters approached, panting slightly after the short run, but he did anyway, out of politeness.

'I'm sorry to bother you, Mr Hart,' said Carol after introducing herself, eyes flitting around, settling everywhere except on Abraham's own. 'I wondered if I could have a word with you for a minute.'

'Of course. Would you like to go back to the church, get out of the cold? Could even get Josh… I mean Father Hart to make us a cuppa. I'm sure he wouldn't mind.'

For a second Carol locked eyes with Abraham and only then did he notice how red they were, the capillaries vivid against the milky white sclera. No sooner had their gazes met than Carol broke away and glanced over her shoulder, back towards the church. 'No. No, thank you, Mr Hart. I just… I know you must be busy, but I just wanted to ask if you might be able to help.'

'If I can, I'd be happy to,' said Abraham, remembering his brother's words but unsure what else he could say. 'But before you do, I just wanted to pass on my condolences. Drugs are unforgiving and remorseless, and I'm sorry it happened to you, and to Alissa, obviously.'

Carol stood silently, once again looking directly at Abraham. The nervousness had gone now, and the frail looking, late-middle-aged woman seemed to harden in front of him. Her jaw clenched and, just as he was about to ask if she was ok, she spoke. Her voice was lower and harder, the previous deference gone.

'She didn't take drugs,' Carol said. 'Ever. I know she wasn't an angel. No teenagers are. I'm not one of those people who believes their child can do no wrong, but Alissa didn't take drugs.'

Abraham didn't know how to reply, and he wasn't about to argue with a recently bereaved mother. Josh had told him that Carol was still coming to terms with her daughter's death, so she obviously didn't want to accept the terrible truth of what had happened. He could understand that, but his understanding didn't help him formulate any words, and he dug around inside his brain for a response.

'I know it must be a terrible shock,' was all he could come up with.

'If Alissa had been a drug user then, yes, it would have been a shock. But she wasn't so, what it is, Mr Hart, is murder. And, please, I'm begging, I need your help.'

Ten

Abraham stared at Carol Peters and, while he felt empathy, he also felt pity. She'd lost a loved one to circumstances beyond her control. She was angry, confused and unwilling to relinquish the memory she had of her daughter before finding out about her addiction. Abraham understood. He'd been through those same emotions after Grace's death, laying blame everywhere but at his sister's door. Of course, someone else *had* been to blame in that case, but even Abraham hadn't stooped to throwing around accusations of murder.

"You're obviously upset, and I completely understand,' said Abraham, a smile halfway between concerned and patronising painted on his face. 'You need to give yourself time to grieve.'

Carol's jaw clenched, the thin layer of skin on her face tightening. 'I don't need time, I need help,' she finally said, her volume rising. 'Didn't you hear what I said? She was murdered. Someone did this to her.'

'And the police? What did they say about it?'

A flash of red hit Carol's cheeks and her stare, until now aimed solely at Abraham, drifted to the floor.

'Nothing,' she said quietly. 'They don't believe what I'm saying any more than you seem to.'

'I'm sorry,' Abraham said. 'No one should have to go through what you're going through, but time's a great healer.'

Abraham winced inwardly as the hackneyed adage sprung from his lips. Did he even believe that himself? Not really, but what else was he meant to say?

Joshua had warned him about Carol's grief and anger, but surely that was only natural. He understood it completely and saw his own mother's suffering in Carol's drawn appearance and anguished tone. But murder?

While the word automatically raised his journalistic antenna, he knew it was nothing more than a smokescreen for a mother's intense grief at losing a child.

'If there's anything else I can do to help, please just let me know,' he added, not really meaning it. 'I'm really sorry about this, but I'm late for a meeting so —'

Abraham threw a thumb over his shoulder and offered an expression that he hoped conveyed sorrow at her loss, empathy for her situation but also a pressing need extricate himself from the conversation as soon as possible.

Before he could make his escape, Carol dug a bony hand into her trouser pocket and retrieved a slip of paper and a pen. She scribbled on the paper and handed it to Abraham.

'Please, Mr Hart, I know you think I'm crazy, but I'm not. If you'll just give it some thought. Please.'

And with that, the steely determination was gone and the frail woman with the weight of the world on her shoulders turned and headed back towards the church.

Abraham stood for a second, watching her retreat, then glanced at the piece of paper, an Aldi receipt, on the back of which Carol had written her phone number.

***

Abraham decided that more coffee was in order and soon found himself back at the same chaotically decorated coffee shop ordering a flat white. It was past lunchtime, so he added a meatball and cheese panini to his order, carrying it to a battered old couch in the upstairs dining area that was filled with mismatched seating, a random selection of old toys and games and, strangely, a large canoe hanging from the ceiling.

It was only then, once settled, that he reflected on the situation in which he found himself. A situation that included being temporarily jobless, currently aimless and, if the first became more permanent, imminently homeless. It was enough to reignite the hangover that was only just abating.ABraham took a sip of coffee and a bite of his sandwich and wondered when his luck might change.

'Abraham? What the hell are you doing here?'

Hearing those words and that voice, Abraham realised his luck wouldn't be changing anytime soon.

Wiping away melted cheese from the corner of his mouth, he looked up to see Siobhan's hazel eyes staring down.

'Shiv!' said Abraham, scrambling to think of an answer.

Siobhan, carrying a mug of coffee, flicked at her mane of perfectly braided hair and pursed her flawlessly lacquered maroon lips, forcing out a sound that was a mixture of annoyance and resignation. 'How long have you been home and when were you thinking of telling us?'

Abraham's heart pulsed with a mixture of misery and longing at the word 'home'. He's started to wonder if he belonged in Southend anymore. The people he loved might live here, but did they want or need him around?

'Yeah, well, I came down to see…' he mumbled.

Siobhan's stare, laser-focussed, had lost none of its ability to unnerve Abraham in the many years since they had first met. 'You'd better be about to say Evie.'

'Of course I came to see Evie. Why else would I come?'

'But you thought a nice sit down, a bite to eat and a coffee in town took precedence over visiting your daughter?'

Abraham sighed. It was becoming a habit. 'Come on, Shiv. I've just got off the train. I thought I'd just get some lunch down me, and then I planned to come over.'

Siobhan lowered herself onto the chair opposite Abraham, releasing a stream of exasperated air as she did so. 'Right, well, it's just, we've not seen you for a while and she misses you. She needs all the support she can get.'

'I know. But she knows I'm always here for her. And, well, it wasn't my decision to move out, was it?'

Siobhan's jawline hardened, and her shoulders stiffened. 'Let's not go into that now. What's up with work?'

Abraham was about to take a bite of his sandwich but stopped, mouth open. 'What d'you mean?' he asked, lowering the sandwich. 'Why would anything be up?'

Siobhan gave him a suspicious look. 'I just mean, it's Friday. You hardly ever take time off. Even when Grace died you pretty much worked the next day.'

Abraham shot his wife a glance that she recognised,

and Siobhan quickly worked to rescue herself from a conversation she'd had too many times before. 'I'm sorry,' she said. 'I didn't mean anything. Just, you lose yourself in work, Abe. It's a shield, a smokescreen and a haven all rolled into one. That's part of the problem, our problem.'

'Might not be for much longer,' he muttered.

'Pardon?'

'Nothing. After we spoke yesterday, I just thought it would be nice to see Evie. Like you say, I'm owed some days.'

'Well, she'll appreciate that. I appreciate it, too.'

'Oh, and Dad said to say hello, as well. And Josh.'

Too late, Abraham realised the mistake he'd made.

'When did you see them? Today? I thought you said you'd just got off the train. Typical, isn't it? Bloody typical,' said Siobhan, her voice rising. 'You were meant to be here yesterday but, oh no, that's too much like hard work, too inconvenient for you. Instead, you wander in more than a day late and, even then, rather than prioritising your daughter you go home for a cup of tea. Then what? Try to beg forgiveness from Josh's big boss in the sky for being a lousy father to your only child?'

Abraham apologised again and tried to look contrite, but he'd already lost his wife to her perfectly reasonable anger.

Siobhan elegantly rose from the sofa, managing to keep the cup of coffee she was sipping from perfectly level, and turned back to her husband. 'Look, I haven't got the energy for this. I just came for a coffee and a break from the office. I'll leave you to it, but just promise me you'll see Evie. Today, Abraham. You might not believe it, sometimes I barely do, but she needs her dad.'

Then, after another flick of her braids, Abraham watched Siobhan turn and descend the stairs, leaving him feeling even lower than when he'd arrived.

Abraham spent another hour in the coffee shop after Siobhan had stormed out, sipping two more coffees and indulging in a slice of banana loaf while he fiddled with his phone, trying to work out the best thing to say to Evie when he finally called her.

His separation from Siobhan had thrown into sharp relief his relationship with his daughter and how, in recent years, it had been too one-sided. Her reaching out to him while he prioritised work, or his mum. Then, when his mum died, putting his focus back onto work. He'd taken her for granted and while he'd been there for most of the myriad milestones - new schools, exams, friend issues, boyfriend troubles - he'd not been there for all of it. Not like Siobhan.

He could feel her slipping away from him and he knew it was his own grip that was loosening, not hers. Unconsciously he clenched his fist, promising himself that he would do better, be better.

At almost 3.30pm Abraham picked up his phone and took a deep breath, scrolling to Evie's number. He stared at the picture of her, the one taken on her tenth birthday, Evie sporting a chocolate smudged grin, eyes sparkling, hair streaked with ribbons, a picture he couldn't bring himself to change.

As his finger hovered over the button to call, his phone lit up, the ring tone sounded, and an image of his dad appeared on the screen. Abraham accepted the call.

'Everything ok?' asked Abraham.

'Fine, all fine. Just wondered where you'd got to, that's all.'

'Just stopped for some lunch. Sorry, do you need me for something?'

'What? No, no. Well, actually, Josh is here, looking for you. And, well, he's brought someone with him, someone he wants you to talk to.'

Abraham nodded to himself, guessing that Carol Peters had returned to the church and spoken to Joshua, maybe asked him to convince Abraham to help with whatever it was Carol thought she needed him for. He wondered whether Joshua would be angry that he'd already spoken to Carol. But he couldn't be blamed for her approaching him. He hadn't done anything wrong.

'Right,' said Abraham. 'Well, I can be back in fifteen minutes or so. That ok?'

'That's perfect,' said his dad 'And Abraham, I know you've turned your back on religion for now, but remember what the Bible says, 'For I will forgive their wickedness and remember their sins no more.' Anger will only eat you up.'

'Ok, understood,' he said, not understanding at all, and wondering what Carol Peters might be about to reveal.

After staring at his phone for a few thoughtful seconds Abraham eventually decided it would be better to call Evie in the privacy of his room, and after he'd dealt with his dad, Joshua and Carol. Arriving at Cambridge Road he unlocked the front door and was immediately confronted by his dad, who stood in the hallway, hands clasped in front of him, feet slightly apart, like he was standing to attention.

Abraham looked him up and down. 'You alright? Looks like you're waiting for the King, or a firing squad. Anyway, I'm here now, where is she?'

Victor Hart drew in a breath, as if preparing to launch into a lengthy speech, but then stopped, wrinkled his brow and instead said one word, 'She?'

It was Abraham's turn to look confused. 'Carol. I assumed it was Carol who Josh brought over. She stopped me earlier, wanted to talk.'

Victor began slowly nodding, absorbing the information. 'I see. But no, it's not Carol.'

'Right,' replied Abraham, the word drawn out, his wariness on high alert. Siobhan? he wondered. Had she gone straight to Joshua after their meeting in the coffee shop in a bid to try to get Abraham to see sense? Or Evie? But his dad was acting too weird for it to be her. Surely not someone from work? Rachel wouldn't have the time or the inclination to visit him at his parent's home, would she?

Father and son stood staring at one another. All they needed were Stetsons and six shooters and it was a scene from *High Noon*. Abraham was about to take the direct approach and simply ask what the hell was going on when someone walked out of the door behind Vic, the one that led from the kitchen onto the hall.

It was Joshua, his dog collar gleaming white against his black attire. 'Ah, Abe, thought I heard your voice. Listen, I don't want you to get upset…'

Abraham cut him off, the sense that he was being ambushed growing. 'Why does everyone keep assuming I'm going to be upset? Are you cutting me out of the will or something, Dad?' Abraham attempted a smile. 'Is there a solicitor back there waiting for me to sign away my inheritance?'

But when another figure stepped out of the kitchen, someone smaller, head bowed, eyes diverted to the floor, Abraham realised it was much worse than that.

From a position of general joviality, if vague unease, Abraham's mood changed, as if someone had flipped a switch. He looked from his brother to his dad, searching for an explanation. When none was forthcoming, he channelled his anger and exasperation into a question delivered at a shout, 'What the hell's he doing here?'

Before either could answer Brody Lipscombe inched forward and, eyes still aimed at the floral carpet, said, 'I don't want to cause any trouble, Abraham. I just wanted to apologise, to explain, to look for forgiveness, and Father Hart, he thought now might be a good time.'

Abraham couldn't think, couldn't bend his synapses to formulate idea or reason. He could only feel. His body seemed like it was on fire, as if it was being heated from within, from his feet upwards. The air around him seemed to vibrate until it was buzzing in his ears.

'Abraham,' said Joshua, stepping forward, 'I know you hold anger in your heart. I understand, we all do. But the only person it's hurting is you. None of us stay the same through our lives, not me, not you and certainly not Brody.'

'Anger?' shouted Abraham, no longer able - nor wanting - to regulate his volume. 'Anger? This bastard killed our sister!' He turned to his dad. 'Your daughter! He helped her get addicted to something that could kill her. That *did* kill her! I'm not just angry, I'm apoplectic. I'm enraged. You should be too. And now he's in our house! In *her* house!'

Abraham could feel the heat inside his body rising, in both temperature and in level. The rage moving up until it was stinging his eyes. He felt the familiar prick of tears and tried to calm down. He didn't want to cry, not in front of them, not in front of Brody Lipscombe.

'I am truly sorry, Abraham,' said Brody.

He still hadn't looked up and his tone was meek, respectful. He almost sounded sincere, thought Abraham, almost believable.

But Abraham wouldn't be fooled.

'You're *sorry*? *You're* sorry? Well, that's ok then. Let's just forget it, shall we?'

Abraham moved forward, jaw clenched, fists balled.

His seventy-eight-year-old father stepped in front of him and placed his thin, pale arms against his son's chest. He looked at Abraham, willed him to turn his furious gaze from Brody to him, saw the tears in his eyes, felt the anger vibrating from within him.

'Abraham,' he said quietly. 'Son, look at me.'

Abraham flicked his eyes towards Victor, holding his stare, wanting his father to know how upset he was, how hurt he felt at what he considered to be an unforgivable ambush.

'It's not your fault, Abraham,' whispered Victor. 'It was never your fault. Before you can forgive anyone else, you need to forgive yourself.'

The tears that were threatening to leak from Abraham, the ones he'd tried to hold back, now rolled out, like a dam had been breeched. He turned from his dad and shot a look of contempt at his brother, one of murderous rage at Brody, then spun around, opened the front door and strode out, slamming it as he left.

Eleven

*I*t was already gone 6pm as Alissa headed down Crowstone Road. The wind had picked up and, as she crossed the footbridge over the train tracks and towards the flat, she pulled the collar of her coat up around her ears, hunkering down into it for warmth.

She was only paid until five o'clock, but Lewis had arrived with David just before she was leaving and asked if Alissa could get them coffee from the cafe. She'd made it just before they were closing for the day but, after delivering them back to the office, Lewis then asked if she could also get some sandwiches from the local supermarket, which she had dutifully done, wondering what was wrong with Francesca's legs that she couldn't carry out this particular task.

The hours before that had been taken up with some research on a big shoot the company was undertaking in South Africa the following month. Lewis had asked her for images of large houses in Cape Town which had uninterrupted views of a sandy beach. She'd not been told what the location was for exactly but had set about the assignment with verve and had produced a folder full of images she hoped would be useful.

All during her time at the office she'd been eager to check the footage she'd recorded overnight but hadn't had the chance. She'd noticed the cobwebs above the boardroom's TV the day before Lewis had reviewed the *work-in-progress of her and Em's Halloween project. Only after that conversation did it occur to her she could use the slightly dusty room to her benefit.*

At the end of the previous day's shift, when the office was all but empty, only David still at his desk, headphones on as usual, she'd placed her phone up on the top shelf. She used some books to keep it steady, which also had the added benefit of concealing all but the lens, and pointed it down towards the cobweb-strewn screen. She'd angled a desk lamp that sat on a side table so that it pointed up to the cobwebs, backlighting it, hoping it would help the camera pick up the image.

She wasn't sure how long the battery would last or exactly what she'd capture, but she kept her fingers crossed that the spider would make an appearance and that the video could be used to add some of the creativity Lewis said it lacked. She imagined slowing the footage down, maybe playing with the filters and adding some creepy music. She knew it wouldn't be anything to rival an Attenborough documentary but, if she was lucky, it might be a nice addition to the finished film.

Craig hadn't said what time he'd be home that evening, but he usually arrived around seven-ish which, once back in the flat, had given her some time to make a bolognaise, which she'd left to simmer on the hob, planning to put the pasta on as soon as Craig walked in. She then laid on the sofa to check the footage on her phone.

She was rewatching it for the tenth time when Craig trudged through the door. But, so engrossed in what she was watching, Alissa didn't hear him.

'We're going to have to rein in the spending,' Craig said in place of a greeting, walking to the fridge to grab

himself a beer. He rummaged through the kitchen drawer for the bottle opener then leaned against the countertop in the kitchen. 'You hear what I said, Al? It's odds on those smarmy twats in head office are letting half of us go and you can bet that it's last in, first out.' Craig took a swig of his beer, his anger building at his girlfriend's lack of response. 'Al!' he shouted. 'What? You're more interested in some bloody TikTok video, are you? It's just my bloody job!'

It was only at the raised voice that Alissa realised someone was talking to her. She looked up from the phone she'd been staring at and towards the voice. 'Pardon? Sorry, babe, it's just, well, something weird's happened.'

Craig gave an exaggerated sigh and threw his head back. 'Oh right! Weirder than me losing my job?'

'What? You've lost it? Oh no, I'm so sorry. What happened?'

'Not yet, but it's pretty likely. If it happens, you're going to have to get something with more hours and more money than that production thing.'

But Alissa wasn't listening. She'd gone back to looking at the phone, her mouth slightly open, her stare intense. 'What the hell are you looking at?' said Craig, walking towards his girlfriend. As he got closer Alissa turned the phone to face him. He kneeled to get a closer look.

On the screen was what looked to Craig like part of an office. It was a downward view of a flat screen television hanging on a wall. Beyond it was the edge of a table with a couple of chairs facing each other, and a light that was shining into the lens, making it hard to see what the light source was, or what it was resting on.

Towards the top of the image was a spider's web. The intricate pattern was picked out by the light and the white, backlit silk strands were very thin, but still visible.

'What am I meant to be looking at?' asked Craig.

'Just wait. I've fast forwarded it a bit.'

Craig waited and within a few seconds another light came on, this one brighter and seemingly coming from overhead. Then there was a voice, off screen.

'Who's left the lamp on in here?'

It was a man's voice. One Craig didn't recognise, but Alissa helped him out.

'That's Lewis. The owner of the company, the one I told you about,' she said.

Alissa saw Craig bristle. When asked about her new boss, she had described Lewis as rich, successful and still relatively young and, on that evidence alone, she could tell Craig had immediately disliked him. The owner of the voice then walked into shot, heading for the lamp to turn it off. Lewis was tall, thin, had blonde hair and, if you liked that sort of thing, was objectively good-looking. Alissa knew that would rile Craig even more.

When the lamp was switched off everything else became clearer, the flare no longer distorting the image. The next voice belonged to a woman who was still off screen.

'Probably that silly mare, the work experience one. Don't know what you were thinking giving her a job.'

Alissa turned red with embarrassment. 'That's Francesca,' she mumbled.

'Not getting jealous, are we, Fran? She is rather attractive,' *said Lewis.* 'Bit young, mind, even for me.'

Alissa went an even deeper red while, on the screen, Francesca pushed Lewis against the wall next to what they could now see was a small table on which the lamp sat, alongside some bottles of water and a TV remote. She pressed herself against him then kissed him. It was a long, lingering kiss that lasted a few seconds, and which Lewis eased himself into.

'Slow down, tiger,' *said Francesca, drawing away and turning around. When she turned, they could see Lewis had undone half of her shirt buttons, the tops of her breasts now showing, along with the edges of a purple bra.*

'We haven't got long,' *said Lewis, starting to undo his own shirt and slipping off his brown brogues.* 'And I've been wanting to do this all day.'

For the next five minutes the video showed Lewis and Francesca come in and out of frame, each time in different states of undress. They heard the telltale noises that suggested they were having sex. Sometimes Lewis's head came into shot, sometimes Francesca's. There was never a full-length image of both of them, but at various points both were topless. Alissa noticed Craig's attention intensify each time Francesca appeared naked from the waist up and felt her own pang of jealousy.

The action abruptly ended when the entire screen went black. It seemed that the phone had somehow fallen over and the lens had landed flush against the shelf it had been resting on. Voices could still be heard for a few minutes, snatches of mumbled conversation, then they too disappeared. It had been a short video, the definition of a 'quickie', Alissa supposed, and though she fast forwarded for five minutes, the black screen remained unchanged. She dragged her finger along the play bar all the way to the end of the recording, which was nearly two hours in total, but no one and nothing entered the frame.

'Where the hell did you get this?' Craig eventually asked.

Alissa explained what she had done and why.

'Jesus! Did you know they were together?'

'They're not together,' replied Alissa. 'She's, like, twenty-three or something. And he's old, married. To the co-owner of the company.'

'Dirty bastard,' said Craig, but with a lascivious smile which insinuated to Alissa that her boyfriend thought Lewis might also be a lucky bastard. 'What're you going to do?'

'I'm not going to do anything. It's none of my business. I didn't ask permission to set up the phone and I don't want anyone to think I was trying to film them doing — that. I want to keep this job.'

'What about his wife? Doesn't she deserve to know?'

Alissa paused, biting her lip. It was exactly what she had been thinking, and though it felt like a betrayal to leave her in the dark, she couldn't see any other way around it. 'Probably,' she answered, 'but it's not my fault she married a cheating shit.'

'So, you're just going to leave it? Pretend you never saw it?'

Alissa was getting annoyed now, with herself as much as with Craig. She was starting to wish she'd never mentioned it. Never showed him the video. 'That's exactly what I plan to do,' she answered, throwing the phone onto the sofa and levering herself up. 'I'll put the pasta on while you have a shower,' she said tersely. 'Dinner will be ready in ten minutes.'

Craig shook his head slowly, making a show of his disappointment as Alissa retreated to the kitchen to ready dinner. She moved to the sink to fill the kettle with water, turning her back on him.

If she hadn't done so, she would have seen Craig glance at her phone, which was now laying face up on the sofa. She would have seen him quickly look from the handset to the kitchen and back again as he noticed that the floral background image she used, and the various app icons layered over the top, were still illuminated because she hadn't locked the screen.

But Alissa's back remained turned and, instead, all she heard was Craig lever himself off the sofa, mumble something about a shower, and make his way to the bedroom.

Twelve

Abraham had no destination in mind, he just knew he needed to be somewhere else. The scorching anger was still flowing through him as he marched down Cambridge Road and back towards Southend. The wind had picked up and a cold breeze attempted to cool the rage inside him, but it would be a slow process.

He constructed conversations in his head, with his father and with Joshua, trying to make them see how wrong they were, how much damage had been done by Brody Lipscombe. How allowing him to be forgiven, allowing him to forgive himself, was like condoning what had happened.

'It's not your fault, Abraham.'

He tried to push his dad's words to the back of his mind and concentrate on the fury. Who the hell did they think they were? They knew his feelings on this. Just because they'd been drawn in by Brody's charade, it didn't mean he needed to be. And today, of all days. He hadn't even told them about the outcome of Nikolova's trial, wasn't sure, now, if they'd care either way.

He continued walking the quiet back streets of the neighbourhood. He could see the glow of TVs behind curtains, hear the indistinct conversations of families leeching out from homes. He walked past a playground, one he and his siblings used to visit when they were kids. It had been made over since those days; a new slide, more modern swings, a climbing frame in the shape of a train, all resting on a red, springy rubber surface. But the space held memory, regardless.

He saw the ghosts of him and Joshua teasing their much younger sister, annoyed that they had to look after her. He saw the joy on her face as they pushed her higher and higher on the rickety old swing. Remembered her clinging to him when she came tumbling off and cut her knee, Joshua carrying her home in his arms.

'It's not your fault, Abraham.'

The images haunted him, not just now, but often. They would catch him unaware, creeping up on him when they were least expected. Sometimes they would retreat to the darker recesses of his mind, overshadowed by other things, but eventually they would crawl back out to bask in the light, upending his day.

There was nothing he could do about it though. No way back from what had happened. No way of fixing the past. But, he thought, dipping a hand into his coat pocket, revelling in doing something his sanctimonious brother had asked him not to, maybe he could fix someone else's.

After one phone call and ninety minutes of aimless walking it was almost 5.30pm by the time Abraham made it to Southend's main high street. The town centre was getting busy. Groups of people milled around - mainly teenagers and early-twenty-somethings - dressed in their Friday night finest, jeans and shorts with box-fresh trainers for the boys and figure-hugging dresses and vertiginous heels for the girls. Some were already drinking from bottles of lager or colourful cans of cocktail mixers. They were laughing, shouting and readying themselves for whatever the night ahead might offer. Abraham envied their freedom and their youth.

At various points during the previous hour and a half, when the storm clouds of his anger occasionally cleared and he saw a sliver of calmer skies, he had considered calling his dad, or Joshua. He wondered if he'd overreacted, thought about trying to apologise. But obstinance, or pride, or the reformation of darker skies prevented him from doing so and, with each step he took, the farther away from them he got and the harder it was to wrestle that pride into submission.

'Bollocks!' he said under his breath as he approached the Starbucks at the top of the high street. The shop was empty, the window was dark, a hand-written sign telling him an electrical fault had caused an early closure.

Abraham pulled his phone out, tapped the number he'd recently dialled and waited for a few seconds. 'Sorry, it's me again. Starbucks is shut. I know it's maybe not ideal, but how about The Last Post. If we can't get a table, we'll think of something. I'm almost there, so what can I get you to drink?'

Abraham entered the large Wetherspoon's pub, bought a pint of Guinness and a glass of orange juice and sat at a small wooden table on a stained upholstered chair. After five minutes, during which the pub got steadily busier and noisier, Carol Peters appeared, smiling nervously, and sat down opposite him.

'Sorry about this,' said Abraham, gesturing around at the teeming space and the noisy chatter. 'Least we're unlikely to be overheard.'

'I'm not ashamed of what I think, or what I have to say,' countered Carol as she removed her beige overcoat and green scarf, placing them on the back of the chair.

'Not suggesting you are,' replied Abraham, wondering if he'd made a mistake in calling her.

'I'm sorry,' she said, softening as she slumped into the chair. 'It's just, no one's listening. No one cares. It's easier for them not to. More straightforward. But I know…' Carol's features hardened for the briefest of moments. 'I *knew* my daughter.'

'Tell me about her.'

Carol took a sip of her drink then drew in a deep breath. She told Abraham about marrying young, and to a man who turned out to be less than she thought he was. She talked about having a child quite late in life, and about the joy it brought her. She talked about how Alissa's father was often the cloud covering the sunshine of their daughter's existence. She crossed herself, ashamed, as she admitted that her husband's death, two years previously, had been a blessing not a curse. She talked about Alissa as a vibrant, joyful, outgoing and creative young woman. How she loved reading, writing, art. Carol explained how the church, and Abraham's own brother, had been there for her when times were tough. How her religion had comforted her and about her disappointment in her daughter's estrangement from the church.

'What caused that?' Abraham asked.

'Nothing. Everything,' answered Carol. 'Young people have other things to worship these days, don't they? Celebrity, money, social media. She was like most other kids her age, God wasn't a necessary part of her life. God isn't cool.'

Abraham nodded, taking another sip of Guinness. He wondered if Carol thought he was religious too but didn't feel now was the time for a confession of his own.

'She moved out earlier this year,' continued Carol. 'To a pokey flat in Westcliff with Craig. That's her boyfriend. Sorry. Was her boyfriend. She was a student at college in Benfleet. Was in her final year there and got some work experience at a place in Leigh called Spotlight Design and Production. Did it over the last couple of weeks of the summer and they kept her on for a few evenings a week. Paid, like. Not much but she was happy about it.'

'What was she studying?'

'Media, film and art. Wanted to get into TV or film production.'

'How could she afford a flat? Did she have another job?' asked Abraham.

'No. Craig paid the rent. He's a bit older. Not much. Twenty-three, I think. Works in the city. Or did. Haven't seen him since Alissa died.'

'You haven't seen him at all? What about Alissa's funeral?'

Carol shook her head, the memory of that very recent day still a raw, exposed nerve.

'She sounded like a lovely young woman, and I'm incredibly sorry for your loss. I have a daughter myself and can't imagine what you're going through. But what you said earlier today,' Abraham lowered his voice, even though the noise around them was overwhelming. 'About murder. What did you mean?'

'They say it was an overdose. Heroin. Craig found her in the bedroom, a needle in her arm, all this drug stuff around her.' Carol was no longer upset, instead she was angry. Abraham could hear it in her voice, could see it in her clenched jaw and hard, unblinking stare. 'They found more of it in the drawer beside her bed.'

'Craig told you this?'

Carol shook here head. 'Never spoke to him. Never saw him. The police told me. Open and shut, they said. I asked about him, about Craig, but they said he'd been at work all day, had a whole office to back that story up, plus a bunch of CCTV footage. She was a secret addict, they said.'

'But you don't believe them?'

'Of course not. You might look at me and see a grieving, old-before-her-time God-botherer, but I was young once. Young around here, too,' Carol said, glancing around at the men and women noisily enjoying their Friday night. 'Drink, drugs, sex. I'm not naive, you know, and nor was Alissa. We talked about it, all of it. What it could do to you, how it could control you and ruin you, as much as it could help with a good night out. She was ambitious. More than I ever was. She wanted a life I never had. A career, money, fulfilment. She was clever. Too clever by half to take heroin.'

'So, what do you think happened? What is it you think I can do to help?'

'Someone killed her. I don't know why but I know what you do. I've read the *Chronicle*, I've seen the people you've helped, the things you've uncovered. I asked Father Hart about it, whether he'd ask you to help me.'

'And?'

'He said he'd talk to you,' replied Carol. 'He said he'd ask, but he hasn't, has he?'

'No.'

'I think he's afraid of getting my hopes up. I think he believes what the police have said. That Alissa did this to herself.'

'Carol,' Abraham said, 'I'm flattered you think I can help, and obviously you knew Alissa better than anyone, but what if it *was* drugs? What if the police are right and she was using? What if it was just a terrible accident?'

Carol Peters was small, and thin and looked as if a stiff breeze might carry her away, but the stare she gave Abraham was strong, like oak, immovable. 'I know about your sister. I wasn't working at the church back then, but I was a parishioner. I saw what it did to you all. What it's still doing.'

'We're ok.'

'Father Hart says you've never been to visit her grave.'

'Yeah, well, Father Hart should learn when to keep his nose out of other people's business.'

Carol looked embarrassed, a flash of red striking her cheeks. 'I'm sorry, I didn't mean to pry.'

'Look,' said Abraham, not wanting to take his anger at his brother out on Carol, 'the difference is that Grace *was* an addict. She *did* overdose.'

'I know. And it didn't just kill her, it killed a part of all of you. Alissa's death is killing me too, but I know, I'm absolutely certain, someone else is to blame. Nothing can bring Alissa back, I know that, but I want my memory of her to be pure. No,' said Carol, dabbing a tissue at her eyes, tears now leaking from them, 'I want other people's memories of her to be pure, and I want whoever did this to her to face justice.'

Abraham sighed, though it was lost beneath the laughter and noise, the shrieks and yells of the pub. He took another sip of his drink to buy him some time. 'I'm not a policeman,' he finally said. 'I have no authority, no power, there's no reason for people to talk to me.'

'You're a journalist for a big national newspaper. That's reason. That's power.'

Abraham didn't want to admit to himself, let alone to a relative stranger, that currently he was no such thing, and that the only words he would likely be committing to paper in the near future would be ones to update his CV.

'I can pay you,' said Carol. 'I have savings. I can get a loan, too, to tide you over.'

Abraham looked at Carol, saw the intensity in her eyes and heard the desperation in her voice. He recognised it, not just in his mother, but in himself. He had wanted to believe that Grace's death had been someone else's fault, too. That the final, fateful plunge of the syringe had been the work of an unseen hand. That the cravings she couldn't turn her back on were due to someone's else's weakness. Most of all he recognised the futile hope for an outcome different to the one that had already happened, and he knew nothing good could come of agreeing to help.

'Ok,' he said, because nothing good would come of not helping, either. 'I don't want money, but Carol, understand that there is a ninety-nine per cent chance that what the police say happened, happened. That as much as you want this to be some big conspiracy, the odds are this is just a tragic story that happens more often that we'd like to admit.'

Carol Peters was nodding and, for the first time since she'd started talking, smiling. Abraham knew the only thing she had heard him say were two letters, 'Ok'.

'Thank you, Mr Hart, thank you so much,' she said, leaning across the table to shake his hand.

But, as she did so, her fingers brushed against his half full pint of Guinness, tipping the glass and spilling its contents across the table. Abraham instinctively jumped up from his seat to avoid getting his trousers soaked, inadvertently knocking into a man behind him whose own drink sloshed over the rim of his glass and landed down the front of his unusually patterned shirt.

'The fuck!' shouted the man who, Abraham now saw, was less a man and more a teenager with aspirations. A teenager, however, who looked like he spent more time at the gym than most Olympians.

'Sorry about that,' said Abraham. 'My mistake. Let me get you another one.'

'Was your fucking mistake, mate,' said the not-quite-adult, the veins on his neck throbbing with hostility, or steroids, or possibly both.

'Prick!' shouted someone, Abraham didn't know who, or if it was aimed at him.

'Knock the old bastard out, Harry,' came another cry.

This time Abraham was certain he was the 'old bastard' and wanted to point out that forty-six wasn't actually that old, certainly not these days. But lessons in civility were unlikely to help matters at this point and, despite his age being the butt of jokes, the situation actually made him feel young. He had been in this pub many times in his youth; for mid-week sessions or pre-club weekend drinks, back when Southend had nightclubs, that was. More than once he had witnessed alcohol-fuelled men (and occasionally women) start fights they had no chance of finishing over arguments they had no hope of remembering.

It usually involved posturing, swearing and the occasional shove in the chest before bystanders would intervene, allowing both potential pugilists to save face by saying something along the lines of, 'Good job you stepped in or I'd 'ave…' followed by some violent colloquialism or other. Abraham knew how it went. He'd danced this routine before.

The man-boy called Harry stared at Abraham, shoulders pulled back, chin pushed out, hands balled into fists, like someone was about to ring a bell. Abraham turned to Carol, who was still sat, wide-eyed, shrinking into her chair, both hands wrapped around her half-empty glass of orange juice. She may have been young once, he thought, but scenarios like this were a distant memory. He mouthed the words, 'It's ok' to her, before turning back to face his would-be opponent.

'Look, mate,' he said, 'I've apologised, said it was an accident. Do you want another drink or not?'

'And what about me shirt?'

Abraham's general inclination was towards peacemaker. But, after the last couple of days, and the very recent argument with his family, he didn't feel like playing the conciliator, certainly not to a teenager with more muscles than brain cells. He'd had enough and though he knew he was playing with fire, he put his faith in the onlookers doing their part as firefighters.

'My dad's got some curtains just like that shirt,' he said, taking a step forward so their protruding chests were now touching. 'Gimme your address and I'll pop them over tomorrow. You can knock another one up.'

Some people around them loudly drew in a breath, a co-ordinated and exaggerated gasp. Others laughed, some cheered - ironically or otherwise, Abraham wasn't sure. Harry, for his part, did not see the funny side.

'I'll rip your fuckin' 'ead off,' he said, shoving Abraham in the chest, making him bang into the table he'd stood up from and causing Carol to let out a small yelp.

The crowd sensed this wasn't the usual charade that men - and it was always men - went through, and the ripple of expectation from those watching fanned outwards like a restless wave, tapping the next person on the shoulder, and the next, until a ring of twenty to thirty people fixed their eyes on the spectacle playing out. Abraham's hope that the firefighters might intervene was gone. Pyromaniacs surrounded him.

He could hear the blood in his ears and felt his heart beating fast in his chest. He didn't fancy his chances against someone more than two decades behind and probably four weekly trips to the gym ahead of him, but he wasn't about to back down.

He turned slightly to his right, keeping his left foot forward, staying on the balls of his feet. He clenched his fists, raising them slightly, hearing the crowd around him become louder, jeering and swearing, apprehensive and excited in equal measure.

'You ready, old man?' Harry asked.

He was as ready for a fight as he'd ever be, he supposed. But he wasn't ready for a voice shouting above the noise and cheers of encouragement. A voice he recognised.

'Hart-breaker?' it shouted, from somewhere to Abraham's left. Which is the way his head turned an instant before a fist connected with his right ear and the sounds around him faded into nothing.

Thirteen

'Some fings never change eh, Abe?' said Tony Stone. 'Mind, it used to be you trying to steer me clear of trouble, not the other way round.'

They were sat in Tony's car, a sleek S-Class Mercedes, Abraham in the passenger seat. The motor was purring quietly, the cream leather seats starting to warm up, soothing the posterior that Abraham had recently been knocked onto. Tony had fished around in the glove box and pulled out a crumpled packet of travel tissues, one of which Abraham had wedged up his nose in a bid to mop up the blood still leaking from it.

'Get blood on the seats and it's not just your nose you'll be worrying about,' said Tony.

Abraham glanced at him, causing Tony to break into a broad grin, his very white, very straight teeth on full show.

'Just kidding. Can't believe we bumped into each other after all this time. Mind you, wasn't hard to find you in there, most of the pub was looking your way.' Tony laughed, a guttural noise that sounded like bubbling tar. 'Don't get many fights in pubs anymore,' he added wistfully, 'not like the old days.'

Abraham wasn't sure whether to feel thankful that Tony had intervened after the first - in fact, the only - punch had been thrown, or annoyed that it had been his former friend's shout that had distracted him in the first place. Once Tony had stepped forward though, the crowd very quickly dispersed, and Abraham's assailant was equally fast in offering his apologies.

Tony Stone had that effect. Not just because he was 6'3" and built like a dump truck, but also because most people in Southend, certainly most people who looked for trouble in Southend, knew who Tony Stone was.

'So, you still in the press game?' he asked, looking in the rearview mirror as he straightened the collar on his black Hugo Boss shirt.

Abraham nodded, not wanting to get into a conversation about his current employment status.

'Shame. I mean, I know it's worked out for you, I've seen some of your stuff, the rags you've worked for. Even saw you on the telly once, but, well, you know my feelings about snitches.'

'I'm not a snitch, Tony,' replied Abraham, his voice sounding nasal, 'I'm a journalist.'

Tony just shrugged is large shoulders. 'S'been a while,' he said. 'Still with Siobhan?'

Abraham nodded, not wanting to get into a conversation about his current marital status either. 'Gemma?' he asked in return.

'Yep. Married now. Better late than never, I suppose. Two kids; Matty's eighteen, Daisy's ten. Late arrival, you know. Something of a surprise. Heard about Grace, and your mum.' Tony was staring out of the windscreen at the rows of cars in the car park and at the people walking by. 'I'm sorry, Abe. Grace was a nice kid. And I know your mum wasn't my biggest fan, but still.'

'Thanks,' Abraham said. And then, because this was yet another topic he didn't want to get into, 'Nice car.

Must be lovely to drive.' Abraham knew next to nothing about cars, but felt this was safe ground.

'Yeah, I think so. To be honest, I don't drive it much me self. Got a guy, you know.'

'A chauffeur?'

Another shrug of Tony's shoulders. 'Night off. Fancied a couple of shandies, so here I am.'

'Doing well for yourself then.'

This wasn't a question. Abraham knew exactly how well Tony Stone was doing for himself. He owned a good portion of Southend's nightlife, a couple of bars, at least one of the many arcades that lit up Southend's seafront, and he also had most of his sausage-like fingers in a variety of illicit pies. He was no Hristo Nikolova, even Tony Stone knew better than to encroach on that particular territory, but as shady characters went, he had darker hues than most.

'Can't complain, Abe. Can't complain. And just fink,' he turned to the passenger seat and smiled, 'you could've been on this gravy train as well.'

Tony was the reason that Abraham had almost given up his journalistic aspirations just as the national papers had dropped the ladder for him to climb. He and Tony had been friends from childhood and while their backgrounds, their families, and often their outlook on life couldn't have been more different, the two young boys had bonded and, until Siobhan had guided Abraham onto a different path, had both walked precarious ground. Tony was still walking it.

'Well, thanks for stepping in, Tone,' said Abraham, 'in the pub, I mean. Might've been more than a bloody nose if you'd not been there.'

'Nah, ole Abraham Hart-breaker can handle himself. You'd 'ave been ok.'

Abraham smiled at the long since abandoned nickname he'd acquired in his youth. 'Sorry to have interrupted your night. You heading back in?'

'Don't reckon so. Had a couple and don't want to give the rozzers any good reason to pull me. You wanna lift. Eastwood, innit?'

Not wanting to say he was staying at his dad's house Abraham declined the offer. 'Think I'll walk actually, thanks all the same,' Abraham said, opening the door to the expensive car, letting the cold evening air slide in. 'Bit of fresh air might blow away the cobwebs.'

'Fair enough,' said Tony, as the door slammed shut. 'Oh, and Abe,' he added, buzzing down the passenger-side window. 'Hope Evie's job interview comes good.'

Abraham, one hand on the car's roof, stared back at Tony, a quizzical look on his face.

'Daisy told me. She and Evie know each other from college. Like history repeating, innit? Anyway, see you around,' laughed Tony, pulling away with a rev of the engine and a parting honk of the horn.

***

Abraham found himself once again walking along the high street, past shops closed either temporarily due to the hour, or for good because of the times.

His only company was other Friday night drinkers making their way to or from pubs and restaurants. Some were in groups, shouting and laughing, others on their own, eyes down, doing their best not to attract attention.

A train clattered across the overpass that spanned the street, heading towards London, ferrying Southend's more monied occupants to brighter lights and a bigger city. A busker stood beneath the bridge, an acoustic guitar slung over her shoulder, a passable rendition of John Lennon's *Imagine* decorating the night air. Abraham threw a pound coin in her open guitar case as he passed.

He had apologised to Carol Peters after Tony had helped him to his feet, telling her he was fine, despite globs of fresh blood dripping onto the table they had been sharing, that he would call her for more information in the morning. But the morning seemed a long way away, and who knew what it might bring? So, he decided that now was as good a time as any.

Twenty minutes later, and after Carol had repeatedly asked if Abraham was ok, she had reminded him of the name of the company Alissa had been working at in Leigh and told him that Alissa's boyfriend's full name was Craig Atherton. She also gave him the address of the flat he and Alissa had, up to recently, shared in Westcliff, and the name of the building's live-in caretaker, a Mr Langton.

Abraham reiterated that, in all likelihood, he would find nothing untoward, and he asked Carol again if she was prepared for that to be the case.

'Are you prepared for it not to be?' had been her candid reply, which was a fair question, though not one Abraham believed required much thought because the odds were very much in favour of any digging he did unearthing nothing of note.

By the time he'd ended the call he was strolling along the barely lit pavement of Cambridge Road and towards the untidy front garden of his childhood home. He knew he'd have to face his dad at some point, his brother too, but he hoped that point wouldn't arrive until the morning.

The outdoor light automatically came on as he approached the house, spotlighting him in the doorway. Abraham slipped his key into the lock and took a deep breath before pushing the door open. Inside the house was quiet and still, the only sound coming from the steady hum of the central heating.

'Abraham! I was starting to get worried.'

Abraham hadn't heard his dad tiptoeing down the stairs and the sound of his voice made him jump. It also made him realise that consequences would have to be faced sooner than later.

He looked up at his dad. He looked tired. He looked old. Older than Abraham remembered. His face, half-lit by the outside light leaking through the glass of the door, was drawn and thin. He had a thick brown dressing gown wrapped around him, and a pair of moccasins on his feet that looked like they'd seen better days.

'Alright, Dad?'

'I'm fine, son. You?' Victor squinted in the half light. 'What happened to your nose?'

'Oh, nothing. I'm fine. Walked into a door.'

Victor looked unconvinced. 'Sure?'

Abraham nodded and smiled. 'Look, about before, you have your ways, I have mine. And I don't like being ambushed.'

Victor Hart nodded. 'I know you think we're wrong, that we're somehow disrespecting Grace, but if you can see that the Grace we lost wasn't the real Grace, not the one we knew and loved, then you should be able to see that Brody was different then too. He's worked hard to change.'

Abraham screwed up his face and was about to reply, but his dad beat him to it.

'But both Joshua and I understand, and we shouldn't have gone about it the way we did, so we're sorry. I'm sorry.'

Abraham narrowed his eyes in the half light, closed his eyes and took a deep breath. 'Yeah. Me too. Go on, get back to bed. I'll see you in the morning.'

But Victor insisted on coming down to make tea. Wouldn't be able to sleep anyway, he said. And so the pair sat sipping PG Tips from faded mugs in the small kitchen that, apart from a new dishwasher, looked the same as it had almost a quarter of a century ago.

Abraham had been sat in the same chair when Joshua, at twenty-three-years-old, told his family over dinner that he was entering a seminary and planned to become a Catholic priest. His parents had been overjoyed. More than half of their own lives had been devoted to the church and to think their son would be a bona fide man of God was, for them, like winning the lottery.

Abraham had been almost twenty when Joshua made his big announcement and would much rather have won the actual lottery than have a sibling who was a God botherer. It hadn't always been the case that his brother was a latter-day saint; Abraham supposed it rarely was for any priest. In his teenage years Joshua had been something of a rebel. Nothing too outrageous, but drinking, smoking the occasional spliff and sleeping with the even more occasional girl had been the normal course of things, as it was for many teenagers.

Joshua didn't make a habit of filling his younger brother in on his extra-curricular activities but, as Abraham got older and when he managed to get served, they started drinking in the same pubs and going to the same nightclubs, he and his brother grew closer and stories that might previously have been kept secret became either cautionary tales or instructions for success.

But then Joshua's outlook changed. He began telling Abraham about the lessons taught by the Bible, started warning him about the dangers of excess and the immorality of promiscuity. Abraham might not have minded but at that point he'd never even had sex so was disinclined to turn his back on it so soon.

Joshua had been even more sententious with their sister. Grace was only ten-years-old when her oldest brother's personality began to morph. It wasn't that he was strict, nor was he judgemental, at least not outwardly, but he was moralistic and high-minded and while his parents both delighted in his newfound theology, his siblings found he had become a pain in the arse. No one knew what had caused this change. Possibly Joshua didn't know himself, but instead of having a brother, Abraham and Grace found that, soon enough, they had another father.

'How well do you know Carol Peters, Dad?' asked Abraham, as much for something to say as to find out the answer.

'Such a shame,' said Victor, shaking his head slowly. 'And even younger than Grace was. Such evil things, drugs.'

'So you were close, then, you and Carol?'

Victor took a sip of tea. 'Close? Not really, no. Acquaintances I suppose you would say. But then everyone at the church is. Times have changed. It's a small community now, so everyone knows everyone. And, obviously, she works for your brother, so I hear things from him.'

'What sort of things?'

Victor gave his son a quizzical look. 'Why the interest in the Peters all of a sudden? You're not going to muck-rake are you?'

'Is that what you think I do, then, "muck-rake"?'

A flash of embarrassment skirted across Victor's face, a hint of red blooming at his cheeks.

'No! No, of course not. I just meant —' He paused, unsure where his words were taking him. 'I just know how she feels, don't I? I know the pain, the disbelief. Me and your mum both did. We knew the sideways looks and whispered conversations; the "How could they not have knowns" and "Why didn't they do something mores". It's like a second bereavement. First we lost your sister, then we lost part of ourselves, the part that was a parent. And I know that sounds terrible. Egotistical. Un-Christian. We were still parents, of course, but a part of us died with Grace. You can bet Carol Peters feels like that too, and Alissa was her only child. I just don't want to see her suffer any more than is necessary.'

If you're lucky, your parents are made of Teflon, thought Abraham. Things just slide off them. They are strong and resilient. They are impervious to worry and anxiety. Immune to fear and pain. At least, they are when you're young, when their place in the world is immutable and their time here unending.

But Abraham was no longer young, and neither was his father. He was small and frail and, for the first time he could remember, he saw him not as his parent, but as another person. Even when his sister had died it was him looking to his parents for comfort and understanding, for sympathy and strength.

But, sitting in this tired house, on these worn chairs, drinking tea from discoloured mugs, he realised the man in front of him was just Victor Hart, and that Victor Hart went far deeper than simply being 'Abraham's dad'. He wanted to say something. He wanted to acknowledge his own understanding. To apologise, or correct, or atone.

'I'll get us some biscuits, shall I?' Victor said, standing up. 'There's some chocolate Hob-Nobs in the top cupboard. Don't tell Joshua though, he keeps telling me I need to cut down on my sugar intake.'

And the moment was gone.

His dad was back, and the fleeting glimpse of the man beneath retreated to some unseen region. Abraham promised himself that he wouldn't forget this moment, but then Abraham promised himself a lot of things.

'Have you spoken to her about it?' he asked. 'Carol, I mean. About what you just said?'

Victor shook his head. 'I don't want to butt in, and it's not really my place.'

'But Josh has been helping her, has he? I suppose it's in his remit.'

'It's not his "remit", Abraham, it's his nature. To offer solace, comfort, spiritual advice, it's what he's there for.'

'Right. Yeah, of course. But it's not like he knew Alissa, is it?'

'Why do you say that?' asked Victor. 'He knew her well enough. She wasn't a regular churchgoer, what kids are these days? But, no, she came with her mother sometimes, and Joshua was on good terms with the Peters. Still is with Carol, obviously.'

'Right,' replied Abraham, wondering why his brother would tell him that Alissa Peters wasn't a parishioner and that, baptism and confirmation aside, he'd little to do with her.

Fourteen

*T**he following morning's lessons went by in a haze. Alissa usually enjoyed Film Studies, especially as they were concentrating on German expressionism and the director Fritz Lang, but even while watching* Metropolis *she couldn't keep her mind from wandering back to the video, and of what she should do about it.*

Before leaving for the bus that morning Craig had been uncharacteristically pleasant, at least compared to the previous couple of weeks. She should probably be happy about that, but all she could think about was the video on her phone and of how she might deal with it. Or not deal with it. She'd considered confiding in Em, explaining what had happened and getting her opinion but, knowing Em, she'd side with Craig and think that the best thing to do, the only thing to do, was to confront Lewis and tell his wife. So, she'd said nothing.

She really did want to keep her job, and knew that confessing to videoing Lewis and Francesca, however unintentionally, could only end in her losing it. She'd only met Mrs Maynard-Jones a couple of times. She was a partner in the firm, but seemed to have little input in the business and, when she did, it was more around finances than the creative side of things. As well as being a similar age to her husband she was also, like him, tall and blonde. They made a striking couple and she found herself wondering why on earth Lewis would want to cheat on her. Then she remembered that Francesca was beautiful too, and twenty years younger than his wife, and that Lewis was a man.

Alissa suddenly became aware that the students all around the room were looking at her. She wasn't sure why, but could feel the slow burn of embarrassment as her face grew red.

'Miss Peters, are you still with us?'

Alissa looked from the smirking faces of the students to the annoyed stare of Mr Halthorpe, who was holding the remote control, a static image of a fantastical skyline frozen on the TV screen.

'I was asking about the representation of the urban future showcased in this film and why it was so believable for people in 1927. And I was asking you, specifically.'

The slow burn sped up and Alissa felt a combination of panic, fear and the even more serious sensation of mortal embarrassment. She opened her mouth unsure what might come out but knowing it would be nothing of note. Then, not for the first time, Em saved her, launching into an insightful answer that Alissa barely took in but which encompassed phrases including 'flourishing economy', 'utilitarian architecture' and 'future urban reality'.

'You ok, Al?' Em asked as soon as the class had finished and they were filing out into the narrow corridor. 'Not Craig again, is it? What's the silly twat done this time?'

Alissa laughed, though wondered if she too often painted Craig as the bad guy, even when he wasn't. 'No, no, it's not him. Well, not directly. Just something at work.'

'Sharing is caring.' Em tilted her head and smiled, widening her large brown eyes.

Alissa laughed again. 'Thanks, but it's fine. Don't want to bore you. I'm heading there now, actually. I'll sort it out.'

'What about this secret project you mentioned. Any news?'

Alissa's stomach dropped at the thought of the video. She hadn't even considered what the thing she was actually meant to have been filming looked like. As soon as she saw Lewis and Francesca, the spider and its web seemed insignificant. 'Funnily enough, that's part of the problem, but like I say, I'll sort it. I'm still working on it, and as soon as it's ready, you'll be the first to know.'

Em nodded. 'We still on for tomorrow night thought, yeah?'

'God, yeah. Craig's leaving for Newquay tonight so it's all systems go. Can't wait.'

The two friends hugged and Alissa once more headed for the bus.

***

Her jaw clenched, knee unconsciously bouncing, Alissa spent the whole journey from college wrestling with her conscience.

She knew the right thing was to own up to what she'd done and tell Lewis's wife what she'd captured. The only positive she could think of coming from that scenario though, was that Francesca would be as unemployed as her. She also reprimanded herself for feeling even a twinge of remorse for Lewis, whose life she would be turning upside down but whom she liked and respected, at least as a boss if not, now, as a man.

Despite all the inner turmoil and the weighing up of scenarios, deep down Alissa knew she would say nothing. Not just because of the fear for her job but because, how do you broach such a topic? How can you start a conversation with a woman that ends with a video of her husband having sex with another woman? She couldn't imagine it and so, before she even got off the bus, stopped trying.

Pushing open the glass door of Spotlight she saw Francesca on reception. As usual she gave Alissa a cursory glance, one with all the warmth of an Arctic winter, before returning to her screen. Alissa didn't even try to engage her in conversation, didn't plaster on an insincere smile, instead just walked to her desk with the aim to continue her trawl of South African beaches.

'Alissa, I need to talk to you.'

Alissa jolted at the sudden voice, which had come from Lewis's office. She turned towards it and saw him standing there. His face was unreadable but also tense, his jawline pulsing slightly as he ground his teeth.

'Right now!' Lewis said.

It was almost a shout, something she'd never heard him do and, as she trudged towards the glass office, she caught Francesca looking at her, face contorted into a half-smile-half-sneer that Alissa knew only meant trouble.

Fifteen

Victor said goodnight around 10pm, leaving Abraham in the living room with a second cup of tea watching Leonardo DiCaprio coming off badly in a fight with a bear, though not as badly as the bear. During the point at which DiCaprio hollowed out a dead horse to use as an equine sleeping bag, Abraham decided it was time to finally fold himself into the single bed in his old room.

He didn't sleep well, and it wasn't just because the bed was almost as old as him, and the mattress was softer than a whisper at a funeral. At first, he'd lain awake staring at gaps on the wall that used to contain posters of Halle Berry and Kurt Cobain thinking about what he was going to do about his job, and whether he should have just punched Spencer Milton, even if it might have worked against him in future interviews.

After switching the bedside light off, sleep eventually came, but not for long, because at 3am he was awake once more, this time laying in the inky blackness, listening to the occasional passing car and wondering why he had agreed to help Carol Peters, and what exactly that help would entail.

At 5.30 he finally crept downstairs, the cold gnawing its way beneath the blanket he had draped around him, its teeth biting at any exposed flesh. Three hours later, a cup of cold coffee on the table next to him and a segment about the war in Ukraine playing quietly on the breakfast news in front on him, Abraham prised his eyes open, wiped a strand of dribble from his chin and levered himself to his bare feet.

He could hear voices and, after discounting the ones coming from the television, padded from the living room to the kitchen where he found his dad eating toast and drinking tea. Opposite him, her back to Abraham, was his daughter.

'Morning,' said Victor in the bright tones of someone who was clearly a morning person.

'Evie!' said Abraham, his own voice sounding like a broken engine. 'I didn't know you were coming.'

Evie turned to face her father. Her dark, curly hair was shoulder length, with a fringe that framed her face. Her dark skin was bare of make up apart from a daub of mauve lipstick. She was her mother's daughter.

'Could say the same to you,' replied Evie. 'When did you get home then, Dad?'

The tone was less than cheerful and also indicated to Abraham that Evie knew the answer to her question before she'd asked it.

'I was going to call you today, love,' he said. 'I only got here yesterday and, well, some things cropped up. Any news from the interview? Mum said you aced it.'

'Nothing yet. It's the weekend, so…' Evie shrugged. 'Though, Mum wouldn't have needed to say anything if you'd have been there yourself. You didn't even come over yesterday.'

If it had ben a physical blow, then Abraham would have been on the ropes. As it was, it still stung.

'My fault,' chimed Victor. 'I asked your dad for some help. Something for Carol.'

109

As Evie turned to look at her grandfather Abraham mouthed a 'thank you' to him. He needed all the help he could get and wasn't going to look a gift horse in the mouth.

Evie quickly turned back. 'Carol Peters. God, yeah, terrible what happened to Alissa. How's she doing?'

'Still dead, I'm afraid,' said Abraham, immediately regretting his attempt at gallows humour.

Evie gave him a stare that told him she wasn't impressed.

'Sorry, bad joke. Carol's as you would expect; upset, angry, confused. You knew her didn't you? Alissa, I mean.'

Evie shrugged. 'A bit. Spoke to her at college a few times. Seen her around the church with Uncle Josh occasionally.'

'Right. She at the church with Josh a lot then?'

Evie gave another shrug, while Victor narrowed his eyes at his youngest son.

'I've actually said I'd help her out,' said Abraham, sounding slightly embarrassed. 'She thinks there's something fishy about Alissa's death and wants me to look into it.'

Victor and Evie simultaneously looked at him, the slices of toast they were eating now suspended a few inches from open mouths.

'I don't think giving the poor woman false hope is going to help her, Abraham,' said Victor.

'I know, I know. But she's distraught, she wants closure. And I told her that it's almost nailed-on that Alissa died because of an unfortunate overdose.'

'What about work?' his father added.

Abraham was momentarily stuck for words and realised he'd not thought this conversation through before launching into it. 'Er, I've taken a few days off,' he said. 'I'm owed some time and thought I could spend some of it with my favourite daughter.'

'Oh yeah,' said Evie, the sullenness returning. 'Didn't realise you had other kids.'

'Very droll.'

'So, that means I can help with the investigation, right?' said Evie. 'If you want to spend some time with me.'

'Um, what about college?'

'Like I said, it's the weekend. And I'm currently free as a bird.'

'Right, but it's not an investigation,' replied Abraham. 'I'm just, you know, looking into Alissa's death for a concerned mother.'

'Sounds like an investigation to me, son,' said Victor.

***

After a cup of strong black coffee and two slices of toast Abraham took a shower then changed into a pair of dark blue jeans he'd left last time he stayed, a plain white t-shirt and a grey cardigan pilfered from his father's wardrobe which was so old that it had come back into fashion. Then he sat on the end of his unmade bed and called Carol Peters who agreed to meet him at the church to hand over the key to Alissa's flat.

In the cold light of a new day Abraham tried to justify the reasons that had compelled him to help Carol.

Doing it in a fit of anger at his brother and father, and simply because Joshua had asked him not to, felt like childish logic, mainly because it was exactly that. But recalling his conversation with Carol yesterday evening, and then with his father last night, reminded Abraham of the pain death could wreak on a family. And it wasn't like he had anything else to be getting on with. Plus, he thought, despite trying not to, worried where such speculation might lead, he had a bad feeling around the inconsistencies in Joshua's relationship with Alissa Peters.

'Right,' said Abraham once he was back downstairs. 'Ready?'

'I can come?' said Evie.

'If you still want to.'

Abraham ended up in the passenger seat of Siobhan's Ford Fiesta with his daughter ferrying him the short distance through the grey streets of Southend to Our Lady of Lourdes. Evie had been driving for less than four months and Abraham did his best to show confidence in his daughter's abilities. Only his left hand tightly gripping the passenger door handle gave him away.

As they approached the church Abraham spotted Carol sitting on the low wall just in front of the cordylines and asked Evie to pull up to the kerb, buzzing down the passenger window as he did so.

'Morning,' said Abraham, more cheerfully than he felt.

Carol nodded in return, a tense smile engraved on her face. She held out a key on a keyring that featured the brooding face of Harry Styles. 'I've not been back there since…' Carol's words tailed off. 'Father Hart collected some of Alissa's things for me, and I don't know what state it's in. Apparently Craig's paid the rent up to the end of next month. After that…' Again Carol's words drifted off, replaced by a shrug.

'Anything that looks important, I'll bring back for you. I just want to take a look, get a feel for who Alissa was, who Craig is. Like I said—'

'I know,' Carol cut in. 'You'll likely find nothing. I understand.'

It was Abraham's turn to show a tense smile. 'OK, well, thanks, Carol. I'll be in touch.'

As Evie drove off Abraham made to wave but Carol's back was already turned as she walked towards the open doorway of the church in which, almost hidden by shadows, Joshua stood watching them pull away.

Traffic was heavy as they made their way towards Westcliff. The London Road, part of the A13 which fed all the way to London, was busy with shoppers, day-trippers and those just meandering.

Abraham stared out of the window at the rows of shops, many of them boarded up or fogged with whitewash as someone else prepared to roll the dice on a business venture. Chinese restaurants, Turkish grills, pubs, off licences, stores selling Polish goods and shops offering African food all vied for custom along this vibrant if grubby stretch of the city.

On the corner of Hamlet Court Road the old Blockbuster rental store was still vacant, as it had been since Abraham could remember, the windows plastered with posters for long departed circuses and comedy acts. Just before passing the Palace Theatre Abraham told Evie to turn left onto Valkyrie Road and, a mile later, they arrived outside Harcourt House, a four-storey, lemon yellow block of flats that overlooked the train line.

The building was the size of a large department store. It wasn't particularly well-maintained, but Abraham had certainly seen much worse places.

'Not exactly the Ritz, is it?' commented Evie.

'Whereas we live at Claridge's, do we?'

'You might, for all I know.'

Touché, thought Abraham.

Evie parked the car and the pair made their way to the entrance. Alissa and Craig's flat was on the first floor, flat 2b. Abraham used the code Carol had texted him to enter the main door and, once inside, they ascended the well-worn staircase and walked along the gloomy corridor.

The paint, presumably brilliant white when first applied, was now a dim grey, peeling where it met the skirting board and low ceiling. A smell permeated the building that Abraham associated with old people and which he could only describe as 'boiled vegetables'.

They soon found themselves outside the sturdy white door of flat 2b, but before Abraham could slip the key into the lock the head of a man appeared from behind the neighbouring door, followed soon after by the rest of his body.

'Help you?' the man said, looking Abraham and Evie up and down.

Abraham retuned the stare, taking in the person in front of them. He was in his mid-twenties, Abraham guessed, and short, 5'7" or 5'8", with a wiry frame and an equally wiry beard that sprouted in patches across his face. He was dressed in grey cargo trousers with DeWalt emblazoned on one side pocket, a blue long-sleeved t-shirt and paint-flecked Caterpillar boots. His hands were folded across his chest, one of them featuring a tattoo Abraham couldn't make out.

'Maybe,' answered Abraham. 'We're looking for Craig Atherton.'

'Police?' said the man, as much an accusation as a question.

'No. My name's Abraham Hart, I'm working for Alissa Peters' mother. You know her?'

'Who's that then?' the man replied, nodding his head at Evie.

'This is my daughter, Evie.'

The man looked Evie up and down then gave Abraham a quizzical look.

Abraham, over the last eighteen years, had become wearily used to this response and had learned to replace his initial flash of anger with a reassuring smile. For some people, Evie's darker skin tone, a beautiful mixture of him and Siobhan, seemed to throw suspicion on Abraham's assertion that he was her father. It had taken him a long time to not take it personally.

The man nodded slowly, still staring at Evie, the hint of a smile on his face. 'Private detectives, is it?'

'Just concerned friends, is all,' said Abraham.

'Bit late to be concerned.'

Abraham drew a deep breath in through his nose and slowly let it out again. He wasn't sure the next words out of his mouth would be particularly reassuring.

'Southend fan,' Evie asked, stepping forward and indicating the man's right forearm which, Abraham now noticed, was the badge of Southend United FC.

'For my sins, yeah. You?'

'Go every now and then with my friends,' said Evie. 'Better season than last year, but the money's still an issue. Who knows if we'll stay afloat at this rate?'

The man's demeanour altered from wary antagonism to a more open disposition and Abraham, not for he first time, marvelled at the ability of sport to so often be the implement that managed to break the ice.

'Tell me about it. Bloody Ron Martin'll be the death of us. Name's Matt,' he said, thrusting his tattooed hand towards them, a hand which Evie shook happily, Abraham more tentatively. 'Sorry about just then. I'm not a racist or anything. Just, you know…'

What Abraham knew was that it was rare for someone who openly professed *not* to be racist to not, in fact, be a racist, even if just a little bit. And as far as he was concerned, just a little bit of racism made you a plain old racist. Instead of airing this insight though, he nodded noncommittally. 'You knew Alissa and Craig, did you?'

'Beautiful girl, Alissa. Beautiful. Could've been a model. I told her that more than once.'

'Right,' said Abraham. 'Mind if we ask you a few questions Mr —'

'Hallstaff. Matthew Hallstaff. But just call me Matt. We're all friends here, right?'

Abraham hoped that wouldn't end up being the case but when Matt invited them in he decided that information took precedence over integrity at this point, so followed into flat 2c, Evie close behind.

Matt's flat was clean and tidy but was also a quintessential example of a young, single man's space. The walls were magnolia and bare apart from a framed poster from the film *Scarface*, and the main living area, which comprised a combined lounge and small kitchen off to the left contained no photos or personal elements. A large TV hung on the right-hand wall, beneath which was a battered-looking PlayStation 4 and, facing the TV, two faux-leather reclining seats that looked like they could have been stolen from the set of *Friends*. A set of turntables was in the far corner, the coiled wire from a pair of headphones snaking across the top of the decks.

The kitchen counter was clear and clean, with a bowl and spoon resting in the sink. Off to the left, past the kitchen, were two closed doors which led, Abraham assumed, to the bathroom and bedroom. Pinned to the wall that led to them was a calendar featuring the model Kylie Jenner squeezed into a yellow miniskirt and matching crop top.

'Tea? Coffee?' asked Matt.

'We're fine, thanks,' answered Abraham, not wanting to stay any longer than was necessary. 'How long were you neighbours with Alissa and Craig?'

'Well, I've been here for two-and-a-half years now. Craig arrived about a year ago, maybe a bit more, and Alissa moved in around February, maybe March, of this year. God knows how he pulled 'er. Way out of his league, the little scrote.'

'You don't get on with Craig, then?' asked Abraham.

'Nah, we got on fine. Didn't see too much of each other, you know, what with work and stuff. I work shifts, he's up in the City every day. Well, he was. Dunno what he's up to now. Hasn't been around since... you know.'

'When did you notice he'd gone?'

Matt slumped back onto one of the recliners and puffed out his cheeks. 'Few days after they found 'er, I suppose. Maybe less, not sure. New start. Grief. Guilt. I dunno. Just hopped it.'

'Guilt? Why'd you say that?'

'I dunno, but there's no smoke without fire, that's what I always think.'

'Smoke?' said Evie.

'Little lovebirds most of the time. Can 'ear all sorts through these walls.' Matt grinned lasciviously. 'But they rowed, like all couples, I suppose. And she could be a bit moody sometimes, bit of a bitch, you know. But not long before she "OD'd"—' and here Matt made the universal sign for inverted commas '—they had a slanging match. Couldn't 'ear the words exactly, but she weren't 'appy about something. Had to bang on the wall and tell them to pipe down. But after ten minutes a door slammed and Alissa stormed out. Day later she was brown bread.'

'Do you know what they argued about?' asked Abraham.

'How would I know?' Matt replied, a little too defensively.

'But you think Craig might have had something to do with it, with Alissa's overdose?'

Matt shrugged. 'I dunno. Known a few druggies in my time. Sneaky bastards, most of 'em. One guy I knew was on the books at Colchester United. Promising career and everything, but also did more nosebag than Shergar, you know. Caught up with him eventually, but for a while you'd never have known. But only a while. Never saw anything that made me think Alissa was a user. And 'specially not H. That's next level shit.'

'Did you speak to the police? Tell them all this?' Abraham asked.

"Course. Don't think they was interested, to be honest. They thought she was bang to rights. Needle in the arm, gear in the flat. Bosh! OD. Fair enough I s'pose.'

'How'd you know it was Alissa?' asked Evie.

'Eh?' replied Matt.

'You said it was Alissa who stormed out after the argument. How'd you know it was her?'

'Was having a fag by the window, Looked out,' he replied, jabbing a thumb behind him. 'Saw her in the street.'

'You see where she went?' asked Abraham.

'Nah. She jumped in a car and off they went.'

'They?'

'Yeah, she didn't drive. Someone picked 'er up. Didn't see who, too dark. Some bloke… well, could've been a bird, I suppose… anyway, someone in a crappy old Volvo.'

Sixteen

After leaving Matt Hallstaff's flat Abraham and Evie stepped a few paces to their left and Abraham slipped the key into the lock of flat 2b. In layout Alissa and Craig's flat was the same as their neighbour's and, likely, the same as all the other one bedroom flats in this building. In design, though, it was wholly different. Photos of Alissa and a person Abraham assumed was Craig Atherton - tall, thin, sober haircut, gap-toothed smile - were in a cluster of small frames on one wall. Other photos of Alissa, one or two featuring Carol Peters, were dotted on cheap-looking but perfectly serviceable pieces of furniture. Abraham removed the smallest of the photos featuring Craig Atherton from its frame and carefully placed it in his wallet.

Like Matt Hallstaff's flat, the wall to the right had a television hanging on it and a new PlayStation 5 resting on a wooden stand below. This wall, though, had been decorated with colourful, floral wallpaper, reminding Abraham of the statement wall in the hotel room he had recently been calling home. A teal futon faced the TV, with a large red beanbag either side of it, the imprint of someone still pressed into the one nearest them. The small kitchen wasn't untidy, but a Nespresso machine took up space, as did a juice blender, and a panini toaster. Utensils overflowed from a ceramic jug next to the electric hob. There was a small dent in one of the cupboard doors. It seemed to be a well-used area.

'Nice place,' said Evie, looking around. 'Apart from the smell.'

It wasn't overpowering, not yet at least, but Abraham recognised it as the beginning of the end for any manner of food stuffs. It was a sickly sour aroma, something you could ignore for a while, but you knew it would get too much for you at some point, like a drunk uncle at a family party.

Abraham walked to the fridge and tentatively opened it. As soon as he did he took a step back and turned his head away. Taking a deep breath in through his nose he glanced back inside: mouldy tomatoes were half-furred on small plate; a section of cucumber looked like it had collapsed in on itself; something that resembled a glass bowl of tuna mayonnaise, the foil inexpertly placed across the top of it, was like a fishy soup; green tinged slices of ham lay like diseased tongues inside a plastic container.

Abraham closed the door.

'It's not just the fridge,' said Evie, pointing to a large bowl of semi-rotted fruit that included blackened bananas and soft, brown apples.

Abraham rooted around in drawers and finally found a roll of black plastic bags. He tore off two, put one inside the other, then braved the fridge again, scooping everything into the bag, plate included. Evie carried the putrid fruit bowl over and dropped the contents into the black bag, then Abraham tied it off and placed it out in the hallway.

'Looks like no one's been here for a while,' commented Evie.

'Certainly doesn't seem like it.'

Abraham began searching the rest of the flat but everything inside was as he would have expected. It was a home made for a young couple, inexpensively but carefully decorated and containing the things that many people own; electrical items, books, a shoe rack full of footwear that seemed mainly to belong to Alissa, a yoga mat and a pair of two kilogram dumbbells. The strongest thing the medicine cabinet contained was a packet of paracetamol and some blackcurrant Lemsip, otherwise it was filled with skin cream and vitamins. There was nothing suspicious, nothing out of place.

The only thing that stood out to Abraham was the space inside the bedroom wardrobe where most of Craig's clothes should have been, and gaps on the bathroom shelf where deodorant, toothpaste and shower gel might usually live.

It hadn't been a rushed exit, he thought. Wherever he had gone, Craig hadn't suddenly left his home in panicked desperation, he'd had time to pack essential items before heading out the door.

'Found anything?' asked Evie, who had been searching the kitchen cupboards.

'No. Didn't expect to. You?'

'Nah. A bottle of champagne in a cupboard, and someone is a big fan of muesli,' said Evie, holding up two large boxes. 'What now?'

'Carol mentioned a caretaker. Said he lived in the building. He might be worth talking to.'

They headed back down the stairs, Abraham holding the black sack out in front of him like it was contagious. On the ground floor there was sign pointing them to the building management officer. They followed a badly lit corridor where they found a pock-marked white door and another sign, this one written on A4 paper and taped to the door; Mr Malcolm Langton. Abraham rapped his knuckles on the door.

They could hear footsteps and a muffled voice approaching, then the door was open and Abraham was greeted by a man in his late-sixties wearing the clothes of a teenager; green cargo shorts, a white Vans t-shirt and a baseball cap with the New York Yankees logo. He was quickly followed by a waft of marijuana smoke that cascaded from the flat, snaked around the man in the doorway and slammed into Abraham's nostrils with such ferocity it made him glad Evie was driving.

Abraham snuck a look at his watch; it was 10.15am.

'Help you?' said the man in a manner that suggested he really didn't want to.

'Hi,' Abraham said. 'I'm sorry to disturb you. My name's Abraham and I wondered if I could ask you a couple of questions about the couple who lived in flat 2b; Craig and Alissa?'

The man stared at Abraham a fraction longer than is normal, like the words he'd spoken were struggling to cut through the fog and penetrate his brain. He narrowed his eyes to the point that they were almost closed. 'Nope, not really.'

'Not really?' repeated Abraham.

'Don't socialise with the tenants.'

'You know about Alissa though, the girl who died?'

Malcolm Langton nodded. 'Druggie. The hard stuff. Shame, but you dance with the devil...' He finished the sentence with a shrug.

'You ever speak to her?' asked Evie.

Malcolm turned his attention from Abraham to Evie. It seemed to take longer than it had any right to. 'Nope. Told you, don't socialise with the tenants.'

'What about Craig?' Abraham persisted.

'That toe rag,' snorted Malcolm.

Abraham and Evie unconsciously leaned in, waiting for more. They had to wait for a few, long seconds.

'Supposed to have come back to clean out the flat. Said he'd empty everything. Starting to turn, I can tell.' He tapped his nose. 'Keen sense of smell.

'When did you speak to him? Craig, I mean,' asked Abraham.

Malcolm gazed at an indistinct spot to his upper left for so long that Evie turned to see what he might be looking at. 'Month or so ago, I s'pose,' he finally said. 'After the death, before the funeral.'

'What did he say?' asked Evie.

'Not much. Wouldn't open the door more than a crack. Paid up to the end of this month, but I told him he needed to sort it all out if he wasn't coming back. S'pect old muggins 'ere will have to do it now.'

'Was he upset?' asked Abraham.

'That he had to clear out? His choice to give up the lease.'

'No, that his girlfriend had just died?'

Another shrug. 'Didn't seem it. Wasn't how I would describe him.'

'How would you describe him, Mr Langton?'

'Well, if I had to put a name to it, I'd say he was scared.'

Seventeen

His cheeks were itchy again. With almost four weeks worth of growth it was the longest his facial hair had ever been and the intermittent scratching was annoying. His beard wasn't even particularly long. But when he looked in the mirror all he saw was a patchy mess that made him look like he was homeless, which wasn't far from the truth.

Everyone else in the squat seemed to have a beard too, or the beginnings of one. Razors were expensive so, maybe that was the reason. And no one seemed to have a job, so it wasn't like there was anything to smarten up for.

How any of them earned money he didn't know. Actually, he did, but he pretended not to. What they did wasn't his concern, he just wanted to be left alone. He had nothing of any real value they could steal anyway.

He'd already sold his watch, his headphones, a pair of trainers and the one suit he'd brought with him. Why he'd packed a suit he couldn't now remember. The only thing he had of any value was his phone, which was secreted in an inside pocket of the overshirt he wore. He patted it for the hundredth time that day, just to be sure.

He'd need to use what was on it soon. He was almost out of money and, after this long, surely no one was looking for him. Maybe they never had been, but it was too risky to assume that was the case. These people didn't mess about. They were dangerous. But they were also rich. He had thought about it for a long time and believed they would play ball. The amount he would ask for was small, tiny really, compared with what they must have, and they would be glad to pay him off to get him out of their hair, he was sure.

No, he wasn't sure. Not after what they'd already done. But what choice did he have? He had nothing, so he had nothing to lose.

'What you got there, Freddie man?'

The question startled him and he looked up to see the thin face and dark eyes of Baz staring down at him. He was still getting used to the name he had given himself. It was his middle name, though he'd realised too late that he should really have chosen something completely alien, just in case; Craig Frederick Atherton. He'd thought that he might have some in-built recognition of it, but each time someone used it, it took him by surprise.

'Nothing,' he said.

'Been watching you tapping your shirt for the last coupla days, man. Somefing special in there?'

Baz's matted hair hung over his eyes and his long beard was twisted into a point and adorned with multi-coloured beads. He had blurry tattoos, an angel on one side of his neck and a devil on the other. They were hard to see in the dim light of the squat, the curtains all drawn despite it being the middle of the afternoon, but they were definitely there.

'Nah, just a nervous tick, I s'pose.'

Baz, who could have been anywhere between twenty and forty-years-old, nodded slowly. 'You're not holding out on me are you, man? Invited you here out of the goodness of my heart, you know. A collective, innit. What's mine is yours and all that.'

'Yeah, I know. Really appreciate it too. S'tough out there on your own.'

And it had been. The money he'd had in his wallet lasted a few days. He'd had just enough for a cheap B&B for two nights and some food, and he had maybe £20 left on his overdraft. But he'd seen the programmes, knew they could track his account, see where he'd withdraw money from, where he might be hiding out. London was a big place, but it didn't feel like it, not now. Every face on the street, every second look or suspicious glance held the potential for trouble. Even for a measly £20, using his bank card seemed too much of a risk.

If they were looking for him.

Baz was still staring, the smell of weed and body odour emanating from him, mixing to create a heady, stale aroma that he'd got used to these past few weeks. Everyone smelled like that. Him too.

'You're one of us, right,' said Baz.

It didn't feel like a question, but he nodded his head anyway.

'Need a piss,' Craig said climbing up from the dirty floor, cursing his stupidity as he automatically placed a hand to his chest, checking that his phone was still there.

Baz continued to stare.

In the bathroom, the only room in the crumbling house that still had a lock on the door, he sat on the toilet lid and took deep breaths. Maybe it was a sign. He'd waited long enough and if he lost his phone, the chance would pass.

He pulled it from its hiding place and sense checked his plan. As soon as he sent the email they'd be looking. But he wasn't stupid, he'd already created another email account, an anonymous one with no indication of who owned it. And he'd been off grid for nearly a month. He was just one of millions of faces in a city that paid no attention to people like him; homeless, jobless and moneyless. But if this went the way he hoped, he wouldn't be moneyless for long.

He looked at the file he had sent to Lewis Maynard-Jones, the one he had then forwarded to himself before deleting it from Alissa's sent items.

The thought of Alissa momentarily rocked him. Over the last weeks he had tried to convince himself that he was doing this for her, that this plan would make sure she didn't die in vain. But those weeks had taught him that it's impossible to convince yourself of a lie.

What happened to her was because of him, although he had no way of knowing the danger his actions had put her in - put them both in - at the time. Maybe if he had, he'd never have pressed that button. But it was too late for what ifs. Alissa was dead and his life was in ruins unless he decided to go up against some dangerous people.

He read through the email he had already typed, retyped and altered more times than he cared to admit. His heart was pounding, his palms sweaty. Once he pressed 'send' there would be no turning back.

His finger hovered over the screen.

He took a deep breath, then he pressed the button.

Eighteen

Alissa couldn't stop the tears. They poured down her cheeks and each time she wiped them away, more came to take their place.

People on the bus were staring at her but no one approached, no one asked if she was ok. She was glad of it, wouldn't have known what to say if they had. Maybe they thought she'd had a row with a friend, or had broken up with her boyfriend. The way she was feeling at that moment, the anger and humiliation that was coursing through her, a break up might be happening very soon.

The bus slowly made its way up towards Hamlet Court Road where she got off, keeping her gaze aimed at the floor all the way home. It was almost October, and the weather had recently turned from a late autumnal glow to the grey and cold of early winter. The biting wind and the mean drizzle that filled the air mirrored how Alissa felt. There was no sunny outlook on the horizon, no warm front moving in, only long and dark months ahead. The weather's only benefit was that the rain hid her tears.

She crossed the footbridge as a train sped past beneath and, for the most fleeting of moments, the thought of flinging herself over the railings and onto the track below crossed her mind. At the front of the lemon-yellow building Alissa sent up a silent prayer that she could get to the flat without encountering anyone, but even God had turned his back.

'Allo, gorgeous,' said a grinning Matt Hallstaff as she reached the final few stairs to the first floor. 'You're home early.'

The politeness that Alissa usually showed, whether she felt like showing it or not, had abandoned her. She'd usually say something insignificant, something which kept the wheels of social interaction oiled. But she had no intention of doing so now, instead mumbling a few words in her neighbour's direction about not feeling well. She then pulled the front door key from her pocket and aimed it at the lock.

If asked, Matt would have admitted that reading had never been his strong suit and, in this instance, he failed to read the signals Alissa was giving off. 'Want me to come in and cheer you up?' he asked, a mischievous grin blooming on his stubble-strewn face.

Alissa just looked at him, hair wet, eyes red, her stare unforgiving.

'Come on, Al. You got to admit, there's something there,' he said this as he waved a finger between himself and Alissa. 'Let me just run you a bath or something, you know? You can relax, have a soak in the tub.'

Alissa's expression hardly altered, only her eyes narrowed. 'Why don't you just fuck off, you pervy bastard? I wouldn't sleep with you if humanity depended on it. Now leave me alone and go and play with your blow-up doll or whatever you do in there.'

As more tears spilled down her cheeks Alissa turned the key in the lock, walked inside the flat and slammed the door behind her.

Matt, whose face was glowing scarlet, was momentarily shocked, then his wounded pride found a voice. 'I'm doin' you a favour, you skanky bitch,' he yelled at the closed door. 'You think you're all that! You should hear what people say about you. What your precious boyfriend says! Stupid slag!'

He was still muttering obscenities as he took the stairs two at a time and made his way out of the building.

***

Alissa didn't know how long she'd been asleep for, didn't know what time it was, but despite the quietness of his entry and the depth of her slumber, Craig's key sliding into the lock triggered something in her brain and she was awake almost instantly.

It was dark outside the window now, the streetlight casting a burnt orange glow into the room. She was on the futon, where she'd slumped after coming in, still reeling from the events at work and the altercation with Matt.

She'd grabbed a beer from the fridge but it lay unopened on the floor beside her, a ring of condensation around its base. She'd attempted to make sense of everything, tried to conjure an explanation that pointed away from the inevitable. When that attempt proved futile she tried to wish the last few hours away like they were a bad dream. When that too had proved unmanageable sleep had come, because what else was there?

From the moment he stepped into the flat and spotted her laying there in the rust-coloured darkness, Alissa knew she'd been right.

'How could you?' she spat. *'How dare you?'*

Craig flicked on a light, but all it did was highlight the anger on Alissa's face.

'You ok, babe?' he asked as he shut the door. But even those three, short words betrayed him, as Alissa recognised the nervousness in his voice, the faux innocence in his tone.

'I told you I didn't want to do anything. I told you I wanted to let it go.' She was close to shouting now, her voice becoming higher in pitch and louder in volume, the words cracking in places as her anger got the better of her. 'But blackmail! And he thinks it was me who sent that email. He thinks I'm the sort of person who would do something like that. If I'd have realised sooner I'd have told him it was you, let you deal with the fallout. But it didn't compute. I was too shocked by what he was saying. Thought there was some sort of misunderstanding. It was only afterwards that I realised.'

'Don't know what you're on about,' Craig said, hanging his coat on the hook behind the door, then walking towards the small kitchen.

'Bastard!' she yelled, picking up the can next to her and launching it in Craig's direction. It missed by more than a foot and crashed into the cupboard door, leaving a dent and a discoloured mark.

'What the fuck, Al!' shouted Craig, flinching. 'You mental, or what?'

Two loud bangs echoed through the room, then a muffled voice could be heard and Alissa realised Matt must have come back and was complaining at the noise they were making.

'And you can piss off, too!' she screamed at the wall before turning her attention back to Craig. *'He wanted my phone. Wanted my laptop. Wanted to call the police to report me. He fired me, Craig! On the spot. Just like that,'* she was shouting again, not caring who heard or what they thought. *'Because of you!'*

The tears returned. She'd told herself she mustn't cry, that tears showed weakness and vulnerability. But there was too much anger and disappointment. They flowed despite her best attempts to stop them, and that just made her angrier. She wanted him to explain why it wasn't him, to give some undeniable reason why he was in the clear. Instead, he picked up the thrown can and placed it in the sink, then filled the kettle and switched it on, like nothing had happened. Like this was a normal evening. She couldn't stand to even look at him so, instead, she stormed into the bedroom, her phone already in her hand, tapping at the keyboard.

'Who're you texting?' asked Craig, trying to get a look at her phone.

'Fuck off!' was all the response he received.

Alissa slammed the bedroom door behind her and, ten minutes later, reemerged with a rucksack slung over her shoulder.

She didn't say anything to Craig, who was sitting on the futon, a mug of half-drunk tea on the floor in front of him, instead she put her trainers on, opened the door to the flat and marched out to the waiting car.

Nineteen

Abraham left Harcourt House feeling more unsure than when he'd arrived. Experience had taught him that people's stories were commonly full of gaps. Sometimes those gaps were filled with assumptions and, often, those assumptions were misplaced. But the story he'd heard from Matt Hallstaff didn't feel aligned to the narrative of Alissa's death. From what he'd said, Alissa didn't come across as someone who took drugs or who was in the throes of an addiction.

'So, what do you think?' asked Evie.

'You knew her,' replied Abraham. 'What did *you* think?'

'Well, I didn't *really* know her, but that flat didn't strike me as some sort of junkie bolt-hole.'

'No, me neither.'

'I mean, I know I'm only going off films and TV shows, but you don't often see drug addicts with a fridge full of vegetables, bowls of fruit, muesli and exercise equipment dotted around the place.'

Evie paused and Abraham could sense her nervousness. He answered her question before she needed to find a way of asking it. 'Your aunt Grace, the places she lived in, near the end, when it was bad, they looked nothing like Alissa's flat.'

Evie gave a strained smile. 'I don't remember her much, not really.'

'You were only young. She loved you, wanted to see you more, but your mum and me, we didn't think that was a good idea. Not while she was like she was.'

Evie nodded. 'So, you think there's something up? That the police got it wrong?'

'Far too early to think that,' replied Abraham. 'I agree, it doesn't look like the home of a hardened drug addict, but if I've learned one thing in life it's that appearances can be deceptive.'

Abraham thought of Gavin Halborough, a sub-editor at a paper he'd worked on who had been a gambling addict. No one had known. He had been professional, exacting, courteous, hard-working. Only when they'd come in one morning to find out he had taken an overdose the previous night did it all come to light. The huge debts he owed, both to banks and loan sharks. The awful state of the flat in which he lived. The crumbled marriage and disintegrating relationship with his children.

All of this had been documented in a neat, carefully written note left on his bedside table and no one at the paper could tally the man they saw everyday in the office to the man whose funeral they would soon be attending.

Sometimes things just weren't as they seemed.

Abraham wondered about Craig, too. Malcolm Langton seemed to think he was scared, but of what? Of being caught? According to Carol the police believe he had nothing to do with Alissa's death. Could he have been supplying Alissa with the drugs and was worried that might come to light?

'Be good if we could find Alissa's boyfriend,' said Evie. 'You know, try to get some more information from the horse's mouth.'

'I was just thinking exactly that,' said Abraham, impressed by Evie's investigative nous, but also slightly concerned at her enthusiasm for the role. Another worry was that Evie might ask about Matt Hallstaff's story of the man who picked Alissa up in an old Volvo. She didn't mention it though, which he was grateful for, because he didn't want to think about that just yet.

Back on the street the wind had picked up and a flurry of fallen leaves were being whisked around in a cyclone of rust coloured foliage.

'Where now?' asked Evie.

'Do film production companies open at the weekends?'

Evie shrugged, 'One way to find out, I suppose.'

Back in the car Abraham looked up the company's website, which was less impressive that he was expecting, but there was a contact page, a short list of employees and an office address and number.

After four rings he was about to give up and ask Evie to take them home, then a woman's voice came on the line, 'Spotlight Design and Production, Francesca speaking, how can I help?'

'Sorry,' said Abraham, 'wrong number.' Then he hung up.

Evie looked at him.

'No point giving them a heads up that we're coming.'

On Valkyrie Road, the car crossed back over the railway tracks and headed along Kings Road, past the large detached houses that seemed like mansions compared to his parents' place, then skirted along the western edge of Chalkwell Park. At approaching 11am the park was busy, despite the cold weather. Kids were kicking balls, dogs were chasing sticks and a handful of hardy souls in coats and hats were sat outside the cafe drinking coffee.

Despite his attempt to ignore it, Abraham's thoughts returned to the car Alissa had got into.

There must be hundreds, probably thousand of Volvos in this area. Tens of thousands in the country as a whole. The chances that the one Alissa stepped into after the argument with Craig was the one belonging to his brother seemed minimal. But then more than a few of his colleagues were proponents of the mantra that there was no such thing as coincidence.

Should he entertain the possibility that Joshua was somehow involved in this? *Could* he entertain it?

They drove past the second-hand car showrooms, DIY stores and supermarkets of the London Road until, less than ten minutes later, they arrived outside Spotlight Design and Production.

'Where shall I park?' said Evie.

'Just drop me off, I'll see you back at Grandad's in a bit.'

Evie laughed. 'No chance. Price of a lift is me coming with.'

He huffed in disapproval, but Abraham knew better than to argue. Plus, he still felt guilty for forgetting his daughter's interview.

'I do the talking,' he said. 'You're my intern, ok?'

'Fine,' said Evie, grinning at the subterfuge, pulling the car into the Wetherspoon's car park opposite the office.

Spotlight seemed out of place along this stretch of commercial businesses. The surrounding shops were all glass-fronted with posters or products in the windows, the occasional neon sign flashing brightly to tempt people in. Spotlight, though, was almost hiding in plain sight. There was a metal door and, around it, whitewashed brickwork with one small window carved into it, frosted glass keeping prying eyes at bay. There was no signage to indicate what the door led to and Abraham only knew they were in the right place because of the number of the building, which had been listed on the website.

They crossed the road and tried to open the door, but it was locked. An intercom buzzer was set into the wall; Abraham pushed it.

'Hello?' came a woman's voice from the speaker.

'Yes, we're here to see Mr Maynard-Jones,' said Abraham, remembering the name from the website.

'Do you have an appointment?'

Abraham ignored the question. 'I'm here about Alissa Peters,' he said.

Experience told Abraham that death - especially sudden death - sucked people into its vortex and, although it felt ghoulish to say, made them interested. Morbid fascination at its finest. He was counting on that being true with the people at Spotlight Design and Production.

'I see,' the voice from the speaker said. 'I'll just see if he's free. Hold, please.'

Less than a minute later a loud buzz sounded, a lock clicked and Abraham and Evie entered the office.

Inside, just beyond the door, was a reception area. An attractive young woman with long, dark hair was seated behind a wooden desk, a screen in front of her and a large sign with the company's name printed on a vinyl banner behind her. Far from looking welcoming, the woman eyed the two visitors with suspicion.

'Mr Maynard-Jones will be with you shortly. Are you with the police force, Mr —'

'Hart. Abraham Hart, and this is my intern, Evie. I'm not, no. I'm a journalist.'

'For?'

'*The Chronicle*,' he said, instinctively, if not entirely truthfully.

'*The National Chronicle*?'

Abraham nodded.

Abraham and Evie were waved by a well-manicured hand towards a bright red sofa next to a circular coffee table a few feet away.

'Would you like a drink while you wait? Tea? Coffee?'

'We're fine. Thank you,' said Abraham as he and Evie took a seat on the sofa as the receptionist picked up a telephone and spoke into it in hushed tones.

Five minutes later a man strode from the rear of the office, his hand extended with at least ten paces left before he reached Abraham and Evie, a look of sombre seriousness on his face.

When he finally reached them he looked to be around Abraham's own age but wore dark jeans that ended just north of his ankle bone, black Gucci trainers and a fitted white Ralph Lauren shirt. He was tall and lean with sandy blond hair, a large mouth that had teeth too neat and too white to be natural and what, thirty years ago, would have been called 'designer stubble'.

'Lewis Maynard-Jones,' said the man, planting a smooth but firm hand into Abraham's own, then turning to Evie to repeat the process, adding a more fulsome smile as he shook her outstretched hand. 'I'm sorry, no one told me you were coming.' He turned towards the woman behind the front desk. 'Francesca. This wasn't in the diary, was it?'

Before receiving an answer he turned back to his visitors. 'No matter. You're here about poor Alissa, I understand.'

'You understand correctly. We just have a few questions if we may.'

'Of course. Please, let's go to my office, we can talk there.' Lewis extended his right arm towards the back of the building and a glass walled office, allowing Abraham to lead the way, Evie followed, with Lewis behind tapping away on the screen of his phone.

Lewis's office was stylish if minimalist. Unlike the wood-effect linoleum in the rest of the building, the floor here was real wood, though a rug the same colour as the reception sofa covered half the floorspace.

A rustic wooden desk sat in the middle of the rug, behind it a leather office chair. The desk contained nothing but a MacBook, a Moleskin notepad with a fat fountain pen resting on top, and a small silver stand that held business cards. The cream-coloured walls were bare apart from a framed poster of *Reservoir Dogs* and a shelf full of books.

Lewis saw Evie looking at the shelf. 'Mainly business books,' he said, smiling broadly. 'Should probably read them at some point.'

'And what business are you in, exactly?' said Evie, garnering a reproachful look from her father as he removed a spiral-bound notebook and a yellow Bic from inside his coat pocket. He didn't need to take notes, but the tools of the trade would at least help keep up the pretence.

Lewis indicated the two seats in front of the desk, both of which were leather, neither of which were as fancy as the chair behind the desk. 'We're a film production company. Advertising, in the main. Some corporate videos, occasional music promos and short films. Drink, Mr Hart? Miss…'

Lewis was standing in front of the only other piece of furniture in the office, a slim cabinet sat against one wall, on top of which were bottles of water, both sparkling and still, and a series of spirits and mixers.

'Evie,' said Evie. 'I'm fine, thank you though.'

'Nothing for me either, thanks,' Abraham said, then watched Lewis mix himself a vodka and tonic before taking a seat behind the desk. 'And, please, it's Abraham.'

'So, Abraham, Francesca says you're here to talk about poor Alissa. I thought that terrible situation was all wrapped up. I'm assuming you're writing a story. How can I help you?'

'No one else here?' asked Abraham, ignoring Lewis's question. 'Just you and Francesca, is it? Just wondering, you know. Wasn't sure you'd be open on a Saturday, so we're lucky we caught you.'

'Filmmaking is not a nine-to-five, I'm afraid,' said Lewis, absentmindedly rubbing his bristly face.

'Your wife must find that frustrating,' said Evie who, Abraham noticed, was looking at the gold band on Lewis's wedding finger.

'Not at all,' came a voice from behind Abraham and Evie, causing them to turn in unison.

In the doorway stood a woman in a sleek, black trouser suit. Her shoulder length hair was blonde and perfectly arranged, shiny wisps of it falling over her shoulders. Her blue eyes flicked from Evie to Abraham, a half-smile playing across her lips.

'I know how hard Lewis works to make this place a success.' The half-smile grew wider.

'This is my wife, Ellie,' said Lewis, standing up awkwardly and banging his knee on the hard desk in the process. 'She's a partner in the business.'

'Oh, that's overstating it, I think, don't you, darling? My name's on the paperwork but I'm more of a silent partner, really. A non-executive director I think it's called, isn't it Lewis?'

Lewis nodded. 'More on the money side of things, I suppose. But money's an integral part of any business.'

'Pah! David takes care of all that.' Ellie placed a hand up to the side of her mouth, as if imparting a secret, then whispered conspiratorially, 'I just like hearing the gossip from the shoots and sprucing up the office decor every now and then.'

'David?' said Abraham.

'Our Chief Financial Officer,' answered Lewis, sitting back down, eyes still planted on his wife.

'I'm sorry,' said Ellie, 'I'm interrupting. Are you here about a project?'

'Actually, no,' said Abraham. 'We're from the *National Chronicle*, we're here about Alissa Peters' death.'

'Oh my God. That poor girl. I couldn't believe it. She was so lovely. So helpful and bright. And such a beautiful thing, just like you, my love,' she said, smiling at Evie. 'If we'd have known what she was going through, the addiction she was caught up in, we'd have done anything to help. And her poor mother. If there's anything we can do, anything we can help with, please, let us know. The more people know about the devastating effects of drug addiction, the better.'

Abraham nodded. 'Thank you.'

'I'll leave you to get on,' she added, nodding to her husband then returning to the outer office.

'I have to say,' said Lewis, still watching his wife retreating, 'I'm surprised that *The National Chronicle* is taking an interest in this. It's a tragedy, of course it is, but hardly of national importance, I would have thought. The local rag's been all over it, as you would expect; pretty girl, terrible addiction, life cut short and all that.'

'What did Alissa do here, Mr Maynard-Jones?' asked Abraham.

'Lewis, please,' answered Lewis, flashing his too-white teeth. 'She began as work experience, towards the end of the summer. She was good; keen, clever, enthusiastic. She didn't have any one role, really. Bit of work on reception if Francesca wasn't here, collating research material for an upcoming project, getting coffee, filing, the usual ephemera that is the wont of a junior member of staff.'

'And you kept her on, after her work experience ended?'

'Yes. As I say, she was a hard worker and we were busy and needed the help. She wanted to be a director. Said she wanted to absorb as much as she could from us. Her attempts were good, what I saw of them.'

'She showed you some of her work?' asked Evie

'At the risk of speaking ill of the dead, I think "work" might be overstating it.' Lewis smiled again, more nervously this time, fewer teeth. 'They were interesting, if amateurish clips. The sort of stuff students make. She needed more mystique, more artistic flair, more creativity. But she wanted to learn, and that's why we liked her.'

'Was there ever any indication that Alissa was using drugs?'

Again, Lewis paused. He glanced over Abraham's shoulder and into the office behind. 'I never caught her doing anything like that. No one did. If we had, well, we'd have offered to help her in any way we could, of course. But, in retrospect, there were maybe signs.'

Abraham waited for Lewis to go on. He was used to letting people take their time and getting to the point in their own way. To keep interrupting or asking questions, he had learned, became distracting rather than helpful. And most people needed to fill the silence.

'She was late a lot. Maybe not a lot, but enough. And sometimes she seemed, I don't know, vacant, maybe? Like her brain had switched off for a little bit.'

'What did you put that down to?'

Lewis shrugged. 'Being a teenager, I suppose.'

'And did you talk to Alissa about this? Did you ask her why she was late, or what her lapses in concentration were about?'

'Well, no,' replied Lewis, shifting in his chair. 'Like I said, it wasn't like I thought she was Aleister Crowley or anything. And her work didn't seem to suffer. As far as I knew, anyway.'

Abraham scribbled a note in his pad, at least that's what it looked like to Lewis, who was now tapping at his keyboard. 'Are your staff away on location a lot?' asked Abraham. 'Seems like a pretty big office for a pretty small team.'

Lewis seemed to take offence, sitting up straighter and leaning forward. 'How do you know how big my team is? We deal with large budget projects that require a series of professional creators and producers. Sometimes they're here, sometimes they're not. What's that got to do with Alissa?'

'You said you thought Alissa was pretty,' said Abraham.

'Pardon?'

'"*Pretty girl, terrible addiction, life cut short,*" you said.'

Lewis didn't answer immediately. He paused for a second or two and Abraham could sense he was looking at him differently now. He stood and walked to the drinks cabinet, refilling his glass with vodka and tonic. While his back was turned, Abraham leaned forward and quickly removed one of the business cards from the silver stand.

'I think, objectively, you could say she was pretty, yes. Are you insinuating something, Mr Hart?' asked Lewis, turning, his drink replenished, first name terms now forgotten. 'I thought you were a serious journalist from a serious newspaper, not some gossip merchant with a tabloid mentality.'

'Apologies,' said Abraham, though his face showed no sign of remorse. 'I'm just wondering if anyone might have taken a shine to Alissa. Someone from the office, maybe? Or a client, or someone who lives or works close by?'

'I can assure you, no one here was interested in that poor young girl in that way. Anyway, didn't she have a boyfriend? I thought I overheard her talking about someone.'

'She did, yes.'

Lewis shuffled in his chair and swept invisible strands of hair from his face. 'Any idea where he might be at the moment?'

'Mr Maynard-Jones, I've taken up enough of your time, I think,' said Abraham, pushing back his chair and standing up. 'I wondered, before I go, whether I might talk to Francesca for a minute or two. They're fairly close in age so maybe Alissa spoke to her about things she might not feel comfortable talking to anyone else about.'

'I'm afraid Francesca's just gone to lunch,' said Lewis, looking at his watch, a Breitling, Abraham noticed. 'Not sure when she'll be back.'

'Ah, shame. I'll catch her another time. And would you be able to furnish me with the names and numbers of the other members of your team who knew Alissa? I'd like to do some more background work if I can.'

Lewis, now also standing, took a breath as if to speak, then held it for a few seconds, mouth slightly open. Abraham tilted his head and raised his eyebrows, an unspoken invitation.

'It's just, background on what?' asked Lewis. 'I don't want to come across as insensitive, but what is there to investigate?'

'Probably nothing,' answered Abraham, no longer completely sure that was the case. 'But my editor wants me to do a piece on the fragile psyche of today's teenagers, so here we are.'

Lewis nodded. 'Of course. I'll ask Francesca to get you everything once she's back.'

'Do you have a business card or something?' asked Abraham.

Lewis looked to his desk. 'I'm sorry, these ones are old now. Details all different. Give me your number and I'll make sure Francesca gets in touch.'

Abraham scribbled his name and number on a piece of paper from his notepad, tore it out and hand it to Lewis, who smiled insincerely, shook hands with Abraham and Evie then walked them through the now empty office and out onto the street.

'Well,' said Evie, 'he seemed nervous about something. And her, Francesca; super-bitch. I reckon Alissa was sleeping with Lewis, Francesca got jealous and killed her and now they're both covering it up. It's the wife I feel sorry for, she seemed nice.'

'Alright Sherlock, bit of a leap, isn't it? People are often nervous talking to the press, so I wouldn't read too much into it.'

'Well, what do you think?'

Abraham pulled out his phone. 'I think that now might be a good time to call in a favour.'

Twenty

Abraham sat at a ring-stained wooden table. A pint of Guinness poured by a bored-looking woman with too much eye shadow was settling in front of him.

The Wetherspoons had a large footprint, taking up a whole block of space on the London Road. The main structure was an old farmhouse with cream paint broken up by royal blue windows and facias, with the lower half of the building made of pleasingly rustic red brick.

Called The Elms, it was named after a tree known as Adam's elm which had stood nearby for many years. The only greenery in sight now was some fume-choked shrubbery at the front of the pub which shielded drinkers from the passing traffic crawling by on the busy main road. Or maybe it was the other way around.

Abraham had told a reluctant Evie that the meeting he was about to have wasn't one she could attend and that she should either wait in the car or meet him back at Vic's. She had argued the point, saying she was now part of the investigation, such as it was.

Abraham couldn't deny she'd been helpful and seemed to have a natural ability to read people and ask the right questions, but his pride was outweighed by his concern. He didn't want to drag her into whatever this was, which, at the moment, was nothing, but still meant digging into the life of a recently dead teenager. Evie didn't need that, and he didn't need the subsequent earbashing from Siobhan when she inevitably found out. So, he had been insistent and, eventually, Evie had lifted a hand in sullen farewell as she drove away.

Martin Palmer arrived halfway through Abraham's pint. He shuffled through the main doors and shook the rain, which had just started falling, from his hair. What was left of it, anyway. It had been almost a decade since Abraham had laid eyes on Palmer and the years didn't look to have been kind. His previously thick head of dark hair was thinner and greyer, his pink-red crown visible and a widow's peak prominent. As he removed his coat Abraham could see that his stomach was stretching at his navy-blue jumper, partially hanging over his trousers like it was making a bid for freedom. Had Palmer worn glasses before? Abraham couldn't remember, but the frames he wore now were almost as thick as the lenses they surrounded.

Abraham wondered what he would look like through Palmer's eyes. Sure, Abraham was a decade younger than the policeman, but ten years is a long time and those years had, likely, been no kinder to him.

'Martin!' shouted Abraham, waving a hand.

The older man glanced towards the shout then ambled across the garish carpet, a coat draped over an arm, a look of disdain spread across his face.

'What do you want, Hart?' said Martin.

'Pleasure to see you too,' said Abraham.

'Thought you'd done with this place,' said Martin in a voice that Abraham was pleased to note still sounded like he'd been gargling gravel.

'The Elms?'

'Southend.'

'Home is where the heart is, Detective Sergeant Palmer.'

'Detective Inspector now,' said Martin.

'Well, in that case, congratulations are in order,' said Abraham, standing up. 'What can I get you?'

At the bar Abraham ordered another Guinness for himself and a pint of lager for his companion who, with the subtlety of a breeze block, looked at his watch and complained about being hungry. After ordering fish and chips for Martin and bangers and mash for himself, Abraham led the way back to the booth.

'So,' began Martin after squeezing himself into the seat opposite Abraham, 'to what do I owe this dubious pleasure?'

'Thought a catch up would be nice.'

Martin laughed, took a slow sip of his drink and shook his head. 'You'll forgive me, Abraham, but cynicism is so deeply ingrained in my being that I have trust issues. It's a hindrance of the profession. You working a story? I thought your focus was much wider than this little part of the country.'

'It usually is, but something came up that's a bit closer to home and I said I'd give it some attention. Plus,' Abraham said with a grin, 'it means we get to rekindle our friendship.'

Martin almost choked on his pint.

'I'm hurt,' said Abraham, smiling.

'Hmm, looks that way,' said Martin, tapping the side of his nose and looking at Abraham.

'This?' he said, dabbing the slightly swollen patch around his nostril. 'Walked into a door.'

'Classic mistake. Look, maybe you've hit that part of a mid-life crisis that makes a man re-evaluate his past and atone for his misdeeds, but I'd suggest saving yourself the trouble and just buying an MR2 or something.'

'A Mazda?'

Martin shrugged. 'Policeman's salary.'

'Anyway,' said Abraham, 'what misdeeds?'

Martin, whose drink was halfway to his lips, froze, then slowly placed his glass back on the pock-marked table. 'You saying you've not invited me here so I can do something for you while you hold that old and spurious information you illegally obtained over me?'

Abraham remained straight-faced. 'Not spurious. Those photos exist and I did you a favour by getting them buried.'

'Right. But not so buried that you won't use them to your advantage. Again. There should be a statute of limitations on that debt. What I did happened a long time ago and I'm not that person anymore.'

'None of us are who we used to be, Martin. For better or worse.'

Martin stared daggers at Abraham then took another draught of his pint. Abraham just watched him, relaxed. He had got to know Martin Palmer when he had been working for the *Southend Gazette*. The police and the media regularly worked together, often with mutual benefit, though even more often with different goals in mind. Sometimes Martin had used Abraham to get a result, sometimes it was the other way around. Both always knew what was happening and, on a few occasions, both got what they wanted.

When Abraham had moved to London the two kept in touch. It was a professional relationship that sporadically blossomed into personal rapport, but when

Abraham began working on a story about sex trafficking while he was at *The Independent*, a story which extended outside the capital and to gangs in neighbouring counties, the relationship changed.

'Anyway,' added Martin, 'I'm a grandad now, a family man. And I've told you before, it was a one-off. Complete madness. Pam and me were having some issues and I lost my head.'

'And most of your clothes. S'what made the pictures so compelling.'

Martin shot another angry look across the table, and Abraham held up his hands in mock surrender. 'I'm joking, I'm joking. I convinced the paper to bury those pictures so we didn't sidetrack the bigger story, and luckily they didn't know you're a copper. They're history. I'm asking about this as a favour from an old friend.'

Abraham knew he'd used the same reasoning before, more than once, he suspected. He doubted Martin trusted it anymore this time than he had in the past. They had been friends once, or professional acquaintances, at least. But whatever their relationship had been before that hidden camera was planted, it had morphed into something else. Something that meant Martin was always the tail and Abraham always the dog. A situation which the older man was always looking to rectify.

'A grandad?' said Abraham, raising his glass in salute. 'Congratulations. Talking of family, you know anything about a recent death? Young girl named Alissa Peters. Mother's called Carol Peters.'

'And there it is.'

'Just a friendly enquiry.'

'Rarely anything friendly about your enquiries.'

'Humour me.'

Martin sighed. 'Wasn't my case. Isn't anyone's case now. An OD, wasn't it? Not too many of them round here. Not with kids that age, despite all the drugs that seem to be kicking around.'

The woman with too much eyeshadow arrived and placed two plates of food on the table, followed by two sets of cutlery wrapped in black napkins. The men were quiet as she did this, only returning to their conversation once she'd left.

'And there was nothing fishy about it? No one was suspicious?'

'Of what? Like I said, wasn't my case, but they found drugs in her flat, needles, all that stuff. Alcohol in her system, too. Best guess is she was new, didn't know her limits.'

'New?'

'No track marks. No history with us. Decent family. Steady boyfriend. People don't often go from zero to one hundred like she did. There's usually a path you can trace; weed, coke, petty theft, shoplifting. She probably fell into something she wasn't prepared for. People do.'

'Did you speak to her employer, a guy called Lewis Maynard-Jones? Runs a production company over the road from here.'

'Maynard-Jones? Sounds posh. But no, like I said, I didn't talk to anyone because it wasn't my case. I'm sure someone did.'

'What about the boyfriend?'

'What about him?' replied Martin, tucking into his fish and chips with the gusto of man who'd not eaten since breakfast.

'He wasn't involved in any way? Has nothing to do with drugs? No record?'

Without looking up, and through a mouthful of mushy peas, Martin replied, 'Can't have been. Contrary to popular belief, we do know what we're doing. If he was involved then he'd have been brought in, questioned, arrested, whatever. If I remember, he was away when it happened. Alibi was corroborated. In the clear.'

'He's gone?'

'Who?'

'The boyfriend. He's moved out of the flat they shared. No one seems to know where he's gone or why.'

'Moving out's not illegal. Poor bastard's probably in shock, or grieving. Gone home or something. Why are you so interested in this, anyway? Doesn't sound like the sort of thing to get your boat floated. Bit prosaic for *The Chronicle*.'

'Like I said, it's something that's hit close to home.'

'Grace?' asked Martin.

'What do you mean?' Abraham sounded more defensive than he meant.

'Heard about your sister. You don't need to be Freud to see the similarities.'

'I'm just digging into this for a friend. Well, friend of my brother's.'

'Why, he got some pictures of you?'

'Very funny.'

'Not much to dig into, so you can consider it job done, I'd say.'

'Maybe. Can you look into him for me? The boyfriend, I mean. Craig Atherton is his name. Twenty-three-years-old. Works - or worked - in the city. Maybe he left an idea of where he went, where he was from. He must have left some sort of contact information.'

'Do I have a choice?'

'You always have a choice, Martin.'

The older man shook his head while wiping the black napkin across his mouth. 'It's good to see you again, Abraham,' he said, deadpan.

Twenty-one

A third vodka tonic, already half drunk, sat on the desk, tiny bubbles exploding to the surface like secrets that couldn't wait to get out. Lewis Maynard-Jones couldn't even remember finishing the second one and it was still only early afternoon. His wife had mentioned to him about cutting down on his drinking just before she left. If she found out she would be disappointed, but there were a lot of things she would be disappointed about if she found them out.

The office was empty now. He'd sent Francesca a text message asking her to make herself scarce just before sitting down with Abraham Hart. He didn't want Hart spending any more time in the office than necessary, and he certainly didn't want him talking to Francesca. He took another sip of his drink, hoping it would calm his nerves, thinking that the visit of a journalist was probably not a good thing. Knowing that the email he'd received that morning definitely wasn't.

Lewis was finding it hard to keep all the threads in his brain separated; what he had said, who he had said it to, and when. The main problem wasn't Abraham Hart, but the email. A journalist had no power over him, no authority. Anyway, the police had ruled Alissa's death as an accidental overdose.

That only left the video.

He scraped a hand across his face, closed his eyes then pressed his index fingers into his temples, kneading them in an attempt at massaging away the stress he could feel building. When that didn't work he picked his mobile up from his desk, hesitated over the screen, then dialled. The call was answered after less than two rings.

'Lewis,' said the voice at the other end of the line. 'Everything ok?'

'Hello, David. Look, I know it's Saturday but any chance you could pop into the office for a bit? I just want to run some stuff by you. Stuff we discussed previously.'

There was a slight hesitation and Lewis could picture his CFO replaying recent conversations in his head. 'The office?'

'No. The other thing. About the video. Remember?'

'I see. Yes, of course. I'm actually at a loose end, so no problem. Give me twenty minutes and I'll be with you.'

David Catton let himself into the office a short time later. Though only four years Lewis's senior he looked a lot older. It was partly the thinning hair, the remainder of which clung to his head more in hope than expectation, and partly his dress sense. Though it was the weekend, David wore an ill-fitting business suit with newly shined patent leather shoes and a rain mac that was less flash and more flasher. Unusually, he wasn't wearing a tie, which Lewis could only put down to it being the weekend.

Despite his sartorial shortcomings, David and Lewis had been friends since soon after the business had begun. Ellie had brought him in, as she had all the money people, and while he had proved himself to be a shrewd and diligent Chief Financial Officer, he had also become a trusted friend and useful sounding board.

'Davey, thanks for coming in, mate,' said Lewis, holding up an empty tumbler with one hand and a bottle of vodka in the other.

'Oh, no, thanks,' said David, in answer to the unspoken question. 'Bit early for me.'

Lewis shrugged and poured his fifth drink, having drunk the fourth while waiting for David to arrive. 'There was a journalist here earlier,' he said. The words sounded thick in the air and he topped the tumbler up with more tonic.

'Why?' asked David, sitting in the seat Abraham had vacated only an hour before.

'Alissa. Looking into it, apparently.'

David was nodding slowly, analysing Lewis's words before answering. It was something he did a lot, was part of the reason Lewis trusted his advice. 'What is there to look into? Alissa overdosed. Didn't she?'

Lewis turned his head to look at David. It seemed to take longer than it should have, a streak of colour trailblazing across his vision as his head moved. He resolved to leave this drink untouched. 'That's the police's belief, and who are we to contradict them?'

More slow nodding. 'You're worried.' It wasn't a question.

Lewis dropped himself into his chair. 'It's the video.'

'You think he's seen it? This journalist?'

'No. I don't know. But why would he be here?'

David remained silent. Lewis had called him as soon as Alissa had sent the original email weeks before. He had been panicked, almost hysterical, and he'd had asked to meet David in a bar on Leigh Broadway. He needed advice, someone to complain to, rant at, and he thought David was the person to take on that role. They'd talked in hushed tones about the potential impact of what Alissa had filmed and the more Lewis drank the more scared he'd become. And the more scared he'd become, the angrier he'd got. It was all David could do to stop Lewis heading straight to Alissa's flat to confront her there and then.

'Look,' said Lewis, leaning forward and resting his elbows on the desk and his head in his hands. 'I got another email. Someone sent me the video again. They're asking for money. A lot of money.'

'Who from?' asked David, his tone serious now.

'Me!'

'I mean, who's the email from?'

'I don't know. It's some random address I don't recognise. There's no name, just a PO Box to send the money.'

'Sounds amateurish,' said David. 'The police didn't recover Alissa's phone after she died.'

'No, but what does that matter?' said Lewis, raising his voice slightly.

'It matters whether the video has remained on that one phone, or if it's been sent to other people. Harder to contain if it's the latter.'

'Shit!' yelled Lewis.

'What about the boyfriend? Or the priest, the one you sent me the photos of.'

'What boyfriend?'

'Alissa's,' replied David. 'Didn't you say he disappeared after her death? Could it be him emailing you?'

Lewis rubbed a manicured hand over his face. 'That's what I heard. No one's seen him since. But if it is him, why wait till now?'

'I'm not sure,' said David. Then, after a moment of silence, he asked another question. 'Which part did this anonymous person send?'

'What do you mean?'

'I mean, is it the video of you screwing the receptionist, or is it the recording of us?'

Lewis picked up the tumbler, some of the liquid slopping over the sides and onto the red rug. He drank half of it in one gulp. When he'd swallowed the rest, he spoke. 'All of it,' he said. 'They sent all of it.'

'Right,' said David. 'Then we have a fucking problem.'

Twenty-two

'There might be a problem,' said Erjon who had appeared at the door.

They were at the house in Hampstead, Hristo at the antique desk in his study. Since arriving home the previous day he had re-familiarised himself with his work, with what needed doing, with who needed his time and his focus. Things had carried on without him, but there would always be nervousness without his presence. His, or someone else's. Someone as yet nameless and faceless who would be waiting to force his way into Hristo's shoes when he was looking the other way.

But no one had, because he was cautious.

There were many things that Hristo wasn't - emotional, apprehensive, acquiescent, patient - but he was always cautious.

Being cautious was smart. It showed shrewdness and the ability to think ahead. It was the one thing which had kept him in business, kept him free and kept him alive for so long.

Erjon was cautious, too.

'Tell me,' Hristo said.

'There's a situation with some of the money,' said Erjon in his heavily accented English.

'Serious?'

Erjon's face was unreadable, as it always was. Before answering he fastened the middle button on the jacket of his charcoal suit and shot the cuffs so that half an inch of white shirt showed around his wrists. Hristo still found the sight of Erjon in a suit unusual, even after all these years.

'I'm not sure. A case of, how do you say in English; loose lips?'

Hristo shut the laptop he had been staring at then picked up the crystal tumbler that had been sitting on the desk in front of him, the two fingers of Glenlivet now just one. He took a sip. 'Should we be worried?'

'You needn't be. I will do the worrying.'

'You have someone feeding you information?'

'Of course.'

'And it's being handled?'

'It will be.'

Hristo raised an eyebrow.

'Better for you not to concern yourself,' said Erjon. 'But I should tell you, the problem is in Southend.'

The name caused Hristo to glance up from the tumbler of amber liquid and narrow his eyes at his friend. 'Is Diellza ok? Do I need to pay a visit?'

'I do not think that would be wise,' said Erjon. 'It could get complicated.'

'How so?'

'The journalist is there. And it seems that the journalist's brother may be involved.'

'Involved how?'

'I intend to find out. Do you trust me?'

Another one of the many things which Hristo wasn't, was trusting. Most people, in his experience, didn't warrant his trust. The last person in whom he had placed it was Mariana, and that had not ended well, at least not for her. Other than himself, there were only two people he truly trusted. One of them was in a small city on the south east coast of England, the other was standing in front of him.

That trust had been borne of more than thirty years of friendship. They had been mercenaries in a life before this one, soldiers in a time before that. After leaving the Albanian army both had been recruited by a specialist group looking for young men who were happy to fight for a living, but unafraid to die doing it. They had travelled together to Somalia, Angola, Afghanistan, Peru and many other countries that neither of them had any burning desire to see again. They had worked for monsters, megalomaniacs, freedom fighters, latter day missionaries and more than a few drug cartels.

Security was what they called it, but killing, or preventing someone being killed, was what their work usually entailed. Hristo got no real thrill from it. It was neither something he enjoyed, nor something he excelled at. It was simply a means to an end. He was proficient with guns, knowledgeable on military tactics, and was handsomely paid for his part in whatever assignment they were hired to undertake, but the work was simply that; work.

For Erjon, though, the work was all. Hristo knew that he would have laboured for free because Erjon had told him. The money Erjon had accumulated over the years they'd spent in jungles and deserts, rainforests and dusty, bombed-out towns was sitting somewhere, gathering either dust or interest, but largely untouched.

Hristo had once asked him what he would do if he could do anything, if he could click his fingers and make a dream come true. 'This,' Erjon had said, before he carried on digging the fox hole in which they were to sleep that night.

Hristo had saved Erjon's life once or twice, but Erjon had returned the favour many times over. He should be dead in Beirut, or Kosovo, in Kinshasa or São Paulo but each time Erjon would appear, almost from nowhere, like the wind. In any other field of work - music, or art, or mathematics - Erjon would have been described as gifted. Killing was something he simply excelled at. But it was never indiscriminate, never haphazard. Erjon was not, Hristo believed, psychopathic; he was too controlled, too disciplined, too organised. No, Erjon was simply a survivor.

'I trust you,' Hristo finally said.

Erjon nodded. 'Then trust me to deal with this. The less you know, the better. But I need to ask; are there any boundaries?'

'Diellza.'

'Of course, but that was not what I meant.'

'Then, no,' said Hristo. 'Do whatever needs doing.'

Twenty-three

Abraham kept having to remind himself that this wasn't a story, it was a favour. But a favour that was gradually revealing interesting new elements, and which continued to expose further detail the more stones he overturned.

Martin Palmer had agreed to check out Craig Atherton's statement and let Abraham know if there was anything untoward, or if there were any details about where Craig might now be.

Martin had told him not to get his hopes up. 'Atherton's not a suspect,' he'd said, almost scraping the pattern off the plate as he finished his fish and chips. 'Never was, so it's not like we'd have given him the third degree.'

He stayed at the Elms for a while after Martin had left, flicking a 'v' as his goodbye. He made his second pint last as he digested both his lunch and the information he had uncovered. The most difficult element so far was the Volvo. Could his brother's battered car be the one which had picked up Alissa after her row with Craig? He'd need to broach the subject with Joshua but knew it would be a thorny topic, one that could, whatever the answer, stoke the fraternal fires to the point of explosion.

The rain was still falling when Abraham finally left the pub and rather than get wet walking back to his dad's house he instead got wet waiting for a bus, which turned up late and overcrowded.

Thirty uncomfortable minutes later he unlocked the front door and trudged inside, rainwater soaked into every fibre of his being.

'That you, Abraham?' called Vic from the kitchen.

'Yeah,' he shouted in return. 'Evie still here?'

Vic appeared at the kitchen door, a cup of tea in one hand, a Digestive in the other. 'No, she got fed up of waiting. And Siobhan called, wondering where she was, so she went home. How's it going between you two?'

'Me and Evie?'

'Well,' said Vic, carefully dunking his biscuit and taking a bite of the sodden end, 'take your pick, really; you and Evie, you and Siobhan, you and Joshua.' Vic smiled.

'Very droll, Dad. Evie? I'm not sure. We seemed ok this morning, but then we didn't part of the best of terms. Shiv's mad at me, so no change there. Joshua? It remains to be seen. Though I'm not entirely sure it's him who should be angry.'

'You haven't contacted him since yesterday, then?'

'No,' replied Abraham tersely. 'And he hasn't contacted me. Hardly the behaviour of someone who's meant to turn the other cheek, is it? Anyway, he's probably too busy making sure the man who killed Grace is feeling ok.'

Victor shot his son a look of contempt, a rare occurrence from a man who didn't see tolerance as a benefit, but a prerequisite. 'He's not the same person now. He was ill, Abraham. So was Grace. Anyway, I thought your anger was aimed at those higher up the narcotics food chain; the importers, the distributors.'

'My anger's aimed at all of them,' he said, and stomped up the stairs for a hot shower and a change of clothes.

***

Abraham slept no better on Saturday night than he had the night before. He had come down after his shower the previous evening - warmer, more comfortable and feeling less hostile than when he'd arrived home - and had flopped onto the sofa, saying nothing, while his dad watched repeats of *Only Fools and Horses*.

They ate Vic's famous - or infamous, depending on your point of view - shepherd's pie, which hadn't helped with Abraham's sleep, the rich gravy and mash that was at least a third cream, sitting heavy on his stomach.

But that was only part of the problem. Abraham couldn't help thinking he had stumbled from the car crash of his career into a situation that was soaked in petrol and situated perilously close to an open flame.

He had lain awake, staring at the ceiling, listening to distant engines and muffled voices drifting in through the cracked window, wishing he could rewind his life. But rewind to where? To the argument about Brody Lipscombe? To agreeing to ask questions for Carol Peters? Or maybe further; to forgetting Evie's interview? Or to when he first met Brody and made the decision he'd regretted ever since?

Like the previous night, he'd drifted off in the early hours but woke again close to five and, abandoning any hope of sleep, sat up to use his phone to search for the name 'Craig Atherton'. Google told him there were almost two-and-a-half-million results. He narrowed the search to 'Craig Atherton Southend', which cut the results almost in half, but didn't get him any closer to finding his Craig Atherton. A half-hearted look at a handful of Facebook, LinkedIn and Instagram profiles yielded no joy, none seeming to be the person in the photo with Alissa.

At 6am he began scrolling through job sites in anticipation of his suspension eventually being made more permanent. He scanned journalism.com, the *Guardian* and the usual employment apps, but the process made him feel depressed, so he decided to get up.

He dressed in the same clothes as the previous day, the ones his father had washed, dried and placed on the dresser in his room. It reminded Abraham that he needed to either pay the coming week's hotel bill, or pick up the stuff from his room and find somewhere else to live, assuming Siobhan wasn't going to welcome him home anytime soon. Once dressed he quietly made his way downstairs to get himself breakfast, where his father almost scared him to death.

'Morning,' Vic said as Abraham opened the kitchen door.

'Jesus!' said Abraham, clutching his chest. 'What is it with old people and getting up before the sun?'

'When you realise you're running out of sunrises, it makes you appreciate them more,' answered Vic.

'Cheery,' said Abraham.

'You asked. Anyway, I'm going to the church early, help your brother out.'

'I've been thinking,' said Abraham, 'maybe I'll come too, if that's ok.'

Vic looked at Abraham and smiled. 'Of course it's ok. I can't remember the last time we were all at Mass together.'

Abraham immediately though of Grace's funeral, then tried to push it out of his mind just as quickly.

'You're ok, are you?' asked his dad, suspicious now. 'Nothing bothering you?'

'I'm fine,' replied Abraham, thinking that if he needed to see Joshua then church was as good a place as any, but also wondering whether Carol would be there, because there was something he wanted to say to her.

***

According to Vic the church was busy, but the forty or so people sat in the cold filled only a quarter of the large space, maybe a third if they hadn't been so huddled together for warmth.

The congregation consisted mainly of people over fifty. Some a long way over. There were a couple of young families, babies being held and shushed, older children looking bored and unhappy. Most people were in groups, only a few sitting alone, two elderly women who looked like they may have just come in for a rest, and one middle-aged man in a green baseball cap.

Abraham had driven them in his dad's old Corolla. That morning he had decided to tell Carol Peters that he could no longer look into Alissa's death. He knew Carol would be upset and, if he were honest with himself, he was upset too. The people he had spoken to so far painted an inconsistent picture that set off his journalistic curiosity. But he had made up his mind.

He needed to sort his life out. He needed to prove he could do the job he, for the moment, was employed to do. He needed to see his daughter more often, his father too. He needed to mend his broken marriage. He needed to grow up.

He was thinking all this when everyone in the church stood and his brother, dressed in green and gold vestments, glided down the nave, a young girl dressed in a white robe ahead of him. As he reached the end of the nave, Joshua first bowed to the crucifix hanging above the alter then made his way behind the alter and turned to face everyone.

'In the name of the Father, and of the Son, and of the Holy Spirit,' he said, making the sign of the cross.'

'Amen,' the congregation replied in unison.

Forty minutes later, after numerous prayers he semi-remembered, a series of turgid hymns sung with mumbled embarrassment by most and candid enthusiasm by a few, and a sermon from Joshua about The Prodigal Son, which Abraham hoped was coincidental, even though he didn't believe in coincidences, the service ended and the congregation slowly filed out of the church.

Abraham followed his father back along the nave, Vic stopping every few steps to talk to people and to proudly introduce Abraham to people whose name he immediately forgot.

He wasn't paying too much attention to what his dad was saying because he was scanning the room for Carol. His dad had told him that she was there every Sunday, but he hadn't spotted her yet, and wondered if she had slipped away unnoticed, or whether she was in a different part of the church preparing to clean it.

Outside, on a patch of concrete under a slate grey sky that threatened everything from rain, snow, hail and at least one of the ten biblical plagues, the crowd slowly thinned until it was just Abraham, Vic and an elderly woman who was asking after Vic's health. Carol was nowhere to be seen and Abraham assumed she hadn't attended because, otherwise, she was as likely to seek him out as the other way around. He considered calling her but decided that would best be done in private.

Abraham watched his dad nod goodbye to the lady he had been talking to and wander over towards him. 'I wonder where Joshua is,' he said. 'He's usually out here, shaking hands and checking on everyone.'

Abraham shrugged, wondering if his brother was with Carol, possibly advising her not to talk to Abraham. 'Can't 'have got far.'

They walked back into the porch, past the table with religious pamphlets spread across it, and back into the nave. It was empty. 'Hello!' called Abraham, more quietly than he'd intended, the tranquil nature of the building affecting his voice.

There was no reply.

'Joshua?' said Vic, more loudly. 'You here?'

Both turned their heads slightly, ears primed. It was Abraham who heard it first; a low moan. He closed his eyes.

'What's that?' said Vic, hearing the sound too.

Abraham turned around and faced the pine door of the sacristy. 'Josh?' he said, approaching the door cautiously. 'You in there?'

Another moan. Then a crash, like furniture falling over, followed by a shout, desperate and pleading, 'Help! Please, God, help!'

Abraham turned the handle but the door was locked. He banged on it with his fist. 'Josh!' he shouted. 'What's happening?'

Vic was looking at him, his face white with fear and shock.

Abraham kicked against the door, calling Joshua's name more insistently. More crashing sounds, things hitting the floor. Then a moan, low and drawn out.

Abraham put his shoulder to the door and pressed against it. It gave a little, the wood bending to his weight. 'Stand back, dad.'

Abraham took three steps back, turned so that his right shoulder faced the door and put his full weight behind the run up. There was a loud crack as the flimsy lock broke and the door swung inwards, the latch bolt pulling some of the wooden frame away. Abraham stumbled into the room and almost tripped over Joshua, who was lying motionless on his back, his head angled against the skirting board, blood smeared across his face.

Twenty-four

Hristo had offered his driver, but Erjon respectfully declined. He preferred not to rely on others and, anyway, he always liked to get a feel for a place, for the people, and that was better achieved on public transport than cocooned in a sleek, black car.

Even after all this time Erjon had still not got used to the fineries that this life could grant him. Wasn't sure if he wanted to get used to them. He assumed he could afford his own driver if he wanted one. His own sleek, black Mercedes. A fleet of them, most likely. But who would he be trying to impress by doing such a thing? No, Erjon was not in this for the money.

Hristo would laugh when Erjon reminded his old friend of this. Hristo's laughter was rare, but when it came it was often aimed at Erjon. 'Then why are you in it?' He would ask him. 'What good is the money we make, the money we made before this, if you don't spend it?' Both good questions, but he didn't think Hristo would understand the answer even if he were to tell him, so a smile would always proceed the inquiry, and it would always suffice.

Sometimes Erjon wondered if his friend was getting soft. He knew from experience what Hristo was capable of, the violence he could inflict if necessary. But, back then, it had always been about survival. About the difference between living long enough to take the next job, or being buried in an unmarked grave in a country that held no meaning. If you were buried at all. That choice focussed the mind, brought out the best and worst in someone. Often it was the worst in someone that made them suitable for the job they had both done.

But survival now was a financial imperative rather than a mortal one. The skills Erjon possessed, the ones Hristo had let wane, were still necessary, they were just used less often.

Erjon wasn't surprised when Hristo decided that working for the people who employed them was a fool's errand. Erjon would have been happy to die in a meaningless place, to be buried in an unmarked grave, but Hristo had other plans and Erjon's love for his friend outweighed his own desires.

Initially things had been brutal and bloody. An empire was not given up easily, and when eventually it had been won, it was not expanded effortlessly. Erjon had enjoyed that time, had enjoyed doing what he was good at. The Wind, they called him. Partly a translation of his name, but mainly because he was a force of nature that could overwhelm and engulf. Invisible but devastating. He liked the name, though he told no one.

At Fenchurch Street station he paid cash for a single ticket, his dark green baseball cap pulled low over his brow. He wore dark cargo trousers, a black t-shirt under a black bomber jacket and a pair of well-worn Dr Martens boots. A large neoprene rucksack was thrown over his shoulder. It contained little; a change of clothes, money, a knife, a mobile phone, a high-visibility vest and, hidden in a false bottom, a Beretta Px4 Storm, a favoured handgun since his days in the Albanian army. Erjon was, he hoped, an unremarkable face among the crowd. He checked his watch, a Tudor Ranger which Hristo had bought him, the most expensive thing he owned; it was 4.35pm.

A little more than an hour later he stepped off the train at Southend Central with maybe fifty other passengers and made his way to the exit. The street outside was busy. People laden with bags from different shops; families, groups of women, a handful of men, clusters of kids, all wasting their time and their money on unimportant things that they didn't need. Yet more people were gathering in the bar opposite the station. Mainly young, dressed in clothes that didn't suit the weather. But they looked happy, carefree, a Saturday evening stretching out before them.

Erjon watched them like an ornithologist might observe rare birds. Their behaviour was alien to him. He didn't dismiss it, didn't feel contempt for their actions, it was simply a different life to the one he had chosen.

Or maybe this life had chosen him. He didn't know and no longer cared. Wishing for anything more was pointless. Wondering if different decisions would have made him someone else, someone who worked an office job, who got drunk on a Saturday night with his friends, was futile. 'We are who we are,' Hristo used to say to him. At fifty-three-years-old Erjon would be who he was until the day he died. And who knew when that day might come? To have lived this long seemed impossible.

He walked along the high street in the direction of the sea. He could smell the salt, could taste it in the cold air. Salt and petrol and grease. When he reached the promenade, he was disappointed to find it was too dark to see the water. He could hear it though, lapping against the shore. He understood why people found it calming.

He walked past the bright, flashing lights of the arcades that lined this part of the city, past more pubs and fast-food restaurants, until he came to a cheap bed and breakfast he had looked up online before leaving London. He paid cash for one night to the bored young man on reception and took the stairs up to the third floor where he watched television for an hour. He considered leaving the room to buy food but dismissed the idea. He wasn't hungry, anyway. Instead, he lay back on the too-soft bed, still in his clothes, and closed his eyes.

Many hours later he finally fell asleep.

***

He wore the same clothes, the green baseball cap still pulled low as he entered the church.

There were more people than he expected, maybe thirty-five or forty dotted around the cold interior of the cavernous building. Erjon wasn't religious and didn't know anyone who was. He wondered how Catholicism hadn't already died out, how traditional worship could exist in a modern world that seemed to celebrate individualism and self-expression over deities and divinity. As far as he knew, only celebrities garnered the devotion previously reserved for gods.

He sat near the back, away from the groups of mainly elderly people who were chatting and shaking hands, and close to the room he had immediately singled out as the most likely place to carry out what he had come to do. He checked his phone again, looking at the pictures he had been sent yesterday. She had been pretty, but young. Far too young. But that didn't matter, not in this case. He wasn't here to defend a dead girl's honour. He was here to find out what the priest knew and to make sure whatever that was went no further.

He felt the tingle of anticipation and excitement that always arrived at this time. He had never killed a priest before. He wondered whether it would feel different.

Erjon's involvement in this situation had come much later than he would have liked, and his appearance in this English suburb was far from well-planned. Preparation was always key to success and since receiving a phone call yesterday, then the series of pictures, time had been against him. There had been no groundwork put in place, no reconnaissance or research.

Caution was his watchword, and this approach was unprofessional but, despite this, Erjon felt energised. It was rare for something to happen that needed urgent attention or immediate action, and action was certainly required to keep this situation contained. Once it had been, he would deal with the reasons it had come to light.

The service was long and uninspiring. There were hymns sung and prayers recited, both with turgid monotony, and a sermon that Erjon only partially listened to. He was used to waiting, was good at it. The army had taught him that most battles were fought in the mind. That even fire fights were generally short, explosive events that were stretched out between hours, sometimes days.

'Go in peace to love and serve the Lord,' said the priest, his hands raised, palms up.

Erjon slid out of the pew and made his way to the rear of the church. Everyone's eyes were still on the priest, who was gathering items on the altar. He checked around him, glancing out into the porch.

No one was watching.

Erjon placed a hand on the gold-coloured handle and quietly let himself into the small room at the back of the church, the one he'd seen the priest emerge from at the start of the Mass.

He gently closed the door behind him and waited.

Twenty-five

Vic stood in the doorway of the sacristy staring helplessly at his oldest son. He was frozen to the spot, eyes wide, liver-spotted hands covering thin lips, too shocked to speak, too scared to help.

The room was a mess. A bookcase against one wall had toppled to the floor spilling hymn and prayer books across the thin red carpet. A statue of the Virgin Mary that had been on top of the bookcase lay scattered in a hundred pieces and, among it all, was the supine body of Joshua.

There was a ringing in Vic's ears, like an alarm sounding. It was drowning all other noise, all other thought.

'Dad?'

He could remember the pain he felt at the death of his daughter. No, not remember it, *feel* it. He could always feel it. A gaping hole, an inky black fissure that permanently lived inside him. He couldn't cope with another absence, couldn't bear to think about it.

'Dad!'

Vic noticed that the rear door to the sacristy, the one that opened onto the small courtyard between the church and the rectory in which Joshua lived, was hanging open. He had forgotten it was even there. Joshua never unlocked it in case he forgot to re-lock it.

The alarm in his head was still wailing but, as another sound wrestled for attention in his brain, Vic realised that Abraham had been calling to him from his crouched position on the floor next to Joshua. He turned to his younger son, eyes unfocussed.

'Dad, it's ok,' said Abraham. 'It'll be ok.'

'Is he —' Vic didn't want to finish the sentence.

'No, no he'll be fine,' said Abraham. 'Might have a broken nose and I think he's banged his head, but he'll be fine.'

Vic watched Abraham continue to whisper his brother's name, propping his head up on a pile of robes pulled from a nearby chair. 'Should I call an ambulance? The police? What should I do, Abe?' he said, the panic rising, his voice getting tense, his tone sharp.

'Not yet,' Abraham replied, pulling the chair on which the robes had sat towards him. 'Sit here. Come on, just look after Josh for a minute.'

Vic sat and took Joshua's hand, whispering his name as Abraham had done, attempting to conceal the fear in his eyes and the worry in his voice.

'I'll be back in just a second,' said Abraham, as Vic settled into the chair.

Then he walked through the open door and into the courtyard.

The patch of concrete was empty apart from Joshua's old Volvo and a couple of large flowerpots in which two thin, desiccated stems protruded from dry soil. Abraham crouched to check under the car, then walked around it, but no one was there. He jogged to the edge of the road and looked along it but saw nothing unusual. There was no one running, no figure streaking away from the church in a mad rush to escape.

He made his way to the front of the building, his head swivelling left and right, keeping a close eye out for anything or anyone unusual. The congregation had departed and the church grounds were, as far as he could tell, empty.

He entered the porch with its table of leaflets. Nothing.

He checked under the drooping tablecloth, but just found boxes of more leaflets.

Abraham breathed out heavily and realised his heart was pumping, his pulse racing. He could hear moaning coming from the sacristy and his dad's reassuring words, 'It's ok, Josh,' he was saying. 'You're going to be ok.'

Abraham wasn't so sure.

***

They had locked up the church, Joshua gingerly handing over the keys, then the three of them walked slowly towards the rectory, Abraham propping up his brother, who was unsteady on his feet.

Once inside they went to the living room, where Joshua slumped onto the long sofa, laying on his back, eyes closed. Abraham left his dad to look after Josh while he went to the kitchen to make tea. What else was there to do in such a situation?

The kitchen looked exactly how you would imagine a kitchen in an old house belonging to a priest might look: a white crochet tablecloth; tea, coffee and sugar canisters in the shape of different breeds of dog; pictures of saints and other religious iconography on the walls;

and a French dresser with dainty cups, plates and bowls covered in a green and pink floral design. Abraham felt like he had stepped into the pages of an Agatha Christie novel.

He was about to set three Cath Kidston mugs on a tray before boiling the kettle when he heard a noise above him, a creak of the floorboards and a low drum that sounded like footsteps.

He wondered if it might be his father or brother, but then heard them speaking in low, indistinct tones from the living room. Maybe he was imagining it. He cocked an ear to the ceiling.

Nothing.

Then, another creak. Another set of low drums. Someone was moving around.

Abraham scanned the kitchen surfaces. He couldn't see any knives and didn't want to waste time looking, so picked up the thing closest to him that looked like a weapon, a wooden meat tenderiser.

Stupid, he thought to himself. Why hadn't he thought to check the house before now? If someone was willing to attack Joshua in his church, they'd think nothing of doing so in his house.

He considered calling the police. Maybe getting everyone outside and locking the door. But how long would the police take? Plus, Abraham wasn't sure he wanted to involve the police just yet, not until he'd spoken to his brother about what was going on.

Abraham took a deep breath.

Not wanting to alarm his already unnerved father and injured brother, he crept up the stairs. The meat tenderiser was gripped firmly in his right hand while his left, palm out, skirted the surface of the wall leading up the stairs.

Abraham turned his head as he ascended, checking the landing. As he took each step on the thin beige carpet his grip tightened on the weapon until his fingers were alabaster.

Halfway up he heard footsteps again, louder this time.

He stopped, eyed the area he thought the noise was coming from, then saw the door handle to Joshua's study slowly move. It was being turned from the inside. Abraham watched, the thudding of his heart now the only thing he could hear, as the handle depressed and, ever so slowly, the door began to open.

Abraham was almost at the last step and, as the door opened wider, he made a decision. No longer worried about making a noise, he hurled himself up the remaining stairs and turned his shoulder to the door of Joshua's study, ramming it with as much force as he could muster on the short sprint.

The door sprang open, swinging back and hitting the doorstop with a thud, while Abraham carried on, clattering into the person beyond it, knocking them backwards and onto the carpet.

Abraham raised his right hand, bringing the wooden hammer to its apex. His teeth were gritted, his face a mask of snarling anger.

Below him, hands and knees were brought up in protection and a plea was shouted, 'Abraham! No! Please!'

The use of his name broke through Abraham's burst of aggression and the hammer remained paused in mid-swing. 'Brody? What the hell are you doing here?'

Then a thought struck Abraham and the aggression returned as quickly as it had dissipated. 'Was it you?' he growled through clenched teeth. 'Did you hurt Josh?'

Brody was stunned and, in that moment, abandoned any notion of self-preservation, dropping his hands and staring up with confusion. 'What? He's hurt? What's happened?'

Either Brody was an Oscar-worthy actor, or his bemusement was real. Abraham was reluctant to pick the most likely scenario because of how well this man had duped him in the past.

'What are you doing here?'

'I had a meeting with Father Hart. He's helping me apply for college,' said Brody, still on the floor but slowly crawling away from Abraham.

'Then why are you hiding away up here?'

Abraham realised the hammer was still raised above his head, that he still looked like a man ready to launch an attack. He wondered what it might be like to bring the hammer down on Brody's soft features. To pound at his body until his arms ached and he begged for mercy.

He thought it might feel good. Cathartic.

Abraham slowly lowered his right arm.

'I'm sorry. I was coming to church, walking with Father Hart. But then we saw you with your dad and, well, I didn't want to cause another scene. I came back here. Heard you all come in and stayed upstairs. I'm sorry, I didn't know.'

Abraham's body relaxed, the high state of tension leaking out of him. Behind him he heard footsteps.

'What's going on?' said a concerned Victor as he reached the landing.

'It's just Anne Frank, here,' said Abraham. 'I thought it might be someone else.'

'Who?' asked Vic.

'The person who attacked Josh,' Abraham replied, pointing back down the stairs.

'And what, you were going to beat him to death with a tenderiser?'

Abraham turned to look at Brody, who was levering himself off the floor. 'Maybe I still will.'

'Abraham,' said Vic gently, moving towards Brody, a hand outstretched to help him up, 'remember what I told you?'

'I remember. It's not my fault,' said Abraham, dropping the kitchen utensil-cum-weapon to the floor, throwing a look towards Brody that was as deadly as the hammer he'd just discarded. 'It's his.'

***

Abraham continued to seethe while sat in one of the Chesterfields in Joshua's front room. He'd lost track of why the rage was still simmering inside him; Brody's presence, Joshua's attack, a failing marriage, a disappointed daughter, a dead girl.

Maybe all of it.

Once Joshua had convinced Brody that he was ok, Vic offered to walk to the local chemist to get some paracetamol and maybe an ice pack. Realising he'd be left alone with Abraham and an incapacitated Joshua, Brody volunteered to accompany him.

'What the hell's going on?' Abraham asked Josh as soon as Brody had pulled the front door shut.

'I'm helping him with applications to adult education classes, like he said. He's different, Abe, honestly. I know it's tough for you to see but—'

'Not him!' Abraham spat. 'You! This!' Abraham waved a finger at his brother's face.

'I was attacked. Pretty obvious, isn't it?'

'Yes, but why? This wasn't random, was it. Wasn't some opportunist thief who just happened to be walking by, because who the hell thinks they're going to make a score by mugging a priest?'

Joshua closed his eyes. 'How on earth should I know?'

'Fine,' said Abraham, shuffling in his seat and reaching into the pocket of his jeans. He tapped at the screen harder than he might usually and saw his brother's right eye creep back open.

'What're you doing?'

'Calling the police. Dad's right. This needs to be reported.'

'No!' said Joshua, too quickly and too forcefully. 'No, don't do that.'

Why? You want to turn the other cheek?'

'No, I...' Joshua found words hard to come by.

'Look,' said Abraham. 'Either you tell me what's going on, or you tell a copper. When Dad gets back he'll call them himself if we don't give him reason not to. So, come on, what's it going to be?'

Abraham watched his brother deflate in front of him, like someone had pulled the stopper out. 'I can't...' The words still weren't there.

'Josh, whatever's happened, whatever this is about, we'll work it out.'

Slowly, carefully, Joshua sat up. His eyes were open, but his head was bowed. Some dried blood still clung to his face and a crimson stain was showing on his white shirt.

'It's all a big misunderstanding,' he said. 'I was just trying to help.'

Twenty-six

Joshua kneaded his hands and looked to the ceiling, as if the words he was looking for might be written there. His usually pristine white shirt had blobs of red dotted over it, a vivid and creased Rorschach test. He had removed his dog collar and it lay on the floor like a curled up booked mark. Abraham realised how worn out his brother looked. His thick glasses, which had miraculously survived the attack, were perched on the end of a swollen nose that was surrounded by pale, wrinkled skin. His eyes were dark and sunken and his beard contained more flecks of grey than Abraham remembered.

'Who were you trying to help? Alissa?'

Joshua's head shot up and he stared at Abraham, eyebrows furrowed. 'What makes you say that?'

'Dad mentioned that you were closer to the Peters than you let on to me. That you knew Alissa well enough.'

'What are you insinuating? You're just like them.' Joshua was getting upset, defensive. Abraham needed to tread carefully.

'I'm not insinuating anything. Like you, I'm just trying to help Carol. I know you asked me not to, but she practically begged. She's grieving, what was I meant to do?'

'You were meant to say no.'

This wasn't getting them anywhere, Abraham thought. 'What did you mean '"*You're just like them*"?' he asked, looking at his watch, hoping Joshua realised their dad would take no longer than he needed. 'Just like who?'

Joshua blew a stream of air through pursed lips. When he spoke his eyes were locked onto an indistinct point of the carpet. 'Alissa and Craig had an argument the day before she died. All couples argue, all families argue.' Here Joshua flicked a look at his brother before aiming his gaze back at the carpet. 'But this one sounded big.'

'How do you know?'

'Because Alissa told me. Look, Carol's had a hard time of it. She's a single parent with a husband who wasn't the most pleasant man in the world but whose death affected her, affected Alissa too. And, before you ask, I wasn't trying to replace him. I didn't consider myself to be Alissa's surrogate dad, but I wanted to help. And Carol, well, sometimes she can be too proud for her own good. She couldn't see that Alissa needed someone else to talk to other than her mother. I'm no expert, but teenage girls and their mothers are *meant* to be at each other's throats, aren't they?'

'Is that what was happening?'

'No, no. I just mean that Alissa needed someone other than her mum to talk to sometimes. Someone to discuss things she either didn't want to worry her mum with or was too embarrassed to mention to her.'

'Like arguments with her boyfriend?' asked Abraham.

Joshua remained impassive. 'Something happened at her work.'

'Spotlight?'

Joshua's eyebrows furrowed once more. 'You know it?'

'I spoke to the owner.'

'Yes, well, he accused Alissa of recording him secretly and then trying to blackmail him.'

'Recording him doing what?'

'Something of a sexual nature. She didn't tell me the details and I didn't ask. But while she admitted to the video she swore to him, and to me, that she hadn't tried to blackmail anyone.'

'Why record him at all?'

'She wasn't trying to. She set her phone up to record something else and he made an appearance. Him and a woman who works there. She didn't know till she watched it back.'

'She told Craig about the video?'

Joshua nodded.

'And, what, she thinks he might have tried to blackmail Lewis?'

Another nod. 'They argued. Craig apparently denied everything and got angry that she'd accused him. Alissa said it got heated and she stormed out. She texted me, asked if I would pick her up.'

It *had* been Joshua's Volvo.

'So, you think the guy who attacked you is Alissa's boss? What, to get the video back, or to make sure you never use it?'

'I don't *have* the video. I've never seen it. And I don't think it was him who did this,' he said, pointing at his own face. 'When we spoke on the phone Alissa's boss was English, or sounded English, whoever attacked me had an accent.'

'You spoke to him? To Lewis?'

'Yes. I wanted to help. To explain the misunderstanding.'

Abraham had questions jostling for room in his head. 'What sort of accent?'

'I don't know!' replied Joshua, his voice rising. 'It wasn't the thing I was concentrating on at the time and, sorry, I forgot to ask after he headbutted me in the face.'

Abraham raised his hands in conciliation. 'Maybe he was putting an accent on, to hide his identity?'

Joshua shrugged.

'Had Lewis fired Alissa?' asked Abraham.

'Yes. But even if he hadn't, she knew she couldn't stay, not with that hanging over her, with what Lewis thought she'd done.'

'What did Lewis say when you spoke to him? Did you tell him it was a mistake, that it was Craig who sent the email to him?'

It was as if a cloud had drifted across his brother's face. His already pale skin grew more sallow and his eyes seemed to darken. 'No, I didn't get that far. As soon as I introduced myself, said I was calling on behalf of Alissa, he just told me he had pictures.'

Abraham could sense the pain this was causing Joshua. He could hear the tremor in his voice. He knew he'd need to tread softly, but he also knew he had to ask, 'What pictures?'

'Of Alissa and me.'

Abraham tried not to show any reaction. He obviously failed.

'Don't look like that,' said Joshua, angry and defensive at the same time. 'Whatever your warped mind is thinking, you can wipe it clean. I would never…' he trailed off. 'They were simply pictures of us together. He said that in one I had my arm around her shoulder. It would have been the night I picked her up. She was too upset to go home to Craig, and didn't want to burden her mother, so she stayed at the rectory. In the spare room, before you ask. There was nothing untoward, nothing…' he spat the next word, 'sexual. I was comforting her, attempting to be a shoulder to cry on, that's all. But Lewis Maynard-Jones just laughed. Said a picture was worth a thousand words. Asked what my parishioners would think of the images. Of me sneaking a pretty teenager into my home late at night.'

'Where did he get the photos?'

'He took them. Said he had been waiting to speak to Alissa when I turned up at her flat. He followed us back here. Used his phone.'

'He was waiting outside Alissa's flat? Did he send you the images?'

'No. I told him he was being ridiculous, that even if he had photos, no one would believe such a story.'

Abraham smiled grimly at his brother's naivety.

'He asked me to get the recording from Alissa, to convince her to hand over her phone, to promise it hadn't been sent to anyone else. He even gave me his address for the swap, like we were in some cheap spy movie.'

'And did you?'

Joshua put his hands over his face. 'I would have. At least, I'd have tried. But I was scared after that phone call. I did nothing wrong. Nothing,' he repeated vehemently. 'But who am I kidding? If those photos of Alissa and I were seen, people would draw their own conclusions. Even Alissa's own denials probably wouldn't have been enough. I avoided her the following day. She called and I didn't pick up. She texted and I didn't reply. I was trying to work out what to do, what to say to her. And then…'

'She died.'

Joshua shook his head from side to side, as if by doing so he could shake out everything that had happened.

When it stopped shaking, Alissa was still dead.

'Were you suspicious? About her death, I mean?'

'No. I don't know. She was very upset. She thought it was something that might impact her career, her future. I tried to explain that Lewis Maynard-Jones was not the gatekeeper of the film industry, that she was putting too much stock into his influence. But what do I know? She asked me that; *What did I know about the film industry?* And she was right. I don't know anything. She was inconsolable.'

'If it wasn't Maynard-Jones who attacked you this morning, who do you think it was? What did he say to you?'

Joshua leaned back on the couch and closed his eyes again, his head tipped over the back, stretching his neck out, his Adam's apple pointed at the ceiling. 'He asked about the video, if I'd seen it, whether I had a copy. He asked why I was trying to blackmail his associate. That's the word he used, "associate".'

Abraham furrowed his brow and ran a finger over his lips, something he often did when thinking.

'What?' asked Joshua.

'It's just odd, isn't it? Lewis thought it was Alissa blackmailing him, but that was weeks ago. And it obviously can't be Alissa anymore, but if this person who attacked you, whoever they are, thinks you're the blackmailer, then it means there's been another extortion attempt. Maybe they think you and Alissa were working together.'

Joshua straightened up, wincing at the pain it caused him. 'I can assure you I have nothing to do with this.'

'I believe you. But if I'm right and there's been another email to Lewis, and you're right - or, at least, Alissa was - and it was Craig who sent the original email, then maybe Craig's chancing his arm again.'

'So, what do we do?'

'We need to find out what's on that video and, ideally, we need to find Craig Atherton. What do you know about him?'

'Not much. Alissa said he worked at a bank in London, somewhere in the City. He was adopted. Never knew his biological parents, and his adoptive ones have both passed. I only met him a couple of times. He seemed nice. Quiet. Certainly not some sort of criminal mastermind.'

Abraham showed his brother the picture he'd taken from Alissa's flat. 'This him?'

Joshua lifted his glasses and moved closer to the image. 'Yes. Where'd you get this?'

Abraham was about to respond when a loud knock interrupted him. He looked at his watch and smiled. 'Blimey, they must have run,' he said. 'Anyway, doesn't he have a key?'

'Probably forgotten it,' replied Joshua.

Abraham pushed himself up off the chair and walked towards the front door, hoping Brody had decided to call it quits and head home. 'Alright Usain,' he said as he twisted the lock and pulled the door open. 'You trying to break records?'

But standing on the doorstep was not Victor Hart. Instead, a tall figure dressed in dark blue jeans, a white, cable-knit jumper and a green padded gilet, like a farmer dressed by Ralph Lauren, looked at Abraham through bloodshot eyes.

Lewis Maynard-Jones stood with his mouth slightly open, a mixture of surprise and fear unfolding on his face. 'What the hell are you doing here?' he said.

'Was just about to ask you the same thing,' replied Abraham.

Twenty-seven

After their conversation the previous afternoon, and after David Catton had left the Spotlight office, Lewis spent his time doing two things. The first was sobering up. The second was worrying about the conversation he'd just had with David Catton.

Lewis used David as a sounding board because he was good at offering impartial and, usually, helpful advice. But he also liked talking to David because he didn't get unduly flustered by bad news.

He had hoped that relaying his troubles to his CFO and friend would somehow calm his own mind and also elicit some useful tips on how to deal with the problem at hand. But David's reaction had only served to further unnerve him. David rarely swore and to be told by him that the email Lewis had received was, 'a fucking problem,' meant that it was, in all probability, more serious than that.

When pressed for advice on how to proceed, though, David had been much less forthcoming than usual. Lewis had tackled the problem by drinking yet another vodka and tonic in an attempt to forget the problem even existed. He couldn't remember exactly what time David had left but, at 8.40pm, Lewis had come to on the red sofa in reception with what felt like a nail gun firing repeatedly into his brain, an empty bottle of Absolut on the floor next to him, and a stoney-faced wife looming over him.

She had been calling his phone, getting no response, so had decided to track him down. It hadn't taken long, the Spotlight offices being her first and last stop.

'Here on your own?' she had asked him, an accusation implicit in the question.

Behind the camera he considered himself something of an auteur, but he knew his acting prowess left a lot to be desired. Luckily for Lewis he'd been too hungover to attempt a contrived act of hurt or a spurious appearance of surprise and, instead, had simply nodded and grunted an affirmation.

'When are you going to grow up, Lewis?' had been the next question. One to which Lewis took exception.

'I had a meeting with David, if you must know,' he replied, his voice sounding like it was coming from the back of a very deep cave. 'About the business.'

'What can you possibly have to discuss with David?'

Lewis had realised he hadn't thought this through and might now have backed himself into a corner. But, he remembered, it was always best to hide a lie within the truth. 'About my film. We were talking funding. Seeing if there's money in the budget to finance it next year. It could be the making of us.'

The sound of laughter this elicited from his wife hurt Lewis more than her anger. 'That's not going to happen,' she had said, matter of fact. 'Not least because, post "hashtag MeToo", your casting methods are now redundant. Was that all you talked about?'

This might have been a good opportunity to admit what had been happening, despite his throbbing head. When Alissa had first sent him the video, in an act of cold-hearted betrayal as far as he was concerned, he had considered confessing to Ellie what he had been caught doing. The consideration was fleeting, though, lasting no longer than the time it had taken for him to mix himself a drink.

But the situation had been resolved quickly, and with Alissa's death, Lewis had thought he was in the clear. A drug overdose had seemed too unlikely, he had initially thought. Alissa had seemed too innocent and clean-living for that to be reasonable. But, like he'd told the journalist, you never really knew anyone and, when he'd added in a few untruths about her timekeeping and her dreamy demeanour, even he thought it could be true.

For a few blissful weeks he had forgotten all about blackmail, deceit and demanding emails. But now he was back where he had begun, with the added complication of not knowing who was behind any of it.

His wife was the brains, he knew that much. He might have the creative flair but she knew how to handle things, how to make difficult decisions and overcome seemingly insurmountable obstacles. If anyone could help sort this problem, she could. But that would necessitate a confession of some description and he knew he didn't have the stomach, nor the backbone, for that. He'd simply have to handle this himself.

Later that night, after forcing himself to drink pints of water, and before he took himself to bed in the spare room of their large house in Thorpe Bay, Lewis had an epiphany. David, as usual, had been right. There was only person who could be behind this attempt to derail his life. One person he knew Alissa had colluded with before her death.

He had woken late, a hangover still lurking in the background, threatening to step forward at any moment. Only after showering and dressing did Lewis realise he was alone in the house.

He walked through the rooms, his bare feet cold on the parquet floor. No one was home. The quiet helped him examine the thought he'd had last night. He moved it around in his head, looking at it from different angels, checking whether it held up to the cold light of day. It wouldn't have been the first time a few drinks had steered him towards an idea that, the following morning, wilted under a sober spotlight. But this one held firm and its solidity made him confident that the next move needed to be bold, decisive and, ideally, swift.

Lewis made himself a second espresso from the coffee machine in an attempt to keep the hangover at bay, slipped on his brogues and closed the front door behind him. In the car he placed his intended address into Google Maps then backed the Range Rover off the drive and made his way to Our Lady of Lourdes Roman Catholic church.

The journey took less than ten minutes, even with the smattering of dawdling Sunday drivers on the road. Along the way Lewis formulated an opening speech. During the brief phone call he and the priest had just before Alissa's death Lewis had mentioned the photos he'd taken, alluded to being more than ready to use them if need be. He could tell, despite the priest's incensed denials, that he was rattled, and reminding him of the existence of the images seemed the best way of getting what he wanted.

But what did he want? The video, he supposed. If the priest had copies he wanted them, and wanted to see them deleted from any device they might live on. But, he thought, the best he could hope for was an uneasy truce, one that saw the video of Lewis remain buried in return for the same outcome for the photos of Alissa and the priest.

He pulled up to the kerb a few metres from the church and composed himself for the confrontation. At the house next to the church, Lewis rapped his knuckles on the door and took a step back, trying to steady both his nerves and his growling stomach, which was still protesting at the excess of alcohol. But the person who opened he door, yelling something about broken records, was not who Lewis expected.

'What the hell are you doing here?' said Lewis, his facade of composure already shattered.

'Was just about to ask you the same thing,' replied the journalist he'd met only yesterday. 'Did you just beat up my brother? If you're back to try again, the odds aren't in your favour anymore.'

Lewis's eyes skittered around, from the man in front of him to the hallway behind to the number on the door. Had he made a mistake? Was he in the wrong place? He turned to look at the large stone structure to his right. It was definitely a church. He turned back. Abraham Hart was still looking at him, jaw set, fists clenched.

'Your brother?' was all he could think to say.

When there was no response to this enquiry Lewis's previous resolve melted away. He wasn't cut out for confrontation. This was all some big mistake. Had he said that out loud? He wasn't sure, so tried again. 'I think there's been a mistake,' he said, taking another step back.

Abraham took a step forward, out of the house and onto the doorstep. 'Damn right there has.' Another step, to within touching distance of Lewis. 'Did you attack my brother?' he repeated. 'Did you kill Alissa?'

This wasn't how this was meant to go, Lewis thought. None of this.

He saw Abraham raise his hands. He'd never been in a fight before, not a real one, and didn't know what to do. His first thought was to run, but his ego outweighed his survival instinct. Instead, he took a step forward and pushed his would-be attacker in the chest. It was a preventative measure rather than an aggressive one. He hoped Abraham would recognise it as such.

He didn't.

Abraham swung a punch which Lewis just managed to avoid. His stomach was churning and he thought he might throw up. 'I made a mistake,' he shouted as he took more steps backwards.

Abraham kept coming.

Behind Abraham, Lewis saw another figure appear at the doorway to the house. He was holding what looked like an ice pack on one eye, and seemed to be limping slightly, but it was definitely the man he'd come to see; Father Joshua Hart. And then, like an incredibly large stone dropped into a very shallow puddle, the realisation hit and, inwardly, he cursed his own stupidity.

'You're brothers!' he said, more to spell out the realisation for himself.

Abraham didn't respond. He'd advanced on Lewis, who had been distracted by the appearance of Joshua, and his next swing connected with Lewis's shoulder, bouncing up off the soft fabric of the cable-knit sweater and brushing the side of his cheek.

The blow wasn't hard, his shoulder taking most of the power from it, but it still stung and was, more than anything, shocking.

It knocked him off his already wavering balance and he fell backwards, landing against the rough bark of one of the trees that stood in the grounds of the church.

Abraham, stood over him now, looking down. His fists were still clenched but his expression had altered. He looked surprised, guilty even.

Lewis saw the priest step out of the house and limp towards his brother. He looked back at Abraham, wondering what happened now. Hoping that if the punches came they would concentrate on his body rather than his face.

He tried to think of something to say. Something to delay what seemed to be inevitable but couldn't think of anything. He was there to threaten a man of the cloth, to accuse him of being a sexual predator, to bribe him into staying silent about something which could threaten Lewis's own happiness. Maybe his life. Where should he start?

But he didn't need to. Instead, as Lewis grappled with words and Abraham grappled with emotions, a thin but stern voice rang out. 'Abraham Hart! What in God's name are you doing?'

Each of the three men turned their heads towards the slight figure of the elderly man walking along the pavement outside the church. He carried a plastic bag, a set of keys and a tone that made Abraham lower his clenched fists immediately.

Lewis didn't wait for Abraham to reply. He used the trunk of the tree to lever himself to his feet, the rough bark, catching on his clothes, then ran to the car as quickly as his brogues would allow, hoping none of the three men, even the old one, followed.

Twenty-eight

The anger was still burning inside her as she pushed open the door and stepped out into the cold evening air. Alissa and Craig had argued before, the same arguments she suspected every couple had - washing up, laundry, late working - but this was less a domestic row and more a betrayal of trust.

Despite Craig's half-hearted denial of any wrongdoing, there couldn't be another explanation. She certainly hadn't sent the email to Lewis, and there was only one other person who could have.

The last few weeks had been tough, Craig's worries about his job causing stress and strain on both of them, but she had always trusted him. She'd felt like they were building a life, now that life lay in ruins.

She should head to her mum's, explain to her what had happened, ask for her advice and sleep in the room that had been hers until she moved in with Craig.

But she knew her mum had disproved of her living with Craig. It wasn't for any religious reason, her mum wasn't a prude. Nor was she unhappy with the age difference between her and Craig, it was simply 'too fast' her mum had told her. She had recommended waiting, making sure, and not rushing into anything. Relationships take time to assemble, she had said, but an instant to destroy. Alissa had smiled, nodded and then completely ignored that advice, moving in with Craig the same week he had asked her.

Her mum wasn't judgemental, not like some of the old biddies at the church who she knew tutted and shook their heads behind her back, but Alissa didn't think she could face any 'told you so' comments just yet. The next best thing was Father Hart. He had been kind to her mum, generous and patient, even giving her a job when it seemed like no one else would. When Alissa's dad had died a couple of years ago, decades of alcohol abuse finally taking its toll, Father Hart had been there to offer comfort.

Not that either of them needed it too much. Cameron Peters had been a terrible father and a worse husband. Alissa knew her mum was acting more upset than she really was. She didn't want to seem callous in front of Father Hart, like someone pleased at the death of a supposed loved one, but neither of them would miss the often drunk, occasionally violent and always unreliable man who had embedded himself at the centre of their lives like a parasite.

She pulled her jacket tighter as the wind swirled around her body and thoughts churned around her head. She wanted to turn and look up to the first floor window, to see if Craig was looking. Whether he might bang on the glass, shout an apology, plead for forgiveness. But she knew none of that would happen, so kept walking.

She'd asked Father Hart to meet her further down the road. It wasn't that she was embarrassed to be seen with him, or worried what others might think, she just didn't want Craig to know who was picking her up and where she was headed. She needed time to think.

The street was almost empty, and eerily quiet. The low, threatening buzz of the overhead power lines above the train tracks creating the only discernible sound.

Opposite the flats there was a Pizza Hut moped, its driver absent, likely somewhere inside the building delivering a Friday night takeaway to some still-happy household.

Parked further down was a large car, its headlights on, hampering Alissa's vision. She raised a hand to shield her eyes then spotted the comforting sight of an old blue Volvo, Joshua sat patiently behind the steering wheel.

She pulled open the passenger door and folded herself into the car.

***

The flat was empty when Alissa returned the following morning, as she knew it would be. Craig had been picked up late the previous evening for a through-the-night drive to Cornwall and would be away all weekend. Alissa had periodically checked her mobile for any messages, though the sight of her phone only reminded her of the reason for their argument in the first instance.

Father Hart had been the calm and understanding presence she had expected and craved. He had listened intently as she had railed against Craig's duplicity, not interrupting or asking her to calm down. He had agreed, if what she thought had happened was true, that Craig's actions had been deceitful, though countered that by saying he was not there to defend himself.

Alissa hadn't explained the full content of her mistaken recording. It didn't seem necessary, plus there was only so much detail you could describe to a priest. Father Hart hadn't pried but had simply listened, only speaking when he thought she wanted him to, and only trying to appease her by telling her that Lewis Maynard-Jones was not the centre of the UK film industry.

Though Matt Hallstaff was the least of her current worries, Alissa was careful to be quiet in the flat. She'd managed to avoid seeing him when arriving back but, if he was home, she didn't want him to know she was too.

With the whole day stretched out before her, she was left in something of a limbo; no work, no college, no Craig and in no mood to see anyone, or go anywhere. She called Em, crying off from their long-planned night out, citing a migraine. She didn't think Em believed her, and could hear the disappointment in her friend's voice, but she would explain everything later. Instead, Alissa wallowed in her own self-pity by putting her headphones on and watching the video again.

It both disgusted and fascinated her, like a car crash on the other side of the road. She sat on the couch and played the clip through, all ten minutes of it, then watched as the phone toppled forward and the screen went black. The stupid spider hadn't even made an appearance, she realised.

For the rest of the morning and through the afternoon, Alissa sat in front of the TV, the volume down low, watching cookery programmes, news bulletins, repeats of Friends *and a documentary on fly fishing, a subject she had no interest in but which was, at least, calming. She periodically padded to the kitchen to refill her glass from the bottle of cheap white wine she'd bought to take to Em's later. She felt she deserved it.*

She again considered calling her mum. She would have to talk to her at some point, tell her what had happened. Or, at least, tell her she was no longer working at Spotlight and that, unless something drastic happened to change her mind, she would need to move back home. But Alissa couldn't yet face that task. There would be plenty of time for such conversations.

At almost 7pm there were three low raps at the door which made Alissa, who was still laying on the futon, raise her head from the cushion.

At first, she wondered if she'd imagined the sound and she aimed an ear at the door, which was a few short steps away, listening intently. A few seconds later she heard the same sound again, low but distinct; knock knock knock.

She had almost managed to convince herself that the outside world, and the problems that accompanied it, had ceased to exist, but the real world wouldn't forget her so easily. She remained still, wondering whether, if she ignored it, whoever it was might go away.

Knock knock knock.

Alissa prised herself from the futon and, as she stood, her hand hit the bottle of wine she had placed on the table next to her, bored of the occasional trip to the fridge. She panicked that it would spill everywhere and darted forward quickly to stop it toppling, but was too late.

It landed on its side and Alissa tensed, waiting for the crack of glass and the slop of wine. But the glass stayed intact and the spillage never came because the bottle was empty. That recognition followed another; that she was much drunker than she first thought.

Rubbing her eyes, steadying herself with one hand on the wall and shaking her head lightly in an attempt to restore some focus, Alissa took a few careful steps towards the door and pushed her right eye to the spy hole. Most of the image was a familiar one; the expanse of hallway running left and right, the pock-marked and dirty walls and the cheap strip lighting, all warped by the fish-eye lens.

But Alissa had to blink a couple of times at the person who stood in the centre of the image, waiting patiently on the other side of the door. And, seeing who it was, she really wished she'd stayed on the futon.

Twenty-nine

Craig had not slept since sending the text message, despite barely leaving the dirty mattress that was laid out on the even dirtier floor of the squat's living room.

He wanted to check and re-check his emails every few minutes, but knew it was impossible to do so. Baz was watching. Or, if not Baz, then one of Baz's tight-knit group. He'd managed to snatch periods of rest when the others went out but his mind wouldn't allow his body to relax, so even when he did begin to drift off it wasn't long before his subconscious jolted him awake.

The only safe place to check the phone was in the toilet but it seemed suspicious to head there too often. So he waited in the dim light of the crumbling house, bodies strewn around him in various states of consciousness. He'd sold his watch so didn't know what the time was but guessed it had been a couple of hours since he'd last moved. A couple of hours that had ticked by so slowly that it felt like days.

Craig stood up quietly. He didn't want to wake those around him who were either sleeping or passed out. The thin curtains drawn across the large bay windows allowed a yellow half-light to penetrate the room and Craig navigated through the cans of cider, half-eaten Pot Noodles and overflowing ashtrays towards the bathroom.

He had been wrestling with his conscience again, wondering if he shouldn't simply call the police and tell them what he knew; that his girlfriend had been an innocent victim of a greedy man. A man who would do anything to protect his marriage and his business.

But the anger directed at Lewis Maynard-Jones was nothing compared to the anger Craig reserved for himself. It was he who had looked to take advantage of the film on Alissa's phone. It was he who placed his girlfriend in danger. He who went to Newquay, leaving her alone in their flat.

He should tell all this to the police, lay out the details and let them deal with it. But what proof did he have? The video of Maynard-Jones and Francesca? What did that prove? Married men had affairs all the time. It might destroy a marriage, but it was hardly proof of murder.

Craig slid the lock across the toilet door, lowered the seat and sat down. No, he lied to himself, money was the only thing that hurt people like Maynard-Jones. He owed it to Alissa to squeeze him for all he could.

He'd already decided that he would give half of whatever he got to Carol. She deserved it, and it would still leave him with enough to start over. He just needed to hear back, to know he was being taken seriously. But the fact he hadn't replied was worrying. What was Maynard-Jones waiting for?

Craig fished around in the pocket of a shirt which was now stained, creased and giving off an unpleasant odour. He turned the phone on and waited, hoping the battery still had some juice. The charging cable was hidden in a slit in the mattress but he couldn't charge the phone in the squat. There was no electricity for a start but, even if there was, it was too dangerous to let anyone see the phone. He would have to head to a coffee shop sometime soon, and hope they didn't kick him out.

The screen glowed white then flashed the Apple logo before bringing up an image of Craig and Alissa at the end of Southend pier. They'd walked along the mile-and-a-half structure over the summer, stopping at the end for ice-cream, Craig had taken a selfie of the two of them, the blue-grey water of the Thames estuary behind them, Alissa holding both cones, a smile that reached all the way to her eyes staring out from the screen. Craig looked at it for a few seconds before navigating to his emails.

There was no wi-fi in the squat, so it took a while for the emails to refresh but, when they did, the inbox showed there were no new messages. Before Craig had time to contemplate this, though, there was a sharp bang on the flimsy, ill-fitting bathroom door.

'You in there, Freddie?'

Baz.

'Just having a piss. Out in a sec.'

'Been in there a while, mate. What you doing?'

There was another slam, followed by a kick. The bottom half of the door bulged inward and Craig heard a crack, the wood relenting at the force of Baz's boot.

Craig scrambled to put the phone back in his shirt but in his haste dropped the handset. He bent down to retrieve it and stepped back in fright as he noticed an eye staring through the inch gap between the floor and the bottom of the door.

The eye, which had been focussed on the dropped phone, disappeared and there was another kick, followed by what sounded like a shoulder barging into the wood.

'You been taking the piss, Fred, haven't you?' shouted Baz. 'Worth a few quid that. More than a few, and I think you've lost sight of 'ow things work round 'ere?'

Craig's heart was pounding now. The door creaked again, wood splitting under the force of Baz's kicks. He stuffed the phone back into his shirt and glanced around the room. There was little to see; a bar of congealed soap resting on the sink edge, a can of dust-covered women's deodorant that looked like it hadn't been used in months, a packet of plasters resting on the glass shelf below the smeared and cracked mirror and, next to the plasters, a pair of scissors.

Craig took the scissors in his shaking right hand. They were kitchen scissors with a blue plastic handle. He didn't know who'd brought them into the bathroom or why, but he was glad they had.

He faced the door, the scissors out in front of him. He could wait for Baz to kick it down but that might mean others coming to see what all the fuss was about, if they weren't there already.

Without thinking about the consequences, Craig slowly slid the lock back and placed his left hand on the handle. He could hear Baz on the other side of the door taking a step back and, in the second before the next shoulder barge, Craig whipped the door open.

The timing was perfect.

Baz was already propelling himself forward and, instead of meeting the resistance of the closed door, now stumbled into the bathroom. Craig stepped to one side while leaving his right foot hanging so that Baz tripped over it and fell to the floor, crashing into the porcelain toilet.

Craig aimed the scissors at the fallen man, who was looking back towards the door he'd just tumbled through. 'Stand up and I'll cut your fucking eyes out,' snarled Craig, as he backed out of the bathroom.

Baz laughed and shook his head. 'Nah. You're a fucking pussy. Gimme the phone and I might let you walk out of 'ere.' He placed a hand on the seat of the toilet and started to push himself to his feet.

Craig stepped forward and slashed the scissors through the air. The blade caught Baz's right ear, taking a chunk out of it. Baz shouted and pulled a hand up to the side of his head. He felt warm liquid on his fingers and, when he pulled his hand away, it was smeared with red.

Craig didn't wait to see what happened next. He turned and ran out of the bathroom, down the hallway and towards the front door. He stepped on plates and knocked over people who had come to see what all the noise was about. But he didn't stop.

At the front door he dropped the scissors so he could turn the latch with one hand and pull the door open with the other. Outside he kept running. Down the rubbish-strewn pathway and through the broken gate, the sound of Baz's shouting following him all the way.

Half an hour and two miles later Craig was hiding in an alleyway behind a shop on the high street. His heart rate had only just returned to normal and his hands had only now stopped shaking. Whether Baz or anyone else from the squat was looking for him he didn't know, but he wasn't going to hang around to find out.

He pulled the phone from his shirt and looked at the screen. There was only twenty-three per cent of power left and he couldn't charge it because the cable was still in the mattress at the squat and he wouldn't be going back there again.

The email inbox remained empty, so there was only one thing he thought he could do. Craig pulled his debit card from the small pouch inside the phone's case and, after checking around him, left the alley and headed for the bank across the road. At the cashpoint he withdrew £20, 'insufficient funds' flashing up when he tried for more. He stuffed the note in his pocket then, head down, made his way towards the nearest Tube station.

As he walked, he stared again at the image of Alissa and him at the end of the pier. He'd messed up, but he wanted to make things right, as much as he could. For him, for Alissa.

He needed to turn off the phone, to conserve the battery, but before he did, he made one call.

Thirty

The first thing Lewis did when he got back to the house, nervous sweat still damp on his back, hands still shaking, was to mix himself a drink. There was no finesse this time, no fancy glass or expensive vodka. He half-filled a coffee mug with Smirnoff, spilled some orange juice over it and drank it down in one.

After the second mug Lewis felt his muscles relax and his mind settle on something like equilibrium. He walked to the mirror hanging in the hallway and stared at his reflection, examining the patch of skin on his cheek that had been in the way of Abraham Hart's fist. It was not noticeably different to the rest of his face and Lewis wasn't sure whether to be pleased to escape injury or annoyed to have no evidence of his assault.

'Hello!' he yelled into the silent house.

'What?' came the response from somewhere above.

He ascended halfway up the stairs again, 'You're here, then? I wasn't sure.'

Lewis heard a door close and then footsteps on the landing. He saw the smooth, bare calves of his wife stride by at eye level, then turned to see her at the top of the stairs. She was dressed in a mid-length, black skirt, a tight-fitting black blouse and a cream jacket. Her face seemed softer than before, less angry. She relinquished a smile. 'I have to go out,' she said.

'Where to?'

'Work. Like always.'

'But it's Sunday. Maybe we could do something. Together.'

She looked at him and smiled again. 'Are you ok?'

Lewis nodded.

'Look, I'm sorry about before,' she said. 'The business has been getting on top of me. From here on it'll be better.'

'Yeah?'

'Promise. I won't be long. I'll miss you.'

He heard the car reversing out of the driveway and, despite what he had said, was pleased to be alone. He didn't want to face any questions just yet, he had too many of his own to consider.

Lewis walked into the living room and dropped into the enormous cream leather sofa, leaning his head back over the edge and closing his eyes, his brain already wondering if there was more alcohol on the way.

If Joshua had mentioned to his brother about the photos Lewis had taken, about the threat Lewis had made, and especially about the video Lewis assumed Joshua had, then maybe it was understandable the Hart brothers would both think Lewis had a motive for attacking Joshua. He had something Lewis wanted, so it made sense.

But he hadn't. Had only ever seen Father Hart from the safety of his Range Rover as he took hurried photos of the priest and Alissa a few weeks ago.

So, who had attacked him? And why?

He searched for avenues to explore and theories to prod that might produce answers, or at least ideas of where and how he might find answers. But Lewis's brain was weary and numbed by the vodka. As he lay on the sofa his body relaxed, his breathing deepened, and his thoughts turned to dreams.

***

Victor had returned with paracetamol, ibuprofen, a tube of arnica and a selection of shop-bought sandwiches from the local store. The only thing he hadn't returned with was Brody, who had decided to go home.

Abraham was perched on the sofa next to his brother feeling like a child again, waiting for a telling off. He didn't have to wait long.

'Since when were you brought up to use violence?' Vic asked, staring down at his two sons, more disappointed than angry. 'And who was that man, anyway?'

Neither of the two brothers spoke, instead their heads remained bowed, their eyes fixed firmly on the floor. Vic continued to stare, waiting for a reply, and Abraham was reminded of the steely determination their father had when it came to getting answers. It hadn't occurred to Abraham before that his whole career might be attributable to his dad.

There were a few seconds of prolonged silence, both men reduced to naughty school children, but Abraham knew their dad would win. He always did.

'My fault,' Abraham said. 'Just a mistake, really. I thought he was someone else. He thought I was someone else. It all got a bit heated and, well, it was handbags.'

'Well, it looked a lot more than handbags from where I was standing,' said Vic. 'That poor man looked scared to death.'

Abraham couldn't deny that. He did look scared. Scared and confused, which wasn't what you would expect from someone who had just given a pasting to a priest, in his own church, in the middle of the morning.

'Yes, sorry, Dad,' added Joshua. 'It was my fault, too. Just a bit shook up still, you know? Saw that man at the door and got a bit worried. But he was just in the wrong place at the wrong time.'

Joshua always did know the right words to use because these ones pacified their father and he relaxed back in the red Chesterfield. 'Poor man. There's enough going on without any other dramas, don't you think? Now, did you call the police, like I suggested?'

The brothers looked at each other, neither sure who should answer, nor what to say if they did. In the end, Abraham decided to break the silence, partly because someone had to, and partly because lying came more naturally to him.

'I talked him out of it. These things, if you make a big fuss, they can just provoke people to try again,' he said, not even sure if he believed what he was saying. 'I think it was an opportunist, some deranged idiot. I don't think they'll be back.'

Vic folded his face into a look of disappointment. 'But he could have killed him! He needs locking up, whoever he is. What if he attacks someone else? I could never forgive myself.'

'Abraham's right, Dad,' added Joshua. 'I'd just like to forget it ever happened, please.' This, Abraham could tell, wasn't a lie.

Abraham knew his dad wanted to argue the point but, instead, said, 'Well, I think that's a stupid idea, but if that's what's happening then I think I might head home.

I've had enough excitement for one day. Could one of you give me a lift?'

'Sure,' said Abraham. 'As long as Josh doesn't mind me borrowing the Volvo. Probably best he rests up for a bit, anyway.'

'And you'll be ok here, Josh? On your own, I mean?' asked Vic.

'I'll be fine,' said Joshua before passing his brother the keys to the car and waving them off from the doorstep.

***

Erjon was good at hiding. Whether it was in plain sight, lost among whatever surroundings he needed to conceal himself within, or buried deep in the background, like a dropped coin trampled and pushed into the earth, he knew he would never be found if he didn't want to be.

He was cold, but the cold would pass. Uncomfortable, but comfort was a luxury. Kneeling on the hard cement floor of the partially built house, he was staring through a large hole that would, at some point, be a window.

He was hidden by the blue-grey breeze blocks of the unfinished walls and the usual detritus that accompanies a building site; pallets of bricks, upturned wheelbarrows, a green Portaloo and grubby wire panels that acted as a deterrent to passers by. A deterrent, but no more.

He had taken the hi-vis vest from his rucksack and pulled it on. He didn't expect anyone to find him, only his eyes were above the level of the unfinished window but, if they did, a hi-vis garment was a passport to anywhere, especially in this environment. He kneeled on the floor, perfectly still, watching the house directly opposite.

He had recognised the building site on the opposite side of the street as the best place to keep watch. He doubted anyone was looking for him, but it paid to be careful, and simply standing, staring at someone's house from thirty yards away was unlikely to go unnoticed.

He needed to be patient, to find the right opportunity because when he did this he needed to be sure that there were no witnesses, no danger of being interrupted, and no chance of being caught.

He had kept his green baseball cap on but as soon as he was finished here, he would discard it. It wasn't distinctive, but it was something people might remember and there was no point in taking chances. For the time being, though, he would keep it pulled low, a physical and psychological shield.

Groundwork and planning was always the key and, when approaching the priest earlier, the lack of it had worked against him. He thought he would have more time. He didn't need much, but the appearance of someone at the door had happened far sooner than he would have liked. He should have waited, found a better opportunity.

Erjon knew he should have killed the priest immediately. The questions had wasted precious seconds. He was angry at himself for falling into the same trap all those stupid films fell into, when someone spent too long talking when all he needed to do was pull the trigger.

If the priest was dead it wouldn't matter if he'd seen the video because he would no longer be able to tell anyone about it. But he did need to know whether the film had been shared with anyone else. In the end, he'd run out of time. But that was the thing about time, there was always more of it.

He felt sure he hadn't been seen, and he certainly hadn't left any indication of who he was. How could he? He was a ghost in the world of the living. But even ghosts were somebody once.

The priest had been terrified. Erjon could tell he didn't know anything just from looking into his eyes, from hearing him speak. '*I never saw it,*' he had said in a high-pitched voice and through a bleeding nose and constricted airway. Erjon believed him, but those four words also meant that, even though he may not have seen the video, he knew about it.

But he shouldn't have left him alive. If only to serve as a warning to the journalist. Abraham Hart had proven to be a thorn in their side over the past couple of years. More than once Erjon had asked Hristo for permission to deal with the situation in a more satisfactory manner. Certainly a more permanent one. Each time he had been told to hold off, that such a course of action might be more harmful than helpful. Erjon couldn't see how a dead journalist could be more trouble than a live one, but he wasn't making the decisions.

The adrenaline that had coursed through him at the church was long gone. His heart rate had slowed to a steady rhythm and his breathing was calm.

He'd been lucky, really. No, not lucky, smart. He'd seen the external door that led out onto a small courtyard and had made the priest unlock it before anything else.

Having one exit was good, having two was better, and that decision had allowed him to slip away Part of him had welcomed the intrusion.

But how had one family been able to cause so many problems? Maybe he should have waited for them both to be in that room together. What was that saying? Two birds with one stone.

But Hristo would be unhappy at such an outcome, he supposed. The priest was one thing; a random, tragic attack by a lone vigilante made aware of the priest's dirty secret. But killing the journalist might have caused questions to be asked. May have illuminated a dark place where light was unwelcome.

And so here he was; waiting, watching. And he was glad he had been, because in the last few minutes a car had left, which meant the target was alone, unguarded.

Erjon waited a little longer and then, when he was sure no one else was around, quietly made his way towards the house.

Thirty-one

The drive back to the house was short and uneventful. Abraham wondered if his dad would again try to convince him to call the police but, if the thought had crossed Vic's mind, he didn't voice it. Instead, he sat in silence listening to Radio 4, which was pre-programmed into his brother's car stereo.

At the house, Vic eased himself into his usual position on the couch, emitting the same groan he always did, and flicked on the TV. Like Joshua's car radio, it was predetermined to come to life on Dave which, at this time of the day, was odds on to be showing re-runs of either *Only Fools and Horses* or *The Good Life*.

Abraham settled into position at the other end of the sofa wondering what his next move should be. He could head back to Spotlight, look for Lewis Maynard-Jones and find out why he'd come to the rectory, and what he wanted. But he doubted Maynard-Jones would go back there, especially if he thought Abraham might come looking for him.

He wondered about talking to Ellie Maynard-Jones, to see what more she might know about Alissa, or why her husband had wanted to speak to Joshua. But, really, finding Craig Atherton now seemed like the imperative. He was a key factor in this.

If Craig was trying to blackmail Lewis, which was Abraham's hunch, then he and the video Alissa had shot, was at the heart of everything that had happened. Abraham didn't know what was on the video, not yet, but he could guess it was something Lewis wouldn't want his wife to see.

Abraham could feel his recent decision to step back from helping Carol Peters wavering. Something was obviously rotten. The accounts of Matt Hallstaff and the caretaker, Mr Langton, were arousing suspicion, as was the attack on Joshua and the appearance of Maynard-Jones. But his brother was involved, which added a layer of complication.

According to Joshua it was all a misunderstanding, but what if it wasn't? Digging deeper posed the risk of finding out things he might regret knowing.

And he'd already involved Evie in this. *Idiot!* He chastised himself. He'd gone blundering into something, dragging her with him, and now it was proving to be far more complex than he'd initially imagined.

He should step back. Tell Carol he was sorry, that he couldn't help anymore. But, despite knowing what he *should* do, there were still so many holes, and the itchy, infectious pull of unanswered questions was something he couldn't resist.

Still considering his next steps, Abraham felt his mobile vibrating in his pocket and mouthed to his dad that he would take the call in the kitchen. Extracting the phone, he saw the name 'Palmer' lit up on the screen. He swiped to accept but didn't get a chance to say anything.

'This is the last time I help you,' said Martin Palmer, his voice low and abrasive, like 40-grit sandpaper.

'You've said that before,' said Abraham, leaning against the kitchen countertop, his free hand opening cupboards and drawers, assembling all the essentials for two cups of tea.

'God, I can't wait for you to mess up. I'll be there with a smile on my face and a spring in my step to see it.'

'Yeah, well, you'll have to get in the queue. Anyway, until then, what have you got?'

Abraham heard indistinct muttering on the other end of the line.

'Sorry, what's that?'

'I said, I think we've found him.'

***

Erjon replaced the hi-vis vest in his rucksack, pulled the green cap down further and made his way across the empty street. He affected the air of a person who had every right to enter someone's property, to let himself through the unlocked side gate and into the back garden. He walked purposefully, gaze seemingly fixed ahead but, all the while, his eyes were darting, searching for people, for witnesses, busy bodies, twitching curtains and nosy neighbours.

As soon as the wooden gate was closed behind him Erjon took careful, quiet steps.

He stopped before rounding the rear corner of the house, listening. He could hear birds arguing in the trees, the low hum of a distant aeroplane sawing through the sky, and the mechanical whir of a lawnmower somewhere off to his right, a neighbour taking the last chance to tend his garden before autumn turned to winter and the elements won out.

There was nothing else. No tell-tale signs of life in the house; no music, no television, no barking dog.

Erjon stepped around the corner and onto a large concrete patio. A metal and glass table sat in its centre, surrounded by six chairs. Plants of various colours sprung up from terracotta pots that bordered the concrete. A brick path cut through the garden and, fifty yards away, an enormous willow drooped its leaves lazily onto the emerald grass.

At the rear of the house were French windows, beyond which was an empty kitchen. Erjon cupped his hands around his eyes and looked through the glass, careful not to touch it, not to leave any trace of himself. He could see no one, but he knew he was in there somewhere.

Erjon reached into his rucksack, ignoring the gun - too noisy. He felt for the hard plastic handle of the knife and removed it from the bag. It fit into his hand perfectly, like the two had been made for one another. It felt comforting to hold.

Erjon checked the adjoining properties. None overlooked the garden, no window visible that could harbour prying eyes. Good, it would make this much easier. He turned towards the large table, quietly withdrawing one of the chairs, placing it six feet from the glass, facing the French windows and the last remnants of purple wisteria that wound its way around thick wooden trellis that was fixed to the rear of the house.

He approached the glass, catching himself reflected in it, a ghostly figure of shadow and light, and rapped the knife's black plastic handle on the glass. Not so hard to break it, but hard enough to be heard. He waited a few seconds, then repeated the action, the glass giving off a dull thud.

Then he stepped back, sat in the chair, and waited.

***

Joshua had returned to the sofa with an ice pack, a glass of lemonade and a packet of paracetamol that was missing the two capsules he had recently taken. His head was still throbbing, but he wasn't sure if it was from the blow he'd sustained or from thinking about everything that had gone on over the last few hours.

He'd been carrying the guilt with him for weeks now. Since the moment he found out about Alissa's death he'd been asking himself whether he could have done more? Whether he could have said something to Alissa? Whether he should have been better at recognising the pain she was in, the help that she needed.

And now, after wondering how he'd missed the signs of her addiction, it seemed maybe all he had missed was the truth of what had happened.

Abraham had thrown real doubt on the story they had come to accept as the truth, and Joshua was having a hard time coming to terms with it. Was it, he wondered, better or worse that Alissa may not have died of a drug overdose - accidental or otherwise - and instead may have been at the heart of something even more sinister? As he lay back on the sofa, the ice pack stinging his skin and dripping cold water down the side of his head, he thought of Carol and of how he'd treated her.

'Were you suspicious? About her death, I mean?'

His brother's question hadn't been purposely hurtful, but it had still wounded because the answer was no, he hadn't been.

Carol's protestations at her daughter's innocence, at the wrongness of the manner of her death, was written off by him as denial. He saw a bereaved mother, a woman whose world had been broken, and he had done nothing to help.

Outwardly he'd been kind and supportive. He'd offered prayers at Mass and words of comfort, but he hadn't *listened*. He hadn't *believed*. And what good was a priest who didn't believe?

Joshua thought of Grace and of how it had upended his world, and the worlds of his family, when she had died. She had lived with addiction for a long time. They had all lived with it through her, too, and he wondered if that experience had hardened something in him. Whether it had calcified his empathy so that he couldn't see past a young woman and a seemingly troubled life that had led to tragedy.

The thinking made his head hurt more and he tried to quieten his mind. Outside he could hear a car driving past, revving its engine too loudly. A lawnmower, or maybe it was a drill, sounded in the distance, it's whirring carrying through the air and piercing the delicate feeling inside his head.

His dad was right, he conceded, they should call the police. Whoever the man who attacked him was, it was something to do with Alissa, that much was obvious. And if talking to the police, telling them what they knew, or thought they knew, got them closer to finding out the truth of what had happened, then they should do it willingly.

Joshua's sudden instinct to do the right thing was interrupted, though, by the sound of someone tapping at the backdoor. He lifted the icepack of his face but kept his eyes shut, tilting an ear towards what he thought he'd heard.

It came again; *tap-tap-tap*. Something hard knocking against the window at the rear of the house. Joshua wondered whether he should be scared as he swung his legs off the sofa, propelled himself upwards, and made his way towards the kitchen.

Erjon had asked the question about what to do afterwards. Occasionally a body was purposely left to be found. A message to others that no matter who you were, no matter how secure you might feel, no one was truly safe.

It was an approach Hristo had rarely sanctioned, though. Despite the fear it might instil in others it was, he believed, an unnecessary risk. A body was evidence and evidence was the only way their business could be thwarted.

And this body would be different from any that went before it. It was an unfortunate but necessary pre-emptive strike that Hristo had wrestled with. He was not a sentimental man, it was impossible to be so in their line of work, but neither was he a person who acted rashly and without due consideration.

There were other people impacted in this decision, too, and leaving any trace of their actions would open them up to examination by those who would dig until they found what they were looking for. So, discretion was called for. If not in the action itself, then certainly in the moments immediately after it.

Erjon could hear footsteps now, coming from inside the house. They were faint but his hearing was good, honed over many dark nights in countless hostile places.

He had long ago realised that your eyes could not always be trusted. That what you saw could let you down, trick you. Your hearing, Erjon believed, was more dependable.

He readied himself not by tensing but by relaxing further into the chair in which he sat, his arms languid, his breathing steady.

A man walked into the kitchen, brow furrowed, a concerned look scratched onto his face.

In the centre of the room, he stopped and stared out of the French window, concern turning to confusion, confusion morphing into anger.

Erjon stayed still.

The man walked to the glass and placed the fingers of one hand around the sleek black handle.

The other hand held a mobile phone, which he gripped tightly while turning a key in the lock.

Then the door was open, only a few inches, but enough for the man's voice to be heard.

'Who the hell are you? And what the hell are you doing in my garden?'

Thirty-two

'Carol! Brody! What are you doing here?'

Joshua, still holding the dripping icepack, looked at his housekeeper and the man whose life he had helped turn around. Despite his vision still being slightly blurry, he noticed straight away that one of them had been crying.

'Is Abraham still here?' asked Brody.

'No, he's taken my dad home.'

Brody relaxed, then said, 'I was just coming over to see how you were doing and bumped into Carol. She's very upset.'

Carol was wringing her hands and not looking directly at either of them. It was only when she stared up at Joshua that she stopped, her eyes scanning his face. 'What happened, Father?'

Joshua automatically raised a hand to his swollen eye and gently touched the bruised skin, wincing slightly as he did do. 'I'll explain everything. But what's wrong? What's happened?'

No sooner had the question been asked than whatever had been holding Carol's emotions inside dissolved and her face contorted into a picture of anguish. Brody put his arm around her and Joshua reached out and took her hands, leading her into the house.

'I'm sorry,' Carol kept repeating, occasionally dabbing her eye with a tissue that appeared from beneath the sleeve of her cardigan. 'I'm sorry.'

In the kitchen of the rectory Joshua led Carol to a chair while Brody filled the kettle with water and clicked it on. Joshua didn't know if it was the company, the location or the very English sound of boiling water and teaspoon clinking on china that settled Carol but by the time Brody placed a steaming mug in front of her she was calmer.

'Would you like to tell us what's wrong, Carol?'

As she spoke, a single tear rolled down her cheek. 'It's Craig,' she said. 'He called.'

Both men remained silent.

'He told me that he'd never once seen Alissa take drugs. That she wouldn't do something like that. He said it was her boss.' More tears followed, a cascade that Carol either couldn't or didn't want to stop. 'He said it was him that killed her because of some video she made.'

The sobs were stronger now, rising up from the depths of her body. 'Do you know what he's talking about, Father?'

'But where is he?' asked Joshua, hoping to avoid answering Carol's question. 'And why did he leave?'

Carol dragged the tissue over her face, trying to compose herself. 'He didn't say where, just that he'd had to leave. That they might have come after him too. But he said he's coming back. To fix things.'

Despite what had happened to Carol in the time that he had known her, Joshua had only ever seen her as resolute and unbreakable, her hard exterior impervious to the things life had thrown at her. Even the death of her daughter, though a cataclysmic event, had not seemed to crush her like Joshua knew it would most others.

But now, sat at the table, the mug of tea untouched beside her, Joshua could see that Carol had been clinging on by her fingertips. Her unwavering belief that Alissa had been taken from her not by God, or even by Alissa's own hand, but by some external force, had kept her focussed. Now, with apparent affirmation of her suspicions, grief had crept through the cracks, filling the spaces where the love for her daughter had lived.

Joshua and Brody did their best to comfort Carol. Brody spoke of spiritual strength, of God's will. For his part, Joshua said nothing but hoped his presence was helpful, at least. Eventually he persuaded her to move into the living room where he insisted she lay on the sofa. He told her they would work everything out. They would get to the bottom of what had happened and why.

When Carol drifted into a fitful sleep, he called his brother.

***

As soon as DI Palmer had hung up, Abraham had made the decision to head back to London in an attempt to speak to Craig Atherton. Why Craig had chosen now to use his bank card neither he nor Palmer knew, but it placed him in the Vauxhall area and, if he was quick, Abraham hoped he might be able to find him, or find someone who could point him in the right direction.

He'd left his dad on the sofa with an episode of *Homes Under the Hammer* and a cup of decaf coffee. He hadn't said where he was going, just that he would be back sometime later that day.

There was a chance, Palmer had mentioned, that the card hadn't been used by Craig at all. 'Could have been mugged,' he'd said. 'Forced to hand over the PIN. S'not uncommon.' But Craig was currently a very big missing piece in the puzzle, and Abraham felt he needed to try.

He'd almost reached the borrowed Volvo when his phone rang again, his brother's name flashing up on the screen.

'How you feeling?' said Abraham, after answering.

'Have you heard about Craig?' said Joshua, ignoring his brother's question.

Abraham stopped walking. 'Yes. But how have you?'

'He called Carol. Said he was coming back to Southend. That Alissa didn't overdose but was killed. By Lewis Maynard-Jones.'

'Shit!' said Abraham, garnering a dirty look from an elderly woman as she ambled past the house. 'Sorry, slipped out,' he added, both to the woman and his brother.

'No, "shit" is about right, I think,' said Joshua. 'Carol's here now. She's distraught, as you can imagine. I'm calling the police, but thought you'd want to know.'

'When did Craig call?'

'I'm not sure. Carol said she came straight here after she spoke to him. Maybe fifteen minutes ago.'

'Right,' said Abraham, pausing to think. 'Didn't you say Lewis gave you his address, for when you got the recording from Alissa?'

It was Joshua's turn to pause now. 'Yes,' he replied, tentatively. 'Why?'

'You still got it?'

'Yes,' he repeated. 'I'm going to give it to the police when I call them.'

'Text it to me, please.'

'Abraham, you're not going to do anything stupid, are you? This is a matter for the police.'

'I know. I won't,' Abraham lied.

The call ended, he replaced the phone in his pocket and decided that if Craig was coming to Southend there was little point going to London. Of course, he could be lying, but to what end? And how did Craig know it was Maynard-Jones who had killed Alissa? Did he have proof and, if he did, why hadn't he used it already?

Abraham remembered that morning, and the shocked face of Lewis Maynard-Jones on the doorstep of the rectory. He pictured the fear on his face as he ran away after the confrontation. Something felt off, though he couldn't put his finger on what.

He needed more information and, as his phone vibrated from an arriving text, he decided there was one man who might be able to provide it.

***

'You have made a mistake,' Erjon said. His voice was soft, barely a whisper, but his words were clear and direct. 'Hristo is not happy. Not happy at all.'

As soon as the name was mentioned, Erjon saw the colour drain from Lewis' face. His jaw slackened and his eyes widened. 'Who are you?' he said, his voice less confident now.

'I am a message,' said Erjon.

'My wife is inside. She only has to make a call.'

Erjon smiled, a dagger slash across his face. 'For someone used to lying, you are not so very good at it.'

Erjon raised himself from the chair, a fluid movement that made Lewis jump in surprise. And then

Erjon was stood in front of him, the smile gone, replaced by a sneer.

The sneer broadened as Erjon saw Lewis's eyes fall on the knife.

As Lewis leant forward, trying to close the back door, pushing it shut with both hands, he dropped his phone. Its fall was broken by Erjon's black boot, which he had already planted in the door.

Lewis backed off.

Erjon watched him turn his gaze back into the kitchen, scanning the room. He assumed he was looking for something he could use as a weapon. But the kitchen was sleek and utilitarian, the surfaces clear except for a bowl of fruit and a row of spotless cookery books.

'Do you know who I am?' Lewis shouted.

Erjon ignored the words but revelled in the fear dripping off them.

Erjon raised a gloved index finger to his thin lips then said, 'I do. That is why I am here.'

Erjon had hoped the target would retreat into the house rather than come into the garden. Clean up would be easier there, more contained. It was always harder to decontaminate outside, where blood spatter could be missed. Plus, though the garden was not overlooked, the confines of the house was safer.

'What do you want? What does Hristo want?' said Lewis, close to the internal kitchen door now, still backing away, not taking his eyes from the intruder.

'We both want the same thing,' replied Erjon. 'What we always want; silence.'

The slash was fast, like a cat slicing a paw through the air. If it hadn't been for the blood Lewis would never have known he had been cut, but the bloom of red on his white jumper spread outward, like a crimson flower opening on his abdomen.

Lewis felt no pain, only panic. He placed a hand over the wound, feeling warm liquid seep onto his fingers, then he turned and ran.

Erjon had hoped this would be easier and chastised himself for not approaching the situation more seriously. He knew Maynard-Jones posed no threat, but the longer this took and the further he ran, the more time it would take to contain the results.

He watched as Maynard-Jones bolted up the stairs and, stooping to pick up the dropped phone, he hoped Maynard-Jones was headed for the bathroom because that was where they would end up eventually.

***

The Sunday traffic was light, and it didn't take Abraham long to get to Thorpe Bay. It wasn't an area he knew well but he'd fed the address from Joshua's text into Google Maps and his phone did the rest. It was a nice area with wide, tree-lined streets and large houses set back from the road. Some had longer driveways than others, but most held at least two cars and more than a few of those cars were worth north of £80k. Abraham could almost smell the money and wondered just how much of it there was in making TV commercials.

At the southern end of Parkanaur Avenue the sonorous voice of the navigation system told Abraham that he had arrived. It was hard to see the numbers on some of the houses as the front doors were a long way from the street but, eventually, opposite a large house that was being completely renovated, he found the one he was looking for.

He stepped out of the car and, for the first time, wondered if this was the right thing to do. If Maynard-Jones had killed Alissa then he was a cold and calculating man who had ended the life of a young woman simply to save his own marriage or, more likely, to keep a hold on his business. But despite what Carol had said - or what Craig seemed to have told her - it didn't sit right with Abraham.

He had met Lewis, admittedly for only a short time, but 'cold' and 'calculating' were not words he would have used to describe him. To Abraham, he had seemed nervous, but maybe that was because of what he'd done, of what he was trying to hide.

Leaning against the car, the dull afternoon clouds hanging morosely above him, Abraham looked across at the handsome house and considered his next move.

If Lewis was inside there seemed to be nothing to gain from a one-on-one confrontation. Joshua had called the police but would they be in a rush to come? Alissa's case was closed and the suspicions of a mother and her preist weren't exactly hard evidence.

The area was quiet, only the low hum of a lawnmower somewhere in the distance eating into the tranquil surroundings. Abraham glanced up and down the street but there was no one around. He retrieved his phone from the cradle that was attached to the windscreen and scrolled to Joshua's number, aiming to check that his brother had made the call and find out what the response had been.

Then he heard it.

It wasn't a scream, it sounded too low for that, more like a yell. Under normal circumstances he would probably have ignored it. But these weren't normal circumstances.

Abraham looked along the road again. No one.

He tilted his head, listening. Nothing.

It had definitely come from the Maynard-Jones house.

Abraham took a few paces towards it.

He heard a noise, a bang, like someone had thrown something heavy at something heavier. He stepped onto the driveway, then crossed the front lawn to approach the large bay window. He glanced in but could see nothing and no one inside, only the dark reflection of his surroundings in the gleaming glass.

Then he heard something punch through the afternoon's stillness again. It sounded like a voice; low, insistent, muffled. That was followed by the sound of breaking glass.

Abraham stepped back from the window and looked to the front door. He considered ringing the bell or banging a fist on the wood, but if someone was in trouble then an answer seemed unlikely.

He reached for his phone. 'Police,' he said, when the 999 call connected. 'I think someone's in trouble.'

He quickly gave the address, hanging up when asked for his name. Then, despite his better judgement, Abraham darted to the side of the house where he'd noticed a wooden gate leading to a side passage.

He tried the metal handle, fully expecting it to be locked and for him to have to vault the gate, but it opened easily. He ran down the passage and came out onto a patio area with a large table at its centre.

He paused, listening, but apart from the distant mower and the sound of birdsong, there was nothing.

He noticed a chair had been placed directly in front of the French doors and then spotted that one of the doors was hanging open.

He approached cautiously, pushing the door open further.

'Hello!' he yelled into the kitchen. 'Mr Maynard-Jones? Lewis? Are you here?'

For a second there was silence as Abraham stood rooted to a spot just inside the kitchen, his heart hammering inside his chest.

Then another yell.

The word wasn't distinguishable. It was more a deep moan, and it was followed straight after by a set of thumps from above. Footsteps.

Abraham remained still as the steps grew louder. He looked around the minimalist kitchen for some sort of weapon, and that was when he noticed the drops of blood on the parquet floor. There weren't many but they were dark red and shiny. They reminded Abraham of the wax used to seal old-fashioned letters. The blood looked fresh and seeing it caused a jolt of fear to pulse from his core to the tiny hairs on his skin.

The footsteps got louder, crashing down the stairs.

Abraham turned to look at the door through which he'd just come.

He should leave, he thought. Get to the car and wait for the police. But while his brain seemed in favour of this course of action, his feet refused to cooperate.

When he turned back toward the sound of the footsteps he found himself staring at a thin man in labourers' clothes. He was holding a clear, zip-lock bag.

Inside the bag was a six-inch knife red with blood. The man wore a green cap and under it were dark, dispassionate eyes. He didn't look alarmed to see Abraham. His stare simply bore into him, like a laser.

'Where's Lewis?' said Abraham. 'Where's his wife?'

The man said nothing but took a step into the kitchen, re-opening the bag, his hand slowly reaching inside.

Abraham backed away, inching towards the door behind him. He wanted to turn and run but felt it would be a mistake to take his eyes off of the advancing man.

'Lewis?' shouted Abraham, as much in the hope of scaring the man as receiving an answer.

'He can't hear you,' said the man. There was a slight accent to his voice. 'Stay still and this will be easier for both of us.'

Abraham's heart felt like it would crash through his chest. He had his arms spread in front of him and had bent his knees slightly in preparation of either running or fighting. His eyes were still searching the room for something, anything, that could be a weapon.

Then he heard it.

It was faint but, in the distance, was the sound of a siren.

Abraham looked at his would-be attacker and saw that he'd heard it too. The change in his expression was almost imperceptible, but it was there. A slight flicker that told Abraham the man had a choice to make.

'I called them,' he said, holding up the phone he still held in his hand. 'They'll be here any second.'

He sneered again, then he bolted for the front door.

Abraham heard it open then slam shut again.

After five seconds, during which time the sirens got louder, he sprinted through the kitchen and took the stairs two at a time.

Thirty-three

At the top of the stairs Abraham paused, listening, though it was hard to hear anything over the pounding of his heart.

The landing was a large space covered in the same deep red carpet as the stairs. A similar red was visible in the smeared fingerprints that were on the wall leading up to the first floor.

A bookcase stood at the top, the spines facing out in colour-coded order, from white at the top left, through to black on the bottom right.

There were five doors leading off the landing. The one to Abraham's immediate right was open and showed a large bedroom with a thick cream carpet. More French windows were at the far end of the room, leading to a balcony that overlooked the long garden. Red cushions were piled on top of the king-sized bed, and mahogany furniture hugged the walls surrounding it.

Abraham stuck his head in the room. It was pristine inside, and empty.

'Lewis?' he said, tentatively.

No reply.

He moved towards the next door, which was closed.

'Lewis?' he repeated, the word aimed into the empty space around him. 'Hello?'

Nothing.

The siren was getting louder now, the two tone noise close by.

Abraham took a deep breath, and turned the gold handle, pushing the door open. Inside was a guest room. Still luxurious, but slightly less so than the previous bedroom. Abraham scanned the space. Again, nothing out of place, no one inside.

Then he heard a noise. It was faint, almost hidden behind the wailing of the police car, but it was there. It reminded him of a radiator being bled, like air was escaping from something.

He moved towards the noise. There was another door, this one ajar. He noticed something on the floor and bent lower. It looked like a penknife, the blades all folded into the black body. He picked it up and placed it in his pocket.

Abraham pushed the door further open revealing a glass shower door, then a sink. What he saw next took what little breath he had left from his body.

The bathroom room was a mess. A ceramic plant pot lay scattered into a hundred pieces, earth and leaves covering the grey slate tiles.

Cans, bottles and other bathroom paraphernalia were dotted around the room, and a glass shelf that had been fixed to the wall was smashed, remnants of it spread across the room and laying on the base of the roll top bath.

Among it all Lewis Maynard-Jones lay on the floor, a pool of maroon encircling him. His face was deathly white and a blood-soaked hand was pressed into his abdomen.

His eyes were open, but staring into space, and his lips were parted, bubbles of red-tinged saliva flecked in the corners of his mouth. Abraham thought he was already dead, but then came that sound. A death rattle. A

245

last gasp in an attempt to hold onto life as it seeped out onto the cold tiles.

Abraham placed his phone on the sink top and stepped closer, the glass and broken ceramic crunching beneath his shoes.

He looked for something to staunch the flow of blood and spotted a pile of towels in the bath that must have been on the now smashed shelf. He shook them into the bath, making sure to remove any slivers of glass, then placed one beneath Lewis's hand, telling him to press, but the hand was limp.

Abraham pressed down on the wound himself. He had taken rudimentary first aid courses, part of the training he undertook when he had visited the front line of the war in Syria, but he knew that nothing bar a miracle could help now.

'Lewis, it's Abraham Hart. The police are coming, an ambulance will be here soon,' he said, not knowing if that was true. 'You're going to be ok,' he added, knowing that definitely wasn't. 'What happened? Who did this to you? Who was that man?'

Lewis took a breath in. To Abraham it looked like it might have been the hardest thing Lewis Maynard-Jones had ever done. For a moment he wondered if any more words would ever cross the man's lips again. He was still, his features white, his skin waxen.

Abraham was about to close the man's eyelids, like he'd seen done in so many films, when Lewis suddenly coughed. When the spasm ended he blinked hard and locked eyes with Abraham, seeing him properly for the first time. He squeezed Abraham's arm, leaving a smear of bloody prints on his jacket, and wheezed one word in a low croak, 'Brother'.

Abraham stared at him, confused. 'Whose brother?' he whispered, lowering his head towards Lewis'. 'Mine? What about him?'

Lewis's eyes remained fixed on Abraham but whatever light had been behind them, whatever spark of life that separated the living from the dead, had gone.

Abraham remained rooted to the spot, staring at the dead man, wondering what he had meant. Then the world beyond the confines of the wrecked bathroom crashed back into focus because the police siren now felt like it was in the room with him.

Whatever thoughts he had about Lewis's last word, whatever emotions he felt at being in such close proximity to a recently murdered man, they all deserted him as he realised that the police would find him leaning over a dead man, covered in his blood. His prints would be in the house, the house of a man he only a few hours ago was fighting in the street.

Panic overtook him, scrambling his brain. Even in the whirlwind of thoughts he recognised this feeling; fight or flight. But with the evidence stacked against him there only seemed to be one logical response.

Abraham gave the lifeless body one last glance before he stood up and hurried out of the bathroom and back onto the landing.

The wailing siren, which up to that point had bludgeoned all other sounds out of its path, had now stopped and the silence that replaced it was even more frightening because Abraham knew it meant that the officers were here.

As if to prove that point, there were two sharp bangs on the front door, followed by the impatient chime of the doorbell.

Abraham considered answering, explaining the situation to the authorities, telling them about the man he'd seen in the house, about the person who'd attacked Joshua, about the run-in he'd had that morning with the now dead Lewis Maynard-Jones. Surely they could see he wasn't a killer. That he didn't have it in him to take someone's life.

Then he thought back to Hristo Nikolova's trial, to the fact that evidence was paramount, that contrary to what the Bible said, the truth didn't always set you free. The next round of banging on the door brought Abraham back to reality and he made a decision, without really considering the consequences.

In the main bedroom, with its cream carpets and red cushions, he navigated to the French windows, offering up a silent prayer to a god he didn't believe in that the doors would be open.

He pushed down on the handle, cursing when his potential escape was locked shut. Then he noticed the key resting in the lock and offered a silent thank you.

On the narrow balcony Abraham could see out over the patio. He scanned across the large table, the willow tree and, beyond that, the fence at the end of the garden that led onto the adjoining property. He glanced over the edge at the ten-foot drop to the concrete paving below.

Behind him the banging on the door had stopped. It would be a matter of moments before the police made their way down the side passage and into the back garden.

He considered jumping but, even in a heightened state of fear, knew that doing so would only end in at least one broken limb and no chance of escape.

Hesitating for only a second, Abraham swung his legs over the black railings of the balcony and, with his hands gripping the upper edge of the metal, placed one foot on the wooden trellis fixed to the rear of the house.

When it didn't immediately collapse under his weight, he manoeuvred his other foot into position, keeping hold of the railing in case the structure gave way.

It held, and Abraham lifted his left hand off the black metal and placed it on the trellis.

The wood groaned and creaked. Abraham heard a crack beneath his left foot and his body dropped two inches towards the hard ground.

He closed his eyes, imagining the trajectory of his fall and the potential damage it would do, not only to his body but to his plea of innocence.

But the trellis remained attached to the wall.

Eyes still closed, Abraham heard a man's voice shouting. He didn't pick up all the words but felt sure someone was saying, 'Round the back'.

It was now or never. Abraham moved his right hand from the relative safety of the railing to the trellis full of wisteria that was now taking his entire weight.

Another creak. The terrifying sound of more wood breaking. A further prayer to an ignored god.

Abraham remained on the trellis, and the trellis, for now, remained on the brickwork of the house.

He began to climb down.

One foot, one hand. Next foot, next hand.

He heard footsteps coming his way, and the sound of the wooden gate at the side of the house being pushed open.

Abraham went faster and, a few feet from the patio, jumped, turned and ran.

As he reached the dense, overhanging branches of the willow tree, he stepped behind them and leant his back on the hard bark, realising that he hadn't taken a breath in what felt like hours.

His heart was hammering so fast and so loud he was sure it could be heard from space, let alone from twenty feet away.

He took two deep breaths in through his nose, breathing out with quiet control though pursed lips.

At the house he heard a voice yelling, 'Dave! Round here!' Then more footsteps heading towards the rear of the house.

Risking a glance back he saw a uniformed policeman round the corner of the house and join his colleague at the still-open French window that led into the kitchen. He watched them exchange a glance and knew they'd seen the blood, just like he had.

One of them spoke into a radio mic pinned to their black vest. He watched them tentatively enter the house, one still speaking into his radio, his head tilted to one side.

Abraham turned in the opposite direction and sprinted.

Thirty-four

It was only after vaulting the rear fence of the Maynard-Jones' garden and creeping along the permitter of their neighbour's fence, coming out onto the road parallel with Parkanaur Avenue, that the full impact of what he'd done hit Abraham.

The previous ten minutes seemed unreal, like a fever-dream from which he would wake any minute. But the blood on his clothes and the dried crimson stain on his hands told him that this was very much a reality; he had fled a murder scene and all he had done was make himself look guilty.

The police would know he'd been there. Not only were his prints in the house and his DNA on the body of the victim, but the car he had been driving was still parked outside the house and, most damning of all, he'd left his phone on the sink in his rush to escape.

It was only a matter of time before they came looking for him.

Abraham became aware of his appearance. He was walking along an affluent street in broad daylight wearing blood-stained clothes, agitated and scared while more police sirens filled the air. The cavalry was arriving. Too late for Lewis Maynard-Jones, but in good time to scour the streets for the perpetrator of his murder.

He considered giving himself up. Returning to the house and explaining everything. Maybe there was

CCTV. Maybe someone had seen the other man entering or leaving the house. But maybes weren't good enough. Abraham had reported on enough crimes and been to enough trials to know that simplicity was key for both the prosecution and the jury and, considering the evidence, it would be far a simpler to affix blame to Abraham than to an unknown man no one else might have seen.

There were two things Abraham knew he needed to do. The first was to get away from the scene as quickly and as inconspicuously as he could. The second was to find out the identity of the man with the knife and why he would want Lewis Maynard-Jones dead.

He looked at his watch. It was 12.33pm and if Craig had called Carol roughly half an hour ago then Abraham maybe had an hour before Craig might conceivably arrive in Southend. That was assuming Craig was coming from the Vauxhall area and that he was telling the truth about returning in the first instance. But before worrying about all the 'ifs', he needed to get off the street and out of the clothes he was wearing.

There was no way he could go back to his parents' house, or to the rectory. That would be the first place the police would visit once they realised the car in front of the house was registered to Joshua Hart.

He wondered if Siobhan would stay calm if he turned up to ask if he could take some of his clothes, and whether she might also dispose of the bloodied ones he was currently wearing.

That thought was quickly dismissed not only because of its unlikeliness and the fact that Siobhan lived miles from where he was, but because he didn't want to involve her or Evie in any of this.

The only person he thought might help, and who also lived less than ten minutes walk from here, was the one person he really didn't want to call on. But, at that moment, and in this particular situation, Tony Stone was the man most qualified to give assistance.

Furtively scanning the street, hoping people weren't brought out of their opulent homes by the sound of multiple police sirens, Abraham broke into a jog and headed in the direction of his former friend's house.

Dungannon Drive was only a few roads along from where Abraham currently was. He only knew the address because Tony still sent his parents a Christmas card each year - or, more likely, his secretary did - and they in turn sent one to him. He'd witnessed his mum writing a card one year and, for reasons he didn't quite understand, had memorised the address on the envelope.

Marion Hart had never liked Tony. She had seen in the boy the man he would become. But, despite that, she would always send a card to him in return, though only once his had hit their doormat. It was strange how outward appearances often overwhelmed internal feelings.

He'd never told his parents about the career path Tony Stone had chosen since they'd left school, nor about the time he'd spend at Her Majesty's pleasure. And he'd certainly never told them about some of the situations they had got themselves into.

He and Tony had long ago drifted apart but, after their unplanned meeting at the pub two nights ago, Abraham felt that showing up announced might at least seem less odd. Until he explained why he was there.

Stone Cold Manor, as the sign on the handsome brickwork supporting the wrought iron gates stated the house was called, was a large three storey structure with a row of conifer trees along its perimeter that acted as a partial screen from prying eyes.

Through the branches Abraham could make out a house that was Tudor in style, with the top half featuring bright white render with dark black wooden beams woven into it. From the red gleaming brickwork though, it was likely built in the last thirty years.

Before he could even cross the sleek lawn that was stretched out between Abraham and the imposing, double-fronted door of the main entrance, he would need to gain access via the intercom system mounted on the wall.

There was a camera positioned on top of the wall, pointing down at the driveway and pavement that led into the house, and a silver button the size of a two-pound coin that had the words 'press for access' printed below it.

Abraham pressed.

After a few seconds a male voice rung out from the speaker above the button. 'Yes?'

'I need to see Tony, please. It's something of an emergency.'

Abraham heard the man sigh. He assumed that he was meant to. 'Mr Stone isn't taking visitors at this time. You'll have to make an appointment through his secretary. Details are on the company website.'

Abraham waited for more but, evidently, the man had finished speaking and returned to whatever he'd been doing before being so inconvenienced.

Abraham pressed again. 'Tell him it's Abraham Hart and that I need his help. He'll be pissed off if you let this opportunity pass him by, believe me. And if I know Tony Stone - and I do - he's not someone to piss off.'

Abraham pictured the man weighing up the pros and cons of what he'd been told. As he waited, he scanned the road and his stomach dropped as a marked police car stopped at the top of Dungannon Drive. It was indicating right, waiting for the traffic coming the other way to pass before it turned into the road on which Abraham stood.

He turned back to face the speaker. He could feel pinpricks of sweat blooming from his forehead.

He had a vision of being forced to the ground, hands on head. Could feel the cuffs being wrapped around his wrists and hear the police caution being recited to him.

He risked another glance towards the end of the road. A red 4x4 drove past then the police car started to turn, pulling into Dungannon Drive.

Abraham's brain told him to run. His muscles were twitching, preparing to feel the burn if he sprinted as fast as he could, which he knew would never be fast enough.

As the car drew nearer Abraham heard a metallic click, then a voice. 'Come on then,' it said. 'He'll meet you at the main door.'

The gate sprung open a few inches and Abraham pushed it as fast as he was able, stepping inside the property's border and slamming it shut behind him.

Thirty-five

Erjon had avoided the blood. The two stab wounds he had inflicted - the first a mere warning, the second a more accurate and deadly incision - meant he hadn't needed to get hands on.

There was no fight, he had simply stood outside the door listening to the flailing man stagger around the bathroom, throwing objects and obscenities before he eventually understood the futility of his actions and lay on the floor to embrace death.

With no visible blood on his clothes, there was little need to change them immediately, but it was the small things that could often mean so much.

So, after walking the thirty minutes back to Southend, making sure to keep to the back streets rather than the main stretch of road along the seafront, he had paid cash in two different charity shops for some inconspicuous replacements - a pair of blue jeans, a plain black t-shirt, a grey Adidas hooded sweater, and a pair of brown Chelsea boots that were one size too big - and changed in the toilets of the shopping centre opposite. The clothes he had been wearing he dumped in two different rubbish bins along the high-street.

The deed itself had gone well but all Erjon could think about was the interruption. It had meant abandoning the body and, hearing sirens in the near distance, the scene, to make his escape.

Hristo would not be happy. This wasn't meant to be a message. There was no warning to be made to rivals or wavering associates. Lewis Maynard-Jones' death was both punishment and insurance, and it was meant to happen with no repercussions. Due to that interfering journalist, that would no longer be the case.

Laying on the too-soft mattress in the room of his bed and breakfast, Erjon now wondered if he should have delayed his escape to deal with Hart. It would only have taken a minute, probably much less. But caution was a watchword both he and Hristo lived by, and delaying may have meant alerting the authorities to his presence. There would be other opportunities.

Reaching into his rucksack he removed his phone and dialled. He didn't have to wait long for an answer.

'Is it done?' asked Hristo.

'Yes. But there were complications.'

Erjon heard the steady breathing on the other end of the line. It was a pause heavy with disappointment and, Erjon knew from experience, no little anger. Despite their friendship and long history both men knew who the senior figure in their relationship was. Erjon was there to do a job and, like any other employee, Hristo expected that job to be undertaken successfully.

'Tell me.'

'An interruption. The journalist again. I was unable to dispose of the body.'

'Police?'

'Yes.'

'And Diellza?' It was the fist time Hristo's voice wavered, something distorting its usual calm and even tone; worry.

'I haven't seen her.'

'His phone?'

'Recovered. I used his fingerprint to unlock it and alter the settings. It's no longer locked. I have left it in the place you mentioned. No one will find it until it's picked up.'

'Can we be sure he didn't share the video?'

'No. But why would he?'

Hristo didn't reply and Erjon could sense him weighing up the situation, working out how much damage had been done and how much might still be possible. 'Witnesses?'

'Just the journalist. I did not have time to deal with him, and wasn't sure if that would be your preferred course of action. He doesn't know who I am, nor about your involvement in this, but he has proven to be problematic in the past. It is unfortunate that he seems to have followed us to this backwater.'

'Followed? No, he's not that smart,' countered Hristo. 'Unfortunate? Yes. For him, at least. I don't like disruptions, my friend. The business does not like them, and nor do our suppliers. Deal with Hart. But, Erjon, no noise.'

Erjon smiled, his thin lips stretching briefly across his face. 'I understand.'

'There is another matter,' said Hristo. 'Equally as pressing. The boyfriend.'

'Of the girl?'

'Yes. Someone called Atherton. He has resurfaced.'

'He did well to stay hidden for so long. You should have allowed me to search him out. Are we sure it's him?

'My police contact believes so. He's involved in this somehow. Find Hart. Find Atherton. I want this finished.'

***

'Well, well, well,' said Tony Stone, smiling as he stood at the front door of his imposing house. 'Don't see you for years and then it's twice in one weekend. You miss me or something?'

Tony was wearing a blue Nike tracksuit top zipped up to his chin, a pair of grey Nike shorts, Nike sports socks and pristine running shoes. In his right hand was a large, clear plastic bottle which seemed to be filled with a thick green liquid. He looked, to Abraham, like something out of a TV commercial.

'Sorry. Am I interrupting?'

'Nah, good timing if anything. The Mrs was on at me to hit the gym, do a few miles on the treadmill.' Tony lowered his voice conspiratorially, 'Had a few heavy nights with the lads recently, you know. But she's out, and I can't do all that now guests are here, can I?'

Tony looked Abraham up and down, at his red stained and dishevelled clothes, then glanced over Abraham's shoulder and back along the driveway towards the now closed gates. He just caught a flash of yellow and blue decals as the police car eased by. His expression altered from a happy welcome to a more suspicious stare. 'What's happened?'

Abraham, too, turned his attention back towards the road. 'Do you mind if I come in?'

In the opulent kitchen Tony's initial *bonhomie* gave way to a more serious demeanour. Despite the perception of local-boy-done-good innocence that he put forward to friends, businesspeople, the authorities Tony was no stranger to the darker elements of life. His business and his wealth, while not necessarily built on blood, certainly had traces of it in the cement that held it all together, and Abraham knew this as well as anyone. It was the reason he was here.

'I need some help,' Abraham said, hating that Tony was currently the only person to whom he could turn.

'I guessed. What you done?'

Abraham glanced around the spacious kitchen. 'Who was the man on the intercom?'

'What, Gary? Don't worry about him, he works for me,' said Tony, tracing an imaginary zip across his mouth.

Abraham nodded. He was too tired and too on edge to work out what he should or shouldn't say. He was taking a gamble that whatever was going on with Alissa's death, with Lewis's murder, and the events surrounding both, wasn't something Tony had a hand in.

His instinct told him it wasn't. Despite all he knew about his former friend's background, Abraham also knew Tony had a daughter not much older than Alissa had been, and that he abhorred violence against women. To Tony, the less savoury things he did were somehow cleansed by his gallant policy on the treatment of women and children.

So, Abraham explained what had happened in its entirety. He told him about Alissa's overdose, about the suspicions of her mother and how he had agreed to look into her daughter's death. He talked about the video of Lewis and his secretary and how Alissa had accidentally filmed their tryst. He explained about how Joshua was assaulted at the church, how Lewis and turned up and how there had nearly been a fight. Lastly he recounted how Lewis had been murdered by a man Abraham didn't recognise, and how he had bolted from the scene spattered with the dead man's blood.

Abraham did all this staring at the kitchen's parquet floor, unable to look Tony in the eye. When he'd finished, he looked up to see Tony staring at him, his expression unreadable. 'I expect you have a lot of questions,' said Abraham.

Tony nodded. 'I do. Firstly, 'tryst'? Where're you from, the fucking eighteenth century?'

Abraham laughed. He didn't want to, but he couldn't help himself. It was less the joke and more to release some tension, so weighed down by fear that it was a case of either laugh or cry.

'Definitely a pickle, isn't it?' said Tony, never one for overstatement. 'Look, before anything else, did anyone see you leave the scene? Does anyone know you're here?'

Abraham shook his head. 'I don't think so. Do you think the police car we saw means they know? It must do, mustn't it?'

It was Tony's turn to laugh. 'Nah, don't worry about that. They like a drive-by pretty often. They think it keeps me on my toes. Not that there's anything I need to worry about. Been legit for a long time now.'

Abraham's eyes widened, and Tony looked offended.

'You want my help or not?'

Abraham nodded.

'Then I need to make sure you're not bringing the police straight to my door. Legit or otherwise, I don't need to get involved in something nasty. If what you're saying holds up, then you're talking about an outfit that's sanctioned a hit on a well-known local businessman.'

At Tony's mention of the word 'hit' Abraham felt a blanket of anxiety envelope him. Hearing the concern in Tony's voice, a man who was far more used to walking in this type of world than him, made him understand the danger he might have put himself - and his family - in. It also made him realise that, while coming to this house and relying on Tony wasn't something he had particularly wanted to do, it was probably the best decision to have made. 'So, what should I do?'

Tony took a swig from his bottle and pulled a face as he swallowed the green concoction inside. 'Christ! I think I've shit things less disgusting.' He placed the bottle on the counter and ran himself a glass of tap water. 'Well, first thing is probably to get you out of those,' he said, sipping from the glass and nodding at Abraham's clothes, 'and into something slightly less incriminating.'

'Like what? I don't have any spare clothes.'

'Don't worry about that. But listen, I do this,' said Tony, waving an index finger between himself and Abraham, 'it's because we go back, obviously, but also, it means you owe me, right? I mean, we're grown ups, I know, but ain't nothing in this world for free, is it?'

And there it was. Abraham should have known that coming here for help would cost him. Maybe not now, but at some point. But, he thought, as the image of Lewis Maynard-Jones popped unbidden into his head, what choice did he have?

Fifteen minutes and one quick shower later and Abraham was sporting a Nike tracksuit like the one Tony was wearing, only with matching trousers instead of the shorts. He also wore a plain white t-shirt and a pair of Nike trainers that weren't just similar to Tony's, but were, in fact, the exact ones he had just been wearing.

Though Tony and Abraham were similar in height, Tony was carrying an extra couple of stone, some of it muscle, some of it muscle-turned-to-fat. Tony had insisted a tracksuit was the best choice because it was more forgiving than the other clothes he owned, plus the trousers had a drawstring waist that Abraham could tighten as needed. 'It's either that, or some Lycra get up from the Gemma's wardrobe.'

Once decked out in what felt like 90s fancy dress, Tony walked with Abraham into the large garden which was surrounded by high conifers. He was carrying a plastic bag filled with the blood-stained clothes, which he tipped into a metal dustbin located on a square of concrete at the back of a summerhouse. Tony then threw some wood on top of the clothes, squirted some liquid in then stepped back.

He produced a box of matches from his pocket, lit one and, from a few feet, tossed it into the bin, which erupted in orange flames and a burst of heat that made Abraham step back in fear for his eyebrows.

After a few seconds Tony turned to Abraham and held up an envelope. 'See that gate?' he said, looking towards the rear of the garden and along a red brick path that cut through twenty yards of perfectly manicured lawn. 'It's unlocked. There's a red Fiat Punto out there. Use it for as long as you need to. Do whatever you have to. Keys are in this, plus a tonne in cash, in case of emergencies.'

Abraham took the envelope. 'Why're you doing this?'

Tony shrugged. 'Told you. Old times. Plus, never know when you might need the help of a well-known and respected journalist. One thing, though.'

Tony took a step closer to Abraham, the extra two stone now feeling like a lot more. 'Anyone asks, you don't mention my name. This sort of thing,' he said, hooking a thumb over his shoulder towards the flames licking up the side of the metal dustbin, 'is something most people would frown upon.'

Abraham nodded. 'I understand. Thank you.'

Abraham made a move towards the rear gate then stopped and turned back. 'Any advice?'

Tony was already staring at the dustbin, entranced by the colour and movement of the flickering flames. Without turning around, he said; 'Yeah. Don't get caught.'

'By whom?'

'By anyone,' he said, before turning back to face the heat.

Thirty-six

DI Martin Palmer nodded his thanks at a uniformed officer as they handed a steaming mug of tea to Ellie Maynard-Jones before retreating from the room.

Palmer sat in the middle of a burgundy leather sofa in the spacious lounge while the distraught woman was slumped in a matching armchair across from him. The tea remained untouched, held so limply in her right hand that Palmer was worried it might drop to the floor.

It had taken some time for her to calm down and the crying had only just stopped. She had excused herself to one of the house's other bathrooms to freshen up, leaving Palmer and his team wondering how many bathrooms the house had.

On returning she seemed calmer, though small, sorrowful sniffs punctuated her speech each time she spoke, which had not been very often. The family liaison officer, a middle-aged woman called Deborah White, who Palmer had worked with before and whom he liked, was standing by the door looking suitably concerned.

'Are you sure there's no one we can call?' asked Deborah. 'Anyone who can come and be with you for a little while?'

Mrs Maynard-Jones shook her head and dabbed a tissue on each of her eyes. 'No, thank you, but my parents are both dead. No siblings, I'm afraid. Just

Lewis.' At the mention of her late husband's name, she once again broke into sobs.

Palmer couldn't blame her. She had arrived home to a circus of marked vehicles, uniformed officers stationed on the driveway, and white-suited forensics officers traipsing in and out of her house.

Shock and worry vied for dominance, the latter winning out as she ran towards the front door of her home only to be barred entry by Deborah White, who accompanied her into the lounge and explained the terrible events that had happened.

'I'm sorry to have to ask you questions at what is an incredibly difficult time,' began Palmer, 'but any information you can give us might help us catch the person who did this.'

There was a nod, but no direct eye contact.

'Did your husband have any enemies that you know of? Anyone who might wish him harm?

'No!' said Ellie, forcefully. 'He works —. He worked in TV and advertising, it's not the mafia. Who would want to do this?'

'That's what we're going to find out. Do you know if your husband had any meetings planned for today, anyone who might have been coming to the house?'

Again, she shook her head. 'It's a Sunday. Even he gets a day off once in a while.'

'And you obviously weren't with your husband this afternoon. Can I ask where you were today?'

'I had lunch with our accountant. I don't usually work Sundays, but we hadn't managed to connect in the week and, for once he wasn't playing golf, so I took advantage of that.'

Palmer jotted down the name of the lunch companion, a David Catton, and proceeded to ask other questions, the answers to which shed no light on why someone might enter a home and fatally stab a man to death. No one else had keys to the house which, on initial inspection, suggested Lewis Maynard-Jones had willingly let his killer inside.

Palmer wasn't too worried that the newly widowed woman's answers weren't getting him anywhere. This case, he thought, would be decided on forensic evidence and even the briefest glimpse of the scene told him that there might be more of that than usual. There was blood, shoe prints, fibres plus the thing he was really interested in, the many smeared fingerprints on the stairway, on the bathroom walls and in the master bedroom.

As the distraught woman dissolved into more tears and Deborah approached to take the mug of tea from her hand, Palmer's DS, a twenty-something fast-tracked graduate called Kirk Court, who Palmer wanted to dislike if only for his name, but who was proving to be annoyingly professional, entered the room and bent towards Palmer's ear.

'There's a car parked outside. None of the neighbours have seen it before. We ran it through ANPR and it's registered to one Joshua Hart, a Catholic priest in Southend.'

'Hart?'

The DS nodded.

'Christ!' whispered Palmer.

***

Abraham pulled the Fiat onto the side of the road, turned off the engine and sat in stunned silence. He couldn't believe what had happened since this morning and that, to all intents and purposes, he was on the run.
He should have stayed at the scene, he thought for the hundredth time, should have explained what had happened, why he was there.

But the more he tried to convince himself that the truth was the best choice, the more he realised the futility of that option. If he came forward then he would be in a police station right now; at best answering questions, at worst laying on a thin mattress in a holding cell. And if Palmer had anything to do with it, it would be the latter.

He checked his watch. It was just over an hour since Joshua had called him to say that Craig Atherton was planning to come back to Southend. Craig was the key to all this. He'd told Carol that Lewis Maynard-Jones had killed Alissa and, if that was true, Abraham's pity for the murdered man was less than it might have been. But, true or not, who had killed Lewis, and why?

What he was doing now was a gamble, not just because the police would be looking for him, but also because there was no way of knowing whether Craig was coming back on the train. Or if he was really coming back at all. But he couldn't think of anything else to do, or anywhere else to go that the police wouldn't think of too.

Abraham reached into the pocket of his too-big tracksuit trousers, grabbed his wallet and removed the picture he had taken from Alissa and Craig's flat. It showed the two of them dressed smartly - her in a black dress, him in dark blue trousers and matching jacket.

Craig was almost a foot taller than Alissa, who Carol had told him was 5'5", which put Craig at around 6'4". He looked gangly in the photo, less confident than the girl he had his arm around, but his gap-toothed smile seemed genuine, and Abraham couldn't help but like him for it.

He had a perfect view of the train station fifty yards ahead of him. The stone steps leading up to it were currently empty, the only people in view a cluster of shoppers walking towards the high street.

Palmer had told him that Craig's debit card had placed him in Vauxhall which meant if he was coming back to the town from that area, and if he left soon after speaking to Carol, and if he took the train, then he might arrive any minute. Abraham shook his head. That amount of 'ifs' didn't instil much hope.

That hope was stretched to breaking point after the arrival and departure of six c2c trains that pulled into the station, expelling passengers through the barriers and onto the steps. Abraham scanned the faces as quickly as he could, glancing from the ambling groups of people to the photo he was clutching in his left hand. Most of the passengers seemed to be elderly men and women, and no one he spotted was above six feet tall.

Ninety minutes passed and he began to feel that he should leave. He was parked illegally and was surprised that a traffic warden hadn't already appeared to move him along, or give him a ticket, or both.

His fear had ratcheted up ten minutes earlier when a man wearing a hi-vis jacket ambled onto the steps and sat smoking a cigarette, staring occasionally in Abraham's direction. He'd tried to look like he was innocently waiting for a passenger, which was half correct, and was glad when, after a few minutes, the man flicked his dog end into a bush and walked back into the station.

It was time to call it quits. Abraham turned the key in the ignition, the engine sparking to life.

He thought about what he should do next, where he should go. There was three-quarters of a tank of petrol, and he wondered if simply driving around for as long as possible was an option, hoping the situation would resolve itself. He put the car into first gear and was about to pull off when he heard the electric hum of the overhead wires and the hydraulic puff of air from a train's brakes. *Last one*, he thought, turning off the engine.

There were more passengers exiting this train than any of the previous ones. Scores of people, from elderly couples to mothers pushing buggies, all coming through the barriers one after the other. Abraham scanned each body type but there was no one who looked like the person in the photo.

As they all made their way down the steps and out of sight, Abraham rubbed his eyes and swore to himself. He really didn't know what to do. He couldn't hide forever, and Craig Atherton was the only link he thought might be able to help. Maybe the next stop *should* be Southend police station.

When he looked up, ready to start the engine again, there was one more passenger slowly making their way out of the station.

He looked older than the person in the photo that had now been thrown onto the passenger seat. He had a short, scraggly beard and wore crumpled clothing. He looked, Abraham thought, like a homeless person. But, crucially, he was tall, the tallest person he'd seen so far. And thin. As thin as the young man standing next to Alissa in the photo.

Abraham craned his neck forward to get a better look. An elderly woman pushing a wheeled shopping bag was approaching the station, struggling to pull her bag up the steps. The gangly man trotted towards her and said something Abraham couldn't hear. She looked slightly alarmed at the sight of the person at her elbow, but Abraham saw her nod and stand aside as the man carried the bag to the top of the stairs. The old lady smiled her thanks, and the man grinned at her in return. A gap-toothed grin that set Abraham's heart racing. He got out of the car and had to stop himself from sprinting for fear of scaring him away.

Abraham ambled towards him, trying to seem uninterested in his target, who was now reaching the bottom step and nervously glancing around.

As Abraham got closer he said, 'Craig? Craig Atherton? My name's Abraham, I'm a friend of Carol's. I need your help.'

***

'Murdered?' said Joshua Hart, his mouth hanging open as his face went white. 'What do you mean, 'murdered'?'

'I mean, as in killed illegally by somebody else, Father,' replied DI Palmer, knowing that being flippant in instances such as this was not wholly professional, but also unable to help himself. 'Do you mind if my colleague and I come in?' he continued as Joshua made the sign of the cross on himself.

The priest stood back and allowed Palmer and DS Court to enter the house, raising an arm to indicate the living room. When they entered, two people were already sitting next to each other on a sofa, opposite two empty red chairs.

'This is Carol Peters,' said Joshua. 'Alissa's mum. She works here from time to time. And this is Brody, a family friend. Brody, Carol, this is… I'm sorry, I've forgotten your names.'

'Detective Inspector Palmer, and this is my colleague DS Court.'

'I'm assuming you're you here about the attack,' said Joshua.

'Attack?' said Palmer. 'Would this have anything to do with one Mr Lewis Maynard-Jones, by any chance?'

Joshua looked from Palmer to Brody to Carol and back again. He sensed he'd spoken too soon and said too much, even in the little that had come out of his mouth.

'In a roundabout sort of way, I suppose,' Joshua said.

And so, as Carol excused herself to make tea, Joshua told DI Palmer all that had happened, relaying everything as best as he could remember it.

'Let me get this straight,' said Palmer, once Joshua had finished. 'It was you who was attacked in the church and, at first, you thought it might be Mr Maynard-Jones but, on reflection, you think that's highly unlikely. But, despite that, Maynard-Jones turned up here to see you, but your brother and him got into a fight that was eventually broken up by your father?'

'I wouldn't really call it a fight,' said Joshua. 'Handbags, don't they call it? Bit sexist, I suppose, but there you are.'

'What did Mr Maynard-Jones want when he came here?'

'I don't know. We didn't get to speak.'

'But you think it has something to do with a video of him and a girl who works for him?'

Joshua blushed at the thought of Palmer - or anyone present - thinking he'd seen the footage. 'I've never seen the video,' he was quick to confirm, 'so I don't know it exists for sure, but I'm assuming that's why he came. And the man who attacked me mentioned it so, again, that's why I initially thought it was Mr Maynard-Jones who had assaulted me in the church.'

'And this was a video Alissa shot? Mistakenly, you say.'

'Yes. Well, mistakenly *she* said, but I have no reason to disbelieve her.'

'And your brother is informally involved in investigating Alissa's death?'

'How do you know that?' asked Joshua.

'It's true,' said Carol who had returned to the room with a tray filled with mugs. 'There's no way that my daughter would have taken her own life. No way! Mr Hart agreed to look into it for me. Nothing formal. He wouldn't take any money, and he was clear that he wasn't convinced I was right. But I was!'

Palmer gave Carol a quizzical stare and was about to ask a question, but Carol Peters, now that she'd started talking, didn't want to stop. The most important thing to her was finding justice for Alissa, and now that she believed justice was on its way, that a crime had been committed and needed to be accounted for, she wanted everyone to know about it. The police more than most.

'Craig Atherton. That's Alissa's boyfriend,' Carol said, a shadow quickly passing across her face. 'Was her boyfriend, I mean. He said Alissa was killed. By Lewis Maynard-Jones. To cover up his sordid affair, I expect. Craig had to leave. Was scared for his own life. But he's coming back to make things right.'

Palmer nodded, made an unspecific noise that gave no indication of what he thought of Carol's revelations, then changed the subject, 'We found your car, Father.'

'I'm sorry?' said Joshua.

'Your car, a Volvo, isn't it? We found it.'

'Is Abraham ok. I leant it to him earlier. Nothing's happened, has it? Where is he?'

'I can't speak to Abraham's whereabouts at the moment. I was hoping you might be able to help with that. As for the car, it's fine. Still parked where we found it, I expect, outside Lewis Maynard-Jones' house.'

In unison, Carol, Brody and Joshua raised a hand to their mouths.

'Now,' continued Palmer, 'tell me a bit more about what Craig Atherton said.'

Thirty-seven

Craig had sat in the last carriage of the train, as far back as was possible, so that he could see everything in front of him and no one could enter the carriage from behind his seat. If someone suspicious did board and make their way towards him, he didn't really have a plan for what he would do, but at least he'd see them coming. On the floor beside him was the phone he'd kept hidden all this time, plugged into an outlet next to the seat and charging via a cable he'd purchased with the last of the money he'd withdrawn.

There was a gnawing in his stomach telling him that coming back to Southend would only end in trouble. The gnawing wasn't new, it had been there for weeks, since he'd packed what little he could and slunk off to London, away from the person he knew would be looking for him. He'd had time to think about what he had done to set recent events in motion, and he couldn't believe he'd been so stupid.

It had been a spur of the moment decision, something he thought might ultimately see him and Alissa able to move forward together. He'd sent the email to Lewis Maynard-Jones for her. For them. He was about to lose his job and, with it, the flat. And with no money and nowhere to live, why would Alissa, who could have her pick of boyfriends, want to stick with him?

He was jealous, too. At first he'd denied it to himself, but when Alissa had talked about her boss, about the successful business he ran, the money he earned, the expensive holidays he went on, and how he'd said she was on the first rung of the ladder that stretched to where Lewis himself was now standing, maybe even beyond, Craig had felt the hot stab of jealousy mixed with the cold thrust of anger.

The video was a way of killing two birds with one stone. A way to bring this man Alissa so respected down a peg or two and attain some financial security that would tide them over until he could find a new job, a better job. Stupid, he knew now.

Stupid he knew then, really. But his stupidity had been no match for that anger and jealously.

What really stung, though, was the depth of his own cowardice. He'd allowed Alissa to deal with the consequences of his actions by letting her go into work the next day unaware of what he'd done. Then he'd simply denied having done it. Had brushed it off as though Alissa was a crazed fantasist for even thinking such a thing. She been blindsided by her own boyfriend's deviousness and paid the price; first with the job she loved, then with something much more precious.

Then he'd run.

The train rolled on, clattering through the grimy, built-up suburbs of outer London before slicing through the countryside of south-east Essex's green fields and golf courses, all the while tracing a line parallel with the Thames estuary as it wound its way out of the big city and towards the North Sea.

The gentle motion rocked Craig into something of a trance, speeding him backwards in time as it carried him forward in space. He thought of the turn of fate he could never have anticipated; that Lewis Maynard-Jones could be capable of committing murder to keep his marriage and his reputation intact. Craig knew it was he who should have paid the price for his own hasty actions, him who should be in the ground. Everything that had happened was because of what he had done and, though he didn't yet know how, he knew he had to try to make it right.

The expanse of green fields morphed into a stretch of a slate grey water as, to his right, the estuary and the train's path came together. Small boats, some that looked to have been abandoned for years to rot into the sea, others with freshly applied coats of paint, dotted the marina at Old Leigh. Stalls selling fresh fish, crab and cockles were scattered between the handful of pubs that lined the cobbled street below him. He was nearly there and, less than ten minutes later, the Tannoy announcement told Craig that he had arrived at Southend Central station.

He waited until the last minute to get off, the *beep-beep-beep* of the sliding doors warning him it was now or never. On the platform he hung back, watching, waiting for the other passengers to move ahead. He wanted to have a clear path in case he needed to run.

He wondered if he was being paranoid. There was no way Maynard-Jones could know he was coming back on this particular train. But he'd used his debit card, had needed money for a ticket, for the charger, and for food. Who knew whether that simple action could tip Maynard-Jones off?

He'd watched the films and TV shows that showed how easy it was to track digital transactions. Whether that was true to life or not, he guessed he'd find out soon enough.

As the harried parents and elderly day-trippers cleared the platform Craig prepared to leave the safety of the station and head into town. Before he did so he felt a vibration in his pocket and automatically reached for his phone. There was a text message from a number he didn't recognise.

I know what Lewis did. I'm so sorry. You don't deserve this. Where are you? We need to meet. Carol deserves more. So do you, and I know how to get it.

Craig stared at the message, reading and re-reading it. There was no indication of who it was from but it read like it had been sent by someone other than Lewis. '*I know what Lewis did.*' Were they talking about the video of Lewis and Francesca, or about Alissa's murder?

Craig's finger's hovered over the screen, itching to tap out a reply, to ask for more clarity, more information. But he held back. This required careful consideration, not a rushed response.

Distracted, he meandered towards the ticket barrier and out of the station. An elderly woman was at the bottom of the steps, struggling with a wheelie-bag. He momentarily forgot his wariness and, instead, went to help, carrying the bag to the top of the stairs.

When he reached the bottom step again, his mind still mulling over the text message, a man appeared next to him, as if from nowhere.

'My name's Abraham,' the man said. 'I'm a friend of Carol's. I need your help.'

***

Despite being dressed like he was about to start the Couch to 5K Abraham hadn't taken any physical exercise for some time, his promised running regime yet to gather momentum. As he approached Craig Atherton he sorely hoped he wouldn't need to start it now.

The young man jumped as Abraham spoke his name, a jolt of something - shock, fear, inevitability - streaming through his body. Abraham saw Craig's body tense, muscles contracting, as if ready to stream away as fast as his thin frame would carry him.

But something stopped him.

Now, sat in the red Punto, which Abraham had tucked into a corner of a car park close by, on Royal Mews, Craig told him why.

'You just don't look threatening, do you? You actually look like one of them old white rappers from… what's it called? The Beastie Boys.'

Abraham wasn't sure whether to be honoured or offended.

'So, you're telling me Lewis Maynard-Jones is dead?' said Craig.

'I am,' confirmed Abraham.

'Who killed him?'

Abraham hadn't divulged to Craig that, in all likelihood, the prime suspect was sitting next to him. He didn't want to spook him any more than he already was. He had, however, revealed that he'd been nearby when the murder was committed. 'I saw someone leaving the house,' he said. 'Wiry looking, thin face, dark eyes. He was dressed like a workman, a labourer or something. Does that ring any bells?'

'Sounds like my neighbour. Guy called Matt Hallstaff.'

'No,' replied Abraham. 'We've met. It wasn't him.'

'Then I've no idea. But this doesn't mean Lewis didn't kill Alissa, does it? I mean, I saw him.'

Abraham whipped his head round to face his passenger. 'You saw him? When?'

'I was meant to be on a stag do. Well, *was* on a stag do. But I felt terrible about what I'd done. How I'd lied to Al, got her fired. I fucked up. Big time. So, I told the boys I was ill. Schlepped back early and arrived Saturday evening. Didn't tell Al in case she left the flat or told me to do one. Wanted to speak to her, apologise properly. When I arrived at the building though, I saw him parked in a Range Rover outside. The racing green one that Al'd mentioned a few times. Tricked up thing. Overfinch, you know?'

Abraham didn't know, but nodded nonetheless, wanting Craig to continue.

'Killed me, it did.' Craig's cheeks flushed red, and he turned to face Abraham. 'Sorry, I didn't mean… bad choice of words. I just mean, well, he's a playboy type, right, that Lewis? Or was, I suppose. Reckoned Al had been in touch with him, begged for her job or whatever, told him me and Al were done, and he'd come rushing round to, you know, console her. But he didn't console her, did he? Instead, he – ' Craig buried his face in his hands again. Abraham didn't think he was crying, more that the situation was too much for him and it was easier to try to hide from it.

'What time was this?'

'Somewhere around seven-ish. The trains were delayed at Fenchurch, so it took me a lot longer to get home.'

'And you actually saw Lewis Maynard-Jones at your flat the day Alissa was killed.'

Craig sat back up, then slumped down in the seat again. 'Well, no. I didn't see him as such, but it's his car. Alissa worked for him. Who else would it be? I wasn't going to hang around to see the smug grin on his face after he'd been with my girlfriend. I mean, if I'd have known what he was really doing, that Alissa was about to… Christ! I should have just gone up there, shouldn't I? If I had, maybe she'd still be alive. Maybe none of this would have happened.'

'It's not your fault,' said Abraham, trying to give some comfort, hearing echoes of his dad's voice in his own words.

'Course it is!' shouted Craig. 'I sent that video, didn't I? I started this whole thing off. Who else is to blame?'

'Whoever killed Alissa.'

Craig gave another snorted laugh. 'Thought you said you didn't think she'd been killed at all.'

And he hadn't. As they'd driven from the station Abraham had relayed how Carol had got him involved, and how he'd been sceptical from the start that this was anything more than a young girl making a terrible mistake. 'You're right,' he replied. 'I did think that. But a lot's happened since then. Even what you're saying now doesn't necessarily mean Alissa was murdered. There's no proof, not yet. And why would Lewis risk everything by killing Alissa? There's so much more at stake with a murder than with an infidelity.'

'Yeah, well, men are stupid, I think we've established that.'

Abraham ignored the comment and continued, talking more to himself than to Craig. 'But then why was

Lewis killed? And why was my brother attacked? It all hinges on this video. It's got to. You still have it, you said.'

Craig nodded. 'Look, there's something you need to know. I tried again. To blackmail Maynard-Jones. I know it's wrong, but I just thought, Alissa's dead, he deserves to be punished. And the only way of doing that to people like him is through their wallet. But now, well, he's not going to pay up, is he?'

'I understand, Craig, I do. But I'm afraid you're not getting anything out of Lewis Maynard-Jones now.'

'Maybe this other person will help though.'

Abraham gave Craig a quizzical stare.

Craig pulled out his phone and showed Abraham the text he'd received.

'And you've no idea who this might be from?' Abraham asked a minute later.

Craig shrugged. 'The girl? From the video?'

'Francesca?'

'Should I meet with them? Would you come with me?'

'I'm not sure if it's a good idea to meet with anyone you don't know, not after all that's happened.'

'You think it could be the person who killed Lewis?'

It was Abraham's turn to shrug. 'None of this is making any sense at the moment. Look, can you show me the video, please. I'm hoping that might help shed some light.'

'I don't see how. It's a film of two people screwing. That's it.'

'Maybe something was missed,' Abraham, said, in hope more than expectation.

For the third time in quick succession, Craig shrugged. 'Unless they're heavy-breathing in morse code, I doubt it,' he said, before pressing some buttons on the screen and handing the phone to Abraham, who then watched as Lewis and Francesca unknowingly played out their sex life on camera.

It was a damning piece of evidence if it did get into the wrong hands. But Abraham couldn't help thinking they were missing something. Infidelity happened all too often, but rarely did it result in murder or, in this case, murders. When the video finished playing and went black, he dragged the player to the start and watched again.

'Anything?' asked Craig.

'No, not in the video, not that I can see.'

'Told you.'

'But,' said Abraham, still staring at the screen, the footage lasts for, what, a few minutes, so why does the play bar indicate there's another nearly three hours of the film to play?'

'Al said the phone was propped up to record a spider's web or something. For her showreel, she said. She reckoned the phone fell over, something knocked it, or it just slipped. Landed lens down and just started filming the shelf it was resting on. It's all just black. I've dragged the player along the whole thing and there're no other pictures on there. You can hear those two for a couple of minutes, then that's it.'

'Have you watched the video the entire way through?'

'Well, no. Told you, there's nothing on it. I've scrubbed through, it's just black.'

283

Abraham began double tapping on the screen, knocking the player on by ten seconds each time he did so, letting it play for a second or two each time before double-tapping again.

'What're you doing?' asked Craig.

'There's got to something else.'

'There's not. I told you, it's just a black screen.'

Abraham continued to double tap while Craig looked on, shaking his head slowly. 'It'll take you ages.'

And it did.

They sat in the car park, Craig nervously looking out of the window, scanning the passers-by as Abraham stared intently at the black screen, the index finger of his right hand rhythmically tapping the glass every few seconds.

After thirty-five minutes of tapping, the play bar was showing that 160 minutes of video had been watched and Abraham was starting to believe this was a waste of time. But, when he double tapped the screen again, instead of black and silence, there was black and sound.

Abraham's body stiffened, his finger now hovering over the screen, waiting. He cocked an ear towards the small speaker and closed his eyes. There was an indistinct sound, like nails being dragged along a blackboard. He continued listening, eyes still shut.

'Chairs,' he finally said.

'What?' replied Craig.

'It's chairs being pulled out from a table.'

Abraham tapped the screen again, taking the video back by thirty seconds. He let it play once more. For three seconds there was silence, then he heard a voice he recognised.

Thirty-eight

While an unbiased outlook and a broad-minded approach was needed for any investigation, DI Martin Palmer put those things aside and looked forward to placing the cuffs on Abraham Hart's wrists. The evidence meant he was their number one suspect and the joy he would feel at finally having the upper hand on him was undeniable.

Hart had been a pain in the arse since that whole business with the photos. While Palmer still felt a tinge of apprehension at what a cornered animal might do with those images if he were able, the thought of Hart bundled into a van and surrounded by officers was a salve to such concerns.

A smile played on his lips as he pictured the scenario but, despite his attempts to ignore them, his copper's instincts were telling him to be careful that he wasn't letting fanciful thoughts get in the way of facts.

'Right, what we got?' Palmer said to a uniformed officer called Cumming who had been dispatched to Southend's two train stations soon after Lewis Maynard-Jones' body had been found.

'Gentleman at the ticket barrier at Southend Central said he recognised Hart from the photo I showed him. Said he remembered him because he saw him get off a train a few days ago, "pissed", in his words.'

'Annoyed?' asked Palmer.

'Drunk,' Cumming answered, holding the photo of Abraham which had been hastily printed at the police station and handed out to officers who had been instructed to head to train stations, bus depots and taxi ranks in the area in case their suspect had attempted to flee the city.

The photo had been taken from a recent byline image in *The Chronicle* because, according to Jacob Hart, no photos of Abraham existed in the rectory. Palmer didn't have the time or the energy to argue so had asked one of his team to source the most recent image they could find.

Palmer thought he'd sent his officers on a wild goose chase, more because people were so unobservant than because Hart was unlikely to go to any of those places. Happily, something was going right for a change.

Cumming led Palmer to a small yellow booth next to the ticket barriers. Stepping inside the tiny space Palmer sniffed the air and wondered if the booth had recently been set on fire. A middle-aged man with hair almost as grey as his skin was sitting on a stool. He was wearing a high-visibility jacket, and his bony fingers were playing with a half empty packet of Benson & Hedges, which likely meant the odour was less about the booth and more about its occupant.

Cumming introduced his DI to the grey man, whose name was Ken, and Ken gave a sullen nod.

'You sure it was this man?' asked Palmer, waving the photocopy in front of him.

'Yep. Never forget a face, me. All I bloody do all day, stare at faces.'

'When was this?'

Ken instinctively looked at his watch, then shrugged. ''Bout thirty, maybe forty minutes ago.'

Palmer gritted his teeth in frustration at such a close call. 'Where did he go?'

'How am I supposed to know?'

Palmer screwed his eyes closed and tipped his head back, mentally counting to ten. He got to two-and-a-half. 'I don't need a bloody address, do I? I mean, which way did he go? Towards London, I'm assuming. And did he buy a ticket and, if he did, to where?'

Ken, who now had an unlit cigarette between the fingers of his right hand, looked at Palmer as if he'd asked for the meaning of life; nose wrinkled, brow furrowed. 'He didn't get on a train.'

Palmer turned to Cumming as if he might provide an answer, but Cumming just shrugged.

'He was in a car, out front,' Ken went on. 'A red Fiat if memory serves. Was having a fag, wasn't I. Saw him just sitting there. Assumed he was waiting for someone.'

Palmer closed his eyes again and hoped. 'Did you happen to get the registration of the car?'

A Bic lighter had appeared in Ken's other hand. 'Nah, sorry.'

It's the hope that kills you, Palmer thought, cheerlessly.

'But the CCTV should have picked it up,' Ken went on, already standing, indicating that it was well past time to light up. 'Covers the whole of the front of the station,' he added.

Palmer clenched a fist in silent celebration. The hope hadn't got him just yet, and he told Ken his fag break would have to wait because they needed to see that CCTV right now.

'Thank for coming so late, David. I'm sure you've got better things to be doing on a Thursday night, but I really do need to speak to you.'

It was definitely Lewis Maynard-Jones speaking. Abraham recognised the clipped vowels and slight air of superiority in the voice.

'Not a problem. Always here to help, you know that.'

David Catton, Abraham assumed. He sounded older, and had a nasal voice that, for some reason, made Abraham picture a man in a suit, pens in his top pocket, pushing spectacles up on the bridge of his nose. Abraham remembered Lewis's wife mentioning him when they'd met at Spotlight. Finance, or something. Maybe that explained the stereotypical mental picture.

There was more scrapping of chairs and Lewis offering David a drink, which he politely declined. Then the sound of liquid being poured. Abraham looked at Craig who was, like him, staring at the dark screen of the phone, absorbed by the sound coming out of it, both momentarily ignoring the world outside the car.

'So, Lewis, what can I do for you?'

Lewis cleared his throat for a few seconds. Abraham recognised it for what it was; nerves.

'It's the money, David.'

'The money?'

'For the film.'

'The film.' There was an undertone of weariness to David's two-word reply, and Abraham got the sense that this wasn't the first time Lewis and David had spoken about this topic.

'You all told me, when this business was started, that my feature script was all but green-lit. That it was my... my bonus, if you like. That, after everything I've done,

that would be the least you could do. It's ready, David. It's been ready for months. Years, really. But every fucking penny that comes through the front door here, goes straight out the back one. When's it my turn?'

Abraham heard someone, he assumed David, take in a breath.

'Lewis,' David was saying, patiently, as if talking to a child. *'There is no "turn". This is a business, and decisions are made based on what's best for that business. You know that. The finances are always a tricky balance. We have to make sure we're serving our shareholder to the best of our ability.'*

Lewis laughed. It was more a snort of derision. Abraham thought he heard him taking a large gulp of whatever drink he had made himself. A betting man would put money on it not being tea.

'Shareholder? Oh, come off it, David. You don't have to keep the act up with me. There's fucking millions coming through here. Millions. And this is one business out of, what, tens? Scores? I just need five mill to make it all happen. I'm a director, David. An artist. I didn't sign up to babysit someone else's money. I've had enough! I want to make my film.'

'You need to talk to your wife, Lewis.'

There was a loud bang, like someone had slammed a fist on the table.

'Oh, fuck my wife. I need to talk to Hristo.'

At the mention of that name, Abraham felt his blood freezing, sensed the hairs on his arms standing up.

He'd spent the last few years hearing it mentioned in passing; at first just whispers here, off the record conversations there. That name was akin to the bogeyman, one people were scared to utter for fear of reprisal. It was only after the police had opened an investigation, brought about mainly due to the information supplied by Mariana Nikolova, that it began to seep into the open, was cast around in the wider world, some of its power now excised.

There were plenty of people called Hristo, but there was no doubt in Abraham's mind that this was the same Hristo that had walked free from court two days earlier. The same one who presided over a drug trafficking empire the tentacles of which spread through most of London and leached into the southeast of England. The sound of that name meant that things began clicking into place, but it also caused panic to circulate around Abraham's body.

He wasn't the only one panicking.

'Lewis,' David hissed. *'We don't discuss our shareholder, you know that. Not ever.'*

'Why the hell not? He's not fucking Voldemort. He's treating me like an idiot. This is my life we're talking about, David. This is my company. Hristo Nikolova owes me. And if he doesn't pay up then, well, maybe more people should know who our so-called shareholder is. Then let's see how much good all his drug money coming through here does him.'

Abraham didn't need the confirmation of Hristo's last name, but knew it was even more damning to have it said out loud. Said out loud and recorded. There was no instant response from David. No sound at all, in fact. In Abraham's mind's eye he saw the two men looking at each other. One shocked at what had just been said to him, the other shocked at having said it.

A few silent seconds ticked by, seconds heavy with apprehension. Then, in one of the men, that shock turned to contrition.

'Look, David, I'm sorry. I didn't mean that, obviously. But, come on, I deserve this, don't you think? I've done everything he's asked, that everyone's asked. I was promised that if—'

And then the recording stopped. Abraham tapped the screen and saw the play bar had reached the end. He assumed the phone had run out of battery. It was the only thing that made sense because if either David or Lewis had found the device then none of this would have happened. Alissa wouldn't have picked up the phone and Craig wouldn't have inadvertently tried to blackmail a man about an affair, not knowing he had something far more explosive to barter with.

Abraham looked at Craig who had, like him, been mesmerised for the duration of the recording. 'Who's Hristo Nikolova?' he asked.

'He's why this video is far more important than a married man's sordid fling with a girl half his age. He's why Alissa and Lewis Maynard-Jones are both dead. And he's why we need to be incredibly careful about what we do next.'

Thirty-nine

Hristo was at his desk, a tumbler holding three fingers of Hennessy resting on a coaster beside him, two ice cubes swimming in the golden liquid. He had not left the confines of his Hampstead house since arriving back there.

He had busied himself with work; phone calls and emails that went some way to resetting in motion the wheels of his business, wheels that had slowed to a crawl over the last few months. He had consulted solicitors, spoken to accountants and contacted suppliers using various phones and multiple SIM cards, many of which were now floating somewhere in London's vast network of sewers.

There was also the matter of Mariana's family. She had not seen her parents for many years, cutting herself off from them as soon as she'd met Hristo, as he had wished but had not expressed in so many words. He had sent a heartfelt letter to Mariana's father expressing his sadness at her leaving him and pledging to do everything to find her and bring her home. He had also included a cheque for $50,000. He knew he would not hear from him again.

Family was important. It grounded people in their past and gave them focus and hope for the future. That Mariana had so easily shaken off her parents when life with Hristo was an option had always disappointed him. It was a life far different from the one her parents were able to offer and, even though her estrangement from them was what he needed from her, he had also wanted his wife to be stronger. Mariana had been beautiful and attentive, but strength had not been part of her character.

Hristo took a sip of his drink. His mind, usually so focussed, was distracted. The court case and the developments surrounding it had preoccupied him for months and had impacted the business. Suppliers were wary and distribution had been disrupted, meaning stock had been depleted across the network.

Crucially, he had also not been present to oversee the management of profits. 'Give them an inch…' was a phrase he had picked up from David Catton, one he had always remembered. He needed to be on top of everything, but the situation with Spotlight had meant his focus was still wavering. He afforded himself a wry smile; he had spent a life attempting to avoid the spotlight, and now that very thing was causing him problems.

Erjon had never let him down before and he felt confident he wouldn't fail him now, but things had already slipped. The police were involved now, and this video could prove to be very damaging to both the business and to Hristo personally. Things weren't being resolved quickly enough. From the desk he picked up one of his mobile phones and dialled a number which was answered after two rings.

'It's me,' said Hristo. 'Are you ok? Have you spoken to Erjon?'

'Ok's not the word I would use, no. Things are difficult, but they'll be resolved. And no, I haven't spoken to Erjon.'

'But you've seen the video?'

'Yes. I'd rather you didn't see it, but I'll send it to you if you wish?'

'No, it's not necessary. David told me what was on it. It's important we deal with this. There can be no traces of it.'

'I know, but what can I do? This boyfriend, Atherton, has disappeared, and now the journalist is sniffing around. You should have let Erjon take care of him when we had the chance.'

'We always have the chance, it's just choosing when to take it. Erjon has been instructed to take the necessary steps, and I know you'll do what you must to find the boyfriend.'

'And if I do?'

'When you do,' replied Hristo, putting the emphasis on the first word, 'then I think we both know what needs to be done to protect ourselves. To protect our business. Keep me informed and don't forget, Diellza, I trust you and I love you.'

Hristo killed the call and took and sip of his drink, enjoying the warmth as it travelled down his throat. He had trust that others could contain this situation, but he also began to wonder if it wasn't something that required the personal touch.

***

Abraham knew that ditching the car was probably in his best interests if he wanted to remain out of police custody, but he didn't have another vehicle and knew that public transport would be too slow and taxis too risky. That meant keeping the bright red Punto for the foreseeable future and hoping that no one they drove past paid any attention.

He had swapped seats with Craig, who now steered the car through the quiet streets of Southend while he fished around inside his wallet for the business card he had picked up at Spotlight. When he found it, he asked to borrow Craig's phone.

The card had both the Maynard-Jones's number on it, labelled as Co-Founders. Beneath their details. In a slightly smaller font, Francesca Newsome's name and number was printed next to the words Executive Assistant. He assumed Francesca's and his wife's contact details were why Lewis hadn't wanted to give him a business card when he'd asked for one.

Abraham dialled.

'Oh, hello, is that Francesca?' he said when someone picked up.

'Yes,' said the voice on the other end of the line, the word elongated, the tone wary.

'We met yesterday, at Spotlight. It's Abraham Hart. Mr Maynard-Jones gave me your number and said to get in touch with you. I'm looking into Alissa's death. Would it be ok to meet?'

Abraham took a chance that Francesca didn't yet know that her boss - her lover - was dead. The murder had only taken place a few hours ago and while she would be someone the police would want to talk to, he hoped they hadn't got around to it yet. He felt guilty about the subterfuge but needed information and, as subterfuge went, she was no amateur herself.

'He did?' questioned Francesca. 'About what?'

'Oh, just Alissa's state of mind at the time. How she seemed. He wants to find out what made her do such a terrible thing. He's a very caring man, don't you think?'

There was a pause. Abraham wondered if he'd laid it on too thick and was about to try a different approach.

'He is, yes,' Francesca finally said. 'Well, if that's what Lewis wants. Shall I give you my address?'

'Actually,' said Abraham, 'could we meet at the Spotlight office? I had questions about some of the projects Alissa was working on and Lewis said you would be able to help.'

Another pause. 'And Lewis said that was ok?'

'Of course,' replied Abraham. 'Obviously you're welcome to call to check with him.'

It was a low blow, and a risky one. It was unlikely anyone would answer Lewis's phone but, if they did, odds on it would be a police officer who would either tell Francesca outright what had happened or raise enough suspicion for her to find out herself.

Abraham held his breath.

'Ok, well, I don't live far from the office so can be there in maybe thirty minutes.'

'Perfect,' said Abraham, giving a thumbs up to Craig in the process and then, before ending the call. 'I'll meet you there.'

Something Abraham hadn't considered was Francesca talking to the police when she tried to call Lewis, then relaying to whomever answered that she had planned to meet Abraham Hart who, unbeknownst to her, was a suspect in the death of the man she had been sleeping with. The thought only served to ramp up his nerves.

Ten minutes after the hanging up on Francesca, Craig parked the car one hundred yards away from the Spotlight office. They waited, watching the building, Abraham alert to any sign of police presence. It was inevitable they would arrive at some point, Lewis's place of work would be a key part of the investigation, it was just a case of when.

After twenty minutes he cautiously walked from the car to the office, his too-big tracksuit and box fresh trainers making him feel incredibly self-conscious.

At the locked door Abraham shuffled around trying - and failing - not to look suspicious until a voice behind him made him freeze.

'Mr Hart?'

Abraham turned to see the long, dark hair and puzzled frown of Francesca Newsome, who was looking him up and down, obviously slightly perplexed to see such a change in attire from the previous day.

'Ah, Miss Newsome. Francesca. May I call you Francesca? Please, call me Abraham.'

Abraham realised he was babbling. 'This,' he added, indicating his somewhat unusual attire. 'Sunday's usually gym day. Headed there after this.'

The young woman nodded slowly. 'Looks like it's working, whatever you're doing. Might need a smaller tracksuit.'

Abraham laughed theatrically and checked up and down the street as Francesca slid the key into the door, stepped inside the office and disarmed the alarm.

Fifteen minutes later, sat in front of a computer at one of the workstations, Abraham was looking through a pile of invoices while the paused frame of a video stared out from a laptop screen. The office was cold and quiet.

There was no mess, no personal touches on the desks, no posters on the walls. It was like a film set, Abraham thought, an approximation of an office.

'So, let me get this straight,' Abraham said to Francesca, who was sat in an office chair next to him. 'You've never met any other members of staff in the time you've been employed, which is…'

'Two-and-a-half years,' replied Francesca. 'No. Well, obviously there's Mr and Mrs Maynard-Jones. And David, the finance guy. And Alissa, of course. But, yeah, everyone else is always away on shoots or location recces or in the edit or whatever.'

'And these invoices,' continued Abraham, flicking through the stack of paper in front of him, 'they come from the clients you work with?'

'Yeah. David deals with most of this stuff, I just file it away.'

'And you've never thought there was something odd about the invoices compared to the work Spotlight makes?'

Francesca looked at him with that puzzled expression again.

'It's just, these amounts are huge,' continued Abraham, leafing through the papers. 'Half-a-million. Eight-hundred thousand. Two-point-three million.'

'We're a successful business,' said Francesca, sounding proud rather than defensive.

'But I've never heard of any of these companies you've made work for. ANR Global Reach, Menenzie Multinational, Caspian McCarthy Incorporated. Who are they?'

'Most of the work we do comes from overseas conglomerates.'

'But what about the work itself, Francesca?'

'What do you mean?'

Abraham turned to the laptop and hit the space bar, unpausing the video and allowing it to play. They both watched the screen as an attractive woman, who was standing next to some large metal shelving units in what looked like a warehouse, smiled vibrantly and continued a speech she had been in the middle of when Abraham had paused the video. She spoke about the dangers of climbing the units without the aid of some steps, which where wheeled into frame by an unseen hand the moment she mentioned them. She lectured on the proper way to pick up a heavy object, demonstrating how to bend from the knees. She showed how to apply the handbrake to the wheeled steps so that they didn't move when used.

She was in the middle of recounting why steel-toed boots were the best option of footwear when Abraham tapped the space bar again and looked at Francesca, who stared back at him blankly. 'It's a demonstration video,' Abraham finally said. 'A safety briefing.'

Not for the first time Francesca eyebrows adopted a position of bemusement. 'So?' she said.

'I've watched a few of the things Spotlight has made,' Abraham explained. 'And for different clients. They're all pretty much the same. Some even have the same actress in them.'

Francesca, now tapping away on her phone, was starting to look bored. 'And your point is?'

'Why do you need people visiting far-flung parts of the world for location recces when all the videos I've seen are either shot in a studio or in a warehouse? Why do you need to pay a visual effects company who, by the way, I can't find online anywhere, £100,000 for "post production assistance" when all I can see is a logo bouncing around at the start of the video like a 90s screensaver? In short, Francesca, why do you need to spend more than two million quid on something that looks like it's shot on an old VHS camcorder?'

Francesca pulled a face that indicated Abraham was an imbecile who spoke a form of gibberish.

When she answered, she said. 'What the hell's a camcorder? Actually, you know what, don't worry, we can ask Lewis when he gets here.'

It was now Abraham's turn to pull a face. 'Lewis?'

Francesca rolled her eyes, done with the pretence of playing nice. 'Yes. You know, the man who owns the company. I texted him after you first called. He's just replied.'

'Lewis?' repeated Abraham, unsure what else to say.

Francesca ignored him and carried on where she'd left off. 'Said he was on his way and that we should both stay here till he arrives.'

Before Francesca had finished the sentence Abraham was out of his seat and running for the door, a clutch of the invoices still in his hands.

'Hey!' shouted Francesca. 'You can't take them with you!'

Abraham ignored her and kept moving, praying that the police had only just replied to Francesca's text message because they'd only just seen it. He knew it had to be the police because who else would have Lewis's phone? They were monitoring it and would be on their way here now. If they weren't here already.

He reached the office door and wrapped his fingers around the handle, closing his eyes as he yanked it open, once again offering a silent prayer to an imaginary god that the police weren't waiting outside.

Forty

Erjon cursed under his breath. It was unusual for him to swear but being ten seconds too late, it seemed an appropriate response.

He watched Abraham Hart careen out of the office then sprint to a red Fiat, where he pulled open the door and jumped in. A man was sat in the driver's seat and the car pulled away before the passenger door was closed. A young woman then appeared at the office door shouting something indistinct in the departing car's direction.

Erjon saw all of this from the back seat of a taxi which was driving past the Spotlight office. The driver, an overweight man with a greying beard and a musty odour, took no notice of these events. It was likely he took little notice of anything, but Erjon didn't want to take that risk. He could have asked the driver to follow the red Fiat. It wasn't the embarrassment of uttering such a cliche that dissuaded him from doing so, but the likelihood that the driver, however unobservant, would remember such a detail and, somewhere down the line, remember Erjon too.

Instead, the driver dropped him off at the nearby bookmakers, as he had originally instructed. The reason he was in a taxi headed to Spotlight was because Diellza had phoned him and, in a call that lasted less than ten seconds, told him where to find Abraham Hart.

Erjon was grateful for the assistance because he had no leads on either Hart or the boyfriend and was beginning to taste the bitter tang of something he rarely experienced, failure.

The usual sources had been unable to supply information on either Hart or Craig Atherton's whereabouts. The pair had so far evaded the network of Southend's underbelly that Hristo - and by extension, Erjon - had access to. Southend police, of which at least one was able to go on expensive summer vacations because of Hristo's generosity, had also been ineffective.

Disappearing into thin air was Erjon's own trick so he was begrudgingly respectful of both men's ability to remain undetected. But maybe, he thought, advancing on the shabby building, this girl knew something.

***

'What happened?' asked Craig, his knuckles white on the wheel and his neck craned forward, almost touching the windscreen, as the car sped down the London Road, towards Southend.

Abraham was breathing heavily and had slunk down low as if he wanted to slide not just out of the car, but out of this whole situation. 'Jesus! Slow down,' he said. 'The last thing we need is to be pulled over.'

'Why?'

'Why what?' asked Abraham.

'Why is being pulled over the last thing we need? Maybe the police are exactly who we should be talking to. It's who I should have contacted ages ago.'

Abraham still didn't think it was a good idea to tell Craig he was ferrying around someone the police were likely scouring the city to find and, until he had found a way to identify the man who had killed Lewis Maynard-Jones, he didn't want to trust his fate to a police force that had taken the easy option and, too quickly, written off Alissa's death as suicide.

'There's something much bigger going on here,' relied Abraham. 'Like I said before, we need to be careful.'

'What did you find out from Francesca?' asked Craig, easing his foot off the accelerator.

'It just confirmed what I suspected,' answered Abraham. 'Spotlight's a laundry service.'

'A what?'

'The company's washing millions of pounds of profits from Nikolova's drug business, processing it through what must be a fleet of shell companies associated with filmmaking; location services, equipment hire, visual effect companies. I think their so-called clients are all fake and Spotlight's paying millions to these dummy corporations and getting nothing from them in return. The films they're making, the adverts and corporate videos, they're no better than you or I could make on our phones with some free software downloads. It's all a front.'

'But what about Alissa's job? Or Francesca's?'

'I think Lewis Maynard-Jones just liked having pretty young women around, and it probably made the company seem legit to anyone from the outside looking in. Spotlight was just window dressing.'

'And Lewis?' asked a confused Craig.

'He obviously knew what was happening. We know that from the recording. It wasn't the sex tape he was worried about. Or, not only that. He mentioned Hristo

Nikolova by name, talked about drug money in the same sentence. That would have got everyone worried.'

'Enough to get him killed?'

'Evidently.'

'Jesus. But why kill Alissa? She didn't do anything. She didn't even hear the recording of Lewis talking to that other guy, David whatshisname.'

Abraham had to tread carefully. Despite his obvious remorse for what he had done, Craig had still set the wheels in motion for what had happened and, while he thought Craig must already know this, he didn't want to compound it. For one thing, Abraham needed him.

'Catton,' he replied. 'David Catton. He's obviously in on it too, but they didn't know she hadn't heard it. They're cleaning house.'

Abraham saw Craig's face twitch in reaction to Abraham's words, the stab of guilt sending slivers of pain through his body. His next words came in a broken voice that was close to tears. 'You think the same person who killed Lewis killed Alissa?'

'I don't know, but it stands to reason.'

'What about Mrs Maynard-Jones?'

Abraham shrugged. 'Don't know that either. I met her briefly. She seemed more worried about the office decor than the state of the business. Said she was a non-executive director, not involved in the day-to-day running of the company. Might have nothing to do with any of it.'

'Yeah,' said Craig, still steering the car through the light afternoon traffic. 'But she must know Catton, so maybe she knows where we can find him.'

Abraham was already weighing up the odds of contacting a recently murdered man's widow. Her number was on the business card, but it wasn't her recently widowed status which caused him to think twice about such a call - he had, for better for worse, doorstopped more than a few grieving families in his time as a reporter. He was more worried that contacting her would alert the police and end with him no longer free to do any more digging.

'You call her,' said Abraham.

Craig almost swerved the car into oncoming traffic as he whipped his head to look at Abraham. 'Me? Why the hell would she talk to me?'

'Why wouldn't she? You're the boyfriend of a recently deceased employee.'

'Alissa. Her name was Alissa,' Craig replied.

Abraham held up his palms in a placatory gesture. 'I know, I'm sorry. All I mean is that she should have sympathy, empathy even, after what's recently happened. When we met she seemed genuinely upset at what happened to Alissa. She might want to help.'

Craig looked unsure. 'She's not likely to answer anyway, is she? She's just lost her husband. Probably in with the police or something.'

Abraham nodded. 'True. But if we don't try…'.

Craig, his full attention back on the road, shook his head slowly, but said, 'I'll find somewhere to pull over.'

***

The door bounced off Erjon's boot a second before the bolt reached the safety of the latch. Francesca was startled by the abrupt obstruction and almost lost her footing, banging her shoulder against the now stationary door. When she realised that the blockage was a black boot belonging to an unsmiling man who had raised an index finger to his lips, Francesca used all of her strength in an attempt to force the door closed.

But it was too late.

Checking no one was watching, Erjon pushed his way into the office as Francesca reeled away from the front door and stumbled toward the rear of the building. He followed her inside, closed and locked the door then tracked the sound of panicked breathing to a back office where he found Francesca desperately moving heavy box files away from an emergency exit.

As he stood over the terrified young girl a section of Erjon's brain wondered why this job in particular had seen him abandon his usual caution and diligence.

Time was of the essence he knew but even so, attacking the priest, killing Maynard-Jones, hurrying after the journalist and, now, brazenly advancing on someone who may or may not be of any use to him was outside the usual strictures he set himself.

Am I getting lazy? Erjon wondered to himself. *Bored?*

This uncommon introspection was interrupted as Erjon watched the young girl, her face creased into a mask of fear, suck in a deep breath and ready a scream.

Without thinking, Erjon jabbed a right hand at her face and, before the intake of breath had been completed, she was a rag doll on the cheap laminated floor, eyes staring at the ceiling, a dark halo of hair splayed around her head, and blood trickling from a porcelain nose that would never again be perfect.

For the second time Erjon swore under his breath, wondering how long it would take her to come to.

Forty-one

Still wary of being seen by a passing patrol car, Abraham instructed Craig to pull into The Royals Shopping Centre multi-storey car park at the bottom of Southend's main shopping street.

It was busy with Sunday shoppers laden with bags and bored looking kids, but there were more vehicles coming out than going in, so it wasn't hard to find a space. They pulled in, nose first, between two other cars; hiding, Abraham hoped, in plain sight.

They had discussed the upcoming call on the drive over and, though Craig was nervous, they both agreed this was the best - probably the only - way to get to David Catton. Abraham typed the number into his phone, put it on speaker and gave it to Craig.

'She's not going to answer,' said Craig. 'Why would she?'

'Let's just see.'

After four rings Craig gave Abraham an 'I told you so' look, but that look quickly changed as the ringing stopped and a voice came on the line, terse and impatient, 'What?'

Craig looked at Abraham who widened his eyes and swirled his index finger in the air, indicating he should speak.

'Oh, er, hello. Is that Mrs Maynard-Jones?'

There was a pause, and both men thought the line would go dead. 'Who is this?'

'You don't know me. My name is Craig, Craig Atherton. I was Alissa's boyfriend, the girl who died. She worked for your husband's company. For your company, I suppose.'

Another pause, longer this time. Abraham wondered if she was alone or was still with the police, whether she was relaying to them who was on the phone.

'Hello?' said Craig. 'Are you still there?'

'Yes, I'm here,' came the reply, softer now, less brusque. 'If you want to speak to Lewis, to my husband, I'm afraid that won't be possible.'

The two men heard the woman's voice crack, small, heart-rending sobs travelling down the line. Craig grimaced at Abraham, his conviction that this was the right thing to do wavering.

Abraham widened his eyes again. Twirled a finger.

'Is everything ok?' asked Craig, stalling for time.

A sombre laugh. 'No. I'm afraid not. Lewis is dead. Murdered.'

Craig did his best to feign surprise. 'Oh my God! I'm so sorry. What happened?'

'A burglary gone wrong, the police think. Whoever did this, they dropped a lock pick set.'

'I'm sorry for your loss,' said Craig. 'I know how difficult it is.'

'Your girlfriend wasn't murdered!' snapped Ellie Maynard-Jones, the curtness returning.

'Actually, I'm not sure that's true,' said Craig.

Another pause. Abraham and Craig could hear breathing, slow and deep. 'What are you talking about?'

'I think Alissa *was* murdered,' said Craig. 'I think there's something going on at your company. Something that got Alissa killed.'

'Are you talking about that disguising video of my husband with that tramp on reception? You're not insinuating that my husband had anything to do with Alissa's death, surely?'

Craig looked at Abraham, who shook his head emphatically. There was nothing to be gained from pointing a finger at this woman's murdered husband, it would only work against them, and they needed her help.

'No, no,' replied Craig. 'It's just — there're some financial irregularities. Something's not right and we think Spotlight's being used as a front for illegal activities.'

'That's preposterous. Where are you getting these ideas? And who's "we"?'

Again, Craig turned to Abraham. Again, he shook his head. Telling her that he was involved, was sitting right here in the car, might only speed up the police's arrival, especially if they had indicted that Abraham was a person of interest.

'There's a recording,' said Craig. 'And other people have been digging into this too. I just want more information. I want to make this right. I just need to speak to David Catton. If you have number for him, an address.'

'David? What's he got to do with anything? He's straighter than a Roman road.'

There was a heavy sigh.

'Look, this is all too much,' she continued. 'I'm not sure I can deal with this now, not after —' Another crack in her voice. 'Not after everything else. But I don't want my husband's company, my company, dragged into something sordid. Despite all his faults, he worked too hard to make it a success. You need to tell me how you know what you think you know.'

'Well, I'm not sure where to start —'

'No,' came the interruption. 'Not over the phone. We should meet.'

'Meet?' replied Craig, surprised at the suggestion.

'My husband was a good man and you're accusing him of – well, I| don't know what you're accusing him of. But I want to find out, and I want to be able to look into your eyes when you tell me. Plus, at least this will keep my mind off everything else. I need to get out, to do something. And I need to know what you think is happening and tell you why you're wrong.'

There was a pause before Mrs Maynard-Jones added, 'It's just gone 4pm now. Can you meet at six?'

Abraham nodded his head at Craig.

'Yes, I think so. Where?'

'Somewhere quiet, out of the way. You know the cafe at the end of the pier? There'll be no one around by that time. There at six.'

Craig didn't have time to reply before the line went dead and both men were left staring at the phone, unsure whether they had made any progress or not.

***

The crime scene team had finally finished at the Maynard-Jones' house and had extracted several prints from the property, most of which Palmer expected to belong to the Maynard-Jones' themselves. He was keeping his fingers crossed though, hoping that at least one set belonged to someone else, be that Abraham Hart or another, as yet unidentified individual.

Hopeful, though not necessarily optimistic.

The coroner had estimated that death was due to exsanguination caused by a wound on the victim's abdomen that had severed the abdominal aorta but, as with all coroners Palmer had dealt with, nothing was official until it was official.

He had returned to the police station after viewing the CCTV footage at Southend Central, footage which had shown Abraham Hart, dressed in an ill-fitting tracksuit, meeting with a shambling, scruffy man whom they had so far not identified but who Palmer believed to be the recently re-surfaced Craig Atherton.

The plate on the red Fiat that both men had eventually climbed into was found to be registered to a local business called Marshall Building and Services, the CEO of which was Anthony Stone, a name which Palmer, along with the rest of the Essex Police Force, knew well.

Whether Stone was involved, or whether Hart had stolen the car, he didn't know but resolved to find out as soon as he could. The priority, though, was locating Hart which was why he had instructed a team of officers to scan real time CCTV, as well as monitor the ANPR system for when the Fiat popped up.

'Guv,' said DS Court, poking a well-groomed head round the door to Palmer's office, which was a mess of files and discarded coffee cups held together by motivational posters and ancient diktats from HR. 'We got something.'

'Well, don't leave me in suspense. This isn't an episode of *Eastenders*.'

'One of the tech guys scanning the cameras has the Fiat pulling into the Royals multi-storey. Hard to see the occupants, but it's two people.'

'When?'

'Car pulled in at 3.58pm.'

Palmer looked at the ancient clock on the wall, then at his watch for confirmation. 'That was over an hour ago. They still there?'

Court, stepping further into the office, shrugged. 'Car should be. There's no footage of it leaving. Whether they're still in it...' The DS shrugged again.

'Come on then,' muttered Palmer. 'Let's not be hasty though, I don't want to scare them off. Assuming they've not already left. Notify the centre that we're coming. Give the security staff Hart's picture and tell them to keep an eye on all exits. Send three marked cars but tell them to hang back.'

'You think it might turn nasty?'

'I think it already has.'

Forty-two

The car glided along the the dirty Tarmac of the A13 like it was travelling on air, as though the surface wasn't fit to host the Maybach's tyres. Hristo didn't consider himself a car man but had been enticed by the quality, comfort and quiet of the sleek, black motor. The salesman at the Mercedes showroom had offered information about the car's performance, its handling, speed, fuel consumption, but Hristo hadn't listened because he didn't care. He would never drive the car, he had people to do that for him. All he was interested in was the softness of the rear seats and the silence it guarded against world outside, both of which were more than acceptable.

'How long, Valon?' Hristo said as he watched the industrial estates, roadside cafes and gigantic warehouses streak by in a blur of grime-covered greys.

'Twenty-five minutes, sir. Give or take,' replied the driver, whose name Hristo remembered, but about whom he knew little else.

He tried not to concern himself with the minutiae of the business. His focus was the product, its acquirement, and the oversight of the distribution channels. Those had been established long ago and, apart from the odd disruption, had run smoothly ever since. Police interference in the UK occasionally stymied profits, as did law enforcement in export territories, but these incursions never lasted long.

Hristo had often thought of the business as a living entity. Sometimes it got sick because parts of it failed, which meant they needed to be repaired. Sometimes it became sluggish because the distribution of its lifeblood slowed or was interrupted, which required careful management to nurture it back to health. More often, elements of it ruptured due to greed or other transgressions; those parts were like a cancer that needed to be excised, often brutally, otherwise there was a risk it would encourage other tumours to emerge.

Hristo rarely dealt with these maladies in person but the situation at Spotlight had become more high risk that usual. Deaths were not uncommon in this line of work, but the deaths of innocent - or seemingly innocent - people threw unwanted light on something Hristo and his associates wanted to stay hidden in the dark. The existence of a recording with Hristo's name on it was a cause for real concern, as was the fact that no one had been able to deal with it satisfactorily up to this point.

Maybe Spotlight had reached the end of its usefulness. It had proved to be an astute acquisition, and replacing the amount of money it was able to wash would not be easy, but if they weren't able to locate the journalist and the errant boyfriend then there could be even bigger problems ahead.

Hristo's thoughts were interrupted by the buzz of his private mobile. Only a handful of people had the number, none of whose names were listed in the contact list, and all of whom knew to say nothing that could be misconstrued.

'Yes?' said Hristo, pressing the phone to his ear.
'I know where he is,' said the voice on the other end.
'Who?'

'One. Maybe both.'

'Have you contacted our associate?'

'Yes.'

'Good. Message me the details. I'm coming to you,' said Hristo, closing his eyes and resting the back of his head on the cold leather headrest. 'I understand this is hard for you, but you've done the right thing.'

***

The day had not gone to plan. Leaving one body to be found by the police was a mistake for which Erjon would not quickly forgive himself. If he left two, he felt his pride might never recover.

The issue he was facing was where a body could be hidden. He was on a main road, surrounded by commercial properties, many with residential flats above them. And while the girl was small, certainly compared to Lewis Maynard-Jones, she was not small enough to go unnoticed.

He had travelled with the neoprene rucksack because he had planned to dismember Maynard-Jones in his own bath then discard the remaining parts at a later time, but he had left the rucksack at the hotel, taking only the knife, gun and his phone. Plus, there was no bath in the Spotlight office. No wet room to contain the resultant fluids.

He needed to think.

A low moan snapped him back from those thoughts and he realised the body in question was still, technically, a living person. There was still a job to be done. He felt the heft of the knife in his pocket but decided against using it. It would only mean more to clean. He decided, before the inevitable, to try waking the girl one last time, gently slapping her on each cheek.

The moaning grew louder and, a few seconds later, one eye opened. Then another. There was nothing behind them at first. Just the empty stare of the newly conscious. A blissful, blank slate.

Then came the terror.

Erjon held a finger to his lips and was pleased to find the girl was clever enough - scared enough - to take note. 'I just want to ask you a question,' said Erjon. 'That's all. Don't be afraid. As soon as you answer, you are free to go.'

The girl nodded as a single tear swept down her cheek. From experience, Erjon knew others would follow.

'Where has he gone? The man who was just here, the journalist?'

The girl was shaking now, fear gripping her. Erjon knew he would get nothing from her, not now. She shook her head, confirming Erjon's instincts. He sighed.

'You have no reason to be afraid. I just need to know where he is.' He was wasting time, but how to properly clean up was still eluding him. Maybe he was wasting time for his own benefit.

Again the girl shook her head, more tears, streams of them, sliding down her cheeks.

Erjon nodded solemnly and brought his hands up to her thin, fragile neck and began to press. He looked into her eyes as they grew wider, filling with dread and the hideous realisation of what was happening.

He would have to formulate a plan after the fact. It was not ideal, not at all, but planning on the move was something he was familiar with. Something would reveal itself, he thought.

But thinking and knowing are not the same, and the sound of the building's front door opening - a door Erjon knew he had closed and locked - made him stop, turning his head to one side, eyes closed, an ear pointed in the direction of the sound.

With his concentration interrupted, the pressure on the girl's neck slackened and she drew in a gasping, painful breath. Though not in itself loud, in the quiet confines of the office it seemed like it had been projected through a bullhorn.

Erjon clamped a hand over her mouth but, sensing a way back, she began bucking her body with what little strength she had left, flailing her arms towards Erjon's face.

'Hello?' Erjon heard a man's voice shout from the front of the office. 'Is there anyone here? It's the police.'

It was then, as adrenalin flooded his system, Erjon realised he had become every bit as soft as Hristo. He had been used to operating in the shadows but, with Hristo's money and connections, those shadows were protected. They were so dark that there was never any light, never any possibility of something else reaching out to help. Here, though, the black was not all-consuming. Slivers of brightness remained, and Erjon had stepped into one.

As the voice called out he realised he was a feeling something he hadn't felt in a long time, something that he thought he had excised from his body; panic. He had abandoned the caution on which he always prided himself and it had lead him to this point.

Erjon released the girl and, no longer worrying about noise, quickly shifted the remaining boxes that were blocking the emergency exit. The girl, wheezing and gasping for the air that couldn't fill her lungs quickly enough, paid him no attention, focused only on the next breath.

He heard footsteps, another voice, a woman's this time, 'Whoever you are, stay where you are.'

Erjon had no intention of doing so.

With the last box moved, he pushed hard against the silver bar set across the door and it sprang open. As soon as it did an alarm sounded, a high, piercing sound that filled all the spaces in Erjon's brain.

He was at the rear of the building, in a paved courtyard big enough for at least six cars. A wall, roughly six feet in height, surrounded the perimeter on three sides, the other was taken up by a large metal gate that had a keypad fixed into the concrete on one side.

Erjon could hear footsteps close behind him now, the male voice shouting to his colleague to call an ambulance. They would be on him soon, there was no time to waste.

For a moment he considered staying, fighting. He knew he would win, that wasn't in question, but going up against one member of the police force meant you would, eventually, be up against every member.

It was a battle not worth fighting. Escape was the only option.

He spotted a wheelie-bin tucked into the corner of the courtyard, pushed up against the wall, and sprinted towards it, leaping on top in one fluid motion. The plastic lid bowed under his weight, but held.

Erjon turned as a voice cried out at him, yelling for him to stop, to stay where he was. He wondered if such commands ever worked. Whether anyone making their escape was ever deferential enough to do as they were told. If there were such people, Erjon pitied them.

From the top of the bin he propelled himself onto the perimeter wall and, before lowering himself to the pavement on the other side, kicked the wheelie-bin away so that it trundled to the middle of the courtyard and into the advancing officer, who again yelled as Erjon disappeared over the wall.

***

Hristo had been to Southend before. Not often, but often enough to know that he would prefer not to have to go there again. An important part of his business was here so occasional visits were necessary, if begrudgingly undertaken. As the Maybach cruised along the promenade, the expanse of gunmetal grey water on his right and rows of waterfront flats and houses on his left, the car garnered admiring glances and Hristo wondered if travelling in such a conspicuous fashion had been a wise choice. There was nothing to be done about it now, so he ignored the gawping faces of badly dressed, overweight men and women and concentrated on the task at hand.

He wasn't one for wishes, for keeping his fingers crossed. That approach was for dreamers and, more often than not, failures. But he couldn't help hoping that he would soon be face-to-face with Abraham Hart, and with the boyfriend of the girl whose death seemed to have sparked this whole situation into life; Hristo could not remember either of their names.

He would not do anything to the journalist who had meddled in his affairs for too long, not personally. Neither would he be present when somebody else did. That would be too risky. But Hristo wanted to see the look on his face when Hart realised that no action against him went unpunished.

'Two minutes, sir,' said the driver, not turning around.

Hristo tapped at the screen of his phone and brought it to his ear. When the call was answered at first there was only heavy breathing.

'Yes,' said Erjon eventually.

'What's happening?' asked Hristo.

'I'm compromised.'

Hristo gritted his teeth. 'How?'

'It does not matter. I have to leave. I need a car.'

'The situation is still active. I know where they are. I'm on my way there.'

'You're here?'

'Yes.'

'Then you can finish it.'

Hristo had to fight to contain his anger, his fingers tightening around the phone. 'That isn't how it works. I'll send you the location. Once you see me leave, you do whatever needs to be done. Then you'll have your car.'

Hristo killed the call then sent the details to Erjon's number.

Forty-three

'We should leave,' Abraham said to Craig, who had slid down in his seat so that is forehead was level with the steering wheel.

'And drive where?'

'No, we leave the car here. It's safer on foot. We can get a coffee or something.'

'You make it sound like we're on holiday.'

Abraham choked back a laugh. 'I just don't want to risk them finding the car, and us sitting in it like lemons.'

Abraham had been thinking of a piece he'd worked on about international credit card fraud The suspect at the heart of the scam had driven his Maserati to Heathrow in preparation for a flight to Saudi Arabia. His first mistake had been using his own car, his second was parking in the airport's official car park, and his third had been waiting in the car. It hadn't taken long for the police to trace his plate, block the exits and surround the vehicle.

Walking along the high street, Abraham felt conspicuous in the gleaming tracksuit that he was at least two decades too old to successfully pull off. And walking next to someone who looked like they'd been sleeping in a dustbin for the past few weeks didn't help either of them blend in.

But Southend's main shopping street had always been a place that represented all walks of Essex life;

elderly couples walking arm in arm, harassed parents with screaming toddlers, teenagers on bikes with their hoodies pulled up and their jeans yanked down below their waist, small groups of homeless people drinking cheap cider and telling jokes.

It was busy, a tide of faces drifting along the wide street, the pair merging into the crowd. Abraham could hear Joshua's oft-repeated line that shopping had long ago supplanted church as most people's preferred form of Sunday worship. In this instance, Abraham was glad of it. If anyone was interested in the mismatched pair then they weren't making it obvious, but both kept their gaze aimed at the chewing gum peppered floor.

'Take this,' said Abraham, handing Craig a ten-pound note from the envelope of cash Tony Stone had given him. 'There's a coffee shop round the corner, next to the Tesco. Get two drinks, sit away from the window.'

'Where're you going?' asked Craig. 'You're gonna bail, aren't you?'

'Of course not. I'll be five minutes. I need to check something, and we're more memorable together than we are apart, that's all. I promise. Five minutes. Ten, max.'

Craig gave Abraham a wary look but took the note and stuffed it into his pocket. 'I'm scared, okay. I'm sorry, but I am. I know I started this whole thing off, and Alissa's the one who paid for it, but these people, whoever they are, they're psychos.'

Abraham stared at Craig. He hadn't worked out who the young man really was. He'd disregarded his girlfriend's feelings, as well as her nascent career, and was willing to torpedo a man's marriage in the hope of financial gain. That suggested a certain level of ego and detachment. But, now, he seemed like a scared child, regretting his impulsiveness and having to face the consequences of his actions.

'What you did was wrong,' Abraham said. 'Actually, not just wrong, but cold-hearted and irresponsible. I've got no sympathy for Lewis Maynard-Jones getting found out, but Alissa obviously trusted you and you let her down…'

Craig looked set to say something. Maybe to protest, maybe to agree, Abraham didn't know and didn't give him the chance either way.

'But the only way to rectify that is to find out who's behind all this, to know what happened and why. You came back. To me, that says something. Two people are dead already and we need to make sure it ends there. If Mrs Maynard-Jones can help then all the better, and if she can't, then we'll have to turn to the police and put our faith in them.'

Craig gave a derisory snort.

'You got a better plan?'

The younger man slowly shook his head.

'Didn't think so,' said Abraham, turning around and heading away from Craig. 'Flat white, one sugar.'

**

Palmer and Court arrived at the Royals at 5.25 and the older man immediately issued instructions for a non-uniform to eyeball the red Fiat to ascertain whether its occupants were still inside. Two minutes later they received word on the radio that the car was empty and neither Hart, the man Palmer assumed was Atherton, nor anyone matching their descriptions were in the immediate vicinity.

'What now?' asked Court as he stared into the rearview mirror to smooth a tuft of hair back into place.

'Any CCTV?'

'Someone's gone to the security office to have a look. Manager's off on Sundays and whoever's in charge isn't quite up to speed on the tech side of things.'

'Christ!' Palmer said. 'Well, there's no point sitting here twiddling our dicks, is there? Come on.'

Palmer swung open the car door, levered himself out into the cold evening air and pulled the collar of his thin rain Mac up to guard against the increasingly strong sea breeze and the spits of rain that were now falling from angry-looking clouds. 'What the hell happened to autumn?' he said. 'We just skipping straight to winter this year?'

Court wasn't sure how to respond, so decided not to. Instead, he followed his superior officer as he trudged towards the high street, wishing he'd brought an umbrella because the rain was going to play havoc with his hair.

***

Abraham couldn't remember using a payphone, nor having the need to use one, since he could afford his own mobile. In fact, he was amazed such things still existed, but was thankful they did.

Stationed outside The Royal Hotel, at the south end of the high street, were two BT phones which were fixed to either side of a brushed metal column that had more dents than a scrapyard. The payphones were something that thousands of people walked past each day but which, if you asked them, only a handful would remember seeing and, likely, even fewer would know how to use.

He could have borrowed Craig's phone but didn't want to have this conversation in front of the obviously nervous young man, and with his own phone left in Joshua's car and now probably in the possession of the police, this was the next best option. He knew he shouldn't be wandering around the town centre, but the upcoming meeting could easily be a police sting, so he wanted to make sure he got his side of the story across.

He grabbed the handset, his back to the shopping street, his view now of the garishly coloured rides of Adventure Island. He could hear the squawk from the park's Tannoy system, someone enticing people to 'take a spin on the Axis', or 'get fired up for Rage'. Next to the theme park was the long wooden pier stretching over a mile out into the brackish waters of the Thames estuary. He couldn't see the end of the pier though, the dark clouds making the structure look like a pathway to the unknown.

He slipped a pound coin into the slot and dialled a number which had always remained lodged in his brain.

'Hello, Our Lady of Lourdes Roman Catholic Church, this is Father Hart speaking.'

The sound of his brother's voice, and of his usual greeting when answering the rectory's landline, caused a wave of nostalgia to crash over Abraham.

'Josh,' he said. 'It's me. Can you talk?'

'Abraham! Where on Earth are you? The police are looking for you, did you know that? They think you killed Lewis Maynard-Jones.' The words left Joshua's mouth in a tumble. Then there was a short pause. 'You didn't, did you?'

'Oh, lovely. Thanks for the vote of confidence. "My brother the cold-blooded killer".'

'Well, it's not cold-blooded, is it? You were arguing with him outside the church not that long ago.'

'Hardly a reason to murder someone is it? Bit of an over-reaction. But no, for the record, I did not kill Lewis Maynard-Jones.'

'Of course, sorry,' said Joshua. 'It's just all a bit of a shock? Alissa, the attack in the church, now Maynard-Jones. It feels like an episode of *Midsomer Murders*.'

'Look, I just want you to know, you and Dad, and Evie, I had nothing to do with Lewis's death. But I was there. I saw who killed him.'

'What?'

'There was a man; thin, wiry, blonde hair cut short, high cheekbones, thin lips.'

'Thin and wiry? Is it the same person who attacked me? And should I be writing this down?'

'No. Yes. Probably. I just needed to tell someone. To explain, in case it helps. In case I didn't get another chance.'

'What do you mean? What's happening? What are you going to do?'

'This thing with Alissa, it's taken a turn. Carol was right all along. Something's rotten and Alissa stepped into it.'

'Then tell the police. Let them deal with it. You don't need to save the world. It's not your job.'

'But it was my job to save Grace, wasn't it? My job to look out for her. And look what happened. I know I can't save her now. Her or Alissa, but I can try to make at least one thing right.'

'Abraham, no one blames you for what happened to Grace. No one. She was an adult and she made bad choices. People do, all the time. You couldn't save her any more than I could. Or Mum. Or Dad. As much as we all loved her, she was her own beautiful, flawed person.'

'But it *was* me,' said Abraham, trying not to shout but failing, the crack in his voice partially hidden by the park's repeating Tannoy system. 'I'm the one who introduced her to Brody fucking Lipscombe. I'm the one who told her to give him a chance, to imagine a future. All I did was take that future away. If I'd never have met Brody, if he'd never come to work at the paper, then Grace wouldn't have met him either, and she might still be alive.'

'You're torturing yourself for no reason.'

'Not for no reason. Look, I'm almost out of credit,' said Abraham, lowering his voice, 'I'm sure it'll all be fine. I just need to do one more thing, then I'll face whatever consequences there are. Hopefully I'll see you all later.'

'Hopefully? Abraham, what are you doing? Where are you going?'

'The tram'll be leaving soon. Tell everyone I'm sorry,' said Abraham before placing the receiver back in its cradle.

Before meeting with Craig, Abraham made one final call, aiming to extract one last favour, then he pulled his hood tight around his face and walked back the way he'd come.

***

Joshua stood holding the phone until Brody tapped him on the shoulder.

'You ok?'

The touch startled Joshua but brought him back from thoughts of what his brother had said about blaming himself for their sister's death.

Joshua had felt guilt too, but he hadn't been as close to Grace as Abraham had. And, if he was honest with himself, he *did* blame Abraham. Partially, at least. It hadn't been Abraham's fault, but blaming someone else meant that Joshua could sleep more easily.

He had always thought himself a good man, a man of God, but the more he examined his behaviour the more he realised that being good was rarely about what you thought, and always about what you did.

Abraham blamed Brody. For introducing him to Grace. For not seeing beneath his surface. For not… what… protecting her? Threatening him? Forcing them apart?

Was Brody to blame? Maybe. He had introduced her to drugs, procured them and administered them. But he had been in the grip of addition too. Joshua wondered whether the time he'd spent helping Brody was as much to do with his own absolution as it was Brody's. He'd taken pride in the man's transformation, but wasn't pride a sin too?

Joshua recognised the splintering cracks that had crept outwards from the death of his sister. Cracks that had swallowed the people around him, plummeting them towards grief, guilt, anger and self-loathing.

'Where once I was blind, now I see,' said Joshua.

Brody looked at him, confused.

'Sorry,' Joshua said. 'Abraham's in some sort of trouble.'

'Anything we can do to help?'

'Maybe. Can you call a taxi?'

Forty-four

Fifteen minutes after leaving, Abraham lowered himself into one of the battered old sofas opposite Craig. The younger man showed a mix of relief and trepidation at Abraham's arrival, as if he was half hoping Abraham had done a runner, giving him the opportunity to follow suit.

'Where'd you go?'

Abraham dipped into the white plastic bag he was now carrying and pulled out a dark blue, zip up sweater, a grey baseball cap, a thin, green cagoule and a pair of navy blue chinos. 'Top and cap's for you. Trousers and rain Mac's for me. Got them from the charity shop over the road. Can't hurt for you to look less like a hobo and me less like Sporty Spice's grandad.'

Craig held up the piece of clothing. 'Looks like something a bank manager would wear at the weekend.'

'Right,' replied Abraham. 'Whereas you look like Harry Styles. Just put it on.'

Craig did as he was told and, after finishing his coffee, Abraham wandered to the cafe's bathroom to change into his newly acquired trousers. 'Come on,' he said, returning to their table, 'we get there a bit early, we can scope the place out.'

'For what?'

Abraham looked at Craig, searching for the right response. 'I have no idea.' Then he ushered Craig ahead of him and followed him out the door.

It had started to rain since they'd entered the coffee shop, the autumn sky a menacing grey that was sucking the light from what was left of the day.

Abraham pulled the hood of his cheap cagoule up. At the end of the high street, where the road became Pier Hill and sloped down towards the rows of arcades, he noticed a distinct increase in men and women in dark suits, some of whom were talking into radio mics. A couple of Ford Mondeos were parked in the dead-end road outside the Royals car park to their left, harried-looking men leaning against them. He quickly decided that Pier Hill was best avoided and instead turned right along Royal Terrace, away from the crowd, Craig jogging to keep up.

Fifty metres along there was a path that cut through the greenery on the steep hill opposite the pier. It ran down to the wide esplanade below and, keeping his head down and his hood up, Abraham, with Craig following, wound his way along the path.

At the esplanade the sprinkling of hardy day-trippers had thinned to a smattering of runners and a handful of dog walkers. The rain was getting heavier and the grey expanse of sea across the road was barely visible through the lashing rain and the darkening sky.

Abraham, thankful for the worsening weather and the need to hide his face from it, beckoned Craig to follow him across the main road. At the western end of Adventure Island, the two men slipped into the near empty theme park and away from the open expanse of the esplanade.

They quickly weaved past the Crooked House, the Twister and the flashing, chirruping machines inside the arcade. They walked beneath the section of the pier that traversed the park then turned left, walking along a sloping path that deposited them back onto the esplanade and opposite the pier entrance.

At the ticket booth they asked for two tickets and the young girl behind the grimy plexiglass, whose badge told them her name was Matilda, looked at them like they'd asked for seats on the Orient Express.

'It's pouring,' she said, as if the drenched figures in front of her might not have noticed.

A soaked Abraham turned around, looking past the glass doors of the entrance to the rain drops that were now hammering into the pavement and exploding like liquid bombs. 'Is it?'

Unimpressed, Matilda shrugged. 'Your funeral,' she said. 'Six pound twenty for a tram return.'

Abraham passed a crumpled ten-pound note through the gap in the plexiglass.

'Each,' said Matilda, looking from Abraham to Craig.

Abraham gritted his teeth and shoved another screwed-up fiver through the gap.

'Next one leaves in one minute. If you make it,' Matilda said, handing back the £2.60 change.

To his left, past a bored looking man in a blue uniform, Abraham saw someone carrying a fishing rod and tackle box enter the green and cream electric tram. A woman wearing an orange hi-vis jacket was walking toward the front of the vehicle.

'Quick,' he said to Craig.

The bored man in blue stepped in front of them and held out his hand. Abraham threw two tickets in his direction as the two men barely broke stride launching themselves into the first carriage they came to a second before the doors beeped and slowly closed.

Six minutes later, after an uneventful journey during which the rain continued to hammer against the side of the tram, and the sea below them, or what they could see of it, broiled and swayed, the doors slid open again and Abraham and Craig stepped onto the wooden slats of the pier.

'Come on,' Abraham said, heading along the walkway and towards the end of the pier where the shops, cafes and restaurants were gathered.

There were a few sightseers sitting under canopied tables sipping hot drinks, and a handful of men dotted around the edge of the pier cloaked in waterproof clothing, nursing Thermoses and fishing rods. Abraham assumed they were men, at least, though it was impossible to tell. The rest of the pier's visitors had trudged onto the tram that would shortly take them the two kilometres back to the shore.

They walked past a restaurant on the left that had been the location for a popular TV cooking show and, further along, saw a larger building which housed the cafe in which they were meeting Mrs Maynard-Jones.

'What now?' asked Craig.

Abraham looked at his watch; 5.43pm. 'We should wait. Check who goes into the building, who's coming to meet with us.'

'You expecting someone other than Maynard-Jones?'

Abraham sighed heavily. 'I don't know what I'm expecting anymore, or who to trust. What if she's brought the police with her?'

Craig shrugged. 'Might not be a bad thing. And, whether we spot them or not, there's only one way off this pier. Unless you're a particularly strong swimmer.'

'Don't even joke,' replied Abraham, staring out at the rolling, foam-flecked waves. 'Ok, you're right. Let's get out of this rain and find a seat inside. When she arrives let me do the talking. We need to find out what she knows about Spotlight, the money and about David Catton's involvement in all this.'

'What if she doesn't know anything?'

Abraham shook his head. 'Then this'll all have been a complete waste of time.'

***

'They're here,' said Erjon, the phone against his ear, hidden from view by the yellow waterproof poncho he had bought on the way to the pier.

He had crept more than a mile away from the Spotlight office, vigilant for any sign of the police, then called a taxi, something he was uncomfortable doing, but there was no other way of reaching the pier in time.

He had paid in cash and asked the driver to drop him off a quarter of a mile from the long wooden finger that stretched out into the unwelcoming grey water of the Thames estuary. Caution had ceased to be relevant, it seemed, but the less information people had, the more comfortable Erjon felt.

Whether the policeman would be able to give an accurate description of him, he wasn't sure. He knew there was no CCTV at Spotlight, but being picked up by other cameras was a distinct possibility. But even if he had been, they could never identify him. There would be no match on any database, no record of his existence because, to all intents and purposes, he didn't exist. But that didn't make him invulnerable. He might be The Wind, a force of nature, but sometimes nature could be tamed.

In a tackle shop across the road from the pier he had purchased the waterproof clothing and the cheapest rod they stocked, again paying in cash. He had been standing at the end of the pier for nearly 15 minutes when he saw Hart exit the tram with a scruffy young man in a blue jumper who, he assumed from Hristo's information, was the boyfriend.

'They're early,' replied Hristo.

'Maybe. But she's already here too. They're heading in to meet now.'

'Witnesses?'

Erjon casually glanced around, careful to keep his face tucked behind the hood of his poncho. 'Some. It's manageable.'

'Good. I'm on my way.'

Erjon killed the call, slipped the phone back into his pocket then turned to his right to look back along the pier where he saw Hristo rise from a canopied table and walk towards the cafe.

Forty-five

Mrs Maynard-Jones was already seated at a table when they walked in. She was in the corner, furthest from the serving counter, wearing a sleek, black waterproof coat and black leather boots. A dark grey silk scarf was wrapped around her long neck, her shiny blonde hair partially tucked into it, and her face bore the merest hint of make up. She looked every inch the beautiful, grieving widow.

The cafe was empty apart from the three of them and a middle-aged woman in a blue apron standing behind the till, looking at her phone.

At their arrival Mrs Maynard-Jones looked up and narrowed her eyes, recognising Abraham. The two men approached the table.

'We've met before,' she said. 'At the office. Mr Hart, isn't it?' Her tone was wary, her manner nervous.

'That's right,' replied Abraham. 'I was meeting with your husband. I'm a friend of Craig's. I was looking into the death of Alissa Peters, Craig's girlfriend.'

'Was?'

Abraham gave a polite shrug. 'Still am, I suppose. Thank you for meeting with us.'

She nodded. 'I'm getting myself a drink. Let me get you one.'

'We're fine,' said Abraham.

'Please. You're soaked,' she insisted. And, with that, she walked towards the counter and, two minutes later, came back with three Styrofoam cups of steaming tea, speaking as she sat in the chair opposite the two men. 'Your name came up earlier. The police mentioned you. Asked if there was anything between you and Lewis. Any history.'

Craig, who had been unsure how to behave or what to say, spoke up. 'We're sorry to hear about your husband. You don't deserve this.'

'What? And he did? To be sliced open like common cattle and left to die in a pool of his own blood?'

Abraham winced at the forthright comments.

'Look,' she went on, 'I just want to hear what you think you know. How you believe Lewis could be involved in whatever you think this is. You mentioned financial irregularities, and a recording. I just… I can't believe he'd entangle us in anything like that.' Her voice cracked and Abraham fumbled for one of the napkins nestled in a silver dispenser, which he handed over.

'Spotlight is a front for a drugs organisation,' said Abraham. 'I think it's being used to launder money and I think your husband realised he'd made a mistake which might have caused problems for those higher up.'

Mrs Maynard-Jones laughed, a bitter sound that crackled with anger. 'My husband was a man of low morals, Mr Hart. He was a cheat, a liar, at times a fantasist, but he was mine, and now he's dead. Likely, in some way, because of all this rubbish you're spouting. Is there any proof of the things you're saying?'

'There's a recording,' said Craig, his voice rising, his palms resting on the table, arms tense as if ready to spring up at any moment. 'Alissa made it, by accident. She was nothing to do with any of this. Just in the wrong place at the wrong time. And I think your husband killed her because of it. He was a murderer and, you know what, I'm not sorry he's dead. He deserved what he got.'

'She tried to blackmail him because of that video. Hardly the behaviour of an innocent, is it?' said Mrs Maynard-Jones, her voice calm and steady.

Craig went red, the knowledge that his actions, his greed and impetuousness, had resulted in Alissa's death was like a gut punch.

'How do you know?' asked Abraham.

'Excuse me?'

'How do you know there was a blackmail attempt?' asked Abraham. 'Did he show you the video and, if he did, why?'

'I have my own reputation to think of Mr Hart.'

'Did you see the whole thing? Did you hear him name names?'

'I have no idea what you're talking about. Have you got the video? Can you show it to me? Can you give any credence to these accusations you're making?'

Abraham hadn't heard the last sentence. His brain had quietened, and he was staring at Mrs Maynard-Jones, a faint smile playing across his lips. 'You're good,' he said.

She tilted her head and stared back at him, artfully plucked eyebrows wrinkling. She was about to say something when the door to the cafe opened. A gush of air swept into the room followed by a man with a shaved head who was wearing a houndstooth overcoat and patent leather shoes.

Abraham and Craig turned and watched as he slowly walked towards their table and carefully pulled out the vacant chair next to Mrs Maynard-Jones. His hands were covered by brown sheepskin gloves, which he used to smooth the seat of his long overcoat before sitting down.

'Hello, Abraham,' the man said.

'Hello, Hristo,' Abraham replied.

***

Palmer's mood, which never strayed far from its default setting of "grouchy", had plummeted towards "belligerent". He and DS Court, along with a series of uniformed and non-uniformed officers, had walked the high street scanning for Abraham Hart and Craig Atherton but, so far, had not managed to locate them.

Palmer had been further riled when PC Alfie Kendrick, a young officer, had radioed to confidently say he had apprehended Atherton under the railway bridge that spanned the high street at its halfway point.

After jogging the 200 yards from outside Waterstones, Palmer, who dismissed the growing pain in this chest as heartburn, found Kendrick smiling as he proudly displayed a dishevelled man with a long beard and dirt-streaked face who was now wearing hand cuffs.

'He's about seventy!' Palmer yelled at the young officer. 'Atherton's been missing for a month, not a fucking century, you donut. Cut him loose.'

'Oi! I'm fifty-eight!' protested the man, who was sporting mismatched shoes and an odour that Palmer, had he been asked, would have described as 'au de urine'.

'Need to ramp up your beauty regimen then, don't you,' growled Palmer as he walked back towards the seafront trying to catch his breath.

'What's next?' asked DS Court.

'Let's get the CCTV from the town centre. Every shop, bar and restaurant. One of them must have picked them up. They can't have gone too far.'

'You really think Hart killed Maynard-Jones? It just seems… I don't know, excessive.'

'I don't *think* anything,' spat Palmer. 'Not paid to think, are we? We're paid to follow the evidence. That's what I'm doing.'

Palmer was about to launch into an oft-repeated rant about how too many coppers were slaves to hunches when his mobile phone rang. He held up a finger to his DS and reached into his inside pocket. 'DI Palmer,' he said, after swiping on the screen.

'I've got some information for you,' said the voice at the end of the line. 'About Abraham Hart.'

Palmer instinctively checked his phone, but all it told him was that it was an unknown number. 'Who is this?'

'Doesn't matter, just listen. He's on the pier, but be careful, he's not alone.'

'How do you know? And who's he with?'

But Palmer didn't get an answer to either question, because the line was dead.

***

'It is a pleasure to meet you in person,' said Hristo. 'Well, I say a pleasure though, of course, I don't mean it. But admiration can still be felt for those we dislike, and I admire your persistence, Mr Hart. You must be disappointed at how that persistence has had no effect on the outcome.'

Before having the chance to reply, Craig, who had been sipping his tea while looking between Abraham and this new arrival at their table, spoke up. 'Who *are* you? What the hell's going on?' The tension in his arms had returned, his palms spread on the table, one leg bouncing underneath.

Abraham placed a firm but reassuring hand on Craig's shoulder and turned to face him. 'This is Mr Hristo Nikolova,' said Abraham. 'The real owner of Spotlight Design and Production.' Turning back to face Hristo, his hand still on Craig's arm, Abraham continued. 'Congratulations on the court case. Well, I say congratulations, but what I really mean is you're a murdering shit whose wife just so happened to go missing at the crucial moment. How lucky for you.'

Hristo shrugged. 'And you must be Mr Atherton,' he said, smiling at Craig. Hristo held out his hand, palm up. 'Your phones please, gentlemen. What a lot of problems your girlfriend's video caused. Especially for Lewis, our dearly departed friend.'

Abraham and Craig both looked at the murdered man's wife who sat impassively in the chair next to Hristo. 'I'm not giving you anything,' Craig said through gritted teeth. 'That bastard killed Alissa and, dead or not, I'm going to make sure people know about it. And about you and your business.'

Hristo laughed, a genuine snort that caught him by surprise. 'Lewis? No, no, no. Lewis wouldn't hurt a fly. How do you say, he was a lover, not a fighter. That, I'm afraid, seems to have been his downfall.'

Still sitting impassively, staring into the distance, a tear welled in Mrs Maynard-Jones' eye and eventually broke cover onto her cheek.

Behind him, Abraham heard the door to the cafe swing open again. He felt the breeze swoop into the room and the heard the rain lashing against the wooden planks of the pier.

Hristo dropped his hand and smiled, looking in turn from Craig to Abraham and back again. 'No matter. Give me your phones, don't give me your phones. My associate here will deal with it. Where you're going you won't have use of them anyway.'

'Was it you then?' seethed Craig. 'She was seventeen, for Christ's sake. She had nothing to do with any of this. You're fucking sick.'

Craig went to stand, a surge of anger propelling him upwards. He only got halfway when a hand clamped his right shoulder and forced him back down.

Turning his head, he saw a thin man in a yellow poncho whose eyes were like coal. In his hand, hidden from view by the waterproof cape, was a small black gun, the barrel of which was aimed at Craig's head.

'Sit,' was all the man said.

'Was it me? No. Though it would be untrue to say I played no part in it. Go on,' Hristo said, 'you can tell them. What harm can it do now?'

Forty-six

Alissa felt unsteady as she pulled the flat's door open, the bottle of wine she'd consumed playing with her equilibrium. She reached for the door frame to steady herself.

'Mrs Maynard-Jones! What are you doing here?' Alissa said, then wondered if her words sounded confrontational, or whether it was just the alcohol affecting her judgement. She decided it was better to err on the side of caution, adding, 'I mean, I just wasn't expecting you, that's all.'

The woman standing in front of Alissa was dressed in a black trouser suit with a dark red blouse and black Gucci trainers. On her head was a black Under Armour baseball cap that covered most of her blonde hair, though a few locks of it spilled out the sides and over the diamond studs in her ears. She smiled, her teeth perfectly straight and perfectly white.

'I hope I'm not disturbing you, Alissa. Do you have company?'

'I, well, no. I mean, no, you're not disturbing me and, no, I don't have company.' The words felt thick in Alissa's mouth, and she wished she had some water. 'I just, you know, I wasn't expecting you.'

Mrs Maynard-Jones gave another thin smile that could have doubled as a grimace. 'I would have called, but I wasn't sure you'd pick up. I needed to see you. To speak to you. I expect you know why I'm here.'

Alissa wasn't sure what to say. She could think of only one reason why the wife of the man she'd just accidentally filmed having sex with another woman would be at her door, but she wasn't sure she could give voice to that thought. She wasn't sure she could speak at all.

'Do you mind if I come in? Just for a minute.'

Alissa hesitated, then stood back from the door allowing the co-owner of the company she'd just been fired from into her flat.

'Do you happen to have anything to drink?'

'Sure,' Alissa replied, closing the door. 'Tea? Coffee?'

'I was hoping for something a little stronger.'

Alissa saw her guest glance at the empty wine bottle lying on the floor.

'I was just finishing that up,' said Alissa, trying to keep from tripping over her words at the same time as downplaying how much she'd already drunk. 'It's been open for a while so, you know, Friday night.' Alissa shrugged then stooped to pick up the empty bottle. 'There's another one somewhere if you'd like a glass.'

'Only if you'll join me.'

Alissa knew she'd already had more than enough. 'Of course. Please, take a seat.'

'I hear your boyfriend is away this weekend,' said Mrs Maynard-Jones as she took the few steps from the living room to the adjoining kitchen.

Alissa stopped what she was doing and looked at her.

'Lewis told me. I expect you must have mentioned it to him at some point.' She paused before adding, 'Or maybe you told Francesca, and she's the one who told

Lewis? Though I'm not sure talking is top of their agenda, is it?'

Their eyes were locked, and Alissa felt the red bloom of embarrassment creep up her neck. She tried to think of something to say but couldn't. She considered acting dumb, pretending to not understand the insinuation. But why bother? This was the reason she was here and there was no point hiding from it. 'You saw the video?'

'I'm aware of it. But even without it, I had my suspicions. Lewis is a complicated man, Alissa. Complicated and, like many men, stupid.'

Alissa laughed. 'Tell me about it,' she said, handing over a glass half-filled with red wine. 'You have to know; I didn't mean to record them. I really didn't.' She took a large gulp of her drink. 'I put my phone in the boardroom for...'

Mrs Maynard-Jones placed a finger with a perfectly manicured nail against her lips. 'It's fine. It doesn't matter. It happened, whether you recorded it or not.'

'Yeah, but sending it to Lewis, to Mr Maynard-Jones, that was... well, that wasn't something I would ever have done,' Alissa tried to explain, taking another sip of wine. 'It was, well, it was something my boyfriend did on the spur of the moment. Like you said, men are complicated, and stupid.'

It was Mrs Maynard-Jones' turn to laugh now, her ivory white teeth framed by dark red lipstick. She walked around to where Alissa was standing and picked up the wine bottle by the neck. 'Sometimes they just can't help themselves, can they,' she said, raising the bottle, refilling Alissa's glass which, Alissa was surprised to see, she'd already emptied.

Alissa smiled her thanks, not trusting herself to speak without slurring.

Mrs Maynard-Jones smiled in return. It was a kind smile, Alissa thought. And she was taking her husband's infidelity much better than Alissa would have done.

'Don't think I'm conformable with what happened,' she said, as if reading Alissa's mind. 'Or that he's not likely to pay for his actions. I just wanted to come over here to make sure you're ok. I know he blames you and that he's asked you to leave, but he's not in sole charge of the company.'

For a second Alissa's eyes grew wide as she latched onto the hope that her job might not have been taken away from her after all. But then, as she swallowed another sip of wine, she realised how awkward it would be to have to work with the man who'd not only tried to fire her, but who'd she'd seen having sex with the receptionist.

'That's very nice of you,' she said, making sure to annunciate each word correctly, 'but I'm not sure coming back would be such as good idea. As much as I'd love to.'

'Just leave it all with me. We'll work something out. Out of interest, Alissa, how much of the video did you actually watch? I'm not judging. If the roles had been reversed, God knows I'd have watched it all multiple times.'

Alissa felt her cheeks grow red again. This wasn't a conversation she wanted to have. It was thoughtful of her to visit, to explain the situation, put her at ease, but discussing that video seemed a little weird. Denying having watched it, though, would seem phoney. She didn't want to come across as untrustworthy, not if there was any chance of getting back into Spotlight. God, she wished she hadn't drunk so much.

'No, no, not multiple times at all,' Alissa decided to say. 'I mean, I watched it, but it was like... it was like I...' She couldn't seem to find the right words.

'Like driving past a car crash on the other side of the road?' interjected Mrs Maynard-Jones. 'Morbid curiosity?'

Alissa gave a nervous laugh. 'Yeah, something like that.'

'And did you watch it all the way to the end?'

'Well, I suppose. Though I fast-forwarded through a lot of it, you know. I was just... I don't know. Surprised?'

'Who wouldn't be? Well, I'm glad you didn't obsess over it, Alissa.' That smile again. Those perfect teeth. She leaned across to top up Alissa's glass. 'A sordid business, the whole thing. But if you have anything you want to get off your chest, let me tell you that you can always come to me.'

Alissa nodded, streaks of light trailblazing in her vision as she moved her head. She needed to stop drinking, but having a successful, sophisticated woman in her flat, someone who could be a useful ally in the future, meant she wanted to seem equally as sophisticated. And wasn't drinking wine sophisticated? Though, looking at the other glass, it didn't really seem like Mrs Maynard-Jones had really drunk much at all.

'I suppose,' said Alissa, the first 's' seeming to drag on for longer than was needed, 'I did want to ask one thing. Well, two really.'

'Of course.'

'It's just, well, who showed you that video, is what I'm wondering? And, the other thing was, who's Hristo Nikolova?'

Across the kitchen, which was only a few short steps but, to Alissa, felt much further, Mrs Maynard-Jones's smile slowly deflated. It wasn't obvious, but the gentle change in demeanour, like grey clouds had blown across a previously sunny disposition, made Alissa wonder whether she'd said something stupid, or asked something inappropriate. She tried to think of something else to say, something to cover up her misstep, but her brain was too foggy.

'That's an interesting question, Alissa. It seems like you were paying attention. I'm impressed. I do like someone who has attention to detail. And, please, stop calling me Mrs Maynard-Jones. We're friends, aren't we? My name's Diellza.'

Forty-seven

Diellza Maynard-Jones quietly recounted how she drugged Alissa by putting crushed Ambien in her wine before administering a lethal dose of heroin into the passed-out teen. She then took her phone, which held the incriminating video, placed needles, a rubber tie-off and a small quantity of the drug in her bedroom, and left her to die on the floor of the flat.

Craig listened, at first disbelievingly, then with his head resting in his hands and his heart shattered into tiny pieces. Abraham felt only anger, but he did his best to hide it. He knew they wanted to see it in his face, feel it vibrating off him, and he refused to give them the satisfaction.

'That's how you had Craig's number to text him about meeting.'

'You have to understand,' said Hristo, 'my sister took no pleasure in any of this. And I took none in asking her to do it. My colleague behind you was absent at the time and, as is often the case, time was of the essence. It was an unfortunate business. Even more unfortunate that you were actually the instigator in this, Mr Atherton, and you are a hard man to find, it seems.'

Craig gave no indication that he was listening. His head still buried in his hands, his shoulders heaving in time to his quiet sobs.

'I recognised you,' said Abraham.

Both Diellza and Hristo looked at him.

'At the trial. Your hair was different, much darker, but you were there. You waved at your brother. I just didn't put two and two together. Not soon enough.'

'My sister has always been a great support to me, Mr Hart,' said Hristo. 'Since we both arrived here, she has been a central part of my life, of my business. She's a nationalised British citizen, and even concedes to having her beautiful Albanian name bastardised into an English one. There is nothing she would not do for her family.' At this, he placed his hand over hers and squeezed.

'Even kill her own husband?' said Craig, his face streaked with tears and his eyes burning with anger.

Hristo laughed again, quieter this time, his patience for the meeting wearing thin. 'Poor Lewis had made one too many mistakes. Thankfully we have eyes and ears everywhere, and I was alerted to Lewis's unfortunate misstep.'

'David Catton,' said Abraham.

Hristo smiled. 'You have been busy, haven't you? Yes, Mr Catton even managed to get hold of some helpful pictures that Lewis had taken. Pictures of young Alissa and a priest. Your brother, I'm told, Mr Hart. Very distasteful.'

'So, that was it,' said Abraham. 'Lewis was expendable.'

'Call it a punishment, call it a pre-emptive strike; sometimes a change is needed. But you are mistaken about my sister. She may be a pragmatist, but she is not a monster.'

Hristo turned his attention to Erjon. 'You have the knife?'

Erjon nodded and Hristo aimed a smile at Abraham once again. 'As far as anyone will be concerned, you killed Lewis, Mr Hart. Anger, revenge, jealously; who knows? Who cares? But when they find you, if they find you, they'll also find a bloody knife with your fingerprints all over it.'

'And you agreed to all this?' said Abraham, looking at Diellza. 'To killing an innocent girl. To allowing your husband to be murdered?'

'You look at me and see what, Mr Hart?' said Diellza, her voice different now, less tremulous, more solid. 'A fragile woman? Someone to be controlled? To be manipulated? You think that men are the only ones able to be strong, to do such things?'

'Killing people doesn't make you strong,' seethed Abraham.

Diellza laughed. 'Maybe you're right, but it keeps you rich, and after the life we survived as children - poor, misused, discarded - we know the value of money. She didn't suffer, for what it's worth. She never knew what was happening, or why. It was like she just drifted off. I'd like to go that way, when it's my time. As for Lewis, yes, he was my husband. Did I love him? Maybe, in my way. But he was weak and stupid. He knew what he was involved with, who I was, who Hristo was. He embraced the money we made but it was never enough, and neither was I. I've shed tears for him, but not many. He didn't deserve more.'

'Bit risky, wasn't it, to go to Alissa's flat?' said Abraham.

'I took precautions, wore clothes not dissimilar to my husband's, dyed my hair to match his, a cap to hide my face. I even took his car, just in case. But none of it was necessary. No one takes notice, not anymore. And the police were quick to jump to the conclusion that we'd hoped for. The only fly in the ointment was this young man's disappearance, and your interference.'

'You lot want anything?' a voice called out across the cafe.

They each turned to see the woman behind the till staring at them. 'Only I'm closing up in a bit.'

'No, thank you,' replied Diellza, her voice and mannerisms reverting again. 'We're leaving in just a second.'

The woman nodded and turned back to tidying the area around her, taking no notice of her remaining customers.

'Are we boring you, Mr Hart?' said Hristo, who was watching Abraham staring out of the window and along the pier's boardwalk towards the shore. 'I came all this way just to see you, did you realise? I wanted to make sure you knew what had happened, and who had made it happen. Closure is important, I think. And, talking of closure…'

Hristo stood and buttoned his overcoat, pulling his collar up around his neck.

'I'm surprised you don't want to stay and gloat some more,' said Abraham.

Hristo smiled insincerely. 'Don't flatter yourself, Mr Hart. I came, primarily, to see my sister in a time of grief. You two being here is just a bonus. It was nice to finally meet you, Mr Hart. Though I'm afraid we won't be seeing each other again.'

'Are you sure about that?' asked Abraham.

'Oh, quite sure.'

'The police might have other ideas.'

Another laugh. 'Of the five of us present, the police are only looking for two people, and, though they'll never find them alive, I'm confident it's the two people sitting opposite me.'

'Can I show you something before you leave?' said Abraham, who motioned towards his right pocket. It won't take long.'

Hristo, sighing, like a frustrated parent humouring a young child, nodded to Erjon who took half a step back and covered both Craig and Abraham with the hidden handgun. 'Be quick, Mr Hart. Though, also, be slow.'

Abraham spread his palms and slowly dipped his right hand into his right pocket.

Erjon shuffled closer, the gun now almost pressed against Abraham's neck.

Carefully, Abraham removed his hand from his pocket to reveal something pinched between his thumb and index finger.

Everyone watched as he deposited a black object on the table.

Hristo looked from the object to Abraham. 'Is it some sort of desperate threat? Are you going to attempt to fight the three of us with a pen knife?'

It was Abraham who smiled now. 'Yeah, see, I thought it was a pen knife too. Looks like one, doesn't it? But do you know what it is?'

'Please, enlighten us,' said Hristo.

'It's a lock pick. I expect your man here - Erjon, did you say? - I think he used it to get into the bathroom that Lewis had locked himself inside. And then Diellza told Craig that the police suspected burglars of killing Lewis because they'd found a lock pick. But they didn't find one, because I had it. Erjon dropped it on purpose to muddy the waters, and you assumed the police found it. And remember before, when I talked about adding two and two? Well, that was when I put them together. A bit late, granted, but not so late that I didn't take the precaution of letting someone know where we'd be. You know, just in case.'

Abraham slowly tipped his wrist to look at his watch. 'And that someone should have called the authorities by now.'

The conceited smile on Hristo's face was gone, replaced with gritted teeth and a scowl aimed at Abraham. 'I think you're bluffing, Mr Hart.'

'You can think what you like.'

Hristo looked through the windows of the cafe, down towards a shoreline that was lost in the darkness.

'They'll be here soon,' said Abraham.

Hristo was nodding his head slowly, methodically. 'Not soon enough.'

A loud crash interrupted the conversation as Craig fell sideways, away from Abraham, and onto the tiled floor of the cafe.

'What's wrong? He ok?' yelled the women from in front of the counter, who was about to pull the steel shutter down.

'He's been feeling ill all day,' said Diellza, standing up and moving towards Craig in a show of concern. 'We'll get him some air. He'll be fine.'

'What have you done to him?' Abraham whispered, not wanting to get the woman from the cafe involved in the situation. There were already enough innocent people caught up in this.

'He's drifted off, just like his girlfriend,' said Diellza.

Abraham looked to the tea she had bought for them. His was untouched, but Craig's showed a muddy brown puddle at the bottom, some white specs floating on top.

'One out of two isn't bad,' said Hristo. 'Take him outside.'

Abraham wrapped an arm around the stricken man and heaved him up. Diellza made a show of helping, standing on the other side and wedging a shoulder into Craig's armpit. Erjon manoeuvred himself so that he was behind Abraham and Craig, the poncho still hiding the gun he was aiming at them.

Outside the rain was still lashing onto the thick wooden planks and the wind was whipping around them as if coming from every direction. The water was lost to the blackness, only white-tipped waves occasionally visible, rolling along the surface. Abraham could see the lights from a container ship further out, its silhouette imprinted on the background, slowly snaking towards the open water of the North Sea. What few fishermen and tourists there had been had disappeared, headed back to the relative shelter of the shore.

'You know what to do,' were Hristo's last words to Erjon. Diellza peeled away from Craig's limp body, leaving Abraham to support his weight, and she and Hristo headed back down the pier.

Forty-eight

'Keep going,' said Erjon, prodding Abraham in the back with the barrel of the pistol.

Abraham dragged Craig towards the RNLI station that was situated at the very end of the pier. Before they reached it, Erjon commanded him to stop. There was a padlocked gate that led to stairs, which themselves led towards the upper level of the pier and, Abraham guessed, to maintenance areas and possibly to the lifeboats.

The strain of carrying a dead-weight had kept Abraham's body and mind occupied but, having stopped, the fear of where he was, of what was all around him, began sticking to his insides.

Even if he couldn't quite see the water beneath them, he could hear it. No longer was it something relaxing, meditative, instead it was the sound of the elements conspiring against him. He tried to block it out, to concentrate on the challenge of keeping Craig upright.

Erjon indicated for Abraham to move to one side. Then, from beneath his waterproof cloak, he produced the lockpick which Abraham had left on the table and, with the gun still awkwardly aimed at Abraham, managed to slide the pick into the padlock. A few deft hand movements later and the it fell to the floor with a thud barely audible above the wind.

The gate swung open and Erjon waved the barrel of the gun from Abraham to the stairs ahead. He could hardly move his feet but eventually shuffled through the entrance and saw the yawning black ascent, heard the waves crashing against the thick uprights of the pier.

Erjon indicated for Abraham to take the stairs, and he carefully manoeuvred both himself and Craig down the steel steps. There were only ten, but it felt to Abraham like the mouth of hell.

At the top they were on another wooden platform, made of the same thick slats, about ten feet by fifteen in size. It was bordered by a low metal fence with a gap at the far end where a thinner section of the platform carried on to what looked like a maintenance shed, though it was too dark to see properly.

'Drop him,' said Erjon.

Abraham hesitated, eyes dancing around the platform looking for inspiration, for help.

Before his gaze returned to the man in front of him, Erjon's right fist smashed into Abraham's nose. There was a crunch and a blinding flash of pain. Abraham's eyes immediately filled with tears and blood started to stream from his nostrils.

Erjon put the gun to Craig's temple and repeated his instruction.

Trying to see clearly through the pain, Abraham gently lowered Craig to the rain soaked floor, propping him against the side of the gate.

'Arms out,' said Erjon.

'Why?'

'Because I asked.'

Abraham reluctantly spread his arms, making a star shape.

'If you try anything stupid,' said Erjon, 'I will kill him slowly, and you even slower.'

Erjon proceeded to pat Abraham down, starting at his ankles and moving up his legs. At the pockets of his tracksuit bottoms he reached in and removed Abraham's wallet. The envelope of cash from Tony Stone he slid into his own pocket, the rest he deposited between a gap in the wooden planks, the wallet and bank cards dropping soundlessly into the water.

Erjon moved further up, his search thorough. At the chest pocket of his recently purchased green cagoule he found something hard. He looked at Abraham then deposited two fingers carefully into the unzipped opening, pulling out a slim plastic and metal contraption the size of a small cigar case.

Erjon took a step away from Abraham and examined the find more closely.

'Always the journalist, Mr Hart,' he said, running his fingers along the small metal buttons of the Dictaphone.

Abraham had bought it in the second-hand electronics store in the high street. Without his phone he needed something to record the meeting with Mrs Maynard-Jones. If his suspicions - which is all they had been at the time - were correct, he'd need evidence. He didn't expect anyone to believe him without it.

He could have used Craig's phone, but it was bulky and he was worried Craig would inadvertently give the game away. So, when he spotted the JVC digital voice recorder, not dissimilar to one he used to own, he bought it, along with two triple-A batteries. He'd slid it into his cagoule, keeping the pocket unzipped in the hope the recording wasn't too muffled.

What Erjon was now holding was the key to everything. The confession to not just Diellza's murder of Alissa but to the subsequent murder of Lewis

Maynard-Jones, and of Hristo's business dealings. It was their downfall and Abraham's saviour.

He looked at the wiry, gun-wielding man in front of him, the man who had already killed at least one person that day, and he knew that this was the moment.

Erjon was going to kill both him and Craig. Whether stabbed, or shot, or simply thrown into the murky waters below, it didn't matter. They would have won, and Abraham would have let down another young woman whose life was ended prematurely because of Hristo Nikolova.

Abraham couldn't let that happen.

***

As Brody stepped out of the taxi in front of the entrance to Southend pier he heard the wail of sirens. Looking back at the steep slope that led up to the high street, he saw blue lights streaking down Pier Hill and towards the seafront.

The few remaining people braving the wind and rain on the promenade stared at the spectacle as it raced by, their faces painted violet by the lights.

From what Father Hart had said, Abraham was heading into trouble and, with the blue lights racing towards him, Brody felt confident trouble was close by. Father Hart had also said he heard the muffled sound of the Tannoy system at Adventure Island and, alongside Abraham's mention of a tram, it seemed that the pier was the obvious place to come.

At the entrance Brody paid his money, receiving his change along with a baffled shake of the head from the young woman behind the plexiglass, then ventured out onto the rain-lashed boards. He considered getting the tram, which would have been quicker, and certainly drier, but the next one didn't leave for 15 minutes, plus, this way, he could scan the faces of those coming back down the pier, in case Abraham was one of them.

But there was hardly anybody around. The darkening sky, battering rain and rising wind had convinced everyone there were far more pleasant places to be than over a mile out into the Thames estuary.

He could see the silhouette of a few people ahead, trudging towards him like shadows come to life. One was a retreating fisherman, a rod slung over his shoulder and a large tackle box hanging by his side. There were two other people much further away, walking together, head down. Brody looked around; no one else was walking the same way as him. He didn't blame them.

Eyes squinting against the wind and rain, he picked up his pace, careful not to lose his footing on the increasingly slippery surface. Soon the fisherman was past him, giving a gruff acknowledgement as they passed each other. The pier stretched out before him; a long, unwelcoming walk that was getting him just as wet as if he were to swim in the dark waters below.

A hundred yards from the small station at the end of the train tracks Brody was approaching the two other people, a man and woman. As they passed each other the man eyed him suspiciously while the woman spoke in an excited foreign language that he didn't understand.

Two minutes later he was nearing the pavilion that housed the cafe, and it seemed he was alone. Despite not yet being 6.30pm, it felt like midnight, the sky the colour of charcoal. Then, out of the shadowy evening, another figure emerged and started walking towards him.

Brody stayed still and squinted into the rain.

'If you're looking for a hot drink and somewhere dry, 'fraid you're out of luck, love,' said a middle-aged woman in a dark coat and sturdy boots. 'Just locked up and nowhere else's open. Best get yourself back.'

She scurried past him, shoulders hunched against the weather.

Brody stood for a minute, wondering if there was anywhere he could have missed, any area of the pier he might have checked. The lifeboat station was closed to visitors and wasn't permanently manned anyway. The windows were all dark in the buildings around him, the lights along the pier's walkway the only illumination. Apart from the screeching gulls that remained hidden from view, and the sound of the water swirling below him, Brody was alone.

Maybe Father Hart had misheard, or maybe, Brody thought, he'd been too late in arriving at the pier?

Then again, maybe Abraham had decided not to come to the pier at all. He felt deflated and only now noticed that he was shivering, the rain having soaked through his too thin coat.

As he looked at his watch, wondering if a train might be at the pier's end, saving him the long walk back to the shore, he heard a crack, like somebody had clapped their hands.

He looked to the sky, wondering if it was thunder, waiting for the fork of lightning. But the sound hadn't been deep or loud enough to be that. It had been sharp and sudden and close.

What it had sounded like, Brody thought, was a gun shot.

Forty-nine

'Right, take three uniforms and cover the two entrances and exits,' said Palmer. 'No one gets on the pier, no one gets off. Not until we ID them.'

DS Court nodded his understanding as he trotted to keep up with Palmer, who he'd never seen move so quickly.

Three marked cars were parked in a row directly outside the pier's entrance, each throwing ominous blue light over the building, the road and the crowd of people that had gathered to watch the proceedings. Two officers were setting up a cordon using police tape, shepherding the growing number of people behind it.

'You believe him then?' panted Court. 'Whoever called, I mean.'

'Can't take the chance of not, can we?' replied Palmer, identification raised as he approached the ticket booth and the startled Matilda sitting behind it.

Once he had explained who he was and why they were there, Matilda relayed to him that only a handful of people had bought tickets in the last forty minutes or so but that she had no idea how many of those had returned already.

'It's not like I count them in and out,' she said. 'And if they don't come back on the tram, they don't come past me anyway.'

'When's the next one?' asked Palmer.

'They run on the hour and half past the hour,' Matilda said, looking at her watch. 'Next one's about to leave.'

'Where's the driver?'

'Probably sitting in the cab.'

Palmer turned to Court. 'Kirk, you're on foot. I'll meet you at the end. If you see Hart, or anyone who looks like him, radio it in.'

'It's pissing down though,' protested the DI.

'Oh, I'm sorry,' said Palmer. 'Shall I let everyone know we're calling a timeout till the weather passes? Ask them to just stay where they are till it clears up? Or maybe we can just pop back to the shops and see if we can get you some waterproofs from TK Maxx?'

Court looked sheepishly from Palmer to Matilda. 'Was only saying.'

But Palmer didn't hear him because he had already walked past the guard, raising his police ID, and was trotting to the front of the train.

Court aimed raised eyebrows at Matilda in a 'What can you do?' expression and started to jog, his shoes squeaking on the rain-lashed surface.

***

Looking at Erjon, a gun in one hand the Dictaphone in the other, all Abraham could focus on was the sound of water crashing against the huge wooden stanchions holding the pier up.

He couldn't see it, but in his mind the sea was a dense and broiling mass waiting to claim him. The churning, rolling waves would crush his body then devour it, dragging him to the filthy seabed where he would suffocate while trying to claw his way to the surface, lungs bursting, eyes bulging.

The sickening thought of it propelled him into action.

Abraham dived forward, eyes closed, arms outstretched, chin tucked down into his chest. He hadn't planned past the fact that it was now or never. He and Craig would both be dead in the next few minutes if he didn't act now.

The sight of the Dictaphone in Erjon's hand had also triggered something in Abraham's brain. Hristo Nikolova's business had already killed his sister and provoked the murder of Alissa. They'd killed Lewis Maynard-Jones, too and though Abraham would not mourn his death, countless other families had mourned loved ones taken by Hristo's operation.

Abraham hit Erjon in his midriff, eliciting a pained grunt as his right shoulder struck hard, knocking him off balance. A burst of noise assaulted Abraham's eardrums as Erjon instinctively pulled the trigger and a bullet exploded from the gun. It sounded like a bamboo cane being rapped against bare skin.

Whether he was hit or not, Abraham didn't know. He felt no impact, no pulse of agony, but he'd seen enough movies to believe that, when adrenaline was pumping, your body seemed impervious to pain.

The gun remained in Erjon's right hand, but the Dictaphone was knocked free, landing a few feet away. It was slim enough to be easily slide between the wooden slats, so Abraham ignored the gun and the man who was holding it and scrambled towards the recorder. He had almost reached it when a foot smashed into his stomach and forced all the air and most of that morning's breakfast out onto the cold and rain-soaked pier.

Abraham turned onto his back coughing and spitting. He looked up at the dark sky and the even darker expression of the man looming over him.

Erjon held the gun in his right hand, pointing it at Abraham, while his left hand hugged his ribs at the spot where Abraham had hit him.

Erjon's face was like a wild animal's; teeth bared, lips flecked with spittle, eyes that were seeing only its prey.

'I've been waiting a long time to do this,' Erjon said. 'You've been lucky that Mr Nikolova is more forgiving than I am, more concerned with consequences, or you'd already be a memory.'

While Erjon talked, Abraham held his stare but slowly crept his hand along the wooden planks till he wrapped his fingers tightly around the Dictaphone.

Erjon laughed. 'You think that's going to help you?' he said. 'Whatever's on there will be lost to the sea. No one will find it, I'll make sure of it. They might find you, though. And if they do, you'll be a bloated, half eaten corpse.'

Erjon's thin lips, barely visible in the gloom, spread across his face in the approximation of a smile. His left hand reached into his jacket, removing a knife stained dark with what Abraham assumed was blood, the knife used to kill Lewis Maynard-Jones.

'Enjoy your swim,' Erjon said as he squeezed his index finger against the trigger.

***

Now, too late, Hristo realised it had been a mistake to come here. Hubris had convinced him he needed to be present to see the look on Hart's face. His ego had persuaded him that consequences were something other people needed to be mindful of, not him.

Looking at Hart when they told him what had happened had been a sweet moment, but was it worth risking everything for?

'What do we do?' asked Diellza, who was hanging onto his arm as they strode along the rickety old pier.

Hristo kept quiet.

'Hristo?' came a more urgent enquiry.

'I'm thinking,' he snapped, staring at the flashing blue lights two thirds of a mile in front of them. He could just make out the illuminated train making its way towards them along the tracks to their right.

There was no one else in sight but Hristo felt confident that if the police were here then at least one officer would be on the train while others walked the pier.

The question was, were they here for Hart, or for him?

Hristo guided Diellza towards the edge of the walkway. He looked over the side but all he could see was darkness. He could hear the water below but hadn't taken notice of how far the tide had come in, how deep the water might be or how far the drop was. Too many variables to risk jumping. He could feel the resistance in his sister's body agreeing.

'We carry on,' Hristo said, leading Diellza towards the shore.

'How will get past them?'

'We've done nothing wrong. We're accused of no crime. You're simply a grieving wife being consoled by her brother.'

Diellza seemed unsure but smiled weakly, allowing herself to be led.

As they walked Hristo recognised a crack in the distance, just loud enough to rise above the gusting wind and the swirling sea. Finally, Hart was out of the way. All they needed to do now was get off this pier.

***

Like most people facing death, thoughts of what might come next swirled around Abraham's head in the milliseconds before his life ended and his existence, his memories and his identity all leeched out onto the wood, dripping into the depths below.

At least he would be dead before he hit the water, he thought. Small mercies.

He had lost and, even in his last moments, that's what stung the most. Pride was a powerful thing and his had taken a beating and, now, would never recover.

He closed his eyes and thought of his parents, of Joshua, of Carol Peters and Craig Atherton, of all the things he'd done wrong.

Then he thought of Evie and of all the things he'd done right.

He heard another crack, the gun going off and the air around him filling with noise.

He opened his eyes.

He was still Abraham. Still alive and, so far as he could tell, still without a bullet in him.

In front of him now were two writhing figures grappling on the hard wood, rolling around, grunting, shouting.

The gun had skidded free and was teetering on the edge of the platform next to the slumped body of Craig, ready to drop. The knife had fallen to the other side of the two brawling bodies, beyond Abraham's grasp.

The two figures were rolling around on the deck. Abraham couldn't see who Erjon was fighting but the other person was now on his back, beneath Erjon, who was kneeling on their arms, raising a fist, then swiping it through the air to connect with their face.

He heard a crack, heard bone breaking, heard the grunt of pain.

Abraham stood up and aimed a kick at Erjon, catching him a glancing blow on the shoulder, dislodging him from his position of superiority but rolling him towards the knife.

Erjon reached for the handle, gathering it into his palm, blade down. In that brief moment Abraham saw Brody Lipscombe laying prone on the floor, his face streaked with blood.

Confusion enveloped him, but Brody's appearance had saved Abraham's life.

For now.

Flushed with adrenaline, Brody scrambled unsteadily to his feet.

He was disoriented and, rather than turning to face Erjon, looked straight at Abraham, fists raised. 'You keep away from him,' he shouted, shaking his head in a bid to clear the fog.

Behind Brody, Abraham watched Erjon stand. One hand grabbed the metal fence surrounding the platform, the other raised the blade.

That same thin-lipped smirk appeared on Erjon's face and Abraham opened his mouth to scream a warning. Before any words came out the air around them exploded with the crack of another gunshot.

The smirk on Erjon's face was replaced with an expression of surprise. He dropped the knife and his hand began grasping at the empty space in front of it.

Erjon staggered sideways, then backwards, leaning on the railing.

He looked past Abraham, to Craig, who was standing now, shivering wildly, the gun still aimed at Erjon, who continued to paw at the air.

Erjon leaned back further, his body straight, his lower back against the railing.

As if in slow-motion he began to topple, his black boots lifting off the slick wooden surface, his head tipping towards the sea.

But, before he fell, Erjon's probing hand clamped its fingers around Brody's thin jacket, pulling him backwards and dragging him over the edge, both dropping out of sight and into the freezing water below.

Abraham heard the splash of water but felt frozen to the spot. The image of Brody's face - surprise, confusion, fear - was replaying in his mind on a loop.

The sound of another thump brought him round and he turned to see Craig collapsed on the floor again, a crumpled mess of clothes and limbs.

'Help!' Abraham shouted. 'Over here! Please! We need help!'

But there was no one around and, even if there was, they wouldn't hear him over the wind and the rain.

He nervously stepped to the railing at the edge of the platform and peered over. It was impossible to tell how big the drop was; twenty feet? Twenty-five? More? It was like looking into a void, a world that had been painted black.

His hands gripped the metal like it was the only thing keeping him grounded to dry land, his knuckles white enough to cut through the inky darkness.

'Hello?' he shouted. 'Brody? Hello!'

Abraham turned an ear to the water, closing his eyes in concentration.

Nothing.

'Brody!' he yelled again.

There was a part of Abraham that prayed for no response, for only the sound of the waves and the gulls crying out in the dark to answer him.

But, out of the black, came a muffled cry.

Abraham couldn't understand the words, only that they had been made by a person. Which person though, he didn't know.

The cry came up again. Indistinct, panicked, pleading.

Abraham wondering if it wouldn't be better to run for help, to find a phone, call the coastguard. He thought of Craig and whether he should check him first?

He shouted for help again.

Or did he? He wasn't sure. Time was becoming warped, his brain leaping from one thought to another.

Abraham tried to control his breathing, sucking in deep lungfuls of cold, salty air. Had seconds passed? Minutes?

Then he thought of Grace. Of the help he couldn't give her. Of the life she might have had. Should have had. Of the pride and love she had for Abraham, that she told him about every time they spoke.

The cry came up again, less distinct now, weaker.

Abraham looked back at Craig, who was groaning, moving himself into a sitting position.

Abraham glanced down towards the water below, then he took off his coat and jumped.

***

At the pier's halfway point Hristo and Diellza, huddled together against the elements and, walking in silence, met DS Kirk Court coming out of the murky night heading the other way. He was jogging, one arm fruitlessly raised to his forehead in a bid to counter the rain.

'Mrs Maynard-Jones!' said the surprised DS. 'What are you doing here?'

Diellza stopped, mouth open, glad that the gloom covered the blood draining from her face. She looked from Court to her brother, but Hristo just smiled benignly, unspeaking.

'Oh, DS Court. My brother here, he came to see me, suggested we get some air. I needed to clear my head.'

'Understandable,' replied Court, nodding at Hristo, his face giving nothing away.

'What brings you here?' asked Diellza.

Court turned to the flashing blue lights filling the sky, then back to Diellza.

'Of course. It's not anything to do with my husband, is it? Oh, God, he's not here, is he? The killer?'

Court looked at Diellza then turned his attention to Hristo, his face remaining neutral. 'I'm afraid I can't discuss any details with you. We'll make sure to keep you informed. When you get to the exit, you'll need to speak to an officer. They're taking names and information. Protocols, you understand.'

'Are you sure that's necessary, Detective Sergeant Court?' said Hristo, speaking for the first time.

Diellza smiled nervously. 'And you know me. You know where I live.'

Court narrowed his eyes at Diellza, then turned his stare to Hristo, shrugging. 'Protocols,' he repeated.

Diellza and Hristo looked on as Court loped away towards the head of the pier. They watched as he pulled a radio mic from his pocket and talked into it.

'We need to go,' Hristo said.

***

Hitting the water felt like being kicked in the stomach again and Abraham's regret at jumping was immediate.

Why had he done it? What did he hope to achieve? The fear was overwhelming, like entering a new, alien world, one that felt unable to sustain human life.

Thoughts of Brody, of attempting to help, had left him. Survival was the overriding instinct. In the darkness he thrashed around, flailing his arms, trying to keep his head from slipping below the surface.

The waves, which in Abraham's head were colossal walls of water, were pushing him against the wooden pillars. He didn't know if holding onto one would save him or crush him.

In the end he latched his arms around a slippery, circular pole and tried to control his breathing. He coughed out a mouthful of salty water and told himself he was ok, that the worst was over, that everything would be fine.

Then he heard it. Someone splashing nearby. Heavy breathing. A faint cough.

'Hello?' Abraham shouted. 'Brody! Is that you?'

He got no answer but wasn't sure how far his voice carried, whether the water and the wind whisked it away.

He tried again, a guttural scream into the blackness.

'Help!' came the reply, feeble and barely audible.

It was to his right, Abraham was sure. He waved an arm in that direction hoping to grab hold of something and pull it towards him, but all he touched was the sea.

It was useless, Abraham thought. He couldn't see anything and if he set off into the black water then the likelihood was he'd drown long before finding Brody.

He tried one last time, screaming into the night, his voice as ragged and broken as his spirit.

The next sound he heard was another loud crack and for a second he thought it was another gun shot, that maybe Erjon had a second gun and was blindly firing. But this boom was deeper, louder, a sound that filled the night; thunder.

He looked out to where he'd heard the cry for help and, in that moment, a fork of lighting cracked open the black night, briefly illuminating everything around him.

He saw the sea, far less rabid than he had imagined. He saw the lights of a passing ship, distant and oblivious. He saw the scores of pillars that were holding up the pier stretching out from the sea like timber tombstones. And he saw Brody, ten feet away, his head bobbing on the surface, sometimes dipping under it, a limp arm still waving forlornly.

Without waiting for thought to paralyse him Abraham pushed himself away from the safety of the pillar and in the direction of Brody. He forced his arms to move past his head; one, then the other, then repeat. His heavy legs kicked as hard as they could, thrashing at the cold water.

Abraham felt as though he were travelling through tar and when, at last, he reached the slowly sinking figure, his lungs were burning, and his body was broken.

He grabbed Brody around the neck, manoeuvring him onto his back, all the while telling him he was ok, that they were ok.

He had done what he set out to do. He had saved Brody.

But, Abraham wondered, who would save him?

***

'Mrs Maynard-Jones is here,' Court relayed into the radio to DI Palmer, glancing back at the two figures walking to the shoreline. 'With her brother.'

'What do you mean, "here"?' replied Palmer.

'On the pier,' said the DS.

Palmer was silent. Thinking. 'Bit of a coincidence. You still with them?'

'Thought you didn't believe in coincidences. And no, told them to see an officer at the exit. I'm heading up to meet you.'

'There's nothing here,' said Palmer. 'Whole place is empty. Seems like a wild goose chase.'

'You think whoever called was trying to throw us off the scent, give Hart a chance to scarper?'

'Dunno. Maybe. If he is trying to do a runner then he's got us chasing our tails,' said Palmer. 'But Maynard-Jones being here too…'

'No such thing as a coincidence?' said Court.

'Exactly.'

'I'm nearly there. Where are you?'

'Not far from the lifeboat station.'

At that moment a thunderclap ruptured the sky and both men looked to the heavens and if they might be able to see the sound. 'Christ,' said Palmer, turning to the head of the pier, 'the sooner we get off this bloody great jetty, the better.'

Before Palmer had finished the sentence the lightning cracked open the night and he noticed a figure on the platform above. It was bent double over the railing, head down as if it were about to topple over.

Palmer squinted but then the lightning was gone and he sky went black again. 'Ok,' he said into the radio to his DS. 'See you in a minute.' Then he started for the stairs, his eyes fixed on the space where he'd seen the figure, the darkness having claimed it.

At the top of the stairs Palmer found the crumpled form of a man laying on the floor. He was moaning, incoherent words bubbling from his lips.

Palmer pulled his phone from his pocked and turned on the torch, shining it in the fallen man's face. Craig Atherton. Dishevelled, unkept and soaked to the skin, but definitely Craig Atherton.

Palmer gently shook him, then held his face, turning it towards his own. 'Mr Atherton? Craig? What's happened? Where's Abraham?"

Craig's head lolled and his eyes were barely focussed, but he raised a hand and pointed a finger towards the far end of the platform, to the railing and beyond, out to the waves.

***

Abraham wasn't sure how long he'd been in the water. Seconds? Minutes? It felt like hours. He was shivering uncontrollably and struggling to keep Brody's head above water.

All the while he was conscious that, somewhere, Erjon could be lurking. The bullet had hit him, Abraham was sure, but where and how seriously, he had no idea.

Not that it would matter. He couldn't last much longer. The tide was pushing and pulling him, ultimately trying to drag him under. It felt like a sentient force, a malevolent entity intent on claiming their lives.

Brody hadn't spoken since Abraham had got to him, his body a dead weight. Abraham tried not to think about whether he was alive. There was nothing he could do at the moment except hope.

But hope was fading.

He felt delirious. For a second, he thought he saw a light above him and wondered if a rescue helicopter had arrived, its light a distant but beautiful sight. The next second he realised that was impossible. No one knew they were here.

He closed his eyes and felt the water claim him.

When he heard a voice, he knew the delirium was taking over. But, when the same voice swore at him, Abraham forced his wandering mind to concentrate.

'If you can hear me, grab the fucking lifebelt,' the voice cried.

Abraham opened his eyes. The tiny light was still there above him, moving from side to side.

'It's me!' the voice shouted. 'Palmer! Can you hear me? Abraham! Can you see the lifebelt?'

Abraham did his best to scan the water without dipping Brody below the surface. It was dark all around apart from the distant glow of a ship.

He tried to cry out, to shout for help, to say that he'd heard, that he was here, that they both were. But no words came out.

Then he spotted something. A glint of orange a few feet off, shining out like a beacon, the tiny light from above reflecting off it.

Abraham kicked his legs, moving them towards it. Slowly at first, the energy in them almost gone, then with more urgency.

He tried not to think about the rolling waves, about the cold, about the heaviness of his limbs.

He tried to ignore the thoughts in his head about who else might be in the water.

He kept kicking.

Fifty

'This is ridiculous,' shouted Diellza. 'Detective Inspector Palmer knows who I am. Knows how and where to reach me. You can't keep us here indefinitely. I've just lost my husband.'

PC Helen Jeffers remained calm, assuming a tone that was polite but firm. 'I'm afraid you aren't able to leave just yet. The DI's given strict instructions that no one is to enter or exit the pier without his say-so. You and your brother are welcome to wait inside the ticket office, out of the wet.'

A few minutes later there was a buzz of activity, people on radios, groups conferring in huddles, others looking towards the water and the pier that stretched out into it.

Two more marked police cars arrived, and the number of officers increased. Diellza could see at least fifteen now, most of them located along a perimeter that was stopping anyone from the large crowd from moving onto the pier.

Hristo had remained quiet, but Diellza could feel the tension vibrating off him. It had been the same when they were younger; any trouble they faced, any scrapes they got into, she would be the one who did the talking while he fizzed with a barely noticeable but easily triggered rage.

'We need to leave,' he growled into her ear as they were moving away from the line of police. It was the only thing he had said, and the third time he had said it.

'What do you want me to do?' she spat back through gritted teeth. 'I can't just barge past them.'

Hristo was considering doing exactly that.

No one knew who he was. His only tie to this whole thing was Diellza and he knew she would never give him up.

But leaving would only make things worse. He knew he needed to stay calm, but so long tied up in the court system with the threat of prison hanging over him had made him jittery.

He again cursed his own decision to come here. Regretted his ego and its need to make sure Hart was aware of who had beaten him.

He took a deep breath.

But, really, what did he have to worry about? He had done nothing wrong. Certainly nothing provable. He was comforting his sister after her terrible loss and as long as Erjon was able to evade the authorities, which Hristo had no doubts about, then he was simply a free and innocent man who happened to be in the wrong place at the wrong time.

'Who are you?' asked a uniformed officer who Hristo thought couldn't have been much more than twenty-years-old. He had wandered into the ticket office from the promenade and was carrying a clipboard, a pen and an air of importance that seemed to outweigh his rank.

Hristo looked around to check that the young officer was addressing him.

'Not sure you should be in here,' said the officer.

'No,' Hristo said. 'I agree.'

'You spoken to anyone? Had your details taken?'

'Yes,' offered Diellza, sensing an opportunity. 'Officer Jeffers has all our details. She said she was just waiting for someone to say it's ok to leave, someone with the authority. Is that you?'

'Well,' he replied, visibly straightening at the word "authority", 'I've been asked to clear the crowd, and as long as Helen, I mean Officer Jeffers, has your details then I think it's best you vacate the area. What did you say your names were, just for the record?'

Diellza repeated their details, handing over the mobile phone number the police already had, then thanked the officer for his time and expediency. The young officer escorted them to where the police tape was fluttering in the stiff breeze, lifted it for them to duck under, then turned back towards the pier.

On the promenade Hristo and Diellza looked at each other, eyes wide, not wanting to verbalise their stroke of luck for fear of jinxing it. They began walking away from the pier and the rows of arcades with their flashing lights. Hristo pulled a phone from his jacket. 'Valon, I need you to bring the car. The pier, where you dropped me off, drive east along that road. There's a casino not far from there. Meet there.'

Hristo pulled the collar up on his expensive coat, as much to shield himself from the streetlights illuminating the promenade as to protect himself from the cold. The casino was a ten-minute walk away and he could feel the tension in his body draining away now that they had left the confines of the pier and the gaze of the police.

'You'll have to drop me at home,' said Diellza.

'Come to London. I have plenty of space. We can celebrate. Maybe even go away. You deserve it.'

'No,' Diellza chided him. 'I'm a grieving widow. I need to be here to answer questions, be consoled. I'll come when I can.'

Hristo was about to reply when the sound of an engine, loud and high-pitched, interrupted him. They both turned to face the water. Two motorboats were making their way towards a boat ramp that dropped down from the yacht club that neighboured the pier.

They were standing directly in line with it and had a good view of both vessels, each carrying a handful of people, though they were still too far away, and the evening too dark, for them to see who the people were.

As the boats grew closer, the whine of their engines increasing, they could see some of the figures on board were wearing white helmets and yellow waterproof outfits. Others seems to be wrapped in heavy blankets. No one seemed to be talking, and one person was kneeling on the floor of the boat, leaning over something.

'We should go,' said Diellza.

Hristo nodded but did not move, his eyes focussed on the flurry of activity.

The first boat pulled onto the ramp, the lights from the yacht club illuminating the scene. Voices drifted across the ramp and towards the promenade. Instructions were shouted and fingers pointed by the throng of police, many of whom were running the two hundred yards from the pier to the boats.

And then Hristo saw what it was that had been laying on the deck.

Two of the men in white helmets carefully picked up a stretcher at each end and walked what looked like a pile of dark blankets along the ramp and towards a waiting ambulance, which has pulled up not far from where he and Diellza stood.

Moments later the second boat came to a stop and again the people on board shouted and pointed.

Though the boats had killed their engines, Hristo couldn't hear what was being said over the waves and the wind. Two men once again stood at each end of a stretcher and carefully lifted it over the side of the boat and onto the concrete ramp.

Hristo smiled.

Erjon had done his job. He wondered which was Hart and which Atherton. It didn't matter. That the job was done was all that did.

'Come on,' scolded Diellza, eager to leave.

Hristo nodded, the smile still playing across his lips. He was about to turn and continue walking when he noticed something; the blankets covering the second stretcher were moving, someone beneath them. Was he imaging it?

He stepped forward, edging into the glow of the streetlight to get a better view.

He looked to the first stretcher which was about to be loaded into the ambulance. Whoever was on it remained still, but Hristo could see part of their head, a bandage, red with blood in places, wrapped around it. Whoever it was, he didn't recognise them.

He scanned towards the second stretcher, this one further back, and the movement he thought he saw was confirmed as the two men wielding it slowly placed it on the red concrete of the promenade and tended to the man laying on top.

It was Craig Atherton.

He was deathly pale and shivering, but he was alive.

Hristo felt a wave of fury flare up through his veins, igniting them, the heat migrating to his brain.

This changed everything.

If Atherton was still alive he could identify Hristo and Diellza. The celebrations would need to be put on hold, there was more work to be done and, this time, Hristo knew he would need to do it himself.

He took another look back at the shoreline, to the group of men and women who had exited the two boats and were making their way to the throng of police officers and medical staff.

One person caught his eye. While everyone else was in motion, absorbed in the urgency of the situation, this person was unmoving. They were standing on the edge of the ramp, blankets wrapped around them.

Someone in green approached and spoke to them. Still the person did not move. Instead, they were staring in the direction of Hristo.

Intrigued, Hristo took another step forward, squinting at the stoic figure.

As he did so, the person raised an arm, slowly at first, then more insistently.

Hristo watched as the person became animated, turning to the man next to him, who was older and larger and who had just descended the ramp carrying something over his arm. The figure was yelling now, the words indistinct but urgent.

The blankets covering him fell way and Hristo saw Abraham Hart pointing and shouting. He watched the older man next to him follow Hart's finger then talk into a radio mic.

He felt the atmosphere around him change as more people in uniforms looked towards the tall man in the expensive coat standing in a pool of light not a hundred yards from where they were.

Hristo stayed still, unsure what to do. The car would be waiting, warm comfortable, secure.

People were advancing towards him. The overweight, bald man was talking to Hart, eyes fixed on Hristo.

He could run, but to what end? They would know who he was, could find him easily enough. Better to stay and answer the questions, clear his name.

He turned back to look at Hart, still stationary by the boat, still staring at Hristo.

He watched him say something to the man stood next to him, saw the man hand over the thin coat he had been carrying in the crook of his arm. Hart's hand dug into it and pulled something free. He held it aloft between thumb and forefinger and turned his gaze back to Hristo.

The object was silver and small, not much bigger than a disposable lighter, but Hristo instinctively knew he what it was; a weapon more powerful than a gun or a knife. The weapon of a journalist that could do just as good a job of ending everything Hristo had worked for.

Hristo thought of the car, wondered how quickly he could get to it, whether Diellza could keep up, whether it mattered if she did. These thoughts were interrupted by a hand on his shoulder and an unfamiliar voice asking him to come with them.

As he turned to face the voice, he noticed a very sleek, very expensive car glide past, Valon in the driver's seat.

Hristo's eyes followed it as it cruised past the casino and out of sight.

Fifty-one

Abraham stared at the ageing wallpaper, its edges worn and frayed. He looked at the gold-plated carriage clock on the mantelpiece that had been there since he could remember, then at the photo next to it.

A much younger version of his father stared out at him, his smile soft and easy, an arm draped over Marion Hart's shoulder. In front of them, locked in time, stood three children. Eighteen-year-old Joshua in a denim jacket, his face impassive, teenage rebellion written all over it. Next to him a fifteen-year-old Abraham trying to mimic his brother's cool apathy, the upward-creeping corners of his lips giving him away.

At the front, nestled between her two big brothers, sat five-year-old Grace in a green dress with flowers embroidered into it. Her grin was almost as wide as her head. Her eyes were aimed up at Abraham, her hand clasped in his.

Abraham had avoided looking at this photo, one of their parents' favourites, for a long time. The happiness it represented had only been matched by the pain it ignited.

But now, sitting on the old couch in his parents' house, the sound of his father's and brother's voices in the kitchen. Abraham looked at his sister and remembered her voice, her laugh, her constant questions, and her unconditional love for her family.

He closed his eyes and tried to recall the Grace he had known most recently and was glad that he couldn't.

In the fortnight since the events on the pier a lot of changes had taken place, many of them inside Abraham. He couldn't explain exactly how his mood had altered, or why he felt as though his mind had been, if not purified, then somehow refreshed.

Joshua was the first to notice. The old antagonism between the two brothers had dissipated, Abraham's wariness and cynicism replaced by gratitude and affection.

'Maybe the cold, grey waters of the Thames estuary have healing properties,' Joshua had said. 'Maybe you've been baptised. Reborn.'

When he had been pulled from the sea by the coastguard, Brody's limp body hauled up after him, Abraham hadn't felt that was the case. He was too tired to feel much at all. He had spent the night in hospital, 'under precautionary observation' the doctor said.

Brody had been kept in for three nights. He had been hypothermic and, in the darkness, and unbeknownst to Abraham, had cracked his head on a wooden pillar, which had knocked him out cold. He'd needed twelve stitches and still had a white bandage wrapped around his skull. Jacob called it his halo. Abraham thought the religious sentiments had got out of hand.

Craig, too, had been hospitalised. Diellza Maynard-Jones had administered a high quantity of crushed temazepam into their tea but, after having his stomach pumped and activated charcoal administered to absorb the drug, Craig seemed to rally. After his release from hospital, jobless and homeless, his prospects looked bleak until Carol Peters stepped in.

Not long after Abraham was released from hospital, sat in the confines of Carol's small but comfortable home, a home in which Abraham could feel the ghost of her daughter, he had told her what had happened.

He had explained the events which had unfolded, and which had eventually conspired against Alissa. Abraham had expected uncontrolled fury and tears of rage, but the tears that did come were as much in relief as resentment.

She relayed to him that a distressed and contrite Craig had already confessed to his part in Alissa's death, calling from his hospital bed as soon as he was able.

In turn she had invited him into her home until he was able to get back on his feet.

He wondered if Craig was the last vestige of Alissa, whether his presence somehow filled a gap in her life. He also wondered at the compassion of the human spirit, and whether he would be so charitable in her situation.

'Tea's up,' said Victor, walking in with a tray, Joshua following. 'Got some biscuits as well. Thought I'd push the boat out.'

'Thanks,' said Abraham. 'Though I've had enough of any water-based references for a while.' He took a biscuit all the same.

'So,' asked Joshua, easing himself onto the sofa, his mouth half full of Digestive, 'will you have to give evidence?'

'I expect so, though the recording's pretty definitive. Though I imagine the defence will try to cast doubt on its authenticity.'

'What about that other one you mentioned,' added Joshua, 'the money guy?'

'David Catton? Disappeared. The police are looking for him. You can bet your life Nikolova is too. Even from prison, his reach is long.'

'And Brody?' asked Victor.

'He might be called, too. Though he wasn't in the cafe with us, and there's no case for Erjon Demiraj to answer. Not as it stands, what with him being missing, presumed dead, so…' Abraham shrugged.

'I wasn't really talking about the court case,' added Vic.

Abraham nodded, a week smile playing on his lips. Brody Lipscombe had undoubtedly saved his life, Craig's too. His actions had been stupid, dangerous, reckless but wholly selfless.

The previous fizzing heat of loathing Abraham had felt towards him had burnt itself out. Or maybe it had been quenched by Joshua's notion of the estuary's healing properties.

Vic and Joshua had long ago forgiven Brody, had accepted him for who he had become, and welcomed him into their fractured family. Abraham wasn't sure he was there yet, despite his brother and father's encouragement. But neither could he'd locate the anger and hatred he'd held onto for so long.

He felt better for it.

'Almost time,' said Vic, finishing the dregs of his tea and standing to gather up the mugs.

As Abraham passed his empty cup to his dad, his phone, returned to him by DI Palmer, began to vibrate, the screen lighting up, 'withheld' showing across it.

Vic looked at his son, wary. 'They'll be here any minute. You're still coming, aren't you?'

'I'm coming,' he replied, picking up the phone and following his dad out of the living room door. 'I'll take this upstairs.'

In the room he had now returned to thinking of as 'his room', Abraham answered his mobile.

'Hello? Abraham?'

Abraham recognised the voice, but it took him a few seconds to place the nasal whine. When he did, his contented disposition took a downward turn. 'Spencer. What do you want?'

Abraham had hardly given Spencer Milton a thought since stepping off the c2c train only two weeks ago and, thinking of the *Chronicle*'s deputy editor now, he could feel some of that fizzing heat returning.

'Just to say, well, the staff here are all thinking of you, of course.'

Spencer paused but Abraham remained silent.

'Anyway, we were wondering if you were coming back. To the office, you know. Rachel asked me to get in touch. She...'

Abraham heard a voice, muffled, in the background.

'That is, *we* would like you to return to the office. And, if you feel up to it, maybe you could continue where you left off with Hristo Nikolova.'

Abraham smiled. He expected this call might come. Expected it sooner, in fact.

With Nikolova back in the news and the drama that had unfolded in Southend recently, the story was a hot topic; a fallen empire, a glamorous sister, a murdered husband, an innocent young victim, and a showdown at a local landmark.

News outlets - both press and broadcast - were clamouring for more. Abraham had spoken to no one and written nothing of his own on the situation. That the pleading call had come from Spencer Milton was more than he could have hoped for.

'We thought that, well, you could put your own spin on it,' continued Spencer. 'Sort of, make it personal.'

'I'll think about it,' Abraham said, then ended the call.

***

An hour later, wrapped against the cold, his hands buried in the pockets of the winter coat he had recently collected from the small hotel room in London, Abraham stood with his family.

Evie was next to him, her right arm looped through his. Beside her was Victor, head bowed, lost in thought, his right hand held tightly in his granddaughter's. Joshua was standing behind them, Siobhan close by.

He didn't think he'd ever see this place. Didn't think the anger would ever dissipate or the guilt ever dissolve. But it had. At least enough.

After a short time, the silent party turned and trudged back towards the car. All apart from Abraham.

He stepped forward, tentative. 'I'm sorry it's taken so long,' he said. 'I'm sorry I've not been here for you. I suppose, really, I'm just sorry.'

He raised a hand to his lips and then touched it on the smooth marble gravestone he'd not been strong enough to visit until now. 'I'll be back again soon,' he added, before turning to catch up with the others, seeing Siobhan standing a respectful distance away, watching him.

'I can't believe it's been eight years already,' she said when he reached her.

Abraham gave a sad smile.

'She'd be proud, you know,' she added. 'Of all of you. Of who you are, of what you've done.'

'I miss her,' said Abraham.

'I know. Vic tells me you've collected all your stuff from the hotel. That you're coming home.'

Abraham turned to face his wife. 'I'm going to stay with Dad for a while. Home, but not quite.'

'Well,' said Siobhan, 'it's a start.'

ACKNOWLEDGEMENTS

Firstly, thank you for choosing this book over the myriad other great books that are available. Time is precious and investing it in *Dark Waters* is a show of faith for which I am extremely grateful. I hope it repaid that faith.

Secondly, I want to thank my wife, Ellie, for allowing me both the time and space to work on *Dark Waters*, as well as giving me the encouragement to keep going when I wasn't sure things were working. This book wouldn't exist without her, and for the avoidance of doubt, she no way inspired the character of Diellza. I promise!

I would also like to thank The Bestseller Experiment, both the podcast and its Academy course, of which I was a member. Mark Stay and Mark Desvaux were - and are - a positive force in the writing world. Their podcast gave me the inspiration to believe I could do this, and the Academy course (and the people on it) were cheerleaders for me and for each other. Also, thank you Mark S for your invaluable editing assistance, and thanks to JF Burgess for the book cover design.

If you enjoyed reading Dark Waters, please think about leaving a review on Amazon. Every review helps, and comments from readers are incredibly useful.

You can find out more about Max Elwood, and join his email newsletter, by visiting;

maxelwoodauthor.com

Printed in Great Britain
by Amazon